THE RIPPER DECEPTION

JACQUELINE BEARD

Vinci Books

vinci-books.com

Published by Vinci Books Ltd in 2024

1

Copyright © Jacqueline Beard 2019

The author has asserted their moral right to be identified as the author of this work in accordance with the Copyright, Designs and Patents Act 1988. This work is a work of fiction. Names, characters, places and incidents are the product of the author's imagination or are used fictitiously. Any resemblance to actual persons, living or dead, places and incidents is entirely coincidental.
All rights reserved. No part of this publication may be copied, reproduced, distributed, stored in any retrieval system, or transmitted in any form or by any means, including photocopying, recording, or other electronic or mechanical methods, nor used as a source for any form of machine learning including AI datasets, without the prior written permission of the publisher.
The publisher and the author have made every effort to obtain permissions for any third party material used in this book and to comply with copyright law. Any queries in this respect should be brought to the attention of the publisher and any omissions will be corrected in future editions.
A CIP catalogue record for this book is available from the British Library.
Paperback ISBN: 9781036701376

Printed and bound in Great Britain by Clays Ltd, Elcograf S.p.A.

By Jacqueline Beard

The Lawrence Harpham Murder Mysteries

The Fressingfield Witch
The Ripper Deception
The Scole Confession
The Felsham Affair
The Moving Stone
The Maleficent Maid
The Disappearing Doctor
The Camden Killer
Shadow Over Malvern

The Denman & Tallis Cotswold Crime Thrillers

The Girl in Flat Three
You'll Never Escape Me

The Constance Maxwell Dreamwalker Mysteries

The Cornish Widow
The Croydon Enigma
The Poisoned Partridge
The Cheltenham Torso

Prologue

Friday 22nd June 1888

The man hunched over a heavy, black-covered tome and scoured the pages through deep-set eyes. He tapped arrhythmically against the dark-stained wood of the table as he read. Quick taps, slow taps, silence. A distracted mind. Raising a cup to his mouth, he gulped the tepid brew and umber coffee grounds flecked the edges of his white walrus moustache. The room was cold, yet sweat beaded his brow, and he swept it distractedly into a receding hairline. His chair was set close to an unlit fireplace, and its proximity tricked him into thinking that the day was fine, but the weather was unseasonably cold for June. The man looked up and snapped the book shut. His eyes were dark, almost black and devoid of compassion. Otherwise, his appearance was unremarkable, although his reading material was not. The title of the book he pored over with studious intent by the fireside of The Cricketers Inn, was entitled 'The Occult Relevance of Blood.'

His black frock coat lay crumpled over a battered leather Gladstone bag at his feet. Both were shabby and second hand, quite likely inherited. Like the man himself, they had seen better days. Roslyn D'Onston placed one hand on the table and heaved himself to his feet. He loosened the lock of the bag and put the black-bound book inside with a certain reverence. He pulled a small, silver timepiece from his breast pocket and scowled. Slipping the frock coat over his jacket, he wound a dark check scarf around his neck and walked to the front of The Cricketers Inn. Then, he nodded to Emily Pitt, wife of the proprietor, lifted his collar over the scarf and set out into the rainy night.

A gas lamp cast shadows across the street illuminating the lanes and alleys of Brighton with a gloomy glow. D'Onston surveyed the front of the Cricketers Inn. Dark painted render coated the curved window bays to the first and second floors. His room was on the second floor at the back of the building, necessitating a regular slog up two flights of stairs. The climb irritated his old leg wound and defeated the purpose of being in Brighton where he had come to relieve the fatigue caused by neurasthenia. Climbing a staircase was not the way to go about it. He had asked for a room on the first floor, but The Inn was full, and his request was denied.

Roslyn D'Onston limped as he picked his way through the alleys. It was eight o'clock in the evening and on a fine day, it would have been light, but today was overcast and wet. He shoved his hands deep into the pockets of his coat and bowed his head against the increasing rain. As he strode down the Old Steine towards Brighton seafront, he thought about the pointlessness of the meeting he was about to undertake. Not that he was confident that the woman he was due to meet would arrive. She hadn't turned up last time. Mabel Collins shared a profession with him, being a journalist too. She also shared his interest in the occult. He respected her theosophist opinions, but not enough to be looking forward to their meeting on such a cold night. Still, The Royal Albion served a particularly fine single malt whiskey which he would, no doubt, enjoy whether he drank alone or in company.

The wind whipped his scarf as he reached the seafront and he gazed towards the Royal Albion Hotel to his right looking forward to an escape from the relentless drizzle. He remembered his first visit to Brighton over a decade ago. Back then, the Royal Albion had epitomised elegance with its large Doric porch and Corinthian columns. Now it looked tired. Patches of plaster had peeled from the walls eroded over time by the acidic kiss of the dogged sea wind. D'Onston stole a glance towards the Aquarium on his left. It was one of the attractions he must see, they told him. It was unlike any other in the country, they said. He would find it tranquil. But like his visit to the Pavilion and all the other places he had frequented in a bid to distract his thoughts, it failed. Nothing shifted his fatigue or quelled his restless mind.

He crossed the street and passed a horse tethered to a post in front of the Hotel. It whinnied and shifted its weight from foot to foot. He paused to pat its soft muzzle before unbuttoning his coat. Then, without further ado, he entered the building.

The guest lounge of the Royal Albion Hotel was a large, airy room facing the seafront. Wall mounted gas lights were plentiful, and the natural light from the expansive windows gave the place a spacious, open feel. A wave of relief descended over D'Onston for the first time in a week as he entered the comfortable room. He wondered whether the size of his quarters in The Cricketers Inn might be making his condition worse. The Inn was well priced, and the food was excellent, but the rooms were small. He considered whether to stretch his funds a little further and move to a seafront hotel for the last week of his stay.

He walked to the bar, ordered a whiskey and sat by the window gazing out to sea. There were only two other people in the bar, none of whom were female. D'Onston looked at his timepiece again. It was precisely eight-thirty, and Mabel was almost late. It did not bode well. He swilled the whiskey around the glass and took a large mouthful. It trickled down his throat like molten nectar.

The door opened, and a man appeared carrying a drink which he took to a table at the other end of the room. He did not see Roslyn D'Onston, but if he had, he would have recognised him. They moved in similar circles. D'Onston noted the man with interest. Edmund Gurney was well known and a founder member of the Society for Psychical Research. Gurney believed in parapsychology and was an intelligent man and a scientist seeking to prove inexplicable events using quantifiable means. Definitely not a fool, or gullible. D'Onston continued to watch. He enjoyed watching people. He was a journalist and was paid for his observations, and as Mabel was now officially late, he had nothing better to do.

He watched as Gurney mirrored his own actions from earlier by opening his breast pocket and checking his watch. Repeat, repeat, repeat. Gurney must be waiting too. Gurney took a final look at the timepiece and thrust it deep into his trouser pocket pushing temptation out of sight. He reached across the table and grasped a copy of The Brighton and Hove Herald, spread it out and began to read.

A sudden sneeze broke the quiet atmosphere of the guest lounge. Gurney covered his nose and reached into his pocket for a handkerchief. He sneezed again and blew his nose not noticing the envelope that fluttered from his jacket onto the carpet. It settled under his chair.

Gurney remained oblivious to its presence, but D'Onston did not. He made his living from being observant, and instinct told him that this small event mattered. He debated whether to retrieve the envelope and hand it to Gurney, find an excuse to pass the time of day with the man and enjoy some company. But Mabel was long overdue and had let him down again. He was irritable and vexed, churlishly preferring to drink alone rather than offer help. He decided not to trouble himself and instead he watched and waited.

Before long, Edmund Gurney folded the newspaper and retrieved his watch for final scrutiny. He nodded imperceptibly and returned the timepiece to its starting place inside his jacket. He wiped his moustache with the back of his hand, displaying an elegant signet ring, then strode towards the door. D'Onston turned away as Gurney approached him. As soon as he left the room, D'Onston walked towards the sideboard and searched an array of periodicals stacked in piles. When no one was looking, he stooped and retrieved the envelope. He placed his empty drink on the bar, fastened his coat and retreated into the hallway. As he appended his vacating time in the red-bound guest book, he glanced up the wood panelled staircase. Edmund Gurney and another man were in earnest discussion. D'Onston could not see the man, who walked ahead of Gurney, but his voice carried in a frank exchange of views. They were not quite arguing, but whatever they were talking about had provoked a passionate response. Roslyn D'Onston tried to listen but heard nothing of note above the noise in the hotel foyer. It was of no consequence anyway. D'Onston dismissed the matter, nodded to the Hotel Manager and retreated into the night.

Saturday 23rd June 1888

Millicent Harvey was fed up. She was often fed up. The life of a hotel maid had not turned out in practice the way she had rehearsed it in her head. She could have gone into service in a nice villa in Hove where she might have worked with a small group of servants. But Millicent had grander ideas. She was a romantic and wanted a husband. The best way forward, in her opinion, was to find an occupation where she would come into daily contact with members of the opposite gender. Sadly, it hadn't worked out that way. Though there were plenty of young men employed at the Royal Albion Hotel, she didn't cross paths with them very often. She was always too busy changing bedsheets or cleaning bathrooms. And the young men weren't that appealing anyway — apart from Douglas, and he was already taken.

Today she was particularly fed up. She had woken to find one crusty eye sealed shut. Another attack of conjunctivitis had conspired to spoil her half day off tomorrow. She had arranged to watch a performance at the bandstand with her friend Nora. Her pretty friend, Nora. A friend who would look much more attractive than she did, if she ended up watching the recital through one eye. No, it wouldn't do. She must find time to slip out of the Hotel and visit the Chemist before she was due in the dining room at three o'clock. It was now a minute past two, and the occupant of room 27 still hadn't surfaced. He had slept through the morning and wasn't answering now. "Idle beggar," she thought as she hammered on the door with the flat of her hand for the fifth time. Silence.

Millicent stomped down the stairs with her dustpan in her hand brandishing the brush. She confronted the Hotel Manageress who was busy hanging keys in the lobby.

"Who's the lazy bones in room 27?" she demanded.

The Manageress put her keys down and pursed her lips. "You mean which of our valued guests is occupying room 27, I assume?"

"If you say so," said Millicent, sullenly.

"I don't know who is staying in room 27," said the Manageress. "The gentleman did not write his name in the guest book. Not that it matters. It's his own business, but tell me, what seems to be the problem?"

It did not take long for the scope of the problem to become evident. The Manageress accompanied Millicent up several sets of stairs before they arrived outside room 27. She rapped smartly on the door and inserted her master key. The door swung open, and they saw, at once, the shape of a man lying on the bed.

The Manageress called out again, then grasped the heavy curtains and flung them open. The afternoon sun streamed into the room as she stepped towards the form lying prone on top of the bed. She examined him. He was a handsome man with a head of wavy hair and chiselled cheekbones which were still visible despite the sponge bag covering his mouth and nose.

"He—he's not dead, is he?" stammered Millicent.

"I'm afraid he is," said the Manageress. "You had better go and fetch Mr Gilbert."

Alone in the room, the Manageress attended to the practical aspects of identifying her deceased guest. She crossed to the table and picked up a dark leather wallet.

There was a large sum of money contained within, but nothing that helped to locate the man's name. She returned to the bed and watched the corpse with an air of detachment. One of his arms hung beside him. She noted the elegant shape of his fingers — musician's hands, she thought. How sad that such a man would end his life in this way. Then she spotted a small bottle, just out of reach of the hanging limb. Gloria Crosby had a sensible head on her shoulders and decided not to touch the bottle. Instead, she knelt on all fours and scrutinised it carefully. It was open and almost empty. The small amount of substance remaining was colourless and odourless.

Her purpose unaccomplished, she rose and opened the wardrobe. She patted down the man's waistcoat, but the only pocket was empty. A search of his jacket proved more fruitful. It contained a letter providing not only his identity but the name of someone they could notify. Gloria took the envelope and placed it on the dressing table. Then, she waited for the Assistant Manager's arrival and all the inevitable furore that accompanied a hotel death.

Roslyn D'Onston leaned over the edge of the pier watching the waves lap gently against the side. It was mid-afternoon, and he had used all the self-discipline he could muster to drag himself away from the Cricketer's Inn. He had endured yet another night of broken sleep, and seldom slept any other way. Last night was an interminable struggle as his restless mind dominated his exhausted body until dawn. If only he had a way to turn off his thoughts. He wondered how other people seemed to fall asleep so quickly. What trickery allowed them to rest on a pillow and drop off to order? His eyes finally closed long after daybreak, and he remained in bed until the best part of the morning had passed. This lapse in routine would inevitably result in another bout of insomnia, and so it would go on. He would much rather read the daily newspaper or work on another article to sell to the Pall Mall Gazette once he returned to London. But he decided to go for a walk instead. And it would be a good long walk, as far as he could manage, given his frail health.

He had trudged around the town for about four or five miles, circumnavigating the centre and was now at the furthest end of the pier, enjoying the soporific effects of the sea swell and the remoteness of the location. His reverie was soon disturbed when two young women arrived and plonked themselves on the bench behind him. Two boisterous young women, one of whom was bordering on hysteria. He sighed and turned to move away when the more animated of the two said something interesting enough to make it worth remaining.

"But I called him lazybones, Nora, and all the time he was lying there dead."

"There, there, Milly. You weren't to know. It's not every day that one of your guests dies."

"Thank goodness," Millicent replied. "I've worked at The Albion for two years, and I've never seen a body or even an injured guest in all that time. Miss Crosby says she has witnessed a few deaths and Mr Gilbert seemed to know what to do about it, but I don't. I dread to think what my mother will have to say. It's not respectable working in a hotel where such things happen."

"How did the poor man die?"

"Mr Gilbert says it was suicide, but Miss Crosby says not to second-guess before the inquest."

"Inquest?"

"There will have to be an inquest, they say. When someone dies unexpectedly, the authorities need to find out why it happened."

"Was he travelling alone?"

"Quite alone," said Millicent, "but he works in London. Miss Crosby found a letter, and now they know how to contact his friends. It's just as well. The poor man forgot to sign the register, and we didn't know who he was until the letter turned up."

"So, he has a family then? They will be sad."

"I don't know about a family. But he works for an organisation." Millicent closed her eyes as she tried to visualise the address on the letter. "SPR," she said. "Society for something or other research. I can't quite remember, but it doesn't matter. The fact remains he is dead, and it is very upsetting."

Millicent continued to complain about her harrowing experience, but D'Onston was no longer listening. It would be too much of a coincidence to suppose that more than one member of the SPR was staying at The Albion on the same night. So, it followed that he knew the deceased. Edmund Gurney, who D'Onston had only seen a few short hours before, was dead. And whatever the contents of the letter held by the Hotel, it was nothing compared to the document D'Onston had in his possession. The beginnings of a plan began to form in his mind. For the first time in days, Roslyn D'Onston smiled.

Chapter One

INQUEST

Tuesday 10th Feb 1891

Lawrence stifled a yawn as he listened to the butcher giving evidence in the same monotonous tone that he remembered from the day of the incident. It was like hearing someone reading a list. The butcher's voice neither rose nor fell, remaining dull like the drone of wasp, and a boring wasp at that.

Lawrence had given his evidence at the beginning of the trial. He was only the second person sworn in by the borough coroner who had asked him to remain close at hand in case they needed him again.

It was pure bad luck that Lawrence was in Ipswich on the day of the accident at all. He would have been in Bury had it not been such a slow day at the office which he now shared with Violet Smith. After the initial surge of interest in their newly acquired shop, all went quiet. The new signage, promoting not only Harpham Private Investigators but Smith as well, did nothing to improve matters. Enquiries ceased, and the door remained steadfastly shut. Violet busied herself promoting their services taking on several jobs that were frankly beneath them, the missing fox terrier being the worst. Lawrence, never one to confront a problem head-on, began feeling the effects of the black dog again. His self-awareness had improved over the years, and he recognised the signs before they overwhelmed him. In the early days, he would start to feel low, before becoming irritable and dissatisfied. Then, he would succumb to a crushing depression that weighed so heavily upon him that he doubted it would ever stop. If he let things get that far, he became numb, introspective and would start wallowing in self-pity. His thoughts would turn, as always, to the night Catherine died and he would agonise about whether he could have saved Lily if he had tried harder. He would relive the night of the fire, smell the acrid smoke and hear the dreadful crackle of the life-snatching flames. Nausea would overcome him as he wondered whether little Lily had suffered as she cried for her Daddy.

Over the years he had learned to cope. Now when he began to feel more irritable than usual, he would do something physical. Something that required him to be active. Something that would counteract the voice inside that tormented him for daring to live. It was the reason that he had left an unimpressed Violet back in Bury Saint Edmunds to attend The Primrose League. She was, going under protest, to lunch with ladies she did not particularly like for the sake of their business. Meanwhile, Lawrence boarded a carriage bound for Ipswich where he intended to buy a new coat.

He had dismounted at the Ipswich Buttermarket, consulted with his tailor, and was preparing to find somewhere to eat lunch when he heard a distant rumble. A horseless cart thundered down the street and headed straight towards him at a lick of speed. He had jumped to one side and out of harm's way, but the elderly gentleman behind him never stood a chance. The cart hit him straight on, bowling him over and running across most of his body. Lawrence rushed to the man's aid as soon as he had recovered his wits, but to no avail. The man, it transpired, had never enjoyed good health and was dead before he hit the ground.

Weeks later, and Lawrence was now giving evidence about the incident. The coroner had called him to the stand at exactly twenty-two minutes past nine. A rapid-fire question and answer session ensued even though Lawrence had seen little of the accident. He had gleaned most of the facts from the butcher on the day. The butcher was a talker, and Lawrence had been a captive audience. Lawrence had rushed over to the victim and tried to make him comfortable in case he was still somehow clinging to life. The butcher took the opportunity to follow Lawrence and unburden himself, giving a blow by blow account of the events leading up to the accident. It started with an accusation about spoiled meat. A long-standing customer complained that his lamp chops were rotten. The butcher, who was the owner of the cart, denied it. Things soon turned nasty. The purchaser spread the word, blackening the butcher's good name. The butcher lost money and reported him to the police. After months of hostility, the accuser passed the shop and could not resist the opportunity to give the cart a good hard shove. Fortunately, the pony was unharnessed, or the situation could have been even worse. Lawrence had listened to the story, trying and failing to feign interest. The man could make a stage play sound dull.

Eventually, Lawrence had drifted into a reverie only

regaining concentration when Police Constable Claude Shalders arrived and took his statement. The part Lawrence played was small, and he did not expect to hear any more about it. Weeks later, a letter arrived asking him to give evidence at the inquest. He came, as requested, to the Woodhouse Street schoolroom where the coroner habitually held court. Lawrence considered it a shocking waste of a day until he thought of a silver lining. The coroner's court was close to Ipswich Police Station, and he was keen to visit an old friend, Inspector Fernleigh. It had been years since they had seen one another, and PC Shalders was one of Fernleigh's men. Lawrence decided to walk back to the Station with Shalders once the tedium of the coroner's court had ended.

It was half-past twelve when the coroner finally concluded matters. His verdict resulted in a gaol sentence for one man and a severe reprimand for the butcher. Lawrence, by then, was fighting to keep his eyes open, despite the draft in the old schoolroom. He had only managed to stay awake by exchanging knowing glances with PC Shalders who appeared to be suffering from boredom too. Lawrence had caught him raising his eyes heavenwards several times while the butcher was speaking. He had smiled his support knowing he should avoid over-familiarity with a junior police officer. But Shalders was almost the same age, and a partner in crime was essential if he wasn't going to disgrace himself by falling asleep in court.

The coroner thanked them for their attendance and permitted them to leave. Lawrence rose, buttoned his coat and left the court immediately. He found a pleasant spot under a tree and waited for PC Shalders to emerge.

Shalders soon arrived. "Are you still coming back to the station, Sir?" he asked.

"Definitely," said Lawrence. "That was hard going. I need to walk off the boredom."

PC Shalders grinned. "I'm sure Inspector Fernleigh will give you something to take the edge off it," he said.

Lawrence nodded. "I can assure you that my visit to Fernleigh is not just because of his exceedingly good taste in port. I wouldn't want you getting the wrong idea."

They traversed Woodhouse Street and passed The John Barleycorn Public House. PC Shalders raised a hand, and a middle-aged woman waved back.

"Do you come from around here?" asked Lawrence.

"No, not me," said PC Shalders. "I'm from Norwich. Can't you tell by the accent?"

"Sorry," Lawrence replied. "You seemed to know the landlady. I thought you might live nearby."

"It's part of my old beat," said Shalders. "But they moved me on six months ago. Being back is nice. They're good folk around here."

They had reached Rope Walk and were strolling towards the town centre. PC Shalders chattered amiably, displaying great enthusiasm for the area.

"You might think that this street is called Rope Walk because of the gaol," he said. "On account of the fact that there were gallows inside, but that's not the reason. It was once called Rope Lane and, as you might expect, there was a rope yard here too. Then the potteries arrived, and Rope Walk pottery became popular. I'm not sure why. It was remarkably ugly. My aunt kept a few brown earthenware pots with some sort of glaze on top. Not my cup of tea at all. There was a factory here right up until a few decades ago." Shalders beamed, delighted to be able to share his knowledge of the local history. They passed another bystander, and Shalders waved for the third time. PC Shalders was a warm, friendly man popular in the little community he had served until recently. A good policeman, Lawrence thought. He warmed to him.

"Almost here, sir," said Shalders as Lawrence spotted the familiar door of the Ipswich Police Station. Lawrence had entered that door many times while serving in the force. Though stationed in Bury Saint Edmunds, there had been many reasons to visit Ipswich. He still knew officers in the Suffolk Police force and had travelled extensively during his time in uniform. But that was before Catherine had died when he was open to the idea of sharing ideas and experiences with his fellow policeman. At one time he had a vast range of police colleagues to call upon for advice, from as far as Liverpool in the north to Exeter in the south-west, and good old Henry Moore in London. He had even collaborated with the Isle of Man constabulary on one notable occasion. But he had known Tom Fernleigh better than any of them although it had been a long time since the two had met. Too long. Lawrence's fault. Fernleigh, like many others, had been at Catherine's funeral and had tried hard to keep the friendship going afterwards. But Lawrence could not bear his grief, much less the pitying glances of friends. He had avoided their invitations, their offers of help, their visits even, opting instead for a self-imposed exile. That was over three years ago, and it was time to start re-building old friendships. Fernleigh would be the first. Lawrence smiled to himself as he followed Shalders into the Police Station.

The Police Station in Princes Street was comfortably familiar, but the smell hanging in the air by the front desk was not. Lawrence glanced at PC Shalders with an air of puzzlement.

Shalders nodded to the Constable standing behind the reception desk. "Old Morris been in again?" he said, more in the form of a statement than a question.

Benjamin Chenery raised his hand in acknowledgement and nodded. "Yes, the poor old boy's a bit ripe today. I gave him a shilling for a bath, but I don't suppose he'll bother."

Shalders sighed. "The usual problem?"

"As ever."

Shalders opened the door to an inner corridor, explaining as he ushered Lawrence through. "Poor old boy's not the full ticket," he said in his mellow Norfolk accent. "He has two grown children, smashing girls both of them. They would have him live with them in a heartbeat, but he won't hear of it. He sleeps in a run-down old shack at the back of the railway line and walks the town all day searching for his wife. From time to time, he turns up here asking if we have found her yet."

"Poor chap," Lawrence murmured. "I hope she turns up soon."

"She isn't missing," said Shalders. "She's dead. He can't accept it."

They walked up the corridor towards Fernleigh's office. Shalders continued to chat, but Lawrence was silent and deep in thought. Old Morris was wasting his life, unable to move on from the great tragedy that had befallen him. If Lawrence carried on ostrich-like for much longer, he was likely to end up the same way. He needed to stop immersing himself in solitary pursuits and start accepting invitations again.

Shalders reached a door on his right and rapped smartly against the inset glass window.

"Come," a voice boomed, and Shalders waved Lawrence through before retreating to the front desk.

"Lawrence Harpham, well, well." Inspector Fernleigh leapt from his desk and grasped Lawrence's right hand, shaking it for far longer than necessary. "How are you, old man? It's been a long time, a very long time. I am glad to see you. How have you been?" Fernleigh's voice trailed off as he realised that he was beginning to repeat himself.

"I am well," said Lawrence, "and sorry it has taken so long to find my way here. Some things take a while to get used to…" Now it was Lawrence's turn to run out of words.

Fernleigh broke the silence and returned to his desk. He opened the bottom left drawer and pulled out a large bottle of port and two glasses liberally covered in scratch marks.

"Have a drink," he said, filling the glasses to the top. He carelessly pushed one towards Lawrence. A red ring appeared around the bottom of the glass joining many similar ring marks on the wooden desk.

Lawrence smiled and drank a mouthful of Port. It was good, and he took another.

"What have you been doing for the last three years?" asked Fernleigh.

"I left the force," said Lawrence.

"I heard."

"I'm still in the business. I have an office in Bury. I'm a Private investigator."

"Are you now?" said Fernleigh. "That's news to me. Good for you."

Lawrence was about to tell Fernleigh that he had a business partner, and a female one at that, when there was a loud knock at the door. It opened to reveal Constable Chenery.

"There's a report of a dead body in Lower Brook

Street," said Chenery. "It doesn't seem to be a crime, but nobody knows who the woman is, so you might want to attend."

Fernleigh considered the matter. "I do," he said. "Do you want to join us, Lawrence? You can tell me the rest of your news on the way."

Chapter Two

A ROLLING STONE

Tuesday 10th Feb 1891

The route between the Police Station and 45 Lower Brook Street took Lawrence past several pubs. Each one reminded him that he had recently abandoned the best part of a glass of smooth, full-bodied port. His mouth watered at the thought.

Lawrence didn't have much appetite for dealing with the dead body. Under normal circumstances, he would have bypassed the opportunity, made his apologies and gone home. But the earlier conversation about Old Morris had shaken him. He did not want to end up like the old man and wanted to start making more of his life. It would have been useful to catch the earlier train to Bury, but the opportunity to spend more time with his old friend, Fernleigh was too good to miss. He would join them in their investigation and make the best of it.

45 Lower Brook Street was a terraced house like any other in the neighbourhood. Not too shabby, not too tidy

and it came as no surprise when Lawrence learned it was a boarding house. The three men stopped outside and surveyed the building. A curtain twitched in one of the upstairs rooms. "This one's yours," said Inspector Fernleigh. Police Constable Shalders acknowledged his superior, strode ahead and knocked on the door. A middle-aged woman who announced herself as Mrs Welton opened the door straight away. Barely a moment had passed between Shalders knock and her appearance in the doorway. She had evidently been waiting in the hall.

"Thank goodness you are here," she said, "I wasn't sure what to do."

"Is there somewhere we can sit?" asked Inspector Fernleigh. He watched the woman with a concerned expression on his face. She was ashen, with tear stained cheeks. She pointed towards a kitchen table at the rear with a trembling hand.

PC Shalders guided her towards the chair, and she sat hugging her shoulders. A young child, clad in a dirty beige skirt and stockings peppered with holes, perched beside her. Shalders pulled out a wooden chair and sat with them. He patted the girl's hand and smiled. There was only one chair left, so Lawrence and Fernleigh remained standing.

Shalders addressed the mother. "You've had quite a shock," he said. "Tell me what happened? Then we can arrange to have the body removed."

"It was me. I found her." The little girl responded before her mother had a chance to answer. Lawrence watched her earnest face and tried to guess her age.

"Yes, Edith found her," echoed the woman. "She was running an errand but could not get into the room."

"Who for?" asked Fernleigh.

"That's the problem, Sir," said Mrs Welton. "We don't

know. This house belongs to my aunt. I'll take you to meet her in a minute, but even she didn't know the name of her lodger."

"I did," said Edith. "She told me to call her Miss Moss."

"Well, why didn't you say?" Theresa Welton placed her hand a little too firmly on the kitchen table. A spoon lying in a chipped saucer tinkled against the china.

"She told me not to," said the girl sullenly. "She didn't want anyone else to know, but I asked her, and she wouldn't say at first. But then she did."

"Really. You might have told me."

"We know now," said Shalders, "and that's the main thing." He smiled encouragingly at the girl. "When did you see her last, Edith?" he asked.

"Last night, sir," said Edith, "but she was ailing, proper bad."

"How so?"

"She kept holding her side and wincing. She cried out, and I asked her whether I should fetch the doctor, but she said no. She said that she would be better soon."

"Had it happened before?" asked Shalders.

"Yes, but not as badly. Miss Moss often squinted like she was in pain, but she never cried out before."

"And what sort of errands did you run for her?"

"I made her food, sir. Beef and cornflour and tea, always two ounces of tea. But she only asked me to prepare food once a week."

Inspector Fernleigh and Lawrence exchanged glances.

"What did she eat in the meantime?" asked Fernleigh.

"I don't know," said Edith, pulling a thread from her stocking. Another hole appeared revealing a grazed knee. "I bought her other stuff from time to time, but not much of it."

"And did she pay you?"

"Always," said Edith. "The money was waiting for me every time."

"You've done very well, Edith," said Inspector Fernleigh.

"Run along home, now." Theresa Welton had regained her composure. She walked towards the kitchen door and ushered her child from the room. "Follow me, and I'll take you upstairs," she continued.

They climbed the creaky staircase and arrived at a room on the left. A hasp hung uselessly from the door.

"What happened here?" asked Inspector Fernleigh.

"That was me earlier," said Mrs Welton. "The old woman kept the door locked with a nail through the hasp. When Edith couldn't get in, she ran down to me, and when I couldn't make myself heard, I broke the door."

"Are you going to take her away?" A barely audible voice interrupted the discussion.

"This is Auntie Elizabeth," said Theresa Welton, gesturing to an elderly woman.

Elizabeth Baker leaned into her walking stick while clinging to the door frame of the opposite room as if remaining on her feet depended upon it. She was old, and deep frown lines furrowed her face. Silver white hair hung sparsely from her scalp, insufficient to cover the crown of her head. A tattered, old bottle green cardigan covered her from neck to knee. The cuffs reaching over her knuckles were frayed at the edges. She watched the three men through milky blue eyes and spoke directly to Inspector Fernleigh.

"Are you going to take her away? She can't stay here."

"Yes, of course," said Fernleigh. "But I need you to answer a few questions first."

"If you must."

"Would you like to sit down somewhere?"

"No," she said. "Ask what you want and be quick about it."

Fernleigh nodded imperceptibly to Shalders.

The Police Constable cleared his throat. "How long has the deceased lived with you?"

"About three months," said Elizabeth Baker, in a clear, but tremulous voice. "And before you ask, I didn't know who she was. She would not tell me. She was not at all what you would call neighbourly."

"And did she share any of the other rooms?"

"No. I have four guest bedrooms. Each of my tenants has one room each, and the rest of the house is for my use."

"Did she pay her rent?"

"Yes, she always paid her rent on time."

"And did she seem in good health when you went to collect the rent?"

"I do not know. She would not let me in. She put her hand through the door and paid the money when I asked her for it. But she refused to tell me her name, and she did not want to make my acquaintance. As long as she paid her rent, I did not care. Is that everything?"

Theresa Welton smiled apologetically. "Come now, Auntie. Let's get you back to your room. I'll make you a nice cup of tea. Feel free to carry on," she said over her shoulder as she closed the door behind them.

Lawrence was closest to the door. He pushed it open using the highly polished brass finger plate set incongruously above the broken hasp. Lawrence walked inside and peered through the gloom. "Good Lord," he exclaimed.

The deceased woman lay on top of the bed in a room best described as squalid. The bedroom was sizeable which made the absence of furniture more incongruous. Except for the wooden bedstead and one small trestle table upon which a spirit lamp stood, the room was devoid of furnishings. A tiled fireplace surrounded an empty, unlit fire which had not been in use for many months. Five photographs, faded to the point of anonymity, were perched on top of the mantlepiece. The room was malodorous, smelling of destitution and decay.

The woman, confirmed by Edith as Miss Moss, lay directly on a stained mattress. A dirty, threadbare blanket covered her from feet to midriff, and her hands were clasped together as if in prayer. Inspector Fernleigh leaned over the body and tried to prise her hands apart. Her fingers were rigid and cold.

"She's been dead for some time," he said unnecessarily. All three men had a wealth of experience when it came to death and were familiar with the effects of rigor mortis.

PC Shalders walked towards the window. Heavy curtains blocked the daylight from the half of the room not illuminated by the open door. He pulled them apart and heaved the window open. It was winter, but no less cold outside than in the unheated room they now occupied. Letting the outside in might, at least, dispel the unpleasant smell, he thought.

"Hello, what's all this?" Shalders stubbed his toe against a row of boxes stacked beneath the window. He rubbed one of the dusty labels. It read "London & County Banking Company."

"Have you ever seen such a miserable room?" Lawrence exclaimed. "How did she live? There are no candles, no matches. What an awful existence."

"Worse than I have ever seen," said Shalders. "Including the East End of London where the poverty is almost unimaginable."

"Foul." Inspector Fernleigh curled his lip as he spoke. He had opened a canister by the spirit lamp while Shalders was talking and found a mouldy piece of cheese and two rotting chops. The inspector shoved the lid back on and prodded at a lump of bread in a nearby basket.

"Stale," he grimaced.

"She does not seem emaciated," said Lawrence looking at the body. The woman was pallid, but her cheeks were not sunken nor did her arms appear spindly.

"That's because she's wearing several sets of clothes." Inspector Fernleigh had joined Lawrence near the body and lifted the blanket. "It must be how she kept herself warm."

"How unpleasant," said Lawrence. "Two layers of clothes wouldn't offer much protection against the freezing winter temperatures. Poverty is deplorable," he continued, shaking his head. "What terrible conditions this poor woman endured."

"She wasn't poor," said Shalders. "Quite the opposite." While the other two men were inspecting the body, Shalders had opened one of the boxes. "Look at this," he said. "This box is full of financial paperwork. Consols, whatever they are, and dividends. There's even a handkerchief full of coins in here. Well over two pounds in small change."

"Consolidated stocks," said Fernleigh moving towards the window. He picked up a handful of documents and rifled through. "You are right. She wasn't poor. I've seen this sort of thing before," he continued. "Miss Moss was a miser."

"Awful way to live," said Lawrence gruffly. He was

pacing the room and trying to avoid looking at the dead body. Like the decaying food, it was imparting an unpleasant smell. He suspected that Miss Moss had avoided bathing in the same way she had avoided the rest of life's necessities.

He stopped by the fireplace and examined the chimney breast. A framed sampler hung from the wall.

"Curious," he said aloud. The other two men ignored him. They were still discussing the contents of the box and left Lawrence to his musings.

He peered at the discoloured glass again. Its presence was at odds with the rest of the room which was sparse and ill-kept. The dead woman had not spent a penny if she could avoid it. She did not waste money on necessities, never mind trinkets. Even the faces in the row of photographs across the mantle looked more like the dead than the living. Why would she bother to hang a sampler?

Lawrence reached into his pocket and located his handkerchief. He unhooked the sampler from the wall and cleaned the dirty glass.

"Physical comforts serve me ill, in Purgatory by God's own will, relinquish chattels, give me peace, ease my conscience, make it cease."

Shalders and Fernleigh stopped what they were doing. "What did you say?" asked Fernleigh.

Lawrence re-read the verse.

"What do you suppose that means?" asked Shalders.

"It seems like she has deliberately chosen to live this way. She has settled on this half-life, not by necessity, but by inclination." Lawrence stroked his chin as he considered the implications.

"She's probably religious," said Fernleigh, "and has renounced her worldly possessions."

"Except she hasn't, sir, has she?" said Shalders who had resumed his inspection of the boxes.

"I don't follow," said Fernleigh.

"She is still using the money," said Shalders. "I don't know much about stocks and shares, but she has cashed in some of her assets, and some are current. She still has access to a lot of money and uses it when she needs to. I wonder if Mrs Jones knows any more about it?"

"What are you talking about?" Inspector Fernleigh was tiring of the squalid room now. It was evident that the woman had died a natural death — not much reason for them to be there at all.

"Mrs Sybil Jones," said Shalders brandishing an envelope. He passed it to the Inspector.

"I see," said Fernleigh. He scrutinised the letter. "It's from Mrs Sybil Jones of Montpellier Street, Brighton to Miss Ruth Moss of Chelmsford. Good. We now have confirmation of her name. The girl was right about that, at least. There's something else in the envelope — a clipping of The Royal Albion Hotel in Brighton. 'There's a room number on the reverse. 'Number 27'."

Lawrence reached for the envelope. "Now, what's all that about?" he mused.

"It doesn't matter," said Fernleigh. "There will be an inquest, of course, but regardless of her lifestyle, this woman died naturally. There is no need to spend any more time on it."

"The circumstances feel wrong," said Lawrence. "The sampler is out of kilter with the rest of the room. It does not fit. We are missing something."

"But no crime has taken place here, Lawrence," said Fernleigh. "I cannot justify an investigation. We are hard pressed in the force, and there are never enough resources."

"Then let me look into it," said Lawrence.

"Look at what, though?"

"Let me check into the background of Miss Moss and find out why she sacrificed a life of comfort for this. If it turns out that she is religious or a little senile, I will drop it at once. I could go to Brighton and speak to Sybil Jones, and while I am there, I can find out the significance of Room 27."

"I would rather you didn't."

"What harm can it do?"

Fernleigh considered the matter. "Very well," he said. It was a pointless task, but it might be beneficial to Lawrence, and it provided an excuse for keeping in contact, which had to be a good thing. "Three days only, Lawrence. I will not be able to authorise any longer than that."

"Three days is all I need." Lawrence smiled and shook Fernleigh's hand. An investigation that interested him was just what he needed. Lawrence left the dismal room with renewed purpose.

Tuesday 10th February 1891 – Evening

"What do you mean you are going to Brighton? You've only just got back." Violet Smith was sitting behind a sturdy oak desk in the offices of Harpham & Smith. She was holding an ink pen which had leaked. Indigo ink pooled across the ledger which rested on her blotting pad and occupied most of her desk.

"It's a new case," said Lawrence, "and an interesting one."

"But you know we're supposed to be going to Chelmondiston in two days. Will you be back in time?"

"No, of course not. Can't Chelmondiston wait?"

Violet pushed back a curl of hair with an inky finger. "No, the psychic researcher arrives on Thursday. It really won't do, Lawrence."

Lawrence sighed. "Remind me of the purpose of this Chelmondiston case?" he asked.

"The haunting," said Violet, "except it isn't really a haunting. It can't be. That's why the Woodward's have asked for our help. We're going to find out who's been playing silly tricks on the household. At least that's what Mrs Woodward wants. The Reverend is taking it seriously. He thinks there is a ghost and has arranged for a member of The Society for Psychical Research to investigate. It's all set for two days' time."

"Well, it sounds ridiculous," said Lawrence. "How much are they paying us for this nonsense?"

"How much is Inspector Fernleigh paying you?" Violet retorted.

Lawrence pursed his lips and turned away. He did not know how much, if anything, he would receive for his trouble. And he wasn't going to tell Violet that curiosity had got the better of his financial interests, yet again.

"Can't you delay the Brighton job?" asked Violet. "You may not approve of the Chelmondiston investigation, but Mrs Woodward has agreed to pay our fees immediately. The rent is due next week, and we need the money."

"Not possible," said Lawrence. "I have only got three days to investigate. I must go tomorrow. There is no choice."

"What am I supposed to say to Mrs Woodward?"

"Nothing," said Lawrence. "You can go to Chelmondiston, and I will go to Brighton."

"And who will mind the shop?"

"Who would have minded it if we had both gone ghost-hunting?"

"I was going to ask Annie," said Violet.

"Annie Hutchinson? The girl who cleans the office? Do you think she's up to it?"

"She's very bright," said Violet. "All she has to do is take messages if someone calls."

"Doesn't she have other cleaning jobs to go to?"

"Yes, but her sister Mary Ann Bird is living with them while her husband is in London. She will help out when Annie is busy."

"You seem to have it all in hand," said Lawrence. "There shouldn't be a problem."

"Lawrence, you aren't listening." Violet slammed her pen onto the blotting pad. It bounced across the desk leaving a spatter of ink.

"What on earth is wrong, Violet?" Lawrence put his paper down and stared at her. A red flush had settled across her cheeks, and she pursed her lips angrily. "Sorry, but I don't understand why this plan causes a problem."

Violet paused. She was trying not to cry and trying equally hard not to slap him. "You have been a private detective for years," she said. "I was still a lady's companion this time last year. Investigating is new to me. I have never taken a case of my own before."

"Oh, I see." Lawrence's gaze softened. He nodded. "I'm sorry, I did not think. Of course, this is still very new to you. But you know a great deal more about the haunting case than I do, and you are good with people and a sound judge of character. One solves this type of case by asking questions. It's a matter of talking to people and establishing whether their answers are truthful. It is an ideal first case."

"But what if they won't talk freely, or if I cannot tell when they are lying?"

"Then Mrs Woodward is no worse off than she was before. But you will get them to talk. You excel at gaining confidences."

Violet sighed. "I suppose so," she said. "Very well. I will go to Chelmondiston, and you can pursue the Brighton case if you must. When will you be back?"

"Two or three days, at the most," said Lawrence. "I'll leave first thing in the morning. Good luck on your first solo case." Lawrence beamed, and Violet returned a weak smile. The scenario was not what she had envisaged when they opened Harpham and Smith Investigators nine short months ago. For the first time since they began working together, she wondered whether there was any longevity in the partnership.

Chapter Three

BRIGHTON REVISITED

Wednesday 11th February 1891

Lawrence arrived at Brighton Railway station feeling tired and irritable. He had underestimated the amount of travelling time involved and failed to consider the early hour he would need to rise. Fatigue had set in, and his stomach was empty. He had given a passing thought to food when he left his rooms at cock-crow and grabbed a piece of fruit of indeterminable age which he thrust into his pocket. He later supplemented it with a bread roll bought from a stall outside the London, Brighton and South Coast Railway Headquarters. Hungry and tired, he was beginning to wish he had joined Violet on her Suffolk investigation.

Lawrence hailed a cab from the station and soon arrived outside The Royal Albion Hotel in Brighton. It was a handsome building positioned close to the sea. The rear of the Hotel overlooked the coast and a broad road passed between it and the aquarium directly opposite. A further open area to the front of the porch provided a pleasant outlook. Lawrence inhaled the sea air and began to relax. He paid the cabman, collected his case and sauntered into the hotel to find a woman standing on a chair in the foyer.

Nora Knight was slight in build and a shade over five foot tall. As Lawrence entered the reception area, he watched her stand on tiptoes, trying in vain to reach a paper dart. The missile protruded from the top of a tall cabinet filled with pigeon holes. Keys and messages were sparsely scattered inside, with many compartments empty, indicative of the slow winter season.

"Can I help you reach that?" Lawrence asked.

Nora wobbled precariously on the chair as she turned to face him. "Sorry sir," she said, wiping her hands on her skirt as she steadied herself before getting down. "What must you think of me?" she continued.

"I can reach it if you like," offered Lawrence.

"No thank you, sir," she said. "I'll be in enough trouble if old angry wasp sees it up there. Miss Crosby, I mean. Thomas and I were larking around, and it got stuck. Still, she won't know who it was, will she? Can we start again?" Nora flashed a broad smile. "How can I help you, sir," she asked.

"I need a room for two nights," said Lawrence.

"Of course," Nora replied. "You can have your choice. It is out of Season, and we are half empty. What floor would you like?"

"It's not so much a matter of what floor I'm on," said Lawrence, "but I would particularly like Room 27."

"That's impossible," said Nora, biting her lip. "I would have let you have it, but someone has already taken Room 27."

"I see." Lawrence steepled his hands while Nora tried to

ignore the disconcerting sight of one gloved hand and the other bare.

"Why do you want Room 27, if you don't mind me asking?"

Lawrence debated whether to evoke her sympathy by making up a story. A sad story, about a beloved aunt who had a particular penchant for Room 27. A sadly deceased beloved aunt who liked nothing more than to watch the ocean from the window of the aforesaid room. But what if Room 27 faced away from the sea? He settled on the truth instead. "Something happened in Room 27 a few years ago. I don't suppose you happen to know what it was?"

"Oh, but I do," said Nora. "I remember very well. My friend, Milly, found him."

Lawrence set down his suitcase in Room 23, which was the nearest he could get to Room 27. He peered out of the window and considered the information given by Nora. The young woman appeared remarkably well-informed about the death of Edmund Gurney. She had been a close friend of the girl who found him. The sight of a dead guest had so upset her friend, Millicent, that she fled the hotel in search of Nora. A dutiful friend, Nora had offered comfort and consolation before escorting Milly home. Her obligations fulfilled, she had returned to the Hotel and joined the deputy Manager and Manageress. Between them, they relocated the body to a downstairs room where it was discretely collected by the coroner's staff later that day. Nora's next half day fell on the day of the inquest. Being something of an inquisitive girl, she decided to attend. She was not called to give evidence but was keen to find out more about the deceased guest and how inquests worked.

Nora had a good memory and recounted the story to Lawrence in detail. The dead man was Edmund Gurney, and he had been a talented musician and philosopher. When Nora mentioned that Gurney had been a founder member of the Society for Psychical Research, Lawrence raised an eyebrow. By unexpected coincidence, Violet was also working with the SPR in Chelmondiston.

According to Nora, Gurney's death was unusual. He had suffered from neuralgia and was in the habit of self-medicating. On the night of his death, he had strapped a mask to his face, inhaled a substance believed to be chloroform and had consequently overdosed. The hotel staff contacted one of his colleagues who later gave evidence at the inquest. The man, a doctor, had confirmed Gurneys' use of opiates for pain relief and the coroner ruled his death accidental. And that had been the end of it, as far as the authorities were concerned.

Having established the basic facts, Lawrence grilled Nora at length about the details. She seemed happy to talk and held nothing back. Gurney, she said, hadn't registered at reception and it had been the devil of a job to find out who he was. There was no identification on his body, but a later search produced an undelivered letter written on SPR headed paper. Names of the primary committee members were printed across the top of the letter. After a little investigation, they tracked down Doctor Myers and summoned him to the Hotel. Myers identified the body and organised its removal to London.

Lawrence sat on the bed and marshalled his thoughts. It was odd that he had come across the SPR again, but it was only a coincidence. Gurney's death was strange but explicable. There seemed no room for doubt about the verdict. Yet Lawrence felt uneasy. But uneasy or not, if no suspicion was attached to the death in Room 27, there was little point in him being in Brighton. If the death was a terrible accident, what more was there to do?

Lawrence thought about it as he unpacked and washed his hands. The trip to Brighton had been rotten, and it was clear that he didn't have a case to investigate. And his conscience was beginning to trouble him. He had let Violet down by abandoning her in Bury and leaving her to carry out the case alone. Lawrence knew that she was capable of running the investigation solo, even if she did not. But he should not have forced it on her. He would return to Bury with some trinket or other and show his appreciation.

Lawrence unfolded a spare pair of trousers and hung them in the wardrobe. Then, he sat beside the dressing table and opened his notebook. He rifled through pages of spidery scrawl looking for a blank sheet and grimaced as he tried to read his writing. It was poor, even by his low standards. His writing used to be tidy until the fire. The injuries he sustained made it necessary to learn to write all over again. His left hand, with its scarred and twisted fingers, was not up to the job. Lawrence remembered the months of frustration as he relearned this most basic of skills using his right hand. Now, his damaged hand was a little stronger and he might be ambidextrous if he tried. But he still hated the scars on his maimed hand and kept it hidden beneath the glove while continuing to produce an almost unreadable scribble.

Lawrence dropped the notebook and retrieved it from his lap. It opened at the back where he had written a short list. The second item was a note to visit Sybil Jones. He might as well see her now that he was here. Once he had eaten, that is. Nothing would get in the way of a good dinner. Lawrence grabbed his coat and hat and made his way towards the dining room.

It was a pleasant walk to Montpellier Street, despite the weather. The pavements were hard with frost, and there was a pleasing crispness in the air. The faint morning sun had all but disappeared and clouds, heavy with snow, hung low in the sky. Lawrence pulled his collar up and pushed his hat over his dark hair, now greying at the temples. He strode with purpose, long legs covering the distance effortlessly.

He passed through the centre of town listening to the clip-clop of hooves across the streets. It was quiet and hardly anyone was around. As Lawrence walked past the residential houses, he peered inside. Well stoked fires burned brightly in their grates. The inhabitants of Brighton seemed happy to remain indoors and away from the cold. The roads became steeper as Lawrence walked north. The houses were bigger and more uniform. Terraces of identical properties stood sentry either side of the road. He reached Montpellier Street and located his destination. The correspondence found in the squalid bedroom where Ruth Moss passed her final days had been useful, after all.

Sybil Jones lived in a handsome, white, bay-fronted house. It stood three storeys' high and was accessible through a black door containing a large brass door knocker in the shape of a lion's head. Lawrence knocked three times, took a step back and waited. Nothing happened for several minutes. Sighing, he tried again — this time knocking harder. He was about to leave when a voice called, "I'll be with you in a moment." Eventually, the door swung open to reveal an elderly woman with white hair and a bronzed complexion.

Lawrence removed his hat and smiled. "Are you Mrs Sybil Jones?" he asked. The woman nodded. He reached into his pocket and passed over the letter she had written to Ruth Moss three years before. Lawrence had surreptitiously removed the letter on the day Ruth Moss died. He hadn't quite got around to asking Fernleigh if he could, on the basis that Fernleigh was sure to have agreed, and if he didn't, well, problem avoided. "I am Lawrence Harpham," he said. "Would you mind if I ask you a few questions about Ruth Moss?"

Five minutes later, Lawrence was sitting in the parlour in a comfortable armchair in front of the fire. His coat and hat hung on the hat stand in the hallway, and a cup of tea and a fruit scone were on a small table by his side. Having been well looked after, Lawrence felt a pang of guilt about the news he was about to deliver.

Sybil Jones spoke first. "Now, my dear, what do you want to ask me?"

Lawrence leaned forward. "I have bad news," he said.

"She's dead, isn't she?" asked Sybil Jones.

"Yes, I'm afraid so."

"How did she die?"

"She was ill. She passed away in her sleep."

Sybil nodded, sipping daintily from her china teacup. "I hope she did not suffer," she said.

"No," said Lawrence, not knowing if it was true or not. "It was a natural death."

"Then, how can I help?"

Lawrence considered how much he ought to divulge about Ruth's living conditions. He did not want to upset Sybil Jones but felt he should put some context behind his questions. He decided to lead up to it.

"How long did you know her for?" he asked.

"Let me think. It must have been upwards of fifteen years. Yes, that's right. Ruth moved here first. She had the house over there." Sybil Jones pointed through the window to a similar house diagonally opposite her own. "She owned a boarding house, like mine. That's how we became friends. I inherited this house from my Uncle, and it was far too big for me, so I decided to take in boarders. Well, Ruth had been doing it for years, so I asked her advice, and we got along famously. We looked after each other's houses when the other wanted to go away and visit family or friends. The arrangement worked well."

"Good," murmured Lawrence taking a bite of scone. He was not hungry and was eating to be polite, but the scone was delicious.

"Very nice," he said.

Sybil Jones smiled. "There are more in the kitchen."

Lawrence shook his head. "That's kind, but I mustn't be greedy. Now, there was a newspaper clipping in the letter you sent to Ruth Moss. I wondered what it meant?"

Sybil Jones removed the snippet from the letter. "Oh yes," she said. I remember it well. "I sent this to Ruth when poor Mr Gurney died."

"You knew him?"

"We both knew him," she said, "although Ruth was better acquainted than I."

"How so?"

"He was a regular visitor to Brighton," said Sybil. "Mr Gurney and his associates came here often. They conducted experiments."

"Experiments?"

"Oh, yes. Mr Gurney studied hypnotism and telepathy. It was very scientific and quite successful, I believe. Anyway, Mr Smith was one of Mr Gurney's young men, and his mother ran a boarding house on The Promenade. Well, Mr Gurney often stayed there, but it used to get booked up in the summer. One year they were so full that he came to Ruth instead and his visits became regular after that. When Ruth left, he stayed with me a few times."

"So, you wrote to Ruth to let her know about his death?"

"I did," said Sybil. "I thought she would like to know, but she never wrote back."

"Odd that he stayed at The Royal Albion on the night of his death."

"I had never known it," said Sybil. "He always boarded."

"Curious," said Lawrence. He picked up his teacup and put it to his lips, just as a large, orange cat leapt into his lap.

"Marmaduke, get down!"

The cat ignored her and started grooming. Lawrence glared at the intruder in his lap and put the teacup down again.

"Push him off if you like," said Sybil.

Lawrence would have liked nothing better. Cats made him sneeze, and this particular cat was an unfortunate colour. If it stayed in his lap much longer, it would make a nice mess of orange cat hair over his perfectly laundered suit. But he had a series of difficult questions to ask, so he smiled and tickled the cat behind its ears. It settled down and began to purr.

"Did Miss Moss keep a tidy boarding house?"

"Of course, she was very house proud. Why do you ask?"

"I ask because she died in unfortunate conditions."

"You said her death was normal."

"It was, but her room was, well…" Lawrence searched

for the right words. "It was empty, bare. There were hardly any possessions in her room, and the place was untidy, dirty. But she did not lack means. She had more than enough money to live a comfortable life. It was a choice."

"Oh." Sybil Jones eyes glazed over. She stared from the window in silence, her thoughts elsewhere. Lawrence waited.

Eventually, Sybil turned to face him.

"It all stemmed from that man," she said. "The whole thing. He was the reason she sold her house. She was never the same again."

Lawrence sat up and shifted in his seat. The cat scowled. "What man?" Lawrence asked.

"I don't know," said Sybil. "Ruth didn't either. That's how it is with boarding houses. Sometimes people book in advance and sometimes they turn up out of the blue, wondering if you have a room. Well, that's what happened. It was out of season, quiet and a man called and asked if he could stay for a few days. Ruth said yes, and everything seemed fine. On the third night, Ruth went up to bed and passed him on the landing. The man was coming out of his room with a manic look in his eyes, staring as if he wasn't in control of his faculties. Ruth asked him what was wrong, but there was no reply. Then she walked past him to go to her room, and as she walked by, he grabbed her from behind and held a knife to her neck. She cried out, and something changed in him, and he dropped the knife. He shook his head from side to side as if he was trying to clear his head. Then, he noticed her trembling before him and pointed to the knife on the floor. "Did I do that?" he asked, as if thought he might have, but was not sure. Ruth fled into her bedroom and locked the door. By the time she came out the next morning, he had gone."

"And you have no idea who he was?"

"None at all. I told Ruth to go to the police, but she refused. She felt foolish, having a man in the house and knowing nothing about him. What could she tell them, after all?"

"Was there anything about this man to identify him? Did she tell you what he looked like?"

"She said he was well-dressed and intelligent. Oh, and she thought he was a professional gentleman."

"What do you think she meant by that?"

"I took it to mean that he had an occupation, but a skilled one. In hindsight, she may have meant the opposite and that he was a gentleman of means. I am not sure what her exact words were."

"You say she sold her boarding house soon after."

"Immediately after. Ruth sold it within the month."

"And you never saw her again."

"I did," sighed Sybil. "One last time. It was in the Spring of 1888 before Mr Gurney died. He passed away in June that year. Ruth and I had kept in touch a little, sending the occasional letter here and there. Ruth had returned to Essex, you see. She owned a cottage in the village of Tendring. My aunt lived in Manningtree, and I went to visit her that Spring. I didn't tell Ruth because I wasn't sure whether I would have the opportunity to see her. As it happened, I had a spare half a day, so I made my way to her cottage."

"Did you speak to her?"

"Yes, but I wish I hadn't. It was not a happy reunion. She opened the door but did not invite me in. She suggested that we walk across the fields and we did. But she was preoccupied. Ruth had her eccentricities, but everything about her was different from before."

"In character or appearance?"

"Both. She was poorly dressed. Her clothes were old, and her cardigan buttoned the wrong way, but she did not seem to notice. And she was thinner, much thinner than when I had known her. She hardly spoke and took no joy in the visit. I told her my news, but she exchanged nothing in return. After walking for half an hour, we found a hillock and sat in silence for a while. Then she grabbed my hand and told me that I had been right, and she should have told the police about her lodger. He would kill one day, and it would be her fault. She spoke earnestly, but with wild, haunted eyes, as if she carried an unendurable burden. I told her it was nothing. She couldn't have stopped him because she didn't know anything about him. Besides, it was unlikely to happen again, and he could be dead or in an asylum. I told her that she was not responsible and should stop worrying. But she said over and over again, that she should have fetched help when he attacked her. She had woken every day since convinced that she had looked into the face of the devil."

"Poor woman. He must have frightened her out of her wits?"

"I hate to say it about a dear friend, but I believe she was suffering from an ailment of the mind. She fixated on the man. It must have been a terrifying experience, but almost three years had passed since it happened. She ought to have come to terms with it by then. No, the incident affected her sanity."

Lawrence reached into his pocket and pulled out his notebook. He turned a page then cleared his throat. "Does this sound familiar?" he asked, reading, prosaically, from his notes. "Physical comforts serve me ill, in Purgatory by God's own will, relinquish chattels, give me peace, ease my conscience, make it cease."

"I have not heard that verse before," said Sybil. "But it perfectly describes the burden I witnessed in her and could not name. Unimaginable guilt weighed her down from the moment of the attack. Everything you say makes me think that she spent her final years in penance."

Chapter Four

THE CHELMONDISTON HAUNTING

Thursday 12th February 1891

Violet alighted from the horse-drawn carriage and gave a cheery wave to the driver. It was, in her opinion, more than he deserved. From the moment she closed the door he had ignored her, despite her unfailing politeness. He hadn't responded to her friendly hello and had grunted when asked about the length of the journey. She ended up none the wiser about her likely arrival time. Still, she was not going to start her first solo investigation in a bad mood. She had learned that the best way to overcome negativity was by being relentlessly nice. She continued to be pleasant and carried on waving until he was out of sight.

Violet turned her attention away from the grumpy cabman and towards a sprawling ivy-clad building nearby, which she took to be the rectory. She traversed the driveway, walked past the shrubbery, and arrived outside a large wooden door. She stood for a moment, steadying her nerves, then stepped up and rang the bell. Moments later, a young housemaid answered the door. Violet announced herself and the maid escorted her into a large sitting room where the lady of the house soon appeared.

Alice Woodward was a slender woman of about thirty years of age. She carried herself with an almost military deportment. Her blonde hair was braided tightly without so much as one stray curl daring to defy the uniformity of her hairstyle. Her nose was straight and symmetrical, her eyebrows perfectly arched. She was a handsome, self-assured woman. Not at all what Violet expected in a Rector's wife.

"Hello," she said, offering a flawlessly manicured hand. "I am Alice Woodward. You must be Miss Smith."

Violet shook her hand and smiled. "I am," she said.

"Do you mind if I call you Violet?"

"Not at all."

Alice Woodward nodded. "My husband has business at the church," she said. "It is useful as I need to discuss some details with you privately."

"Does he know I am coming?"

"Of course," said Alice, "but he does not know why, or even who you are for that matter."

"Yes, I remember you suggested using my name, but not my profession. You did not embellish further in your letter."

"It is much easier to speak in person," she said. "You will remember that I mentioned a gentleman belonging to The Society for Psychical Research? Well, he will arrive later today. His colleague has been before, but only to make a report. This time he will investigate using the latest scientific means."

"What is the nature of your difficulty?" asked Violet.

"As I said, this household has been subject to strange manifestations, some seen and some heard."

"Have you witnessed them?"

"I have heard sounds with no obvious explanation, but I have seen nothing untoward."

"Yet others have?"

"Indeed. And my husband, The Reverend, is one of them. He is an honest man and not given to fancies. If he says he has seen an apparition, then he believes it. But that is not to say these events must be supernatural. I am firmly of the opinion that someone in this house is playing tricks."

"I see," said Violet. "Would I be right in thinking the manifestations have been going on for some time?"

"Yes, you would. The sightings are not new. People in the village claim that the hauntings, as they call them, began long before we arrived. They saw them during the time of the previous incumbent. I do not believe it. There are no such things as ghosts, although the locals talk of it constantly. With each alleged sighting, the story grows traction. Our last housemaid left because of it. Fortunately, our current one seems more sensible. But I want to put an end to the speculation. It is fair to say that I have different views from those of my husband."

"What is he expecting from the investigation?"

"He hopes to find a way to lay the spirit to rest. He thinks the ghost is a poor tormented soul walking the earth searching for peace."

"He truly believes there is a ghost?"

"Of course, he does," said Alice Woodward, "he is a Minister of the Church, after all. Faith is central to his thought process. It is not so very different from believing in God and the Holy Ghost, is it?"

"I suppose not," said Violet, uncertainly. "Although I am a Christian, yet I could never believe in spirits or apparitions. It does not make logical sense."

"We are of the same mind, then," smiled Alice Woodward. "Nothing will convince me that this is anything other than a prank. But it is useful that we are in the hands of reputable investigators. They have already carried out a lot of work on the effects of shared hallucinations. There will be a rational explanation for the disturbances in this rectory, I am certain."

"What have you told the Reverend about me?"

"Oh, he thinks you are an old school friend from Little Walsingham, the village I grew up in."

"That is ideal," smiled Violet. "I lived in Norfolk for many years myself. I know the area well."

"Isn't that marvellous." Alice Woodward's eyes sparkled." I could hardly have planned it better. Now, let me tell you about the household. There are only a few suspects to consider. The Reverend and I rattle around the property alone. We have no children, and the house is, for the most, quiet. Anne Durrell is our cook and Kate Harris, our housemaid. A gardener by the name of John Daldy comes from the village most days. Finally, there is Frederick — Frederick Lucas. He is our odd job boy and turns up here only when asked. It is Frederick who has raised the most suspicion as far as I am concerned. He is a typical young boy, always up to mischief and without much in the way of a conscience. It will not surprise me in the least if he has some part in this. You should speak to him as soon as possible."

Violet was busy scribbling in her notepad while Alice spoke.

"I will," she said. "I will speak to everyone."

"But covertly," Alice warned, "the Reverend must not know."

Violet nodded and replaced the notebook in her bag.

"Come," said Alice, rising to her feet. "Let me introduce you to my husband."

They walked the short distance to Saint Andrews parish church, chatting as they meandered through the graveyard. The church, set in a tranquil location, was unexpectedly full of people and was anything but quiet. Two workmen sawed panels of wood on a large bench outside the porch, scattering flecks of sawdust over the grass. Another group of workers were sitting cross-legged by the corner of the tower and drinking from wooden cups. Clad only in shirt sleeves, their jackets lay in a jumbled heap on the ground. Violet shivered. It was February and not at all warm.

"Good day, Ma'am," said the older carpenter as Violet and Alice approached the church.

Alice smiled and nodded, then opened the porch door and went inside.

The Reverend George Woodward was halfway up a ladder, pointing to the roof over the chancel. An auburn-haired man, who Violet took to be a carpenter, was stroking his chin and nodding.

"Is it still leaking, dear?" asked Alice as she approached them.

"Yes," sighed the Reverend, as he dismounted from his ladder.

"George, this is Violet, the old school friend I was telling you about." Alice Woodward smiled as she made the introduction.

"Delighted to meet you." The Reverend thrust his hand towards Violet and shook hers firmly. "I trust you had a pleasant journey?"

"I did," said Violet, gazing towards the font. "Your church is lovely."

"It's in a beautiful location," said the Reverend, "but it's terribly run down. We have finally raised enough money to replace the chancel. And it won't be long before our new oak communion rails, and choir stalls arrive. Such kind gentlemen, such generosity."

He did not elaborate on who had displayed the generosity, but his enthusiasm was infectious.

"Now," he said, "give me a moment to talk to Mr Andrews. He pointed at a middle-aged man seated on the front pew. I must schedule bell-ringing practice.

Reverend Woodward strode towards the altar and conveyed his message. He returned to the ladies and checked the time on his fob watch. "Ah, Mr Podmore is due to arrive shortly. You will know about our ghost," he continued as if it was an everyday occurrence.

Violet nodded, mindful not to reveal too much to the Reverend.

"We should go," he said, waving them towards the porch.

They walked the short distance back to the Rectory, while the Reverend regaled them with stories about the church repairs. There had been some disagreement between the different groups of workers, which had ended in fisticuffs the previous day. The Reverend had separated the warring carpenters and given them a good dressing down. All was well today, and they were cooperating again.

By the time they reached the Rectory, Frank Podmore had arrived. The housemaid was waiting by the driveway to tell them that she had directed him to the sitting room. Alice Woodward asked for tea and cake, then joined the Rector to meet their guest.

"Welcome," said the Reverend offering his hand. Frank Podmore stood to greet him.

Podmore was a slight man with a full head of hair and a neatly trimmed beard. "My coach arrived early," he said in a softly spoken voice.

"You are very welcome, Mr Podmore, very welcome indeed," said the Reverend. "This nuisance has gone on long enough. Will you be staying long?"

"Two days should be enough," said Podmore. "My colleague, Arthur Myers, will be joining us. He is travelling up from London on Friday evening and will help with the investigation. I hope this fits in with your plans."

"Admirably," said The Reverend.

Alice Woodward stayed long enough to greet their guest and supervise the tea. Then she made her excuses. "Please carry on," she said politely, before turning to Violet. "We have a few errands to run."

Violet took the hint and joined her.

"I'm sure you don't want to hear lots of scientific mumbo-jumbo," said Alice. "It's better to leave them to it."

"Thank you," said Violet. "I ought to make a start on my investigation. I'll begin in the kitchen if you don't mind."

From the moment she opened her mouth to greet Violet, there was no mistaking where the Woodward's cook came from. Her accent was a warm north Norfolk burr of the kind Alice Woodward might have possessed, had she enjoyed a less privileged upbringing. Anne Durrell was a large woman, not only overweight but bordering on obese. Violet had entered the kitchen to find Anne chopping fat into a bowl of flour, oblivious to Violet's presence. Violet coughed, and Anne visibly jumped. "My heart alive, who are you?" she asked.

Violet apologised. "I am sorry to have disturbed you," she said. "My name is Violet Smith. I'm a friend of Mrs Woodward."

"Oh, yes," said Anne, nodding her head. "She said you would be arriving today. We don't often get visitors in the kitchen, though. It quite threw me."

Violet wondered what to say. It had not occurred to her to concoct a story for the benefit of the domestics, but Anne was right. It wasn't the done thing to go wandering into a kitchen and start questioning the staff without explanation. She chewed her lip. "I hope you don't mind," she said, "but Mrs Woodward told me about your ghost, and I'm a little afraid. I don't want to worry her with my silly fears, but it's an unusual situation. I wondered if you might tell me what has been happening and what I can expect to see."

Anne Durrell listened while she chopped fat into a bowl of flour. She worked chaotically with clouds of flour billowing from the bowl onto her plump arms. "It's something and nothing," she said. "I hear strange knockings and slamming, mostly after nightfall, but I have never seen anything odd. The house is noisy, that's for sure, but it doesn't frighten me. You have nothing to worry about."

"Oh, I thought it would be much worse when I heard that a man was coming to investigate. It sounded very frightening. He has already arrived."

"He's not the first one," said the cook. "Another man looked into it a few months ago. The disturbances have been going on for quite a while, you see. They are annoying, but that is all. It is much worse for the Reverend. The ghost troubles him more than anyone."

"Mrs Woodward doesn't seem worried about it," said Violet.

"She is very practical," said the cook. "She would need a lot of convincing."

"Do you believe in it?"

"No. There are no such things as ghosts. I cannot deny the noises and disturbances, though." Anne Durrell slopped water into the flour mix as spoke, moulding it into a large ball of dough. She slapped it on the kitchen table, brandished a rolling pin and began to roll it out.

"Could it be trickery?" Violet asked.

"What do you mean?"

"Someone playing a practical joke, perhaps?"

"Why would they do that?"

"I don't know. It was just a thought."

Anne placed the rolled-out pastry over a pie tin. "I cannot see how," she said. "As I told you, most of the disturbances are at night. There are only a few of us in the household. The Reverend and Mrs Woodward sleep in the big room and Kate and I have a small room each in the west wing. It is not one of us, I can assure you."

"But if it's not trickery, then it must be a spirit?"

"No. There must be some other explanation."

Anne spooned a red mixture into the pie dish from a large stone jar. She was about to speak again when the door opened. A young woman wearing a black dress and white apron rushed in.

"The cat has been sick in the parlour," she said. "Where is the floor cloth? I must get it up before Mrs Woodward sees it. She got quite cross with poor Monty last time."

The cook gestured toward the sink. The housemaid lifted a gingham curtain, pulled out an old rag and dropped it into a wooden pail by the door.

"This is Miss Smith," said the cook, pointing to Violet.

"She was asking about the ghost. I have told her I do not believe in it."

Kate stopped what she was doing and grabbed the soggy rag. Water trickled through her fingers. "Think what you like," she said looking at Anne. She turned to Violet. "You make up your own mind, Miss, once you've stayed here a night or two. There is a ghost for sure. I saw it again yesterday."

Chapter Five

THE SUSPICIONS OF MR SMITH

Thursday 12th February 1891

Lawrence woke with a start and rubbed his eyes. An unfamiliar noise like a foghorn sounded outside his window. Bleary-eyed, he reached for his watch and found it on the bedside cabinet. He flicked open the cover — half past nine. Lawrence leapt out of bed, muttering beneath his breath. He had intended to wake long before this. The girl in reception would soon be getting a piece of his mind. Then he remembered. He was going to ask for an early morning wake-up call but nodded off while reading the newspaper in front of the coffee room fire. Later, to his embarrassment, a waiter gently roused him by shaking his shoulder. He had retired to bed immediately.

Lawrence flung open the curtains to reveal the source of the noise. A large passenger vessel was manoeuvring past a row of fishing boats. The horn sounded every few minutes, warning of potential danger ahead. Lawrence sighed again. The seaside was supposed to be peaceful, but it was as noisy as Bury Saint Edmunds on market day. Lawrence washed, dressed and coated his damaged left hand in Atkinson's cold cream which he applied from a white stone jar. Then, he placed his ever-present tan glove over the offending hand. Grabbing his coat and hat from the armchair he had draped them on the night before, Lawrence walked downstairs to the entrance hall.

Nora Knight was standing behind the reception desk, as she had been the previous morning and later the same evening.

"Don't you ever get a day off?" he asked.

"Sometimes," she replied, "though it feels like a long time since I have." She smiled at Lawrence. He opened his mouth to ask another question, but the arrival of a young man interrupted him.

"Telegram, Miss," he said.

Nora thanked him and glanced at the missive. She pressed three times on the reception bell, and a smartly dressed porter appeared. "Please give this to Miss Crosby," she asked.

Lawrence was pretending to examine a grandfather clock set beneath a high arched window in the foyer. He waited for Nora to finish her task, but she had already noticed that he was loitering. "Can I help you?" she asked.

"Only if you know anything else about the death of Edmund Gurney," he replied.

"I told you all about it yesterday".

"I know," sighed Lawrence. "I hoped there would be more. I am investigating a case which may or may not be connected to his death, but I am running out of reasons to stay."

"Are you a detective?" Nora's eyes widened.

"I am a private detective," said Lawrence.

"How marvellous. What are you investigating?"

"I'm not entirely sure," said Lawrence, frankly. "It may all be a huge waste of time."

"Perhaps not. I've told you everything I know about Mr Gurney, but if you need more information for your case, I know a man who can help. And he just happens to be back in Brighton for the week."

"Really?" Lawrence watched the pretty girl with renewed interest. Her face lit up, and she seemed keen to assist.

"Oh yes," she said. "The man's name is Mr Smith. He moved away from Brighton, but he is back again. I used to watch him on the stage when he lived here. He was one of the greatest performers I have ever seen."

"Was he a musician or an actor?"

Nora laughed. "Neither. He was a hypnotist. He used to get up on stage and put his partner in a trance. Then he would ask his partner to describe things that couldn't be seen."

Lawrence raised his eyebrows.

"I'm not explaining myself very well," said Nora. "A few years ago, I walked out with a young man called Henry. He was keen on stage shows and often took me to music halls and theatres. Mr Smith and Mr Blackburn were a double act. Mr Smith would blindfold Mr Blackburn, then hide something in the theatre. Mr Blackburn always found it, even though he didn't know where it had been put. The hypnotic trance caused him to think that he had second sight."

"Right," said Lawrence, doubtfully. "But what has that got to do with Edmund Gurney?"

"A great deal," said Nora, crossing her arms and leaning forward over the reception counter. "You see, Mr Smith was

Mr Gurneys' private secretary. And not only that," she continued, "but they carried out a lot of experiments together for their Society."

"Did they, now." Lawrence was alert and interested. "And where can I find Mr Smith?"

"He will be in Saint Anne's Well gardens," said Nora. "He has business there."

"Do you think he will talk to me," mused Lawrence.

"Oh, I am sure he will. He is a very nice man, friendly and not at all self-important. He signed a place card for me last year when I saw him at the Aquarium. I didn't like to trouble him myself, but Henry walked right up and asked if he could sign it and he did not hesitate. Anyway, he turned up at the hotel a few days ago, and I asked after his health. We chatted for a while and he said he had been in Kent for the last few months. He has booked his hotel room until the end of the week, so it looks like you are in luck."

"That's very helpful," said Lawrence, "I am grateful. Just one more thing before I go. Do you keep a record of hotel visitors?"

"Of course," said Nora. "There's a guest register over there." She gestured toward the right side of the counter. "Who are you looking for?"

Lawrence had no opportunity to reply before a waitress bustled into the hallway. She mouthed something at Nora that Lawrence couldn't interpret.

"I'll be back in a minute," said Nora.

Lawrence sidled over to the reception desk. Two large day books lay stacked beside by the bell. He opened the first. It was a register of guests, with space to record names, addresses and comments. It was new, and only the first two pages had been written on. He opened a second book and found a similar register — this time older and crammed to capacity. Lawrence scanned the first page. The date was 1884. Good. He licked his finger and leafed through until he reached the entries for June 1888. Edmund Gurney had died on the 22nd or 23rd of June. Lawrence located the relevant page and reached in his breast pocket for his fountain pen. It was not there. He patted his coat and trouser pockets, searching in vain for a writing tool. He checked behind the counter — nothing. Lawrence sighed, irritated at his inability to locate a pen on a desk, of all places. He was not prepared to waste the opportunity to glean more information and stole a furtive glance around the lobby. There was nobody in sight, so Lawrence ripped out the page, folded it in two and stuffed it into his jacket pocket.

The momentary pang of guilt he suffered, did not prevent his mouth creasing into a smile. Something felt different — a glimmer of hope, perhaps. The thought of going back to Bury Saint Edmunds with his tail between his legs, having followed another false trail, was behind him for the moment. Lawrence felt motivated again and determined to pursue the investigation with renewed vigour. Stopping only to ask a passer-by for directions, he set off towards St Anne's Well gardens.

Lawrence was ten minutes into his walk when it dawned on him that he was re-tracing yesterday's route. He realised that he must be close to Montpellier Street, judging it only a short distance away. If he walked to St Anne's Well gardens as the crow flies, he would miss the opportunity to see the house Sybil Jones had pointed out the previous day. A glimpse of Ruth's home might give him an insight into how she had lived.

He found his way to Montpellier Street and searched for

Number 41. It was a handsome white rendered property almost identical to Sybil's house. Only the bay window surrounds were different, with the ones on Ruth's side painted black. Other than that, the two houses seemed the same shape and size and likely had similar interiors. Lawrence slowed his pace and loitered outside, pretending to check his watch. He saw no signs of life in the property, and, standing on tiptoes, he peered inside.

As he had anticipated, the living room was at the front of the house. It was a long, thin room with an unremarkable fireplace. The decor was drab, utilitarian and unwelcoming. Heavy drapes masked the large bay window, leaving it cloaked in shadow. Lawrence strained to see beyond the front room, but the poor light impeded his view. Even so, he could see enough to form an opinion. Despite the daylight, the room was sombre, and it was evident from the tired looking wallpaper and faded carpet, that the house was in need of redecoration. He must be seeing the room as it was in Ruth's time. The tired building could have been warm and welcoming, like Sybil's house. It had the potential.

Lawrence imagined how Ruth must have felt living alone in this large, soulless house. He thought of her cowering in a locked room, frightened in fear of her sinister guest. The experience must have been unnerving. If Sybil Jones was right, it was understandable that the memory had remained with her.

Lawrence turned away from the drab room. He would learn nothing more from watching the house and he set off for Saint Anne's Well gardens.

Ten minutes and a steep hill later, Lawrence arrived at the entrance to the gardens on Furze Road. An attractive steeply-gabled cottage stood beside the park gate. Nearby, was a wrought iron signpost inscribed 'private'. Lawrence ignored it. He was in no mood for impediments. He strolled down the path towards a large stone structure, built incongruously in the shape of a temple. By the side of the building, a wizened man moved boulders with the aid of a wheelbarrow. He saw Lawrence, stopped and placed his hand in the small of his back.

"That looks like hard work," said Lawrence, trying to start a conversation. The man grunted and grasped the handles of the barrow.

Lawrence tried again. "Do you know if Mr George Smith is here today?"

The man nodded towards the far side of the building and turned away. Lawrence followed his direction to see a curly haired man standing by a large sash window. He was scribbling in a notebook. As Lawrence drew closer, he realised that it was actually a sketch pad. The man was making detailed drawings of the structure in front.

"Good morning," said Lawrence, holding out his hand. "My name is Lawrence Harpham. Have I the pleasure of addressing Mr George Smith?"

The man reached for Lawrence's hand and shook it tentatively. "You do," he said. "Do I know you?"

Lawrence took a deep breath and began the tricky task of conveying the reason for his visit using the least amount of words. He struggled to express himself, cognisant of the uncertainty of his position. He had still not discovered what crime, if any, had taken place and had no expectation of Smith's cooperation. But George Smith was intelligent and grasped the situation before Lawrence became too tongue-tied. His eyes misted as Lawrence spoke of Edmund Gurney and a tic pulsed above his cheekbone.

"The matter of which you speak is painful," he said when Lawrence had finished. "Painful indeed. Edmund Gurney was my friend. I will tell you what I know, and you can decide for yourself. It's chilly out here. Come inside."

They walked through the ionic columns clustered with creeping ivy and entered the building. George directed Lawrence downstairs to the basement. "It's not much warmer here," he said, "but we are out of the wind and away from prying eyes. You know these gardens are private, don't you?"

Lawrence nodded. "I saw the sign," he admitted, "but I wanted to speak with you". He glanced around the room. A circular stone trough housed a bowl into which water bubbled up from a fissure in the rock. "What's all this?" he asked.

"It's the Chalybeate water," said George. "It's a natural mineral spring. People come from far and wide to partake. It's supposed to be very good for you. Try some."

He reached for a glass from a selection lined up on a trestle table by the basement wall.

Lawrence collected a tumbler of water and sniffed. It smelled of sulphur. He took a few sips to be polite, but it tasted as bad as he expected.

"I'm thinking of leasing it," said George Smith.

Lawrence arched an eyebrow.

"The gardens, I mean. I make films. I need somewhere to use as a studio."

"Is that why you are here?"

"Yes. I've been negotiating with the Goldsmid's. They own this place. They have allowed me free access to the gardens while I work it all out. It should do very well."

"So, you have a legitimate reason to be here, unlike me," smiled Lawrence.

George laughed. "Yes, and it's tricky negotiating so it would be helpful if they don't assume that I've condoned trespassing on their land. "Take a seat," he said walking over to one of several wrought iron tables surrounding the well. "It's always devilishly cold in this part of the pump room, but no worse than being outside. Now, tell me what you want to know."

"I understand you weren't here when Edmund Gurney died?"

"No. I had only married a short time before. My wife and I were honeymooning in the Isle of Wight."

"So, you did not see him at any time?"

George Smith shook his head. "He arrived long after we had left Brighton."

"And you never found out why he came here?"

"No. It is a mystery."

"Did he often visit Brighton?"

"Only when he came to see me. I was his Private Secretary, but as I have already said, I was not here.

I heard that he received a letter summoning him to Brighton. Nobody knows why. There were other letters in his possession when he died, but not that one."

"When did you see him last?"

"A few months before he died."

"Was his behaviour normal?"

"In a manner of speaking."

"Explain."

"He had lost his usual ebullience and he seemed burdened, in some way. I do not know what troubled him, but there was a change in the weeks before his death. He was uncharacteristically quiet."

"Could he have killed himself?"

"It is not inconceivable, but I doubt it. No man was

more dedicated to his work than Edmund. There was so much that he wanted to do, to prove. I cannot imagine him giving it all up."

"So, the verdict of accidental death seems most likely."

"Most unlikely." George Smith leaned forward and spoke earnestly. "I do not recognise any of the behaviour attributed to Edmund that justifies a verdict of accidental narcotic poisoning."

A frisson of excitement coursed through Lawrence. "If his death was not a suicide and not an accident, then what was it?"

"You tell me," said George Smith. "I cannot account for it."

"His use of narcotics to ease pain was well known," said Lawrence.

"Pain?"

"Yes, neuralgia."

"What neuralgia?"

"Did you not know of it?"

"He did not complain of neuralgia in the whole time I knew him," said George firmly. His piercing, clear eyes never wavered from Lawrence's face. "And as far as I know, he did not take opiates. It makes no sense."

"You knew him well enough to make that judgement?"

"Yes, but it's more than that. We conducted many experiments over the years and used hypnotism for the relief of toothaches and headaches. The sessions went very well indeed. We made real progress. If Edmund Gurney had long-standing neuralgia, as they say, he would have tried hypnotism."

"He may have tried, and it failed."

"He would have asked me." George Smith raised his voice and tilted his head. He sighed and leaned forward again, clutching his brow. Unruly curls fell across his face. He sat in silence for a moment.

Lawrence waited for him to begin speaking again.

"I take it you know that we were all members of the Society for Psychical Research," he said.

"I do," said Lawrence.

"Edmund was a founder member," George continued. "A few years ago, he wrote a paper called 'Removal of pain by suggestion.' The article concentrated on mesmerism and hypnotism. He had absolute faith in the power of suggestion. There is not a question in my mind that he would have come to me if he was suffering."

"But you were away," said Lawrence.

"Several men participated in the Brighton experiments," said George. "Anyone of us could have helped him."

"To be clear, you do not think he was a habitual user of narcotics?"

"To be even more clear, I do not believe he used them at all."

Lawrence exhaled. He realised he had been holding his breath while George was speaking. The passionate manner in which the young man argued against the verdict of accidental death, indicated he was on to something at last.

"I am leaving the SPR," said Smith. "I have made up my mind. I have obligations towards them until the end of the year, but I will resign immediately after."

"Why?" asked Lawrence.

"I cannot tell you," said George. "Something I cannot explain is making me uneasy. If you want to know more about the SPR, you should go to London and speak to some of the Society members. They all knew Edmund well. Ask for Frederick Myers or Frank Podmore. If you are lucky, Elias will be around."

"Elias?"

"Our doorman, although he is so much more. Elias is loyal to the organisation and with an almost eidetic memory. He is the man to ask and will always be able to reach the others."

"I thought eidetic memory was a myth."

"In its pure sense, it is rare. All members of the SPR have a speciality no matter what function they serve. Elias has spent a lifetime learning mnemonic techniques to improve his memory. He has trained himself to have an almost photographic recall."

"London sounds like a good place to start then," said Lawrence. "I'll go there and search them out."

George stared towards the bubbling water and pulled distractedly at his tie. After a few moments, he looked up. "There is something wrong with the way they reached the verdict, Mr Harpham," he said. "The coroner was veering towards suicide but was heavily influenced against it. Some of my colleagues thought it was an accident. I sometimes wonder whether it was in their interests for the verdict to go that way. After all, it was important not to tarnish the Society's reputation. Or their own. But in the conflict between accident and suicide, was something else was overlooked? Could Edmund Gurney have been murdered?"

Lawrence walked in a daze as he retraced his route to The Royal Albion hotel. It was dusk, and darkness descended swiftly. The rising moon cast the merest trace of light and a murky soup of clouds concealed the stars. The streets of Brighton had become strangers, made hostile by the ghoulish glow of gas lamps. In the distance, a lamplighter hauled his ladder through an alleyway, trudging along frosty streets as he contemplated the laborious task ahead. Lawrence followed in silence considering George Smith's final words. "Could Edmund Gurney have been murdered?"

Lawrence was distracted as he turned into a passageway and found himself in a maze of tiny streets leading towards Black Lion Street. The welcoming lights of The Cricketers Inn appeared a short distance away. Lawrence peered through the windows into the well-lit interior. The glass was clear, but Lawrence could not see inside. His mind played tricks as the word 'murder' appeared and disappeared from the bevelled glass. One minute it was emblazoned in foot-high letters, the next, only a figment of his imagination. He walked the length of Black Lion Street until he reached the seafront. Accusatory voices surrounded him. Lawrence tried to block the sounds, but they echoed in a whisper of 'murder' again and again. Even the waves joined in, sloshing their criminations against the shore. Was murder an option? Why had it not been considered?

By the time Lawrence reached the hotel, he was exhausted, and his mind was ablaze. He decided to buy a glass of brandy to drink before he retired. It would be more effective than counting sheep. He opened his wallet, but instead of extracting money, he grasped the piece of paper egregiously torn from the register earlier that day. He unfolded it without a flicker of guilt.

Some of the names inside were registered against room numbers indicating that they were guests, not visitors. The remaining records were poor, only containing a surname twinned with a town. But two entries looked promising and were annotated with the word, 'visitor'. One of them belonged to a dentist called Daniel Browning. He had given his address as 27 Upper Montague Street, Marylebone. The second man had appended two locations by his name. Roslyn D'Onston was a journalist who lived in London, but was currently staying at the Cricketers Inn, Brighton.

Lawrence stared at the register. He did not believe in coincidences, and he had been standing in front of the Cricketers Inn not more than half an hour ago. Was it a sign? It did not matter whether it was, or not — it was a lead. Pausing only to consider whether he should tell Violet of his plans, Lawrence abandoned the idea of a pre-bedtime drink. He crossed the entrance hall and climbed the stairs, two at a time. The excitement had dissipated by the time he reached his room and practicalities had set in. Lawrence wished he could speak to Violet. Her opinion would be useful. He missed sharing ideas with her, and she was wise in a way that his natural impulsiveness prohibited. But she was in that village whose name he could not pronounce, or even remember. And the thought of her ghost-hunting still set his teeth on edge. It wasn't easy to contact her, and it was risky to try. She might attempt to persuade him to return to Suffolk. No, every lead pointed in one direction only. Tomorrow morning, at the earliest opportunity, he would take the train to London.

Chapter Six

APPROACHING SCOTLAND YARD

13th February 1891

Lawrence alighted at Victoria Station feeling a sense of relief. He vacated the train almost before it stopped and darted up the platform with an unaccustomed lick of speed. He had been sitting, for what seemed like hours, with a large woman and her elderly dachshund. Lawrence liked well-behaved dogs as much as the next man, but this dog was disobedient and overindulged, and had barked through the entire journey. The jarring, yappy noise penetrated his ears like a hammer on wood, and when he politely asked her to quieten the animal, she glowered at him and called him a brute. Worse still, the dog urinated in the middle of the carriage. Every time the train halted and re-started, the puddle of urine edged closer. In the end, Lawrence moved, but not before the woman had the audacity to complain to the conductor about Lawrence's behaviour. The conductor ignored her, skirting past Lawrence with a nod of sympathy.

Lawrence walked past the ticket office and into the

Victoria tube station, a short distance below ground. He purchased a ticket, hopped on the brownish-crimson carriage and managed to find a seat with no other people in the immediate vicinity. He watched the walls of the tube station pass by as the steam train whistled and chugged. Travelling by train was lazy. It would have been easy to walk, but it had been years since he had used the underground and he was eager to try it again. Lawrence appreciated good craftsmanship. It was abundant in the handsome glossy locomotives with their matching gold lined carriages. He stretched his legs and smiled, enjoying every moment of the short journey. After two stops, he alighted at Westminster Bridge.

Lawrence was in a good mood as he sauntered along the Embankment to his destination at New Scotland Yard. He had made an overnight decision to begin the London part of his investigation by visiting Inspector Henry Moore. Henry was an old friend who he met during training, and their paths had crossed many times over the years. Though several counties separated them, their friendship endured. Henry had always been more ambitious than Lawrence and carved a name for himself in the Metropolitan Police early in his career. This led to his current position in the Criminal Investigation Department at Scotland Yard. Lawrence considered how little he had seen of Henry during that time. It had been due, in part, to the distance between them. But also, a reflection of Lawrence's inability to face people after the loss of his family. As Lawrence considered his friendship with Henry, it occurred to him that it had been several days since he had last thought about Catherine. He bit his lip, ashamed of his neglect for her memory and his good mood retreated.

As Lawrence approached his destination, vast chimney

stacks from the building ahead dominated the skyline. The towering seven-story red-bricked building was gothic in appearance and exuded authority. The architecture was exquisite. White stone bands contrasted against tiers of red bricks on top of which were three levels of attics, graced by steep slate roofs. Lawrence had never visited Scotland Yard, but he had followed the relocation with interest. He was confident that the building ahead of him was the correct location and he could expect to find Henry Moore ensconced somewhere inside.

Lawrence walked towards the imposing structure and through a wrought-iron gate. He looked up. An intricately painted Royal Crest illuminated by two large lanterns either side lent further grandeur. Giant urns topped the columns adding another layer of magnificence. Lawrence passed through feeling somewhat intimidated and approached the polished reception desk where a young constable, clad in shirt sleeves, was scribbling into a ledger. Lawrence coughed, and the constable looked up. "I would like to speak to Inspector Moore," said Lawrence.

"You and half the rest of the press," the young man replied. "You'll be lucky if you get to see him this side of Easter."

"Busy, is he?" asked Lawrence.

The policeman put his pen down and looked at Lawrence incredulously. "Are you trying to be funny? Clear off back to Fleet Street with your gutter press friends."

"I'm not from the press if that's what you are thinking."

"Good," said the young man. "If one more reporter comes in today, I swear I'll swing for him."

Two double doors into the main building burst open, and a group of half a dozen men swarmed through. They were talking heatedly but stopped at the sight of Lawrence.

A dark-skinned moustached man walked menacingly towards him.

"Leave him alone," said the uniformed policeman. "He's not from The Press."

The man retreated. "Good day," he said, touching the brim of his hat.

"What on earth is going on?" asked Lawrence.

"Only another murder," said the policeman.

"Where? who?"

"Tell me who you are first." The young Constable closed his ledger and watched Lawrence through narrowed eyes.

"I'm a private investigator," said Lawrence.

The policeman raised his eyes heavenward. "Then you can hop it too."

"I'm a friend of Henry Moore's," Lawrence continued. "And a former Police Inspector. It's the truth. Please let him know that I am here."

The policemen did not reply but pressed a bell on the desk.

"Name?" he asked curtly.

"Lawrence Harpham".

Another uniformed policeman appeared. "Ask Inspector Moore if he knows a Lawrence Harpham."

The second policeman walked through the double doors. The opaque glass panes allowed Lawrence a view of his route upstairs.

"Are you going to tell me who has died?"

"It wouldn't mean anything to you if I did," said the policeman. "Although you will, no doubt, be familiar with the method of killing."

"Explain?"

"He cut her with a knife. It's another ripping," he replied, grimly.

A thrill of adrenaline coursed through Lawrence making his skin crawl with tension. He felt dizzy, disorientated.

"Are you sure?"

The constable was about to answer when the doors opened again, and Henry Moore appeared. "Lawrence Harpham, as I live and breathe. Do my eyes deceive me?" He grasped Lawrence's hand and shook it warmly.

"It appears my timing is poor," smiled Lawrence.

"Dreadful," agreed Henry. "You have exactly ten minutes of my time this morning, but I'll see if I can correct that later depending upon your plans. Come."

The speed with which Henry Moore ascended the stairs, left Lawrence out of breath by the time he caught him up. He followed Henry into an office further down the corridor.

Henry sat behind his desk, and Lawrence sank into the opposite chair. "I would offer you a drink," said Henry, "but I have to be at Swallow Gardens in half an hour."

"I can come back another time," offered Lawrence.

"You must," said Henry. "Tell me your plans. We will get together."

"I will come straight to the point, as you are so busy. I am looking for somebody," said Lawrence.

"A missing person?"

"No, not missing. But I need to find a man. Two, actually; both residents of London. I have got an address for one, but not the other, and I don't know where to begin to look for it. I've found in the past, that the local police station is a good starting point."

"Always wise," agreed Henry. "Give me the name, and I'll pass it to Fred. He's a never-ending fount of local knowledge. If he can't help, he will know someone who can."

Lawrence removed the torn hotel register from his pocket. "Can I borrow a pen and paper?" he asked.

Henry retrieved a pen from the polished wooden holder in front of him. He pushed a scrap of paper across the desk.

"Good Lord," he exclaimed as he watched Lawrence write the first name.

"What?"

"You are about to write D'Onston. Roslyn D'Onston."

"You know him?"

Henry nodded. "Oh yes. That complicates matters."

Lawrence raised an eyebrow. "How?" he asked.

"I'll tell you, but first I need to know why you are asking. It's important, Lawrence. Official business."

"It's probably nothing," said Lawrence. "I am investigating a death in Brighton. It happened a few years ago. The coroner ruled it as an accidental death, but I'm not so sure."

Henry Moore leaned forward. "How does this concern D'Onston?"

"It probably doesn't," Lawrence admitted. "But he was in the building on the night Gurney died."

"Edmund Gurney?"

"Yes, you know him?"

"Only by reputation," said Henry. "He was well known in London. What makes you think this death was suspicious?"

"Nothing I can summarise in the five minutes we have left," said Lawrence, looking at his watch. "I'll tell you everything when there's more time."

Henry nodded. "Fine, and in return, I will use the next few minutes to tell you some of what I know about Roslyn

D'Onston and give you his address. We keep tracks on the man — he's under surveillance. My help is conditional on your cooperation. You must tell me everything, and I mean every single detail, of the conversation that takes place. Now or at any other time. Is that clear?"

Lawrence glanced at his friend, momentarily taken aback. Henry was uncharacteristically curt. His clenched jaw and stony face bore no trace of his usual good humour. "Of course," Lawrence replied.

Henry sat back in his chair and sighed. "Have you heard about the latest ripping?" he asked.

"Yes."

"Well, your man D'Onston became embroiled in the 1888 murders. For a while, we thought he might be the Ripper. We have subsequently settled on a series of more likely candidates and have removed D'Onston from the list."

Lawrence whistled. "I didn't know."

"No reason why you should," said Henry. "D'Onston is a journalist. He dabbles in esoteric mysteries and spiritualism. He came to our notice while we were investigating the Ripper murders due to his bizarre theories. If it wasn't for the fact that he was in a hospital during some of the murders, he could have found himself at the end of a rope."

"But he is no longer a suspect?" asked Lawrence.

"No," said Henry. "He couldn't have done it."

"Then why is he under observation?"

"He is a trouble maker, always stirring up public opinion with his strange ideas. He knows more about it than he ought. Keeping track of him is precautionary. There was a theory that the Ripper may have been more than one person, you see."

"But the Rippings stopped years ago, didn't they?"

"Yes," said Henry. "And the Ripper is most likely dead,

but until we have proof of this, D'Onston and a few others remain under watch."

"What is the nature of this latest incident?"

"In the early hours of this morning, a young woman by the name of Frances Coles met a violent end. Someone cut her throat from ear to ear. God knows it's only been a few hours, yet every blasted reporter in the district seems to know of it. They have attributed it to Jack."

"With justification?"

"No. Because it sells newspapers."

"So, you won't re-open the investigation?"

"Quite the opposite. We have no choice," said Henry. "We cannot satisfy public opinion unless we start from scratch and investigate the slaying as if it was a Ripper murder. It is imperative that we find the killer. Otherwise, we will end up squandering all our resources on this crime for months to come."

"What sort of young woman was Florence Coles?"

"I take your meaning. Florence was the usual type. She had fallen on hard times and was a drinker. She dossed in a common lodging house in White's Row and sold herself for money."

Lawrence nodded. "I see. I won't take up any more of your valuable time. I'll track D'Onston down and speak with him later today. Can we meet tomorrow morning?"

"Yes," said Henry. "Come back here. I would like to know what he has to say for himself."

Henry Moore pulled out a desk drawer and removed a box of cards. He thumbed through them, selected one and copied the contents onto a piece of paper. He pushed it across the desk towards Lawrence.

"Here is D'Onston's most recent address."

Lawrence folded the paper and put it in his pocket. He

smiled at Henry as he walked towards the door. "Until tomorrow," he said.

"Indeed." Henry held the door open and watched as Lawrence walked down the corridor. He still held the card containing D'Onston's location. Henry sighed and put the card back in the box. The Ripper killings were over — D'Onston was no longer a suspect. But the prospect of Lawrence engaging with the sinister oddball journalist left Henry Moore feeling uneasy. Uneasy and powerless. He decided to re-establish control by setting the nearest available constable to keep watch outside D'Onston's hotel.

Chapter Seven

THE BEGINNING

Everything starts with a first. The first breath of a newborn baby, the first snow of winter, the first shattering realisation that life and time are out of control. The first time that I acted unconsciously, my memories returned gradually — not in a sudden rush of recall, but one recollection after another. They dripped back like drops of fetid water forming a puddle of interminable horror. Every single memory felt safe in its individuality. Alone, they were passive, offering false hope and masking the inevitable. It is hard to describe the point at which the memories become complete, so slowly do they recombine. But they always do, and the horror sends a cold dread coursing through my veins. My heart hurts with the pain of remembering. I am a peaceful man. I am not what the memories suggest — I am not.

Was I always so afflicted? Not from birth, but from a young age. The first time I felt different, I was still youthful, still in education. Harry Kersey found me slumped against a wall — upright, but pallid, and confused. He asked what was wrong and I could not find the words to tell him. If I knew then, what I know now, I could have said that my mind had temporarily absented itself from my body. I could have revealed how I fought, in vain, to fill the void with the memories I knew should be there. They returned, eventually, taking far longer to come back than they took to disappear. The attacks have continued haphazardly ever since. Once, an entire eighteen months passed without a seizure, but in 1888 they increased with appalling regularity. Attacks rushed by in waves, month after painful month, recall after horrifying recall.

The automatisms were less frequent when I was younger. Their prevalence has increased with age, culminating in the events of the last few years. They worsened late in 1887, when I took a regular journey on the Metropolitan Railway. I was due to meet friends which involved disembarking at a train stop and walking a short distance to the venue. I recall staring out of the carriage window while listening to the train conductor as he spoke to a young lady a few seats along. His voice, normal at first, began to echo. The girl's voice slowed down. Words dripped from her mouth like sap down a tree. The now familiar feeling of déjà vu came upon me, then nothing.

Nothing, until the next recollection when I reached into my pocket for my watch and saw that it was quarter past seven in the evening. Last time I checked my watch on board the train, the time had been twenty past six. I recalled this because my appointment was just before seven o'clock and I remember thinking there would be more than enough time to get to my destination. As the memories seeped back, I realised that I was walking on an unfamiliar road. I put my watch back in my pocket and searched for my train ticket, but it was gone. It occurred to me that I must have handed it in at the ticket station without remembering. I reached the end of the road and found myself in Smithfield Market. Logic suggested that I must have exited the train at Farringdon Street Station and given my ticket up there. Had I spoken to anyone? A few vague recollections filtered back. My jacket smelled musty, generating snippets of memory. I recalled the slam of a carriage door and the acrid smell of smoke. But was it a recent memory? I often travel by train. They are frequently crowded, buzzing with sounds. The air is stale, clogged by choking fumes. I could not sort this memory into past or present and had to accept that my recall would never be complete.

And so, it continued. I experienced instances of automatisms during which I could be anywhere with no memory or control. There were also lesser events, which I called blanks. Blanks occurred for short periods lasting no more than a few minutes. During these, I had scant, if any, memory and I was always immobile. My profession could have made my affliction untenable, but I was frank with those who needed to know, including a few loyal friends. Though perplexing and at times irritating, it did not cause my colleagues undue anxiety. Their acceptance made me less fearful. Until a particular Saturday in 1888, when the full horror of my illness manifested itself.

Quite how I arrived in Spitalfields, I cannot say, for I had never ventured that far before. And what passed at Aldgate railway station is still a mystery. My first recollection was the cold. It was dark, and I was standing beneath a gas lamp in another unfamiliar area. Through force of habit, I pulled out my pocket watch and checked the time, trying to adjust my eyes to the gloomy light. It was seven forty-five on a cold February evening, and I had lost over an hour of memory. As I returned my watch to my jacket pocket, my fingers closed over the ticket I had purchased earlier that day. I had not surrendered it at the ticket office as I had in the past. It was damp, and I surmised that it must have been raining, but as shards of consciousness returned, I realised that I was not wet. Cold, indeed, but not wet. I held the ticket closer to the light and scrutinised the brown marks covering it. Blood spotted the pale card. I felt the sleeves of my jacket — they were damp with blood too.

I raised my hands to my face and touched my skin — nothing. The blood was not coming from my body, so I removed my hat and examined my head for a bump. Perhaps I had fallen over, but there was no pain or any sign of a wound. Then I tried to make some sense of my surroundings; to work out where I was and how I would get home. The alleyway in which I was standing was deathly quiet, the only sign of life a skeletal alley cat with one torn ear and patches in its fur. To the right of me, in the light of the next gas lamp along, I noticed a bundle of rags illuminated in the hazy glow. Then it moved and emitted a low moan. I gasped. It was a person, a woman.

I ran towards her and knelt by her side. Her face was sallow and lined, her breathing laboured. I gasped as I saw her rucked-up skirts, mottled and smeared with a dark substance. Slashes marked her woollen stockings leaving bare flesh exposed. Something metal glinted in the light, and I scooped it up. Its comfortable, familiar weight triggered a memory that seared through my passive observations. Oh, God. It was a clasp knife. It was mine and the last time I had seen it I was plunging it downwards in a frenzy, with no idea why. One chilling memory after another returned interconnecting into a mesh that did not form a whole but allowed an insight into what had occurred. Boarding a train at Baker Street station, feeling normal, a train ride and a strange taste. A glimpse of Aldgate Station, running, quiet, dark, quiet, walking, walking, thirsty. Stop. A sign, white paint flaking away from a rotten wooden plank. 'White's Row', memories ebbing and flowing — gone again. A woman, middle-aged, asking for something, disgust, revulsion, raging anger, a scream, silence.

The woman was still alive. Injured, but alive. I should have assisted. I am a good man, and I could have helped her. But I ran. And one way or another, I have been running ever since.

Chapter Eight

A SINISTER MAN

The quickest route to D'Onston's hotel was by train, but after yesterday's incident with the dachshund, Lawrence was in no rush to repeat the experience. He decided, instead, to walk along the Embankment before turning north to his destination in Charterhouse Street. It was a crisp, clear day and Lawrence did not detect any fear or panic in the people he passed on his route. Men and women went about their business as always. Young ladies walked without chaperones while shopkeepers enjoyed robust trade. Barrow boys whistled as they carted their produce and the streets were busy with horses and carriages. The day was like any other day. Though Lawrence's journey took him through an affluent part of London, he still expected to hear something about the Ripper horror. But there was not so much as one newspaper boy shouting about the killing in a bid to sell his wares. The concerns of Scotland Yard had not yet reached the good people of the Parish of Saint Sephulcre.

Lawrence continued along Charterhouse Street on his way to Charterhouse Square. As he reached the square, a structure ahead caught his eye. He stared at it, trying to comprehend what he was seeing. The building was narrow, its span no more than the width of the front door. Three arched windows stacked one above another, formed a tall triangle with a stone balcony enclosing the first window. Lawrence subconsciously widened his arms as he walked towards it, wondering if he could touch either side if he tried. He reached into his pocket for the piece of paper Henry Moore had given him earlier that day. The scrawled note gave D'Onston's address as The Triangle Hotel, 88 Charterhouse Street, St Sephulcre. The name of the hotel could hardly be more appropriate.

The closer Lawrence got, the more he could see of the right-hand side. The hotel looked like a wedge of cheese and fitted snugly between two roads veering off at forty-five-degree angles. From the front of the hotel, it was impossible to imagine a functioning boarding house, but from the side, it became viable.

Lawrence opened the door and found himself in a small triangular room. He approached a shabby dark wooden desk, upon which sat an unpolished brass bell. Lawrence waited for a while, but nobody came. He pressed the bell adding his fingerprint to many others. Moments later a white-haired man shambled in accompanied by a young boy. The man yawned as he asked Lawrence how he could help. Lawrence leaned across the counter. "Is Mr D'Onston resident here?"

The hotel manager raised an eyebrow. "He might be."
"Can I see him?"
"It depends."
"On what?"

The Manager stared at Lawrence. After a few moments of silence, Lawrence understood the man's intent. He sighed, removed a note from his pocket and placed it on the desk. The man's grubby fingers closed over the money. "Tell number five he's got a visitor."

The boy returned a few moments later and nodded to the Manager.

"You can go up," he said. Lawrence approached the stairs and stepped on the fraying carpet.

"Wait," barked the Manager. "Tommy will show you."

He retreated and waited for the boy who glowered as he squeezed past.

The boy stopped outside a door midway along the landing on the first floor and held his hand out. Lawrence felt inside his pocket for the smallest denomination coin he could find and dropped it in the boy's palm.

He stood for a few moments before knocking on the door wondering what on earth he was going to say.

He did not have long to wait before a deep voice boomed, "come," and Lawrence entered the dark and dingy room. Though D'Onston's room spanned two large windows, he had purposely excluded the outside. Both window shutters were drawn across, allowing only a chink of sunlight to enter. D'Onston relied on other means of illumination. Several misshapen candles of dubious provenance burned in saucers on a wooden desk. D'Onston was sitting in a worn red leather armchair. A white walrus moustache dominated his square face, hiding his lips and dark bushy eyebrows sprouted over deep-set eyes. Lifeless eyes. Soulless eyes. Lawrence approached him and offered his hand, avoiding eye contact. D'Onston stood to greet him and accepted it. His grasp was firm, his hands clammy. He gestured towards the chair in which he had been sitting. There was no other seating in the room, and D'Onston repositioned himself on the corner of the bed regarding Lawrence curiously.

"Would you like a drink?" he asked.

Lawrence declined. He still wasn't sure how to approach the conversation, but alcohol was unlikely to help. Besides, he did not trust D'Onston. There was something sinister about his demeanour which would have been evident in daylight, but in the manufactured dimness of the room with the flickering candlelight, was almost other-worldly.

"What do you want with me?" D'Onston's voice was low with the merest trace of an accent that could have been northern.

"I have been in Brighton," said Lawrence. "I want to talk to you about an incident that occurred in the Royal Albion Hotel."

The half-smile fell away from D'Onston's face. "What incident?"

Lawrence opened his mouth to reply but noticed a copy of the Pall Mall Gazette laying folded across D'Onston's desk. 'Another Whitechapel Horror,' the headline screamed. 'A woman brutally murdered this morning'.

Lawrence hesitated, and D'Onston followed his gaze.

"Ah. Have you heard about our latest murder?" D'Onston leaned forward, animated.

"A little," said Lawrence.

"Bloody fools," said D'Onston. "The police, I mean. They know nothing."

"Indeed," Lawrence agreed. "Otherwise, they would have apprehended him long ago."

"Not at all," said D'Onston. "They have avoided every well-meaning attempt to guide them."

"Understandably," said Lawrence. "The general public is a little too accommodating when it comes to murder.

They flood the police force with suggestions and theories, and Scotland Yard lacks the manpower to deal with it."

"And there are not enough intelligent policemen to follow a perfectly obvious trail of evidence."

"Why do you say that?"

"They only process what they see, and they do not think like the Ripper. They complain that they cannot catch him and lament their poor luck. But they let a blood-stained man escape repeatedly without ever considering how."

"Go on." Lawrence's suspicion had turned to interest.

"Because there was very little blood on him."

"There must have been," said Lawrence. "The Ripper used a knife. The murders were bloody and visceral, and the perpetrator would have been covered."

"There was no blood on him," D'Onston repeated. "He cut their throats from behind, do you see. He grasped them from the rear and drew his knife across their throats as they faced away. The blood spilt down their bodies leaving his clothes clean. Then he stepped backwards and placed them upon the ground."

"Good lord." Lawrence fidgeted with his gloved hand as he visualised the scene. Perspiration prickled his brow. The atmosphere in the room had changed again. D'Onston was less sinister and more energised, animated by the discussion. "But how do you know?" asked Lawrence.

"Common sense," said D'Onston. "The police should have worked it out themselves. It was no surprise to find that they had not even considered it when I made the suggestion."

"You spoke to them?"

"Yes, I helped with their enquiries."

Lawrence waited for him to continue, but D'Onston

stopped talking. His gaze wandered towards the window, and his eyes became dull again.

Lawrence coughed bringing D'Onston back from his reverie. "You haven't told me the reason for your visit," he said coldly. "I believe you mentioned something about Brighton."

"Yes," said Lawrence. "I would like to ask you…."

He did not finish the sentence. D'Onston stood abruptly and walked over to the desk. He pulled out several drawers, scrabbling for something and cursed under his breath. He rooted inside the third drawer and retrieved a small, brown glass-stoppered bottle. His hands shook as he poured the contents into a glass and he swigged the mixture in one swallow.

"You were saying," he continued as if nothing had happened.

"I was trying to ask you about the Royal Albion Hotel."

"What about it?"

"The evening of the 22nd June 1888. You were there."

"If you say so."

"Well, your name is in the visitor's book."

"Then I must have been there."

"May I ask why?"

D'Onston's eyes narrowed. "What business is it of yours. I don't even know who you are."

"I'm from Suffolk," said Lawrence. "A woman I know died recently in Ipswich. We found items in her room relating to the death of Edmund Gurney."

"Gurney…" The word slithered from D'Onston's mouth. "Was that the date he died?"

Lawrence nodded. "You were there that night. Did you see him?"

"No, I did not."

"Would you have recognised him?"

"No. We were not acquainted, and I only stayed at the Hotel for an hour."

"Why?"

"I was due to meet a woman. A fellow journalist. She did not keep the appointment, so I left."

Lawrence sighed. "Then it seems I have wasted your time."

D'Onston forced a smile and stood. His deportment indicated a military background, but the image was marred by his shabby suit. "It is as well that I have plenty of it," he said. "Time, that is."

Lawrence thanked him and left the room, relieved to be free of the oppressive atmosphere. Lawrence retraced his earlier path down Charterhouse Street not noticing the young man who had been loitering by the Hotel as he followed behind.

Chapter Nine

SETTING THE SCENE

13th February 1891

Dusk was falling as Violet reclined in the armchair of the rectory drawing room, half-listening as Frank Podmore explained how the evening's proceedings would develop. They had eaten heartily at luncheon with high tea delivered within a few hours. The remnants of the cake selection were still on the cake stand directly in Violet's eye line. Her self-control wavered as she fought to avoid the temptation of another slice of fruitcake. Anne Durrell had excelled herself. The cake she produced was one of the best Violet had tasted. For all the mess Anne made, she was a competent cook.

Violet's gaze wandered outdoors where bats swooped low over the orchard. Their movement was hypnotic, and she began to feel sleepy. It would not do to drop off in front of Mrs Woodward, so she turned her attention back to Frank Podmore.

"We will measure everything," he said. "Every sight,

sound and detail. We will even record the temperature. I have already drawn a detailed floor plan of the upstairs rooms."

"What can I do?" asked Reverend Woodward.

"Nothing," said Frank Podmore. "You must go about your business as if it were any other night. Tomorrow morning, I will interview you all, assuming you have no objection. We will include your version of events in our research as well as my observations and those of Dr Myers."

"It sounds very scientific," said the Reverend, nodding approvingly.

"It is," agreed Podmore. "We are impartial and only want to arrive at the truth of the matter. People are sceptical about our organisation. It's unfair. We conduct our examinations in forensic detail and disprove as many claims of spirit activity as those we deem genuine."

"That is why I asked you in the first place," said George Woodward. "You came highly recommended."

"What about the servants?" asked Mrs Woodward.

"The same applies," said Frank. "We will also ask for their accounts in the morning, but they should carry on as usual until then. Have you prepared the guest room as discussed?"

"Yes," said Alice. "Mr Myers has the blue room overlooking the garden. I have put Ms Smith in the other. But that leaves one of you without a room. Where do you intend to spend the night?"

"Myers and I will take turns sitting on the armchair at the end of the passageway, so we have a clear view. We will swap from time to time. Whichever one of us occupies the guest bedroom will keep the door ajar. I asked for that particular room because it gives a generous view of the upstairs landing."

"I see." Alice nodded, her mouth set somewhere between a smile and a grimace. It was clear to Violet that her hostess was struggling to contain her scepticism.

"Excuse me, but I must leave you for a moment." Violet cleared her throat and put her teacup on the table. She left the room and proceeded upstairs. Her drowsiness had not passed, and her frequent yawns were becoming embarrassing. A quick splash of water on her face should improve matters. She walked towards her room and met the housemaid coming out of the bathroom.

"Ooh you made me jump," gasped Kate. "I was away with the fairies."

"I'm sorry," said Violet. "Have you got a few moments?"

"Yes, Miss," Kate replied. "What do you want?"

"I wondered if you could tell me a little more about this ghost."

Kate's eyes widened. "I can tell you plenty. I have seen him several times."

"Him?"

"Most definitely. An old man, he is. Old and sad."

"Is his spirit clear?"

"I don't know what you mean."

Violet tried to find the right words. "I mean, does he look like a person or an apparition?"

"He looks the same as the ghosts you see at a seance. Have you ever been to one?"

"No," said Violet. "I know it is very much in fashion, but a friend of mine went to one in Bury Saint Edmunds recently. She thought that the so-called spirit looked more like a piece of cheesecloth."

"Well, the ones I saw were real." Kate protested. A frisson of hostility settled between them.

"I dare say she chose a disreputable medium," said Violet, trying to diffuse the situation.

"I dare say," said Kate sullenly.

Violet changed the subject. "Tell me, has your gardener or young Frederick seen the ghost?"

"Not that they've mentioned. You'll have to ask them."

"Will they be here tomorrow?"

"Yes," said Kate. "Mr Daldry will be here early in the morning and Fred soon after. You may have seen the ghost yourself by then," she continued darkly.

"Thank you, Kate," said Violet. She left the housemaid outside the bathroom and went to her room to fill the china basin on her dressing table. She washed her face and considered the housemaid's parting words as she towelled herself dry. Violet had not contemplated the possibility of witnessing a manifestation herself. She did not believe in spirits. It was evident that Kate did and might well be suggestible. Violet felt that she was in no position to judge Kate's character, having known her such a short time. Instinctively, she felt Kate was unlikely to be the cause of the disturbances. Whether she was influential in prolonging the stories through gossip, was another matter.

Violet abandoned her assessment of Kate and returned to the drawing room. Another member of the SPR had arrived while she was upstairs. She opened the door, and he jumped to his feet followed by the Reverend and Frank Podmore. "Ah, this is Miss Smith," said the Reverend. "Miss Smith, this gentleman is Dr Arthur Myers."

"Pleased to meet you," said the Doctor offering his hand. He smiled at Violet, and his grey eyes twinkled. He was about forty years old and dressed in a crisp grey suit with detailed gold cufflinks shaped in the symbol of Caduceus. He waited until Violet was sitting down before joining Frank Podmore on the sofa. They chatted enthusiastically about the work of the SPR. The splash of water had done the trick, and Violet's drowsiness had finally vanished. She listened to their accounts of telepathy and found herself unexpectedly interested. Both men were engaging, and Violet became more sympathetic to the aims of the Society. Time slipped by and the clock chiming ten came as a surprise. The evening had flashed by. Violet felt a flicker of disappointment when Alice bade them all a good night. Good manners meant following the lead of her hostess, and she reluctantly retired to bed.

As soon as she was back in her bedroom, Violet located a box of matches and placed candles in various strategic positions until the room was free from shadows. The biggest candle she saved for her bedside table hoping it would give enough light with which to read. She tried to occupy herself while the household settled for the night, unnecessarily tidying and rearranging clothes. Violet thought about getting into her nightdress and decided against it. She did not expect to hear or see anything untoward but wanted a quick and easy exit from the room, if necessary. She also wanted to keep watch over the hallway. Though Podmore and Myers were unaware of her role, Violet had as much to investigate as they did. She needed to be awake and alert to witness any trickery that might occur.

The landing was easily visible from the bedroom, but a sturdy sideboard obscured her view. Podmore's armchair was out of sight and could be seen, at a stretch, if she stood by the door frame at the risk of revealing herself. The Rectory benefited from an upstairs bathroom located opposite her bedroom giving her a legitimate reason to leave her room and look down the corridor without attracting undue attention.

Violet opened one of her gothic horror novels and tried to read by candlelight. She was too preoccupied to follow the story, and the subject matter did nothing to quell her nerves. The windows were old and ill-fitting. Candles flickered and danced, and the curtains twitched as an icy draught crept into the room. Nerves fraying, Violet lay on the bed trying to imagine what she would do if an apparition appeared. The thought of a spirit emerging through the wall sent shivers of fear through her body. Her fingers trembled as she tried to turn another page. She made herself read aloud while she waited for the household to quieten.

Eventually, a murmur of voices proceeded the sound of the three men walking upstairs. Violet heard the Reverend whisper goodnight and a door clicked shut as footsteps passed by. The hinges of another door creaked further down the landing. The brief interlude of noise was distracting. It settled her mind, and her nervousness vanished. Before long, the squeaks and groans of the old house settled. Violet waited a further half hour then tiptoed across the corridor towards the open bathroom door. She ran the tap to make it seem as if she had a purpose for being there, then crept back taking a long look at the armchair where Frank Podmore was sitting. He had removed a thermometer from his briefcase and set it by the wall. Then, he checked the temperature and noted it in a hard-backed book, in which he continued to write by candlelight. Pieces of equipment, which Violet couldn't identify, surrounded the chair. She returned to her room, none the wiser, and sat in silence for a period of time too long and dull to measure. In spite of her best intentions, her eyes grew heavy and she fell asleep.

Violet woke with a start to the sound of rapid knocking.

Hard, sharp knocks echoed through her bedroom. She gasped and sat up. The rapping stopped followed by a short silence. Then it began again intermittently with no real pattern. Her bedside candle, reduced to a stump, flickered. Most of the other candles had gone out leaving her room partly lit and full of menacing shadows. She reached for the dying night light and was about to leave the room when a door slammed shut like a crack of thunder. She almost dropped the candle in fright and with trembling hands, she opened the bedroom door and tiptoed into the corridor. Frank Podmore was staring down the landing. His book had fallen face down, and the measuring equipment lay scattered at his feet.

"What was that?" asked Violet,

"I don't know," said Frank. "I cannot explain it."

"Did you hear the knocking?"

"Yes, and the door slam. But there were only two doors open — yours and Myers. It wasn't your door, was it?"

"No. Mine was ajar. It has been all night."

"Better check Myers room," said Frank. "It must have been his door."

Violet followed him down the corridor. When they reached the blue room, they stared at each other. The door was also ajar.

"Odd," said Frank, knocking on the door. He entered the room.

Arthur Myers was sitting on his bed staring straight ahead at an empty wall.

"Myers," whispered Frank.

There was no response. Arthur Myers grey eyes were wide open, and his face was pale.

"I say, Myers old chap." Podmore shook his shoulder, and Myers gasped.

"Sorry. I was still half asleep," Myers said. "Did I miss anything?"

"Some unusual noises, knockings and the like. And a door slammed, yet I walked the corridor several times tonight, and the only open doors are still open now."

"It sounds like there is something here worthy of our time," said Myers. "I am only sorry I fell asleep and missed it. My turn now. I'll take watch while you rest."

"No," said Podmore. "I'll stay with you for a while in case anything else happens." He turned to Violet. "You should go back to your room," he said. "I doubt there will be any further disturbances, but you will feel safer if you are behind closed doors."

"Where are the others?" asked Violet.

"They will be in bed," said Podmore. "This isn't new to them, don't forget. It's like every other night."

Violet returned to her room. She did not dress but slipped under the cover and dozed fitfully until dawn.

Chapter Ten

LEMAN STREET STATION

Saturday 14th February 1891

Lawrence woke early and pulled back the curtains in the room he had hastily secured the previous evening. His unplanned journey to London left no time to consider accommodation. He had left it too late to find something comfortable and had settled for lodgings in a seedy lane not far from Victoria Station. Outside the lodging house, a brewer's yard abutted an alleyway and several heavy carts had already crossed the pitted road since the early hours of the morning. Although woken by the noise of working horses, Lawrence had drifted quickly back into a dreamless sleep. It was gone eight o'clock when he drew back the threadbare curtains to see a sheen of drizzle across the paving stones.

Henry Moore had invited him to return to his office in Scotland Yard, and Lawrence was anxious to get underway. It was also time to think about returning to Bury Saint Edmunds, in which case he would need to catch an early train. Lawrence wondered whether Henry would have arrived at work yet. He decided to chance it and borrowed an umbrella from the empty lobby of the boarding house before making his way to the Embankment.

Twenty minutes later, he arrived at the reception desk at Scotland Yard to find a letter waiting from Henry Moore who had left the station almost as soon as he appeared earlier that morning. The note apologised for his unexpected absence. Henry was en route to Leman Street Police Station where Lawrence was welcome to join him. A young non-uniformed policewoman gave Lawrence directions. She pointed out Leman Street on the large map dominating the wall opposite the desk. Leman Street was in the East End, and Lawrence would need to use the Metropolitan train service to ensure a swift journey.

He left immediately for the nearest station, disembarking at Aldgate. The route to Leman Street took Lawrence through narrow streets and alleys. It was his first foray into the East End and showed another side of London where people lived in unfamiliar poverty. Terraces of crumbling properties with broken windows and peeling doors were a world apart from the smart homes of Westminster. Poverty stricken groups of people huddled outside. Poorly dressed women and ragged children squeezed together on doorsteps, soaked to the bone from a persistent drizzle that seeped through their clothing and matted unwashed hair. If being out in the cold and rain was preferable to being inside, Lawrence dreaded to think what it was like indoors.

He arrived at Leman Street station, saddened at the conditions he had seen. There was no time for further reflection as he walked straight into the path of Henry Moore who was in a heated discussion with two other men.

"Ah, Lawrence," he said. "This is Inspector Reid and

Doctor Phillips. Edmund, George, this is the fellow I mentioned earlier. We had better discuss our business somewhere less public."

"Come this way," said Edmund Reid, guiding them through a set of double doors.

They followed him into a sparse room with a table and a sink.

"A poor sort of office," quipped Henry.

"It isn't an office," Reid replied. "And don't ask. You don't want to know."

Henry shook his head. "No matter. Now listen, Lawrence. I don't need to tell you that anything discussed in this room, must go no further.

"No, you don't need to tell me, Henry," said Lawrence. "I can assure you of my discretion."

"I know," Henry sighed. "This is sensitive, as you know. Did you see D'Onston yesterday?"

Lawrence nodded. Edmund Reid raised an eyebrow.

"Let's get this out of the way, and you can tell me all about it."

"What's happened?" asked Lawrence.

"We have just arrested Jack the Ripper."

"We have done nothing of the kind," snapped Edmund Reid. "James Sadler is not Jack the Ripper."

"And Frances Coles is not a Ripper victim," insisted George Phillips.

"I say she is," said Edmund Reid impatiently.

"Hold on," said Henry Moore. "Lawrence only arrived in London yesterday. Can you explain the situation to him?"

Reid sighed. "Yes. It might be useful having the view of

an impartial outsider if you don't mind me calling you that."

"Not at all," said Lawrence.

"Frances Coles is, or rather was, a prostitute. We found her in Swallow Gardens in the early hours of Friday morning, with her throat slashed."

"Was she robbed?" asked Lawrence.

"Unlikely," said Reid. "She had hidden two shillings behind a gutter pipe, which we later located. Possibly earnings from her last client."

"Were there any other wounds?"

"No," said Doctor Phillips. "Which is why she is not a Ripper victim. All the others suffered abdominal mutilations."

"Except Elizabeth Stride," said Edmund Reid.

"He was interrupted," argued Phillips. "He didn't get a chance to inflict any post-mortem wounds on her."

"What's to say the same thing didn't happen again?" asked Reid. "PC Thompson insists he heard footsteps as he walked towards Swallow Gardens on his beat. He probably missed the Ripper by moments."

"Except that it was not the Ripper." George Phillips raised his voice.

"Come, now," said Henry Moore. "Why are you so sure?"

"Because he cut her throat from left to right, right to left then back again. There were three clear cuts. It does not compare to the other Ripper crimes."

"But it does," insisted Reid. "All the cuts made by the Ripper started on the left and finished on the right."

"And he had tilted her body to the left, presumably to avoid blood stains," said Henry.

"Precisely. More evidence of someone experienced. Someone accustomed to the problem of excess blood loss."

"I cannot agree," said Phillips. "The killer of Frances Coles had no anatomical skills and his knife was blunt. He was not the Ripper."

"How does James Sadler fit in?" asked Lawrence.

"He knew the dead girl," said Henry. "And they drank together on the evening of her murder."

"What of it?" asked Edmund Reid. "That is not a motive. We have arrested the man, without just cause. And from all reports, he was blind drunk and incapable."

"I understand he had injuries too," said Henry Moore. "Is that not suspicious?"

"It requires explanation," said Edmund Reid, "but it is purely circumstantial."

"Can you be sure he did not commit the crime?" asked Moore.

"Of course not."

"Then he must remain under arrest. And we must consider him a suspect for the Ripper until proved otherwise. We cannot allow this to escalate into the hysteria of 1888."

"It is a grave mistake," said Edmund Reid. "But I will proceed as you wish." He nodded to Henry, shook Lawrence's hand and left the room, shaking his head.

"He is wrong," said George Bagshaw Phillips, looking over his shoulder. "He will not heed the medical evidence." He did not wait for Henry to reply but pursed his lips and walked away.

"Sorry that became heated," said Moore. "They have worked well together in the past but are on opposing sides in this matter. Anyway, how did you get on with Roslyn D'Onston?"

"Perfectly well, for the most," said Lawrence.

"Odd sort of fellow, didn't you find?"

"Indeed. He made me uneasy. I cannot explain why, but there was something sinister in his countenance."

"It's interesting that you thought so. D'Onston is an occult scientist — a black magician. Did you know?"

"Good Lord," said Lawrence. "Everybody I meet seems to have some connection to spiritualism. Violet is wasting her time ghost hunting, and both Gurney and his friend Smith were members of some psychic society or other. Is anybody rational anymore?"

"I am," said Henry. "I don't care a fig for such matters. Who is Violet?"

"She is my business partner," said Lawrence.

Henry raised an eyebrow. "You do surprise me."

"Yes, well if I don't conclude matters in London soon, she may not be."

"You promised me a full account of your dealings with D'Onston," Henry reminded him.

"It was rather a waste of time," said Lawrence shaking his head. "He denied seeing Gurney, and I have no reason to doubt him."

"Pity," said Henry. "Did he say anything else?"

"Not about the Brighton matter," said Lawrence. "He was very knowledgeable about the Ripper murders, though."

"What did he say?"

"He advanced a theory about the lack of blood on the killer's clothes. He thinks the Ripper stood behind his victims to slash their throats, thereby keeping the blood clear from his clothes. Very similar, to how Phillips and Reid described it."

Henry nodded. "He has suggested this before," he said. "He was under arrest at one time. Did I tell you that?"

"No."

"Well, D'Onston teamed up with a private investigator. Not a proper one, just some fellow who had convinced himself that an amateur could do what the police could not. Anyway, D'Onston was residing at a hospital at the time. For reasons best known to himself, he advanced a theory that one of the Doctors might be the Ripper. It was this doctor, a certain Morgan Davies, who suggested that the attacks on the victims took place from the rear. D'Onston used this theory as an excuse to contact Scotland Yard where he reported his suspicions. In the meantime, his amateur detective friend found D'Onston's behaviour equally suspicious and reported D'Onston too. Roslyn D'Onston kept pushing himself forward, eager for involvement in the case. His behaviour convinced us that he was a worthy Ripper suspect until an alibi for one of the murders proved otherwise."

"Now that I've met him, I can see why you might have thought so," said Lawrence, "but he is of no further use to me. My Brighton investigation has come to nothing. I'm going back to Bury. I'll call in at Ipswich and report back to Fernleigh on the way."

"Fernleigh, you say? It's been a long time since I've had the pleasure of his company. Do give him my regards."

"I will, and I trust you will have a quieter time now that your suspect is under arrest."

"No doubt," said Henry. "It is good to see Reid so passionate in his views, but I think we have the right man. The Ripper is long gone, and despite what Edmund thinks, we have good evidence against Sadler. The matter is almost over."

The two men shook hands. Lawrence retrieved his case from the boarding house and caught the next train to Suffolk.

Chapter Eleven

CHELMONDISTON - THE AFTERMATH

Saturday 14th Feb 1891

Violet awoke to the sound of birdsong. The time was almost seven o'clock, and it took her a few moments to recall the events of the previous evening. She rubbed her eyes and pushed her bedclothes away revealing a crumpled day dress. She sighed. Going to bed fully clothed had seemed like a good idea at the time, but her other dress had not travelled well. She had removed it from the trunk the day she arrived to find it badly creased. Violet could not present herself looking as she did. Regardless of the creases, she would need to change.

Light streamed into the room as Violet opened the curtains. She walked towards the window and peeped outside. Trees swayed in a light breeze, and a layer of mist had obscured the rear of the large, flat lawn. The outside beckoned, and she opened the dark wooden wardrobe to retrieve her day clothes, recoiling at the smell of mothballs. The odour clung to her navy day dress as she held it to the window admiring the high lace collar. Some of the creases had dropped out while it had been hanging. The dress was not perfect, but it would do.

Violet finished her ablutions, left the room and traversed the empty landing. The armchair was vacant and all the notebooks and equipment from the previous evening had gone. The house was quiet and peaceful. Violet struggled to remember why she had been frightened last night.

She went downstairs and opened the drawing-room door, but it was dark. The maid had not yet drawn the curtains. There were no signs of life in the dining room or the breakfast room, so she wandered into the kitchen where Anne Durrell was standing with her hands deep in a sink full of water and singing to herself.

"Good morning, Anne," said Violet.

Anne smiled. "Good morning, Miss Smith. Would you like a cup of tea?"

"I would love one." Violet sat at the kitchen table and watched Anne pour two cups of tea from a tarnished metal teapot pitted with dents. The kitchen was warm and homely, and a well-established fire burned brightly in the grate. Anne placed the teacups on the table, then tossed another log onto the fire. She prodded it with a well-worn poker, and it settled with a satisfying crackle.

"Where is everyone?" asked Violet.

"Still abed, Miss. Sunday is an early start in this house and Saturday is what you might call their day of rest. Breakfast is set for eight-thirty today."

"I see," said Violet. "And the others?"

"The men investigating the Reverend's ghost?"

Violet nodded.

"I haven't seen them," said Anne. "But then I've been in

the kitchen since cock crow. No fancy gentlemen from London are likely to disturb me in here."

Violet smiled. "I suppose not. Did you hear the noises last night?"

"Only the usual knocking sounds," said Anne. "Nothing out of the ordinary."

"They were loud," said Violet. "A door slammed. It would not have been unusual, except that Mr Podmore had closed all the doors. Only two remained ajar, and they were still open after the slamming stopped."

Anne shrugged. "It's the same every night," she said. "It doesn't mean anything."

"What do you think caused it?"

"It's an old house, Miss. There will always be noises, and they seem worse in the dark. As for the rapping — well, it's a rummin, and that's a fact. But there's no use thinking too hard about it. It is what it is."

"It doesn't scare you?"

"No. Were you frightened?"

"A little," admitted Violet. "Though in the light of day, it seems silly. But I can't think of an explanation for it, and that troubles me."

"Not everything has an explanation," Anne replied. "As I said, best not think too hard about it. It is a pity that the Reverend called the investigators again. Better left alone, in my opinion."

"You don't think they can help?"

Ann drained her teacup and placed it on the table. "No, I don't," she said. "All that writing and measuring squit. Pah! Such pretty men and so well educated. But what would they do if there were such things as ghosts and they came upon one? They do not look the type to fight it or even outrun it. Especially the pompous one. No, they should leave well alone."

Violet laughed. "Which one is the pompous one?"

"Mr high and mighty Podmore," said Anne. "Though don't tell the Reverend I said that. Mr Podmore clicked his fingers at me last night before I turned in. Clicked them in my ear and asked for a cup of cocoa. He nearly had one upturned on his head." She crossed her arms and tucked them under her huge bosom.

"Not a very polite thing to do," said Violet. "He behaved so courteously to me last night."

"He claimed he called my name twice," said Anne. "When he couldn't make himself heard, he clicked his fingers. That what he said, but I did not hear him. I told him straight. "I am the cook, not the maid but I will fetch your cocoa anyway."

"Oh, dear. Just a misunderstanding surely?"

"Pompous," said Anne.

"Well, thank you for the tea," said Violet, "but I think I will go for a walk before breakfast. I need to clear my head."

"Very well, Miss," said Anne. "There's a nice carved ham and eggs to look forward to for breakfast."

"Thank you." Violet smiled as she left the kitchen. Anne Durrell had been exceedingly frank in her opinions. Violet wondered if she was always that way, or whether their shared Norfolk connection had made her more open. Anne had been bordering on disrespectful to her employer, but her candid observations were refreshing. Violet was grateful that she did not need to interpret Anne's motives.

Violet walked through the breakfast room into the rear hallway where she unlatched the door and let herself into the garden. The mist had lifted. After a quick promenade of the lawn, she opened the side gate and set off down the path towards the village.

Violet shivered as she walked towards the Church. The warmth of the kitchen had masked the cold February morning. She pulled the fur collar of her coat higher and fastened the topmost button. Violet decided against walking to the village and chose a new route instead. She turned into a narrow lane running past the Church and opposite the rectory. The winding tree-lined road was pretty, and Violet momentarily forgot that she was here on duty. She refocussed her thoughts and contemplated what she had learned from her time in Chelmondiston. Apart from a little insight into some of the occupants of the rectory, she had not achieved much. She had managed to exchange a few words with young Frederick Lucas the previous morning but had yet to meet the gardener. Nothing she had seen suggested any trickery behind the recurring noises in the Rectory. Quite the contrary. It seemed likely that the sounds arose from the age and composition of the building. If not, they were, as Anne Durrell suggested, inexplicable.

Violet was deep in thought, only registering the presence of another person when she heard noises coming from behind her. A quiet tread of boots interrupted her reverie, and she turned to see Doctor Myers clad in a long brown coat, striding in her direction.

"I thought I recognised you," he said. "Do you mind if I walk with you?"

Violet smiled. "It will be lovely to have some company," she said, glad of the distraction. She was becoming despondent about the investigation and losing faith in her ability to bring it to a satisfactory conclusion.

"Where are you heading?" asked Myers.

"I don't know," she replied. "I'm not familiar with Chelmondiston."

"The Rector suggested a walk by the river when we spoke last night," said Arthur. "It's quite a long way, but well worthwhile, if you fancy it."

"That sounds ideal," said Violet. "A long walk might keep out the cold. I have managed to leave my gloves behind."

"Have mine," said Arthur Myers removing them from his hands. "They may be a little large, but they will keep you warm."

Violet started to speak, but Myers interrupted. "Please take them. I won't enjoy our walk knowing you are cold, and I do not feel it myself. Besides, I have deep pockets."

Violet accepted the gloves and thanked the doctor. They turned off the narrow lane and walked together onto another straight path that stretched into the distance.

"Tell me about your work," asked Violet. "A life spent in medicine must be fascinating."

"Oh, it is," Myers agreed. "I always wanted to become a Doctor, although it was a close-run thing between that and being a professional sportsman."

"They are two very different occupations," said Violet.

"Indeed. But I always enjoyed cricket and had some success at tennis," said Myers. "I played at Wimbledon when I was a younger man in better health."

"How fascinating," said Violet. Her walking companion was slim and wiry. She could easily imagine him participating in sporting events. His demeanour suggested that he was of a similar age to Violet and probably in his forties. He showed no signs of middle age spread or any outward sign of aches or pains. His hair was grey and slightly receding and his complexion fresh, although bags beneath his eyes suggested a lack of sleep. Violet could see no evidence of poor health and his appearance suggested otherwise.

"But you chose to become a Doctor," said Violet.

"I did, and I am glad of it," Myers replied. "A sporting occupation is a short-lived thing, so I studied medicine and became a physician. I am currently working at the Belgrave Hospital for Children," he continued.

"Do you enjoy it?"

"I do." Myers smiled warmly. "It gives me the opportunity to practice medicine and conduct my research. It is a good life."

"What do you study?"

"Have you heard of Raynaud's disease?"

"Is that something to do with your hands?"

"Yes. It is a condition causing pain to the extremities."

"Is that why you gave me your gloves?"

Meyers laughed. "I gave you my gloves because you were cold. There is no evidence of Reynaud's disease in your hands."

"Oh, look." Violet pointed ahead. They were nearing the end of the road, and the River Orwell was in sight. A small clutch of thatched cottages and an Inn bordered the lane and a brick-built boathouse nestled on the bank to their left. Wooden boats dotted the shore, some intact and some lying broken on the river bank. The choppy waters of the Orwell were murky blue. The riverside was bitterly cold yet bursting with life. Ahead, a young boy steered a rowboat to the shore where a woman was waiting, arms folded over her stiff white apron. Cattle grazed in a field which reached almost to the river banks where they were tended by a farmer, clad in layers of patched up clothes.

Violet and Arthur reached the river's edge and surveyed the scene in silence. The Orwell heaved and churned to the rhythm of the wind as dark clouds rolled across the sky. Violet brushed a drop of spray from her face and then another before realising that it was a gentle scattering of snowflakes.

"We had better go back," said Doctor Myers.

They returned up Pin Mill Lane, each distracted by their thoughts. Violet broke the comfortable silence that descended. "What made you interested in Psychical Research", she said. "It is so very different from science. It's nebulous, illogical and relies entirely on faith."

"No, it doesn't," said Myers. "I became involved because of Frederick, my older brother. He has had a life-long fascination with spiritualism. But our research isn't illogical and is quite compatible with my medical experience. There are scientific grounds for the study of hypnotism and more than adequate proof of the powers of faith healing. The mind is a powerful engine and belief in a cure can aid most conditions."

"Do you believe in spirits?" asked Violet.

"It is not important one way or the other," said Meyers. "I believe in scientific study and quantifiable results. It is important to approach these matters without prejudice and be circumspect and rational."

They were back in the village now and walking towards the Rectory. It was bitingly cold, but the snowflakes had petered out almost as soon as they began. Since they left, a shabbily dressed man had appeared in the front garden of the Rectory and was squatting by the side gate oiling a pair of shears.

"Are you Mr Daldy, the gardener?" asked Violet.

"That I am," he replied.

"Good morning. I am Violet," she said, "and this is Doctor Myers."

She hesitated. This might be her only opportunity to question the gardener, and she was going to have to do it in front of the doctor without arousing suspicion. In the short time, she had known him Violet had already decided that she liked Doctor Myers. She hoped to portray curiosity rather than nosiness while appearing amiable instead of a gossip.

The gardener stood and faced Violet. A web of crow's feet surrounded his pale blue eyes, and his tanned skin was almost leathery. Deep laughter lines furrowed his face. "John Daldy, Ma'am. What do you need?"

"Doctor Myers and his companion are investigating the noises in the Rectory," said Violet. "I have found their accounts very interesting. Have you have ever heard any strange sounds yourself?"

"I have heard them all right," said Daldy, "and a worst night's sleep I have never had in all my life."

"You stayed in the Rectory overnight?" asked Violet.

"For one night only," said Daldy. "Never again. It was just before Kitty left," he continued. "Last year, before your lot came for the first time."

"Yes," said Myers, "I remember reading the report. I believe Barkworth wrote it. I don't recall reading an account from you."

"I left long before he arrived," said Daldy. "Other gardening jobs to do, but the Reverend will have told him what happened."

"What did happen?" asked Violet.

The gardener placed his shears on the floor and cleared his throat. "I have worked here for a long time," said Daldy. "And the disturbances are nothing new. They happened a lot when Reverend Beaumont lived here, but he was never bothered. He had a big family, you see. His children were loud, always larking around and making noise. It drowned out the knocking and rapping, and it was only the servants that ever mentioned it. Well, eventually Reverend Beaumont left, and Reverend Woodward arrived. There were no children this time and the Reverend and Mrs Woodward rattled around the place alone. They bought their servants, of course, but none of them knew anything about the noises. Then one night the Reverend heard footsteps in the passageway. Doors began opening and closing when there was nobody around."

As the gardener spoke, Arthur Myers removed a notebook from his jacket pocket. He patted his coat, searching for a pencil, located one and began to take notes.

Daldy continued. "Reverend Woodward asked his servants if they had heard anything, and they said they had. Kitty was especially upset. She had kept her fears under control while she thought the sounds were only in her imagination. As soon as the others started talking openly about a ghost, fear got the better of her. She was so distressed that the Reverend asked me, young Frederick and another man to search the house. We started in daylight so we could see clearly, and we examined every corner of the house, inspected the drains and took up the floorboards in one of the bedrooms. Even the ivy on the outside wall did not escape our notice. We pulled it away to make sure there was nothing beneath. And still, the noises continued."

"What happened on the night you stayed at the Rectory?" asked Violet.

"It was the smell that did for me," said John Daldy. "The bedroom reeked of sulphur, and all night I was disturbed by slamming, banging, rapping and footsteps. I did not sleep a wink. Then in the early hours of the morning, Kitty screamed and woke the whole household. Mrs Woodward was furious."

"Why?"

"Kitty said she woke to see the shadow of a small grey-bearded man in shabby clothes standing by her bedside. Mrs Woodward did not believe a word of it. She threatened to dismiss Kitty, but it was too late. Kitty had already made her mind up. The house terrified her, and she said she wouldn't stay a moment longer. She didn't. She packed her trunk and left the very next day."

"It is odd that Reverend and Mrs Woodward have such diverging views," said Violet.

"She hears the sounds the same as the rest of us," said Daldy. "She cannot explain it so she will not admit it."

"What do you think it is?" asked Violet.

"I think it's the previous rector," said Daldy looking down at his feet, embarrassed.

"Reverend Beaumont?" asked Violet.

"Not him, he's still alive as far as I know," said Daldy. "I mean old 'cabbage' Howarth, the one before. He was a rotten old miser. Never spent a penny while he was alive and then his will went missing after he died."

"You think he has come back to haunt the Rectory?" asked Violet.

"It's what they say in the village," muttered Daldy. "They think it is the Reverend Richard Howarth risen from his grave in the churchyard. He has come back to claim his money."

"Have you ever seen this apparition?"

"No," said Daldy, "but old man Thompson saw it in the churchyard on the morning Reverend Howarth died in '63.

Reverend Woodward may have seen the ghost and Kitty did. They're all the sightings I know of."

"Well, thank you for explaining," said Violet.

The gardener tipped his cap, collected the shears and trudged off muttering below his breath.

"Oh dear," said Violet as they entered the Rectory. "Completely deluded."

"But quite compelling, from a parapsychological point of view," said Myers.

"It sounds rather unlikely," replied Violet, dubiously.

"It's the first sighting, that interests me," said Myers. "It's as good an example of a veridical hallucination as one could ask for."

"I don't know what you mean."

"A veridical hallucination is one that corresponds with a real event — generally something that we can corroborate later on. In this case, Thompson saw what he thought was the ghost of the Rector which coincided with the Rector dying. It is all there in my brother's book, Phantasms of the Living."

"Complicated, but fascinating," said Violet. She was about to ask a question when Frank Podmore came down the stairs carrying a large leather bag.

"Ah, there you are," he said, addressing Myers. "I have been looking for you everywhere. I was getting worried."

Meyers retrieved his pocket watch. "Good Lord, is that the time?"

"Yes, it's nine thirty," said Podmore, "and high time we were off. Sidgwick is expecting us for supper."

"I must be on my way too," said Violet.

"How are you travelling?" asked Myers.

"By train," said Violet.

"We are too. Our carriage to the station has arrived, and there is plenty of space. Would you care to join us?"

"Oh, thank you, but no. I must speak with Mrs Woodward first. I will catch an afternoon train."

"Then I wish you a good day," said Myers doffing his hat. "I enjoyed our conversation. The Headquarters of the SPR is in the Adelphi. If you are ever in London, do look us up."

"I will," said Violet. The two men loaded their cases onto the carriage and Violet watched as it pulled away. She sighed. 'Now just the small matter of what to tell Mrs Woodward', she thought.

Chapter Twelve

BACK IN THE BUTTERMARKET

Monday – 2nd March 1891

Violet stared out of the window of her office in the Buttermarket and reminisced about the previous year. She missed her employment as Mrs Harris's companion and felt her absence keenly. Violet often remembered her former employers' quiet fortitude in the face of poor health. She remembered every corner of the home they shared in Fressingfield. Mrs Harris had been formidable but kind, and Violet had felt useful and secure in her employment. When Mrs Harris died, it had been no less upsetting than it would have been for Violet to lose one of her kin.

Lawrence's offer of work had come as a surprise, all the more so when he suggested a partnership. Violet had accepted it gratefully, believing she could perform the task well. That certainty had dwindled lately as she felt Lawrence's regard for her slip away.

Violet realised early on that Lawrence was a complicated man, but the extent of his capricious nature came as a surprise. Violet was steady and not given to extremes of behaviour. She was always courteous, generally content and saw no reason why Lawrence should be otherwise. He was moody and downright rude when provoked. He had been unpleasant to their domestic last week. Poor Annie was only singing as she worked, and not very loudly. But Lawrence had thumped his fist on the table, then stalked into the yard where he admonished her loudly. Violet hoped it would not put Annie off coming in tomorrow. Good cleaners were hard to find, and Annie was very thorough.

The bell jangled, and Lawrence strode into the office with a newspaper under his arm. "Good morning," he said curtly, hanging his coat and hat on the stand by the inner hallway. "Good God, but it's cold in here." He walked towards the fireplace and prodded the fledgling fire.

"It hasn't been going long," said Violet.

"We should get that girl in to set it," Lawrence replied. "What's the point of having her if we need to set the fire ourselves."

"We don't make up the fire," said Violet. "I do. I can't remember the last time you did it. Annie deals with it on the days that she is in and there isn't enough money to pay for her to come more often."

Lawrence sighed. "I am expecting payment for that forgery business in Shottisham. Hasn't it arrived yet?"

"No," said Violet. "The only fee that came in last week was from the Chelmondiston job."

"I'm surprised she paid that," said Lawrence. "It was hardly the outcome she wanted."

"I did what she asked," Violet replied. "There was no proof of any trickery. I wasn't going to invent it. How are you getting on with your half of the ledgers?" Violet hastily changed the subject. She had not told Lawrence about the terse note Alice Woodward had sent with the fee. The letter made a pointed reference to Violet's lack of progress and Alice made it clear that she was only paying under sufferance.

"I've nearly finished," said Lawrence. "I've found some more anomalies. You?"

"Yes, I found another discrepancy on Friday," said Violet, "while you were in Norwich. Remind me what you were doing there? Another case, was it?"

Lawrence ignored her. "Get your notes ready, and I'll drop in and see Challoner later this afternoon. There's no doubt that his clerk is fiddling the books. I will never understand why these people don't check their employees work."

"He can't check," said Violet. "He is barely literate. His abilities lie elsewhere. That's why he employs a clerk."

She took a clutch of papers from her drawer and dropped them on Lawrence's desk. "It's all there," she said. "I've checked every line of the ledger. There's nothing else to find."

"Good," said Lawrence. "Good that something has gone well, for once."

"What's wrong now?" asked Violet.

"Nothing new. Just problems," he continued. "Hello, what's this?"

"Post from Friday," said Violet. "I didn't feel I ought to open something addressed to you marked Private and Confidential."

Lawrence grasped a brass letter opener in the shape of a sword and slit open the envelope. He removed one sheet of fine-lined paper and smoothed it over his blotting pad."

"Damnation," he said, screwing the letter into a ball. He hurled it towards the fireplace, and it bounced off the coal pail.

"Another problem?" asked Violet

"It's from Fernleigh," said Lawrence gloomily. He put his head in his hands and sighed. "He's read my report and doesn't think there's any point in investigating the Moss case any further."

"You can't blame him," said Violet. "It's hard to understand why you took the case in the first place, not that there was a case, there being no fee involved."

"We've had this conversation before," snapped Lawrence. "But Fernleigh is wrong. There is something inexplicable linking Ruth Moss to Edmund Gurney's murder."

"Murder," exclaimed Violet. "It's an accidental death."

"No," said Lawrence shaking his head. "It's not, I'm sure of it."

"Why?"

"Because George Smith says so," said Lawrence. "He knew Gurney better than almost anyone."

"Remind me, which one is George Smith?"

"He worked with Gurney at the Society for Psychical Research," said Lawrence. "Smith was Gurney's secretary."

"It's odd, isn't it," said Violet.

"What?"

"Both our cases involve the SPR to one degree or another."

"Oh yes, I think you mentioned it, but I wasn't paying much attention at the time. Purely coincidental though."

"I'm making a cup of tea. Do you want one?"

Lawrence nodded. Violet walked towards the stove in the rear kitchen that they shared with Mrs Wise who sold millinery in the other half of the shop. It was a useful division of space that kept both their bills low.

Lawrence had opened his copy of the Bury press and

was scanning the headlines when the doorbell rang. An errand boy burst through the door, panting. "Telegram for you, Sir," he said.

Lawrence dropped a few coins in the boy's sweating palm and watched him leave the shop. He gazed at the telegram. It had been a long time since Lawrence had received one in the course of his work. He slit it open, read the contents and hot-footed it into the back room.

"It's nearly ready," said Violet.

"I don't care about the tea," Lawrence replied. "This is a telegram from Henry Moore." He brandished the message in the air. "He wants me to go back to London and speak to Roslyn D'Onston again."

"Why?"

"They've released James Sadler. He is not the Ripper, and he did not kill Frances Coles. The hunt is on, and they don't trust D'Onston anymore than I do."

"You're not going, are you?"

"Of course."

"What about me?"

"You can stay here and mind the office."

"No." Violet put her hands on her hips feeling an unfamiliar surge of anger. "I am not staying here on my own again," she snapped. "We are either a partnership, or we are not. Make up your mind."

"Fine, come with me then. We've finished Challoner's case. Get your girl to look in on the office and join me. It's important, Violet, just you wait and see."

Chapter Thirteen

AN UNANNOUNCED VISIT

Tuesday 3rd March 1891

Lawrence hailed a cab outside The Regal Hotel on the Lambeth side of Westminster Bridge. The Hotel in which they were staying was not at all regal, more closely resembling an upmarket lodging house, but it was respectable, clean and cheap. The cab driver acknowledged Lawrence's raised hand with a nod and stopped the carriage. Lawrence opened the door and helped Violet inside before exchanging a few words with the driver. They climbed on board and set off for a brief journey terminating at Montpellier Square in Westminster.

"Where are we?" asked Violet, suspiciously. "This doesn't look like the Embankment."

"Slight detour," Lawrence replied, fishing in his pocket for change. He paid the cabman and gestured to the black door of a large four storey building. "This way."

"Where are we going?" asked Violet.

"Don't worry. It's just an idea I had."

"Who lives here?"

Lawrence sighed. Violet had proved an amiable and interesting travelling companion. The strained exchanges they had become accustomed to of late, vanished as soon as they left Bury and the train journey was unexpectedly enjoyable. He had purposely delayed telling Violet about the visit because he knew she would not approve.

"It's Kate Grove's house."

"Who is she?"

"Edmund Gurney's wife. Or rather she was. She's Archibald Grove's wife now."

"Does she know we are coming? I can't imagine what you want with her, and I'm surprised she has agreed to it."

"She hasn't, exactly."

"She doesn't know, does she?"

"No."

"I can't believe you, Lawrence. What do you hope to find out from her?"

"I want to know what was in the letter summoning Gurney to Brighton. The one that went missing."

"Oh really." Violet's tone was terse again. "You're not working on that case. It's over. Forget it."

"I can't yet. I will if nothing more comes of it. I want to find out why Gurney went to Brighton before I see D'Onston again."

"But D'Onston doesn't know anything about Brighton."

"I know. I know. Speaking to Kate Gurney, I mean Grove, is too good an opportunity to miss. The more facts we uncover, the more we can find out."

"This is turning into an obsession," Violet complained. "Not to mention embarrassing. Calling without notice — it's too much."

"You will come with me though? I need your help. She's much more likely to speak in the presence of a woman."

Violet shook her head. "If I help you, can we go straight to Scotland Yard without any more distractions?"

"I promise," said Lawrence solemnly. He strode to the door, rang the bell and waited. A butler wearing tails appeared in the doorway. Violet bit her lip — the encounter was going to be worse than she thought.

"Yes?" said the butler in a strongly accented voice.

Lawrence offered his card. "Is Mrs Grove at home?" he asked.

"One moment," said the butler, leaving them standing on the doorstep.

"French?" asked Lawrence.

"I think so," said Violet. "Not that it makes things any less awkward. I can't bear it."

"You'll have to," said Lawrence. "He's coming back."

"Mrs Grove will not see you," said the butler.

"It's important."

"She is unwell. She does not know you and will not see you. Kindly leave."

The butler pushed the door too.

"Please," said Violet. "It concerns the health of an old lady."

"Wait," a voice boomed from inside. "Inghelaine, you can leave this to me."

The butler nodded and retreated. A handsome, fair-haired man in a brown suit replaced him in the doorway.

"Archibald Grove," he said, offering a hand.

"I am Lawrence Harpham, and this is Violet Smith."

"You seem eager to see my wife. May I ask why."

Lawrence opened his mouth, but Violet spoke. "It's in connection with an elderly lady," she said. "A friend of ours.

She recently became quite distressed about a matter concerning the death of Edmund Gurney. She knew him well when she lived in Brighton, and we hoped to give her some reassurance."

"Kate, my wife, she's not in good health," said Archibald, "and she doesn't like talking about her late husband's death. It was a difficult time."

"We understand," said Violet. "But Ruth is ailing and…." She looked downcast as if she might cry.

"I'll see what I can do," said Archibald. "Come and wait inside." He directed them to an occasional room at the front of the house.

Lawrence turned to Violet. "I don't know what to say."

"I'm sorry. It was an awful thing to do. I don't know what came over me."

"Violet, it was perfect. I didn't know you had it in you."

"Neither did I," Violet admitted. "I don't like lying."

The door squeaked open, and Inghelaine appeared. "Come this way," he said, directing them to an opulent drawing room. Archibald stood as they entered while his wife reclined on a chaise lounge.

Lawrence approached him and shook his hand again. "Thank you for this," he said.

"Kate has agreed to speak with you, but only for five minutes. That is all. Please do not overtire her. I have to leave now. Inghelaine will see you out when you have finished."

Violet smiled at her host. He was a pleasant looking man, well-mannered and amiable, though a good deal shorter than Lawrence.

"Sit down," commanded Kate Grove, gesturing to the armchairs opposite. Her appearance was markedly different from that of her husband. His face was open, with a full, generous mouth and he exuded charisma. She was sallow-skinned with dark patches under her eyes and bristled with undisguised resentment.

"Archie has asked me to help you," she said querulously. "He says it would be public-spirited, which matters to him. It matters less to me."

"We understand," said Lawrence. "This will be quick."

"Very well."

"Our friend, Ruth Moss, knew your former husband in Brighton. His death upset her, and now she is older and coming to the end of her life, it has become a terrible burden. We don't know why, but she feels responsible."

"I cannot see any reason why she should," said Mrs Grove.

"Nor we," said Lawrence. "But when we said we were coming to London, she asked if we could contact you. She hopes you can answer a question that would put her mind at rest."

"What do you want to know?"

"Ruth said Edmund received a letter asking him to come to Brighton. Do you remember anything about it?"

"A little. Edmund had been out to dinner with Mr Flower. Do you know him? He is the Liberal Member of Parliament. They dined at the House of Commons, that night. Edmund came home to find a letter waiting for him which he read in the hallway. He didn't even pause to exchange pleasantries but had the maid pack a bag. He left for Brighton early the next day."

"Do you know who sent the letter?"

"I assumed that it was George Smith. He often wrote, but I later learned that Smith was on his honeymoon at the time so it couldn't have been him."

"And you don't know who it was?"

"Sorry, I do not."

"And you can't think of anyone it might have been?"

Kate sighed. "This is getting tedious," she said. "Are you finished?"

"If that is all you know," said Lawrence, "then, yes."

"Thank you for trying to help our friend," said Violet. "We appreciate your kindness."

Kate Grove's stern face relaxed for a moment. "I don't know who sent the letter," she said. "This may not help, but I am certain that it came from someone well known to Edmund, most definitely not a stranger."

"How do you know?" asked Lawrence.

"I caught a glimpse while it was in his hand," she said. "The salutation was to 'My Dear Edmund'."

Chapter Fourteen

HEADQUARTERS OF THE SPR

"I still don't understand why we had to go through that charade," said Violet. "What have we gained?"

"Something we did not know before," said Lawrence. "Definite proof that a stranger did not write the letter."

"I would not have considered otherwise. Why would he leave home within a few hours of receiving a letter from someone he didn't know?"

"He might go if it involved a professional matter," said Lawrence. "It would be perfectly reasonable to investigate something interesting at short notice."

"But surely his colleagues were also his friends? It makes very little difference."

"Violet, please don't be so obstructive."

"I am using logic, which is why you asked me to be your business partner in the first place. And there is another thing I don't understand."

"What?"

"How many letters were there?"

"Only two. I have told you often enough. The first

letter summoned Gurney to Brighton. We now know that it was from a close friend or colleague. This letter is missing. It was not on his body when they found him. Gurney himself composed the second letter and never took the opportunity to post it. He had written the letter on headed notepaper. It bore the SPR crest and address, and more importantly, the names of each member of the council. The Hotel staff used this letter to contact a colleague to help identify him."

"What was in the second letter?"

"Nora did not say," replied Lawrence, "but she made it clear that the letter was routine and unimportant."

"What happened to it?"

"I have no idea. Does it matter?"

"Probably not, said Violet, "but I think I will pay a visit to the Society for Psychical Research. I would like to know more."

"You can't just go wandering in there," said Lawrence.

"I can. I was invited to visit."

"When? By whom?"

"In Chelmondiston, and by Doctor Myers. He asked me to look him up if I was ever in London."

"I'll come with you."

"No, Lawrence. You have already delayed your appointment long enough. Henry Moore is expecting you at Scotland Yard."

"But I know more about this business with Gurney than you do."

"Then you will have to trust me, won't you? I am the one with the invitation, and you are not."

"Where is their building? I can meet you when I have finished with Henry."

"It is in Buckingham Street, Adelphi."

"That is only a short distance from Scotland Yard. You go, and we'll compare notes later."

Half an hour later Violet left Lawrence at the entrance to Scotland Yard and walked the short distance to the Adelphi district. The Society's headquarters took up most of an imposing flat fronted terraced house — a grand building with expansive sash windows and wrought iron railings. Violet approached the entrance. The door was wood panelled with side windows and a fanlight, both set beneath an archway. She rapped on the brass door knocker, but nobody replied. Violet peered into the arched window on her left. A bald man with a neatly trimmed beard gestured as he walked around the room. She raised her hand and waved gingerly. He saw her, left the room and moments later the door opened.

"My apologies for keeping you waiting," he said. "Our doorman is unavailable today. Can I help?"

"I'm sorry to bother you," said Violet, "but I met Mr Podmore and Doctor Myers recently. They asked me to call in if I was ever passing, and I am. I hope it isn't inconvenient."

"No, not at all," said the man, "although neither Frank nor my brother is here, and I do not know whether to expect them today. I only called in on the off chance that Arthur would around. I am going back to Cambridge tonight and won't be available for a few days. Come this way. Sorry to have kept you waiting. Under normal circumstances, the door would be open, but Elias is unwell, and we lock ourselves inside."

The man ushered her into the room with the arched window where a second man was reading a newspaper while he reclined on the sofa. He was smartly dressed and also wore a beard.

Violet spoke. "If you are Arthur's brother, you must be Frederick Myers. Arthur mentioned you."

"Did he now? Yes, I am Frederick Myers, and this is William Crookes. Pleased to meet you Miss — sorry I don't think you mentioned your name?"

"I didn't. I'm Violet Smith. I was in Chelmondiston when they conducted the investigation last month. I found it very interesting and hoped to learn more about your organisation."

"Ah, yes. The Chelmondiston case was quite unusual. I don't know if Frank explained, but we dedicate much of our work to the psychology of spiritualism. The cases we investigate are those involving participants of flawless reputation. There must be no evidence of suggestibility or any intellectual infirmity. As you will know by now, we cross-examine everyone and take as much empirical proof as possible. This method sometimes results in the detection of trickery."

"Yes, I am unfamiliar with your methods, but I greatly admire their scientific basis."

Frederick Myers nodded. "We take steps to understand the psychology of error and perception. Not all trickery is intentional, and we have found no evidence of it in Chelmondiston. The events at the Rectory have so far proved inexplicable. It is rare for us to witness a manifestation. Our involvement usually comes afterwards when we collect and analyse the evidence. William examines much of the documentation when he is not busy with other matters. He is a Professor of Chemistry but still finds a great deal of time for us."

William lowered his paper and smiled. "I have not spent as much time as I would like on the Rectory case," he said, "but I am aware of it. There is undoubtedly something worthy of explanation."

Violet turned to Frederick. "Do you believe there is a ghost at the Rectory?"

"It is too soon to be sure. First, we must rule out all non-paranormal explanations. As I said, we are confident that we have ruled out fakery, but we must conduct further research before ruling out misperception."

"How will you do that?"

"It's too big a question to answer quickly, Miss Smith," said Frederick. "I have limited time at my disposal today. As I said, I only dropped in to see my brother and borrow a few books from our library. I must return to Cambridge in an hour. Please allow me to lend you a book on the subject. We will need it back eventually, but you may keep it as long as you need."

"Thank you. I would like that. Do you have a big library?"

"It has grown every year," said Frederick Meyers. "My great friend, Edmund Gurney, founded the library. Keeping it well stocked with books has always been an important part of our work. Since his death, it has assumed even greater significance."

"Edmund Gurney? Oh, that's interesting. My friend met a man in Brighton who knew Mr Gurney."

"Edmund spent a lot of time in Brighton. He knew many people. Did your friend mention a name?"

"George Smith," said Violet.

"Oh, yes. Smith was one of Edmund's young men. Quite the expert on mesmerism. He is still part of the SPR, but we don't see much of him in London, now."

"That is a pity. Lawrence found him charming, though saddened by the death of your mutual friend."

"Poor Edmund. We still feel his loss. It was a testing time for all."

"He died unexpectedly?"

"A tragic accident," said Frederick. "Anyway, time marches on and so must I. Now, William, would you mind showing this young lady to the library? She might find one of our methodology guides useful. Please excuse me, Miss Smith."

Frederick Myers gave a little bow and disappeared across the hallway.

"This way," said William Crookes. Violet followed him down a small flight of steps and into the rear of the building.

"I hope I am not taking up too much of your valuable time," said Violet. "You all appear to be very busy."

"I am not as busy as Frederick gives me credit for," said William. "And have no involvement in any formal chemistry research at present. It is poor Frederick who suffers from not having enough hours in the day. He has less than an hour to finalise the programme for our next committee meeting. It's at Westminster Town Hall on Friday and time is precious. Whenever he makes a start on it, he loses the thread."

"Oh. The poor man must have been working on it when I interrupted."

"My dear Miss Smith. You have taken up no more than ten minutes of his time. He spent a far greater part of today speaking to a representative from the London Spiritualist Alliance. The man left moments before you arrived. He bought a donation for Frederick to present at our next meeting — a volume of works we were particularly keen to acquire. He was a most affable chap, but fond of the sound of his voice. It took a combined effort to get him to leave."

"I am surprised to hear that there is more than one spiritualist organisation in London. Wouldn't it be better to have all the expertise in one society? Or are you rivals?" Violet asked mischievously.

"There is more truth in that than you could know," said William. "As Frederick said, our methods often uncover fraudulent accounts of supernatural activity. There was some unpleasantness a few years ago and a growing suspicion that the SPR was becoming too sceptical. Some said that the Society took more interest in disproving spiritualism than investigating it. We lost a few well-regarded members that year. Some left to form other societies and some abandoned spiritualism altogether. One of them is in the library at the moment," he continued. "Harry Kersey. Moved up north, to Newcastle, I think. He has made quite a name for himself there. But we are all friends now. He was in London on business and has come to use our facilities."

"Did you say you were a chemist, Professor Crookes?"

"Yes. And I am also the President of the Institution of Electrical Engineers."

"I wonder how you manage to find time for anything else. What does the occupation of Professor of Chemistry entail?"

William Crookes laughed. "I spend more time teaching and researching these days," he said. "But I was an inventor in my younger days. I doubt you have ever heard of it, but I invented the radiometer."

Violet bit her lip. "Sorry, no."

"And I discovered the chemical element Thallium."

"I have heard of that. How fascinating. There seem to be a lot of well-educated men in The Society."

"There are," agreed Crookes. "Many of us have occupations."

"Like Arthur?"

"Yes, he practices in Belgravia. He is one of many doctors in the Society. There are at least five in London."

They had been chatting outside the door to the right of the hallway. The Professor pushed the door handle. "This is the Edmund Gurney library," he said.

Violet walked through to find herself in a large room with four desks set in a square in the middle. Two men were hard at work in front of the desks working diagonally opposite each other. Books and jotters littered the space.

"Excuse me," said Professor Crookes. The men looked up and nodded before continuing their work.

"Here," he said, passing two small volumes to Violet. "Read that one first, then this one. He reached to a higher shelf containing a pile of bound papers. "Here is one of our journals," he said. "You should find it interesting. There's lots of information about our aims and aspirations, and a good helping of case studies as well."

"Thank you," said Violet, leafing through a copy. There was page after page of letters and accounts. "How do you accumulate all this information?"

"Our Society is better known than you might think. We invite people to submit accounts of their supernatural experiences. There are thousands of letters in that office waiting for analysis." He pointed to a door at the rear of the library. "I won't show you. I can only describe the room as a disorderly mess."

"Have you ever received any letters about the Ripper murders?"

The question was out before Violet had time to consider the wisdom of it. Nobody in the Society knew that she was a private investigator, so it should be safe to ask. In the worst case, the Professor might assume that she was nosy.

"There were a few," he said. "Not as many as you might

expect and most came in 1888 or early 1889. There was nothing of any relevance though. Only a few reports of anecdotal dreams and forewarnings, all conveniently received after the murders."

Violet nodded. "Well thank you so much for the books. I will return them as soon as I can. Do thank Mr Myers for his help."

William Crookes escorted her to the front door. Frederick Myers was nowhere in sight. As the Professor offered his hand, the front door creaked open.

"Miss Smith," a familiar voice exclaimed warmly.

"Doctor Myers. How nice to see you."

"Are you staying in London?"

"I am here for a few days," she said. "Your colleagues have been very kind. They have loaned me books and journals so I can understand your work better."

"Wonderful," said Arthur. "You wouldn't be free? No, I don't suppose you would if you are only in London for a brief time, but if you were free…?"

"When?"

"Tonight. If you were free tonight, perhaps we could talk about it over dinner?"

"I am free tonight," said Violet.

"Well, that's marvellous. Let me know where you are staying, and I will collect you later."

Violet scribbled the address of The Regal Hotel in the notebook she habitually carried. She removed the page and passed it to Myers.

"Splendid," he said. "Until tonight then."

Violet left the building barely noticing the chill wind as she sauntered towards the Embankment with a broad smile on her face.

Chapter Fifteen

A REPORT OF THE STRANGEST NATURE

"I'll come straight to the point," sighed Henry Moore resting his chin on steepled hands. "This D'Onston character is still getting in the way of our investigation. Every time we eliminate him, his presence manifests itself in another way. I could ask him to assist with our enquiries, but I don't believe it is the right approach."

"And you think I can help?" asked Lawrence.

"Yes, I do. It's a shame that you have given up on the Brighton investigation. Perhaps you could pretend otherwise and introduce the matter again. Let him think it is the focus of your visit."

"Why?"

"Because we have received a report of the strangest nature. An account which is hard to believe. In fact, I do not believe it, but I have to take it seriously."

"Go on."

"D'Onston was, until very recently, involved in a business. The Pompadour Cosmetique Company, to be precise."

A slow grin spread across Lawrence's face. "You mean makeup? Not something I would have associated with him."

"Yes, hard to believe, isn't it? And I do mean cosmetics — beauty creams, elixirs and the like."

"A strange occupation for a Satanist."

"I wouldn't know," said Henry, stuffily. "This is serious, Lawrence."

"What has he done?"

"He was in partnership with two women, Vittoria Cremers and Mabel Collins. Both were business partners, and both are as peculiar as he is. They describe themselves as Theosophists."

"Explain."

"Good Lord, I don't know. Some esoteric religious movement, I suppose. Anyway, that is beside the point."

"Which is?"

"Which is that their business relationship has disintegrated. Miss Collins has recently expressed an irrational fear of Mr D'Onston."

"Henry, I am afraid of Mr D'Onston myself. He is extremely odd."

"Well, yes. But it is more than that. A friend of Mabel Collins turned up here a few days ago. Miss Collins had told her that she thinks D'Onston is Jack the Ripper."

"Why are you surprised? He has been under investigation for the very same thing. It is quite likely the accusations have followed him."

"We didn't announce it," said Henry. "Her fears were not provoked by gossip. Regardless, Miss Johnson, who reported the event, says that Miss Collins will not approach us herself. She is too afraid. But she has told Miss Johnson that she saw a collection of bloodied neck ties hidden in D'Onston's trunk."

"I have been in his room, and I don't recall seeing a trunk."

"It is small tin trunk apparently."

"Can't you simply search his room?" asked Lawrence.

"We have questioned and cleared him once already," said Henry. "Besides, he isn't The Ripper, assuming that the Ripper committed all the crimes attributed to him. No, it would be easier if you were to gain access and satisfy yourself that there is nothing to this report."

"You want me to search his room?"

"I don't think it will be necessary," said Henry. "Let me know if there is a trunk, of course. The real purpose is for you to talk to him. Find out if there is another reason for Miss Collins to make a spurious claim against him."

"The failed business partnership sounds like a good starting point."

"Really?" I have known many unsuccessful business ventures, but never one that has resulted in an accusation of mass murder."

"Very well," said Lawrence. "I take your meaning. I will endeavour to find out more about his dealings with Miss Collins under the guise of investigating Edmund Gurney. Though I warn you, he was quite hostile when I asked him about Brighton, and he denied seeing Gurney. It is going to take a lot of imagination to ask him a question that he hasn't already answered in the negative."

"I'm sure you will think of something."

"Is there a tram stop nearby?"

"Go through the gates and turn to your right. Are you going now?"

"Yes. Whether D'Onston will be in or not is another matter."

"He will be there. We are keeping an eye on him, and he is a man of routine."

"Good." Lawrence looked at his watch. "It shouldn't take too long. I'll let you know what he says."

"Ah, Blake." There was a knock at the door, and a young constable dressed in plain clothes entered the room. He looked vaguely familiar.

"Show Mr Harpham to the nearest tram stop," asked Henry.

PC Blake was a man of few words and guided Lawrence to the tram stop in virtual silence.

Lawrence arrived just in time to see the tram pull away.

"Damn," he said, perching on a low brick wall near to the tram sign, but Blake had gone. Lawrence stared idly into the distance for a moment, failing to spot a shadow creep into his proximity.

"Hello, Lawrence."

He clutched at his chest. "Violet — what are you doing here?"

"I said I would meet you."

"You did. I forgot. We've got to go to Charterhouse Street again."

"Now?"

"Of course, now."

"I can't."

"Why ever not? Have you got a better place to be?"

"Yes, as it happens."

"Oh. Where are you going?"

"I have been invited out for dinner."

"By whom?"

"Doctor Myers."

"That chap you met at the Rectory?"

"Yes."

"Oh."

The sound of hooves interrupted their conversation as another tram drew up beside them.

"You had better get off then," said Violet.

"Are you really not coming? I thought you wanted to be more involved."

"I do, but you don't need me, and if I go to dinner, I will have another opportunity to find out more about the SPR."

"As you wish." Lawrence turned abruptly and ascended the curved walkway of the tram. He strode towards the back and stared pointedly at Violet who was still watching from below.

"You can tell me all about it later," he called from the top deck of the tram.

"I don't know what time I will be back. Don't wait up," said Violet. She gave a carefree wave then walked away.

Lawrence pulled his collar up and rubbed his gloved hands together, as he muttered under his breath. It was bitterly cold. He watched Violet as the tram pulled away trying to assess why he was so irritated at her dinner engagement. It was the selfishness of it, he disliked. She knew he was keen to find out more about the SPR. She could have manipulated Myers into making a joint invitation, yet she was going alone. He felt excluded from part of his own investigation. It wouldn't do, but it was a conversation for tomorrow. He had better things to do this afternoon and would devote the rest of the journey to planning his conversation with D'Onston.

Chapter Sixteen

AN ANGRY MAN

"This is becoming a habit," said D'Onston opening the door. Lawrence had asked the hotel errand boy to instigate a meeting. It was a gamble as D'Onston could easily have refused the approach, but Lawrence detected a note of loneliness in the older man. It was hardly surprising given his disquieting demeanour.

"Come in, then." D'Onston beckoned Lawrence inside. The curtains were open this time, and the ugly unlit candles were now little more than burnt out stumps. A pile of books covered one side of D'Onston's desk, and a dark mahogany wooden mask of African origin lay against the wall on the other side. It had fallen to the left and Lawrence felt a familiar surge of irritation as he contemplated the lack of care. It took all his self-control not to straighten it. He tore his gaze away from the desk and towards D'Onston.

"It's good of you to see me again," he said.

D'Onston nodded. "I was curious," he replied.

"As I am," said Lawrence. "Curious about Brighton,

that is. You have said that you didn't see Gurney, but I forgot to ask you if you recognised anyone else in the Hotel that night."

"I did not," said D'Onston. "I rarely visited The Albion and had few acquaintances there."

"But you had been in the Hotel before?"

"Only once during that particular visit. And a few times on prior occasions. Why? Does it matter?"

"It might," said Lawrence, trying and failing to keep the conversation going. He had to do better than this if he was going to fulfil his obligation to Henry Moore. He gazed around the room looking for inspiration and signs of a trunk. Unless it was in a cupboard or hidden beneath the bed, there was no possibility of a container in D'Onston's room, tin or otherwise.

"Why would my prior visits be important?"

Lawrence hesitated. "Edmund Gurney spent a lot of time in Brighton, conducting his experiments. You might have run into him."

"I have already told you that I did not."

"Do you know anything about his experiments?"

"A little."

"Did they have any scientific value?"

"They had some merit," said D'Onston. "I have studied the occult in depth. You could say I am something of an expert. I have acquainted myself with the methods and ideology of Gurney's organisation." He smiled self-importantly.

"Could I prevail upon your expertise?" said Lawrence.

"Of course."

"Were the Ripper murders connected to the occult?"

"That is an excellent question," said D'Onston, his eyes

shining with enthusiasm. "It depends upon how many murders you credit the Ripper with."

"Why?"

"Because if you discount the Dorset Street murder, which happened indoors, the other six form a perfect cross."

"And what is the significance of that?"

"It was a profanity. It implies that the killer deliberately murdered according to location. The victims were incidental, or so I thought. But now I realise I must have been wrong."

Lawrence nodded. "I agree. No reason to suppose the murders are location based."

"The locations are not the problem," said D'Onston impatiently. "It's the other attacks that do not fit."

"What other attacks?"

"Annie Millwood and Ada Wilson," said D'Onston.

"Who are they?" asked Lawrence. "I admit I don't know much about the Ripper murders, but I haven't come across these names before."

"I told you the police were fools. They still don't know how many women the Ripper murdered. I know without a doubt that Annie Millwood and Ada Wilson were among the first victims."

"And how would you know that?"

D'Onston stopped talking. His mouth set in a thin line and he stared at Lawrence through narrowed eyes.

"You seem strangely curious about the Ripper murders."

"It is hardly surprising. Half the population of London talks of nothing else."

"Yes, well, how I came by that knowledge is immaterial. What matters is that the two attacks disrupt the pattern and do not form a new one."

"Where did they die?"

"They found Annie Millwood in White's Row lying in front of the lodging house where she lived. The location was logical geographically speaking if you count the death of Mary Kelly into the series. I don't, as it happens, but 8 White's Row is only a short distance from Dorset Street. The other murder creates a bigger problem. Ada Wilson was in Stepney when her throat was cut. She lived much further away than any other victim, and her attack is out of sequence with my theory. Ada Wilson survived, but her attacker left her for dead. She lived to tell the tale but did not know who he was or why he wanted to kill her."

"And you are certain that she was a Ripper victim."

"It is beyond doubt. And now there is another unexplained murder."

"Frances Coles. Do you think she is a Ripper victim? How can that be? Jack the Ripper is dead."

D'Onston's face darkened. "Maybe he is, maybe he isn't. I do not know whether Coles fits the pattern," said D'Onston. "It cannot be, and yet, and yet… Do they think they can make a fool of me again?" He slammed his hand onto the desk. The African mask clattered to the floor, and Lawrence jumped backwards.

"Who?"

"Get out," shouted D'Onston. A red flush of anger stole across his face. "I cannot trust anyone."

Lawrence opened his mouth to protest, but D'Onston was moving towards him with hatred spilling from his bloodshot eyes.

Lawrence darted from the room. He walked quickly without turning back until the Triangle Hotel was safely out of sight.

It was nine-thirty in the evening, as Lawrence turned

the pages of a book in the inappropriately named reading room of the Regal Hotel. His chair was by the window and uncomfortably close to two elderly ladies who were gossiping in the corner. The other occupant of the room, a sullen young man smoking a pipe, stared balefully towards the door. The reading room was furnished with eight uncomfortable high-backed chairs, a low coffee table and a half-empty bookcase. A deck of cards, a dozen dog-eared books and a worn planchette littered the middle shelf. Lawrence picked up the only book of interest, a newly published work by Bram Stoker hoping it would prove a suitable distraction, but it was almost impossible to concentrate with all the noise and chatter in the room.

Lawrence repositioned himself in the chair in a futile attempt to get comfortable and tried to read a page for the third time. Before he had reached the end of the first paragraph, one of the women rose from her chair, grabbed the poker and prodded at the sparse fire. "There is no more coal, Ethel," she said.

Her companion joined her, and they both inspected the fireplace. "No dear, no more coal. And it is freezing. What will we do?"

Lawrence sighed and placed the book on his lap. "Would you like me to get some?"

"Yes, my dear — if you would be so kind."

"I'll do it." The young man placed his pipe in an ashtray and left the room abruptly.

"What a nice young man," said Mrs Guymer, the larger of the two ladies. "Isn't he a nice young man, Ethel."

Lawrence tried to ignore them as they spent the next five minutes extolling the virtues of the man that they had ignored for the previous half hour.

"Here he is," said Ethel as the door swung open. A ruddy-faced man entered carrying a small bucket. He emptied a few coals into the fire, placed the bucket by the poker and left without saying a word. Ethel examined the pail. "It's only half full, Doris," she said.

"Oh dear, I don't think the fire will last long." They exchanged anxious glances.

Both Lawrence and the younger man turned away, determined not to get involved. Lawrence opened his book again and continued reading. The story was progressing. Jonathan Harker had just woken after a sleepless night and was about to board a train.

"Oh Ethel, what was that?"

Ethel shrieked. "A spider. How I hate spiders." She held her arms protectively around her sides and shrank into the chair.

Lawrence closed his book and tossed it on the windowsill. He left the room without a backward glance and strode down the hotel steps and into the street. Marching past the hospital next door, Lawrence made his way towards an ugly commercial building when the cold hit him. He had left his coat and hat inside the hotel, and it was freezing. Lawrence wasn't going to lose face by returning, and he carried on regardless. After a few hundred yards, he began to calm down. His irritability vanished, and he felt sheepish. He was generally more tolerant and respectful of the elderly and tonight's behaviour was uncharacteristic. He was angrier with himself than he was with them. Lawrence sighed. He hadn't made any progress with the case, and his lack of discretion during his chat with D'Onston was unprofessional. Lawrence had been imprudent. He might as well have come clean and revealed that he was a private investigator. Remarkably, D'Onston had believed his story, or so it appeared. At least Lawrence had not indicated that he had any connection to Scotland Yard.

Lawrence had walked a circular route and was now at the back of the hospital. The conversation with D'Onston kept replaying in his mind. He hadn't found a way to introduce Mabel Collins into the discussion before D'Onston had asked him to leave. And D'Onston's rise to anger puzzled Lawrence. He needed someone to talk to. Where was Violet? What was the point of having a partner who was gadding about when she ought to be helping? He looked at his watch. It was after ten. What on earth could she be doing at this hour? She had been out since six-thirty, and it didn't take over three hours to dine.

Lawrence continued his walk until the hotel was in sight. A Hansom cab alighted outside, and a man and woman disembarked. He peered at the couple and realised that it was Violet and her doctor friend. Lawrence watched as the doctor took Violet's arm and guided her up the steps of the Hotel. He stood shivering in the shadows, not wanting to meet them in the foyer. It would look as if he was spying and there really wasn't anything to see. Violet barely knew the man — there was no question of intimacy on such a short acquaintance. Lawrence wondered if Violet even thought of men romantically. She was over forty, and as far as he could tell, destined to remain a spinster.

It was too cold to stay outside, so he walked towards the hotel entrance. The door opened, and Lawrence turned away just before Violet's dinner companion left the building. The doctor climbed into the cab which sped hastily away. Lawrence negotiated the hotel steps and entered the foyer looking for Violet. She wasn't there. He heard voices in the reading room and opened the door to find Violet chatting to the two ladies who had caused such irritation. They eyed him suspiciously and left the room.

Lawrence picked up the book he had discarded earlier and pretended to read.

"Good evening," said Violet.

Lawrence grunted. "Ah, you're back at last. You've been a long time."

"I told you not to wait up."

"Did you have a good evening?"

"Very pleasant, thank you, Lawrence. The meal was lovely and the company excellent. Mr Crookes joined us. I have had a very entertaining evening."

"Well, perhaps you can spare a few minutes now. I need to marshal my thoughts."

"Can't it wait until the morning?"

"I suppose so, but I am meeting Henry for an early lunch in Regent Street. I won't have much time."

"That is just as well. Arthur has invited me to St Bart's Hospital tomorrow afternoon."

"Whatever for?"

"To look around. It is a splendid building, steeped in history."

"You seem to be spending a lot of time with him."

"He is a fascinating man, and it's kind of him to offer. Besides, we won't be in London very long. I have to make the most of it."

"Yes, but dash it all Violet, we are here on business."

"How much is Henry paying?"

"Don't start that again. There will be a fee. I haven't discussed the details yet."

Violet removed her coat and placed it on the coffee table. She perched on the chair nearest the fire. "You can at least tell me if you have finished your investigation."

"I don't know," said Lawrence. "I don't have much to tell Henry. The conversation took an unexpected turn."

"Did you find anything out about Mabel Collins?"

"No," he admitted. "It was always going to be difficult. I thought there would be more opportunity to introduce her into the conversation."

"What are you going to tell Henry?"

"I can tell him not to worry about the trunk. There's no space in the room for one," said Lawrence.

"Could he have hidden it?"

"I don't think so. I knelt to tie a shoelace so I could look under the bed. There was nothing but dust beneath. There were only small items of furniture in D'Onston's room. There wasn't space to fit the smallest of trunks."

"Your visit wasn't entirely fruitless, then."

"Not completely, but D'Onston is a complex character and deceitful. There is something that he isn't telling me. Whether he is lying or being evasive, I'm not sure, but I wish I could have asked more questions. I doubt I'll have another chance. I have never seen a man rise to temper so quickly."

"What did you say to upset him?"

"I'm not sure. I wasn't rude or pushy. D'Onston seemed happy to talk, at the beginning of our conversation. He is a man of great self-importance and enjoyed discussing his theories. It is obvious that he has spent a lot of time studying the Ripper murders."

Violet grimaced. "I can't imagine why."

"No. Nor me, but I have learned a few things that might be of interest to Henry. D'Onston knows of two other murders but the police have not connected them to the Ripper."

"How would he know?"

"He refused to say," said Lawrence. "He mentioned

their names, though. One was Annie Millwood and the other, Ada Wilson. D'Onston says they were among the first Ripper victims. I walked back via Fleet Street and discovered that both attacks took place early in 1888."

"Did D'Onston get angry talking about these murders?"

"No, it was when we were discussing Frances Coles?"

"The latest murder? Does he think the Ripper killed her too?"

"He does not know. He said it wasn't possible, but it was obvious that he fears it might be. I think it was the uncertainty that drove him to anger."

"He sounds dangerous, Lawrence. Are you sure he isn't the killer?"

"He has certain characteristics that set him apart from other men. You would have to meet him to understand how sinister he is. The way he moves, his dark, unreadable eyes — and his interests, Violet. He is a self-proclaimed Satanist and has studied most of the esoteric religions in detail. But Jack the Ripper? I am not sure. Henry says he cannot be, but even Henry keeps him under surveillance. There must be some doubt."

"You should stay away from him."

"He wouldn't have me back now. D'Onston is a clever man though. He said the Ripper kills by location, not by choice of victim."

"That makes no sense. Someone who uses a knife kills out of passion, not planning."

"D'Onston plotted the locations onto a map, and they made a cross. He thinks — oh! That's peculiar."

"What?"

"Locations. It is about locations, Violet. D'Onston said that Annie Millwood lived in White's Row. I knew there was something at the back of my mind. Frances Coles dossed in White's Row too. Henry told me the other day."

"It's hardly surprising. There are not many places that take in women of their kind."

"It's still a coincidence, and I don't like coincidences. I'm going to take a look at the place tomorrow evening. There should be plenty of people who knew Frances Coles there."

"I'm coming too."

"No, you're not."

"We've been over this before. I am your business partner. I will go where you go."

"Please, Violet. These are rough areas, and they are dangerous. You will stand out in your clean clothes with your nice manners. It is not safe."

"I'll change clothes," she said. "You will not know me."

Lawrence sighed. "I would prefer it if you didn't," he said, but if you insist, then we will have to take great care.

The door handle turned, and the young pipe-smoking man joined them. He started rifling through the bookcase.

"Time to go," whispered Lawrence. "We'll leave here at five tomorrow evening."

Lawrence prepared for bed with a feeling of foreboding. He was far from satisfied with the decisions he had made and was still not sure where it was all leading. Taking Violet into Whitechapel was foolhardy, yet what choice did he have if she insisted? His earlier request that she accompanied him had backfired. He could hardly refuse when she chose to go, just because it was too dangerous. His mind churned, and he knew he wouldn't sleep. He opened his notebook and read through. Lawrence was a disciplined note taker and had faithfully recorded the conversations with Henry Moore, Roslyn D'Onston and Kate Grove. He found the entry he was looking for and circled it — proof that he was right about White's Row. There was a definite connection between the first and last crime, even though they were committed three years apart. Lawrence set his reservations aside. They would visit White's Row tomorrow night and take their chances among the impoverished inhabitants of Whitechapel.

Chapter Seventeen

THE MONSTER INSIDE

The horror of that first night stayed with me, and other fears soon joined it. My hope that it was a singular aberration vanished late in March 1888 when I found myself outside number 19 Maidman Street, Mile End. I was holding a knife in my hand, and a woman screamed blue murder in front of me.

Once again, it started with a train journey. Once again, the hypnotic chug of the Metropolitan railway triggered a seizure. But the distance involved was fearsome. I was miles away from my home in an area of complete unfamiliarity. It was like waking from somebody else's nightmare. I did not belong there. I had no desire to be there and no conception of how my unconscious mind had transported me to this area east of Whitechapel.

Somewhere deep inside me lurks a monster. Something unaccountable drives me to acts of violence I would not contemplate in my right mind. It brings me, unbidden, to a destination in which to commit them without detection. I cannot attribute it solely to my illness. Other men are similarly afflicted but do not resort to violence. An inner demon drives me. It must. There is no other explanation.

I may be a savage and every kind of coward, but I am a logical man. *I have concluded that I must keep a journal of these events so I can prevent myself from being in a position to commit such acts again. Though sickening to endure, I scoured the local newspapers looking for reports of my crimes. I discovered that my first victim was a woman called Millwood. I killed her, though not immediately. She died later in a workhouse from her injuries. The second woman, Ada Wilson, survived, thank God. I deduced, from newspaper reports, that I had knocked upon her door. When she opened it, I burst into her room and demanded money before stabbing her twice in the throat. Do I remember any of this? Yes, there were snatches of recall. Not enough to form the whole picture but sufficient to be in no doubt of my guilt. I was conscious by the time I ran away and remember two of her friends in rapid pursuit. But I bolted towards the west and somehow escaped. Remarkable considering that I had no geographical knowledge of the area. But desperate men make good survivors, and I found my way home. There was a minimal amount of blood, not enough to make anyone look twice. It could have been my blood for all anyone knew. Of course, it was not. I had once again attacked a random stranger with no consequences.*

I have done my best to order these memories into sequences. Listing them might reveal commonalities, triggers. Not only does this interest me, but it is also a means to prevent future occurrences. I find my condition fascinating and can detach myself and observe it rationally. I have concluded that I must stop using the railway line which is a pity as train travel has formed part of my routine for some considerable time. I have journeyed abroad lately, and not been similarly affected, though this may be because I was always in company. Railway travel is convenient, but it has been a catalyst for both my crimes, and I must desist. I have further concluded that I cannot keep sharp objects on my person any longer. It will be inconvenient, but if I stop carrying a knife, then I cannot use it. I hope these two decisions are enough to prevent any further incidents. I will not succumb to these unconscious urges again. I will not.

Chapter Eighteen

SAVING VIOLET

Wednesday 4th March 1891

Lawrence disembarked from the train at Aldgate station already regretting his decision to question the inhabitants of 8 White's Row in the evening. It was a dark, moonless night and the skies were heavy with unshed snow. Lawrence wore a greatcoat and Violet a full-length black coat with a winter bonnet. Neither was sufficient to keep them from shivering as they walked north along Commercial Street.

"I don't like this," said Violet as they passed a shop doorway. A man dressed in rags lay in a foetal position in the recessed porch. A puddle of vomit glistened in the light of a nearby gas lamp.

"Should we help him?"

"No," said Lawrence. "Can't you smell the fumes? He has been drinking. I can see him move. He needs to sleep it off."

Commercial Street was quiet. Small pockets of people

passed here and there, but the cold evening seemed to have deterred all but the neediest from straying on to the streets.

They passed an alley and heard muffled voices. Lawrence glanced towards the sounds and turned abruptly. "Don't look, Violet," he said softly, taking her arm.

"What's wrong?"

"I would rather not go into detail. Some commercial transactions in this part of London are not fit to discuss in front of a lady."

"You are chivalrous, Lawrence, but I know how things work."

Lawrence guided Violet towards a gas lamp. He stopped and removed a scruffy piece of paper from his pocket, smoothed it out and scrutinised it.

"What's that?" whispered Violet.

"It's a map. I asked the hotel manager for directions earlier.

Violet examined the crudely drawn sketch. "It doesn't make much sense," she said doubtfully.

"He explained it as he drew it," said Lawrence. "It's pretty straightforward. Not far now by the look of things."

"What's that?" asked Violet.

"What?"

"That noise?"

"I can't hear anything."

"I'm sure I heard footsteps, but there is nobody behind us."

"I didn't hear them."

"It's not the first time. I heard something when we left Aldgate station."

"Violet, it's not a pleasant area, and it's dark. You must not worry if it sounds and feels different to West London. I will look after you, I promise."

They continued along Commercial Road until they reached a pile of boxes scattered across the pavement. The decaying carcass of a recently butchered animal lay beside the wooden crates, and a black rat squatted on the ribcage and chewed the body. Entrails crawling with maggots fell into a squirming heap on the floor. The rancid smell hit Violet like a wall.

"Oh," she raised her hand to her mouth in horror and turned her head towards Lawrence. "Oh, it's disgusting."

Lawrence pulled a handkerchief from his pocket and held it over his nose as he steered Violet away. "We won't go past that. Come with me."

They turned into a narrow lane off Commercial Road which opened into a small square with an alleyway at the far end. A chink of light coming from a narrow window cast weak illumination for a few yards. They were alone, and it was deathly quiet.

Violet leaned into Lawrence. She was still shivering.

"We can go back, Violet," he said, reaching into his coat pocket. He withdrew a candle from a small tin and set it on the ground. Then he struck a match and squatted on his haunches, trying to protect the flame from the chill air. The match went out. He lit another, and this time it remained alight long enough to ignite the candle. He held it in one hand and grasped Violet's hand in the other.

"Do you want to go on?" he asked.

"Yes," she whispered. "I'm better now."

They walked hand in hand across the silent square. A sliver of moonlight cut through the darkness. Lawrence and Violet continued their journey without speaking. The narrow alley magnified the sound of gravel crunching beneath their feet. They finally emerged at one end of White's Row and looked down the street towards the lodging house. Two men were outside a building that could have been their destination. They were bareheaded with no coats and clad in shirts with rolled up sleeves, despite the bitter weather. Light from the two windows overlooking the street illuminated their sweaty, grimy faces. The taller man began to shout. He walked up to the other and pushed him squarely in the chest. The second man reached into his pocket and pulled out a chunky metallic object which he fitted over his hand and ploughed into the stomach of the taller man who dropped to the floor. The fallen man clutched at his stomach, gasping while the other stood above him. He crossed and turned full circle to face the building behind and gestured towards the window goading the watchers inside. The man on the ground took advantage. He lunged towards him, seized his leg and pulled him to the floor. The two men began brawling, flailing around on the frosty ground, fists flying. The door to the building swung open, and a motley crowd of men and women piled into the street. They surrounded the two shirt-sleeved men, shouting and swearing words of encouragement.

Lawrence pulled Violet away. "We can't go there now," he said. "They must be drunk as lords. Anything could happen."

He guided Violet into Crispin Street and towards a brightly lit Public House. The battered sign above the door read "The Paul's Head."

"We can wait here for half an hour," said Lawrence. "The worst of the trouble should be over by then. And there may be someone in here who can tell us more about Frances Coles."

Violet tiptoed towards the grimy window of the Public House. Even from the outside, she could hear a cacophony of voices and the screech of a poorly played fiddle. She rubbed the glass with her glove, and a circle of light appeared through the dirt. She peered inside. The large room was full of people. Two men in grubby jackets leaned against the bar. A small, squat dog stared possessively towards his master who wore baggy trousers and a wideawake hat. He listened intently to another man who sloshed the contents of his glass over the floor as he spoke. Large barrels occupied one side of the bar. A group of women rested their drinks on top while they chatted. All were unkempt, with dirty clothes and matted hair. Another barrel propped up a skinny man, almost insensible from drinking. His glass lay upended on the sawdust floor.

"I'm not going in there," said Violet.

Lawrence looked inside. "It's not that bad," he said.

"Look," Violet pointed. At the far end of the room, a man's fleshy hand gripped a girl by the throat. She was young, in her teens. Her older and rounder companion waved a chubby finger menacingly in her face, his own a mask of rage.

"Perhaps you are right," said Lawrence.

"We should go back. It isn't safe anywhere."

"Hang on a minute. That's D'Onston in there."

"It can't be?"

"It is, I tell you. I wonder what he's doing. He looks a mess."

"Are you sure it's him?"

"I think so, though his clothes are different. He must be in disguise. He's talking to another fellow. A real ruffian."

"Then you had better leave him alone."

"I want to know what he's doing here so close to White's Row."

"I doubt it matters."

"Give me five minutes, Violet. I want to get close enough to hear what they are saying."

"Don't be ridiculous. D'Onston was furious last time he saw you. Anything could happen."

"He won't see me. I'll walk around the bar and stand by the pillar. I should be able to hear them without them noticing me."

"What about me?"

"Come along. You're wearing black. I don't think you will stand out. Just don't get too close to him."

"I'm not going in there, Lawrence, and you shouldn't either."

"Well, stay here then. There's plenty of light from the window. You can come and find me if you get worried."

"You're impossible," said Violet turning her back against the window. She crossed her hands and stared across the street as Lawrence walked into The Paul's Head. The door banged shut, and Violet was alone. The road was empty save for a grey-haired woman hobbling in the direction of Bell Lane. The temperature had dropped further, and clouds covered the moon. The raucous sound of the fiddle that had irritated Violet before was strangely comforting. She returned to her spy hole in the window to check Lawrence's progress. He was still close to the door and a woman was talking to him. She had evidently been drinking, and Lawrence was trying to disentangle himself from her clutches. He looked impatient and angry, his plan thwarted. Violet turned away and sighed. It would be a long wait.

"Help me."

Violet spun around as she heard a faint voice. It was childlike, pitiful.

"Help me, Miss."

She stepped away from the Paul's Head and looked around. There was nothing — not a person in sight.

"I'm frightened." The voice was crying. She could not see the owner, but as she moved to her left, the sobs became louder and more urgent. Violet edged closer. She was stepping away from the illuminated window panes of The Paul's Head towards inky blackness. Loud sniffs accompanied the muffled sobs.

"Help me." The voice led Violet towards another narrow alleyway. She peered around the corner. There was still nothing in sight, but she could hear the whispered gasps of someone trying to stifle their fear. Violet's eyes adjusted to the dark. At the bottom of the alleyway, she saw a little girl. The child stood alone, clutching what looked like a hat. She trembled so hard that Violet could see her shake in spite of the darkness. The child was almost choking with distress.

"Oh, come here." Violet held her arms open. The girl did not move.

"Come to me. I can help you."

The child remained where she was, rigid with terror.

"I'll find you, then." Violet edged her way down the dark alley reaching out towards the terrified girl. She was nearly close enough to touch her. Glistening tear tracks ran down the sunken-cheeked, dirty face. The little girl wore rags, and a pool of liquid surrounded her holed boots where she had wet herself. Her eyes were round and anguished. As Violet knelt, the girl gasped. A sudden force propelled her forwards and bought her to her senses. She shrieked and darted up the alleyway leaving Violet sprawled on the ground. Violet stood up, disorientated and a shadow loomed ahead. It was a man, tall and menacing. She stepped back, sick with terror as the man moved towards her. A scarf covered his lower face, and his eyes were dark with malice. Before Violet could react, his arm snaked out and pulled her back into his chest. She heard a scream and realised it was coming from her mouth. Something cold pressed against her throat. She screamed again. A volley of footsteps thundered down the alley.

"Stay away," hissed a voice as Violet's assailant slunk into the shadows and vaulted a low wall at the end.

"Are you alright, Miss?" Violet stared uncomprehendingly at her rescuer. He was a night porter and was holding a lantern. His face was kind. "Did he hurt you?"

Violet clutched her throat. It was wet. She looked at her hand and placed it in the beam of light. Blood.

"He cut me. Did you see him?"

"I did. Let's get you out of here."

He escorted Violet onto Crispin Street and towards The Paul's Head. The doors were open, the drinkers now outside on the street, curious about the source of the screams.

"Oh God, Violet." It was Lawrence. He rushed towards her. "What happened?"

"There was a man in the alley, a stranger. He cut me." Violet's hand was still over her wound. She was trembling.

Lawrence took her hand and examined her neck. "Still bleeding, but superficial," he said. "Here, hold this over the cut." He passed her a clean white handkerchief. Violet held it to her neck and stared dumbly at Lawrence.

"Oh, Violet." He pulled her towards him and held her in his arms. He stood a head taller, and he rested his chin against her head. Her hair smelled clean, her skin fresh, but he could feel her fear. She was trying hard to be brave while shaking involuntarily. He kissed her on the forehead. "We need to get you to hospital."

"No. You said it wasn't serious."

"You won't bleed out," said Lawrence, "but it needs cleaning up, and we ought to find a policeman."

"Did you get cut by the Ripper?" The woman who had accosted Lawrence in the bar tugged at Violet's cloak. Violet recoiled at the stench of alcohol and rotting teeth.

"Go away," said Lawrence angrily.

"Oh, my gawd," cried the woman. "You've been got by Jack. He's back."

Lawrence pulled away from Violet and faced the crowd.

"Was it Jack?" asked the owner of the dog.

"It ain't safe," said another woman. "And nobody cares about us."

A tall man brandished a piece of lead pipe. "I'll kill 'im, so I will."

"It wasn't the Ripper," said Lawrence. The mood was turning ugly. The situation would be easier to manage if the rowdy, unpredictable occupants of The Paul's Head weren't afraid.

"Get back inside," said the night porter. "Leave the lady alone."

The man with the lead pipe spat on the pavement. He glared at Lawrence then threw the weapon on the floor before returning to the bar. The other drinkers followed.

"Do you have a whistle?" asked Lawrence. "We need a policeman."

"You'll see one any minute," said the night porter. "Crispin Street is on his beat."

"Did you see what happened?"

"A little. I heard the lady scream. A small child tore out of the alley — nearly knocked me off my feet and I saw him with a knife to her neck. One more minute and it would have been, well, you know."

"God." Lawrence put his hand to his mouth. "It doesn't bear thinking about."

"Hey — you." The night watchman darted across the street. "Rachel, come here." He knelt by a large metal container on the other side of the road. "It's alright. You're safe. Come with me." He returned to the front of the public-house hand in hand with a little girl.

"Oh, you poor thing." Violet reached towards the girl and stroked her cheek.

"Who is she?" asked Lawrence.

"Solly Cohen's youngest," said the night watchman. "I didn't recognise her when she was running full pelt towards me."

"She was at the bottom of the alley — with him," said Violet.

Lawrence dropped to one knee. "Did you know the man in the alley?" he asked.

The girl shook her head.

"Why were you with him?"

Rachel turned towards the night watchman and buried her head in his coat.

"Don't worry. You aren't in trouble young Rachel," said the watchman. "Tell the gent what you were doing there."

The girl sniffed. Her bottom lip trembled. "I was walking past the alleyway, and the man said he would give me a penny if I helped him look for his dog. I went with him, and he pointed to the coal cellar and said the dog was in there. I took my hat off and was about to go inside when he grabbed me and put a knife in my neck."

"Are you injured?"

"No. I don't think so. It doesn't hurt. The man said he wouldn't hurt me if I did as he asked."

"What did he want?"

"He said I was to shout for help, but not too loudly, so I yelled, and it wasn't loud enough. He kept saying shout louder or shout softer and jabbed me in the neck with the knife until I was so frightened that I couldn't make my voice change. I couldn't stop crying. The child sniffed again, and tears fell silently down her cheeks.

"Do you know where she lives?" asked Lawrence. The porter nodded.

"Better get her home."

"There's your policeman now."

The soft glow of a bullseye lantern proceeded PC141. "Come on Violet. We'll get you to the police station then straight to a hospital.

Violet opened her mouth to protest.

"I mean it," said Lawrence. They watched the night watchman and the little girl fade into the night. Violet removed the blood-stained handkerchief from her neck. Her legs almost gave way at the sight of her blood. She had been seconds away from death, and it was no random attack. "Stay away," the man had said. It was personal.

Chapter Nineteen

PREVENTION IS BETTER THAN CURE

Thursday 5th April 1888

Thank God I keep a journal. There has been another attack on a woman in Whitechapel, this time in Wentworth Street. It is only a short distance from the place that the unfortunate Annie Millwood met her fate. Or rather, that she met me. Not the real me, but the brute that wakes during the attacks.

I have spent the short time since the last event, cataloguing my memories, such as they are and continue to analyse my behaviour and my symptoms. I have always found my condition fascinating right from the early days when it was of short duration and barely noticeable. I have never been afraid of it and even now, knowing the full extent of my actions, I no longer rail or panic as the memories return. Instead, I am passive, almost detached. The self-loathing comes later, usually as a result of reading newspaper reports.

But I digress. I had not killed this time which meant that the preventative measures I employed were working. I no longer carry a knife, and I keep the tools I use in the course of my trade at work. They are not taken with me, as was my custom. I have stopped using the railway and, most usefully, I keep a detailed log of my movements. I note the time I leave, where I go and even how long I take to get there. It is all in my journal.

The murder in Whitechapel took place on Tuesday. Another fallen woman, another alcoholic, felled by an unspeakable act in the dead of night. I heard about it as I walked through Holborn yesterday. The newspaper boys were chanting 'another Ripper murder' in their high-pitched cockney voices. Men and women flocked towards them to buy a paper and indulge in their unsavoury thrills. I was one of them, of course. I do not enjoy gratuitous violence, which might seem like a strange thing to say after recent events. I purchased the paper only because I needed to glean enough details to rule out my potential involvement.

I felt sure of my innocence this time. There were no snatches of memory, nor recollections of my journey home from somewhere unfamiliar. I bought a paper and took it into the coffee room of the nearby Crown Hotel and spread it across the table while drinking the steaming liquid to steel myself. I scoured the paper, looking for the time of day for which I would need to account. When I found it, I took my journal from my coat pocket which I kept on my person at all times for obvious reasons. It was the work of a moment to establish that I was, as I already thought, at home that night. Not only had I stayed at home, but I even recorded the time that I retired to bed, which was a little after ten o'clock. I was not involved in the murder of Emma Smith, and it came as an enormous relief.

Chapter Twenty

THE MISSING PAGE

Wednesday 20th June 1888

Something dreadful has occurred — a calamity, a dire situation that I cannot see a way through. It was all going so well. My journal keeping, avoiding the railway — everything worked as I planned. There were no further repetitions of the incidents of February and March.

My illness lay mostly dormant with only one or two new episodes lasting a few seconds at most. I was in full control of my faculties until this afternoon.

I travelled to Westminster, as usual, walking instead of using transportation. I had come to deplore transport of any kind. It might have been an overreaction on my part, but I concluded that the sounds and motion of mechanical carriers precipitated my attacks. The most severe incidents had happened during train travel, and it struck me that they could be similarly induced in a tram or carriage by the clip-clop of hooves. It was possible, and I wasn't prepared to take the chance.

I arrived at my destination in good time and joined the meeting, alert and interested. The June weather was fine and sunny. The windows were open, but I found my eyelids growing heavy, and my concentration began to lapse. I removed my jacket and hung it over the back of a chair, immediately feeling much better. The talk was fascinating, and at the end, I met the speaker, and we discussed the merits of his theories. We talked for half an hour, and one by one the other members slipped away until there were only four of us left in the room.

I said goodbye and went to retrieve my jacket. Fear slithered through my chest as I saw that the journal had fallen from my pocket and lay splayed across the floor underneath the chair. I grabbed it and frantically stowed loose newspaper articles back into the notebook. I turned to see if anyone had noticed. Nobody was facing me. As my heartbeat slowed, I realised that it wouldn't matter if they had. There was nothing untoward about the journal, and it would not have looked suspicious even if they had seen it on the floor. I was panicking for nothing.

I put my hat on and said farewell, before returning home once again, by foot. And here I am now, in my bedroom in my night attire, pen in hand about to journal the day's events. My notebook is intact and exactly as it should be, but one of the three newspaper articles is missing. And it is damning. It was the first, the death of Annie Millwood and I noted my movements around the outside of the newspaper text. I jotted all my loose thoughts on that piece of paper. Untidy speculation in spider scrawl filled the empty spaces. And now it is gone. It can only be where it fell from my jacket. The speaker is unlikely to find it, and another man followed me out leaving only one other in the building. He is the only man who could locate the cutting tonight.

What is the worst that would happen if he did? I cannot remember precisely what I wrote, but I am sure that I did not identify myself. I may have referred to my affliction in passing, but I did not name it. I scribbled my notes in a frenzy, and they bear little resemblance to my usual writing. So, what chance is there of detection?

I have concluded that it is not worth the risk and I will return this evening. I have a key of my own. We all do. It will be late by the time I get there. Everyone will be long gone, and the building will be empty.

I will find the clipping, or I will not. And if I don't, I can be reasonably sure who took it.

Of one thing I am certain. Though my conscience pains me, I will do everything I can to prevent an intrusion into my written thoughts. If the wrong man reads my journal, he may talk. I will be shut away and examined like an animal at a zoo. I will do whatever it takes to remain at liberty.

Chapter Twenty-One

A DIFFICULT DECISION

Prowling around London in the middle of the night bought back painful memories of my initial foray into the East End earlier that year. I remember feeling disorientated and frightened with no real idea of how to get home. Tonight brought back those feelings of guilt and wrong-doing, but this time I had prepared. I knew where I was going and how to get there without drawing undue attention to myself. And even if someone saw me, I had a ready explanation at hand. Still, I would prefer to remain undetected, so I slipped down side streets and cut-throughs. Before long, I found myself outside the Society Headquarters determined to find the newspaper cutting.

I crept around the outside and established that it was empty, as anticipated. I located my key, unlocked the door and stepped inside. I had never been alone in the building that late at night. Despite the familiarity of the rooms and layout, I found the emptiness unsettling. I opened the door to the meeting room and lit the gas lamp nearest the door. My stomach knotted when I saw two stacks of chairs at the end of the room. Someone had taken the time to clear up at the end of the meeting. It did not bode well.

I discarded any further concern about the possibility of detection and lit every gas lamp in the room so I could see without impediment. I searched the floor, behind the curtains, and under the circular mat in the centre. I even unstacked the chairs, hoping against hope that the clipping had fluttered onto the seat and become sandwiched between two of them. It was a waste of time and energy. The cutting had gone.

I extinguished the lamps and slammed the door then opened another and collapsed on the settee with my head in my hands. There were people I could rely on to protect my best interests, regardless of my actions, but if the wrong person found the clipping, the game was up. The man I left in the building was as straight as a die and law abiding. He was unlikely to keep any misgivings provoked by the article to himself. Even if he did not mention his suspicions immediately, he would be sure to discuss them sooner or later. It was in his nature to deliberate and consult.

I sat in the darkness for half an hour, wrestling with my conscience. The man was my friend. But something had altered in me, and my overriding aim was to avoid detection, come what may. The man was past his best. He had not enjoyed the success or renown he might have expected from his latest venture. He had feared, for some time, that he has been defrauded and made a fool. The thought of these things made my decision bearable.

A plan was formulating in my head. I discarded it at first, but after fifteen minutes of deliberation, I realised it was the only way. I could not achieve it alone and would need help. Could I reasonably expect to get it? I was adept at understanding the nuances of human nature and had built strong friendships. The men I knew had seen me through difficult times. They might be ready to help without the need for explanation. They already knew of my affliction and were protective, as true friends ought to be.

More importantly, it was in their interests to help. They were intelligent men. The less they knew, the better. I could credit them with the sense to know that they should not ask questions for which they would undoubtedly regret knowing the answers. There would be safety in *numbers. I decided to rally their support as soon as I could. But first I needed to write a letter.*

I moved across the hallway and into the library then sat at one of the reading desks where I lit a lamp. An inkwell was in front of me. I reached into my pocket and retrieved my fountain pen. I opened the box in the centre of the desks, extracted a sheet of headed paper and began my missive. "My dear Edmund," I wrote.

Chapter Twenty-Two

WHAT D'ONSTON KNEW

Thursday 5th March 1891

Lawrence paced the floor in the bedroom of the hotel he had grown to loathe. It was drab, noisy and full of people for whom he had no time. It was only the presence of Violet that made the place bearable, and she had spent the night in a hospital. He could not face the reading room again and kept to his bedroom, forcing himself to remember details of every conversation that had taken place over the last few days. Why was Violet attacked? Was it a random event? She maintained otherwise. Violet said that the menacing man in the top hat had warned her to stay away, but Violet had been disorientated and fearful of losing her life. Now that she was out of the oppressive darkness and no longer terrified, could he rely on her memory? Lawrence felt there was room for doubt.

Even so, he would treat the matter as she had reported it. He would assume that the assailant had lured her to the alley as she supposed, but he could already see flaws in the scenario. How would the man know she would be there all, never mind alone? And how would he know there would be a child conveniently available at that time of night?

Lawrence drew the curtains and watched a horse plod along the lane below. A boy in a flat cap wandered ahead of it, pulling the rope on its halter without ever looking behind. The boy's ill-fitting attire was threadbare, and though it was February, he was not wearing a coat. His head was down, he did not smile, and his demeanour suggested that he was carrying an unendurable burden. The horse appeared equally defeated by life. The disheartening scene reminded Lawrence of his first impression of the East End. There were groups of people everywhere, come rain or shine, by day or deep into the night. The pavement life had been one of the most noticeable features of the area. Whole communities congregated on front doorsteps outside their lodgings. It would be easy to find a child, even at night. The hour hadn't been especially late. In Spring, it would have been light. True, some of the smaller streets they had passed through were empty. But once they reached the larger roads, there were many more people, particularly near the public house. Violet's attack was opportunistic. It had to be. The man used the child because she was there. Had she not been, he would have found another means of enticing Violet away. Which suggested that he was already in the vicinity before they arrived.

Now Lawrence considered it Violet had mentioned hearing footsteps several times. He had dismissed her fears as an overactive imagination, but perhaps she was right? Who knew of their intention to journey to the East End? Who could have followed them? Well, Henry Moore knew, because Lawrence had discussed it over dinner. Henry was not at all keen on the idea, but he would not have intervened and had no wish to see Violet harmed. Had Violet told anyone? Lawrence did not know and could not ask, not until she left hospital anyway. Oh dear. Violet may not have said anything, but now he came to think of it, he might have done. He remembered asking the hotel porter about stations and railway lines, though he could not recall whether he had mentioned White's Row. But he certainly asked for directions to Aldgate which placed them in the East End. And there was the small matter of a map, which the porter had drawn. Not only did the porter know where they were going, but any one of the guests could have overheard the conversation. Not that there was any reason for them to take an interest in Lawrence's business, but it was fair to say that other people had known where they were going.

And D'Onston was aware, wasn't he? He had given Lawrence plenty of information about White's Row. Could he have deduced that Lawrence would visit? And what was D'Onston doing in The Paul's Head? Lawrence raised his eyes at the memory of that nuisance woman in the Public House. He had tried to get closer to D'Onston at the back of the room before she waylaid him by the door. He could not shake her off in time to identify the man before hearing Violet's screams. Lawrence screwed his eyes tightly and tried to visualise the scene from the previous night. He couldn't remember seeing the man who resembled D'Onston again, after he encountered the over-friendly woman.

Lawrence sat on the bed and picked at the candlewick bedspread. He wondered whether The Paul's Head had a back door and concluded it must. The public house was located on the corner and would need a rear entrance to take delivery of stock. D'Onston could have slipped outside undetected and attacked Violet in the alley. It all made sense. God, he could have killed her. Lawrence didn't give much thought to Violet half the time, and she irritated him the rest. It had taken the attack for him to appreciate the extent of his regard. It wasn't a romantic interest, at least he didn't think so, but she meant a lot more to him than he had realised. And someone had hurt her — possibly a man who looked like D'Onston.

Lawrence gritted his teeth as anger rose in his breast like the first flush of fever. How dare D'Onston think he could behave like this and get away with it. Lawrence flung open his wardrobe and extracted his coat and hat. He strode from the room, slamming the door behind him and exited the hotel almost walking into the path of a hansom cab. The driver pulled up.

"Going somewhere, gov'nor?" asked the cabman.

"The Triangle Hotel," snarled Lawrence, "and make it quick."

Lawrence jumped from the cab and pressed a few coins into the driver's hand without checking how much it was. Value for money was the last thing on his mind as he stormed into the entrance of the hotel. Lawrence strode past the man at the desk without acknowledging his presence and ran up the stairs two at a time. He hammered on the door of D'Onston's room and waited a few seconds listening for signs of life. Nothing happened, so he hit the door again. It opened, and D'Onston stood there, pallid and with a puzzled expression on his face.

"Mr Harpham, again. What can I do for you this time?"

"Why did you attack Violet? What has she done to you?"

"What are you talking about? Have you lost your mind? Leave me alone."

D'Onston tried to close the door, but Lawrence put his foot between the door and the jamb. "Oh no, you don't."

"Get out."

Lawrence lost his temper, grabbed D'Onston by the throat and pushed him into the room. He shoved D'Onston backwards and pinned him to the wall by his throat, just like the girl he had seen at The Paul's Head.

"I have had enough of your lies," spat Lawrence. "You nearly killed her, you bastard."

D'Onston gasped. He tried to speak, but Lawrence's hand constricted his throat, and all he could do was splutter. Lawrence released his grip, still incandescent with rage.

"You had better start talking, D'Onston."

"I would if I had the first idea what you are speaking about," he said hoarsely.

"You know perfectly well. You were at The Paul's Head last night."

"I was not."

"I saw you."

"You did not, I tell you. I never left this room. Whoever you saw, it was not me."

"I don't believe you. You have been lying to me since the moment we met. The White's Row connection was your idea, not mine. But for you, I wouldn't have been anywhere near the place."

"Why did you go? I thought your interest was with Gurney?"

"Start talking now." Lawrence forced D'Onston deeper

into the wall and glared at him. Their faces were almost touching.

"Let me go. I'll tell you what I know, but I can't talk like this."

Lawrence released his grip, and D'Onston coughed and rubbed his throat. Lawrence picked up a walking stick which was propped up by the window and pushed it towards D'Onston's chest. "Sit on the bed," he commanded. "And start talking."

Lawrence backed towards the open bedroom door and shut it. He did not take his eyes from D'Onston as he brandished the walking stick in front.

"Put it down," whispered D'Onston, his voice still hoarse. "There is no need."

Lawrence pulled the chair from the desk and turned it towards the bed. He sat facing D'Onston with the walking stick held across his lap.

"Why did you lie?"

"Because my life depends on it."

"Go on."

"Look, I did see Gurney that night. I cannot imagine how you knew."

"I didn't." Lawrence blurted it out without thinking, surprised at D'Onston's admission. He had known all along that D'Onston was being evasive, but it hadn't occurred to him that it was about seeing Gurney.

"Isn't it Edmund Gurney that you're interested in?"

"Never mind that. Tell me what you saw."

"It might be easier if I show you." D'Onston stood and faced Lawrence. He raised an eyebrow and Lawrence nodded.

"Go ahead. No funny business, though."

Roslyn D'Onston walked to his desk, took a key from

the empty inkwell and unlocked a small drawer. He withdrew an envelope and handed it to Lawrence before sitting back on the bed.

Lawrence opened the envelope to find a letter written on SPR headed paper.

"My Dear Edmund

It has come to my notice that someone close to the heart of our organisation has committed a criminal act, an act so heinous that I cannot overlook it. Unspeakable violence has been perpetrated against two women, Annie Millwood and Ada Wilson. I have been gathering evidence for some time now in support of my suspicions. Unfortunately, I mislaid an item that may lead to the transgressions becoming public knowledge. I had hoped to have more time to consider the matter and investigate it thoroughly before bringing it to the attention of the authorities. Edmund, I fear I cannot make this decision alone. Reluctant as I am to place my burden in the hands of another, I beg you to help me resolve this dilemma. Meet me in the foyer of the hotel where we stayed when we conducted the first of our investigations into post-hypnotic states. I will be there at nine o'clock on Friday evening. Tell no one.

Yours ever"

Lawrence turned the page over. The reverse was blank.
"Who wrote this?"
"I don't know," said D'Onston.
"Have you told the police?"
"No."
"But these names — they are the women you mentioned yesterday."
D'Onston looked sombre as he nodded his head.
"You've been helping the police with their enquiries.

Why didn't you tell them about this?" Lawrence searched the man's face, perplexed. D'Onston had been a suspect himself. Production of the letter would have guaranteed an immediate release.

D'Onston sighed. "I wrote to the Headquarters of the SPR," he said, "advising them of the contents of this letter and that I had seen the writer in Brighton. They suggested I never spoke of it and offered a large sum of money in return."

"Blackmail," gasped Lawrence.

"If you like. I thought it a fair exchange," said D'Onston.

"But those poor women."

D'Onston eyed him coldly. "They were dead. I could hardly bring them back."

"Did you find out who wrote the letter?"

"Never. As you can see, it was not signed. Presumably, the reference to the hotel was enough for Gurney to know who wrote it."

"Who did you contact at the SPR?"

"I don't know. I wrote a letter and posted it to the Society's Headquarters. A day later I received a note telling me to look out for instructions in the personal section of The Pall Mall Gazette. I did, and that is the way we communicated."

"Are you telling me that the SPR is concealing the man who murdered these two women?"

"They are concealing far more than that."

"Why have they paid you if you don't know who wrote the letter?"

"They believe I do know. I have never indicated otherwise."

"Then you are in grave danger."

"Not necessarily. My solicitor has instructions in the event of my sudden death. I made sure the SPR were fully aware of this when I wrote to them."

"But you said the deaths were part of the Ripper killings. They cannot be."

"They are, Mr Harpham. The killings never stopped."

"Good God, man. You allowed him to go on when you could have intervened."

"I repeat, I did not kill them. Who knows what would have happened? The SPR has many members. It could be any one of them."

"Scotland Yard would have unmasked the killer."

"Really? The men at the top of the SPR have conspired to keep this secret. They closed ranks. Any evidence will be long gone."

"You wanted to prolong The Ripper's capture for money."

"There has been no money since the end of December 1888, and I had to fight to get that. You may have heard of Montague Druitt. He died that month by drowning. He was a Ripper suspect, and the SPR refused to pay any more money on the strength of his probable guilt."

"The name sounds familiar."

"It should. Druitt was one of only a few suspects seriously considered by Scotland Yard. There was good reason to suspect him. The timing was right, and the SPR claimed to have proof of his guilt."

"What proof?"

"They did not say, and I could hardly press them. But I do not believe Druitt was the murderer."

"You were a suspect for a while. You knew so much, yet you allowed them to arrest you."

"I encouraged it, Mr Harpham."

"Why?"

"Money. Why else?"

Lawrence stared at D'Onston unable to comprehend the coldness of a man who put money ahead of life.

"I don't understand."

"I will explain. First, I need a drink. Do you want one?"

Lawrence shook his head. D'Onston grabbed a glass tumbler and filled it with a dark liquid from a chipped decanter. He knocked it back and filled another glass."

"Well, it's like this. The SPR paid me after the murders of Millwood and Wilson. Later there were several other killings which seemed like the work of the same man, but it was far from certain, and I gave them the benefit of the doubt. Then Polly Nichols was killed in Bucks Row. Her throat was slit, and her abdomen ripped apart just like Annie Millwood. There were too many similarities to ignore. And look at this."

D'Onston stood up again and walked to the wall by his desk. Above the African mask, was a map of the world. He detached the two top corners and folded them down, revealing a large map of London on the rear with strategically placed red ink markers. "Look, here, here and here," he said, pointing to the most easterly marker and working towards the west. This one is Ada Wilson in Maidman Street. This one in the west is Annie Millwood in White's Row and this one," he held his finger over the middle marker. "This is Polly Nichol's in Buck's Row."

"They are all along the same line," said Lawrence.

"Quite. The location is significant."

"The Ripper is a madman," said Lawrence.

Quite possibly. I did not say what significance. Perhaps it is a matter of transportation, or the Ripper might have had business in one of the local buildings. Maybe the area was unfamiliar, and he kept close to Whitechapel Road. Who knows? But I had time on my hands. Did I mention my confinement to the London Hospital throughout the latter half of 1888?"

"No."

"I suffer from, well, you don't need to know the details. It is enough to say that I was at a low ebb, lethargic most of the time and bored with life. But I am, as you know, a journalist by trade and I still required an income. The hush money from the SPR did not last long and hospitalised or not I had bills to pay. And so, I lay there, confined to my sick bed, embittered and angry. I am a clever man, Harpham. I decided to put my intellect to the test and resolved to unmask the murderer. I already had a head start on all the other amateurs, knowing, as I did, the connection with the SPR. But which one of them was it?"

"You say you were in a hospital. Could you not leave?"

"It was not a prison, but nor could I come and go at will. There were ward rules to follow."

"Did you make any progress?"

"It was easy to get hold of copies of the SPR journal. They publish it monthly, and they name all members and associate members. But as for the identity of the Ripper, I am no further forward now than I ever was, though I have a greater understanding of how he did it."

"There must have been further communication from the SPR if you received another payment?"

"I did, but it was torturous. I left messages in the personal column of The Pall Mall Gazette, as before, but they ignored them, damn their eyes. At quite a risk too. A less patient man than me might have given up and taken the matter to the police."

"Hardly," said Lawrence out loud. The narcissistic man

in front of him was not awash with morals nor the type to walk away from a lucrative venture. "How did you gain their attention?" he continued.

"I waited to see if there would be another murder and there was. Annie Chapman, Hanbury Street died within a spit of White's Row. And another left to right cut to the throat with slashes to her abdomen. This time, he took her uterus. Cut it right out. Cleanly."

Lawrence swallowed. He did not appreciate the evident glee in D'Onston's voice. The more revolting the details, the more animated D'Onston became. He was enjoying it and bragged like an actor at the denouement of a stage play.

"There was no doubt in my mind that it was the same man. I brooded over the matter for the rest of September, angrier than you could know. If the Ripper was on the loose again, I wanted more money. I attempted one more contact through the personal pages, but nothing came of it. On the last day of September, the double event occurred."

D'Onston was striding around the room now, red-faced and enraged as he recalled the impotence of his position. Lawrence watched him in disgust. His greed was unpleasant enough, but it was more than that. D'Onston disliked being ignored. Self-centred and vain, he had struggled to maintain the secret he badly wanted to share.

D'Onston stopped at the window and took a few deep breaths, trying to calm himself. Finally, he returned to the map and placed a finger over a marker just south of Commercial Road and another to the west of Aldgate Station. "Elizabeth Stride, Berner Street and Catherine Eddowes, Mitre Square. The Ripper walked in a straight line from one to the other. Cut the first throat left to right, no further damage."

"Not the same as the others," said Lawrence.

"Exactly the same. The Ripper must have been disturbed."

"And he murdered the other woman the same night?"

"Yes. And he did it properly, this time. Throat ripped, abdominal injuries and he took a kidney."

"Revolting," said Lawrence, feeling queasy.

D'Onston ignored him. "I acted at once. They would not disregard me again. I wrote to the police and copied my letter to The Pall Mall Gazette. Here..."

D'Onston wrenched open a desk drawer and removed a handful of clippings. He selected one and thrust it towards Lawrence.

It was a short article directed towards the SPR, goading and taunting them. The writing was derogatory and designed to provoke. The letter openly mocked the organisation, suggesting they use their influence to identify the Ripper. But it was the last few lines that were revealing. Their meaning would be apparent to anyone concealing the murderer. Lawrence read it aloud.

"Clairvoyants, even if the mere local influence be insufficient to unseal their spiritual eyes, might set to work upon 'Jack the Ripper's letter and determine whether it be genuine or a hoax. Why does the Society for Psychical Research stand ingloriously idle?"

Lawrence whistled. "Publishing that letter was risky, but they must have understood the warning."

A self-satisfied smile played on the edges of D'Onston's mouth. "They did. They contacted me through the personal columns the following day. I collected an envelope from a butcher's in the Strand with promises of money. They asked me to wait as it was a substantial sum to raise and they needed time, so I did."

"And they paid you."

"They did not." D'Onston slammed his hand on the desk. "They reneged. And in the meantime, Mary Kelly died in Millers Court."

"I remember," said Lawrence. "It was the only Ripper murder with which I was familiar. I remember reading accounts in the Bury Press. The violence and destruction were incomprehensible. I have never read such awful details."

"It was all wrong," said D'Onston. "I still have doubts."

"But it was the final murder. The Ripper indulged himself until he could endure no more. Then the killings stopped."

"It does not fit the pattern," said D'Onston. "I don't believe it was the work of the Ripper and the killings never ceased."

"But you contacted the SPR again?"

"Yes. I gave them until the end of November, but nothing transpired." D'Onston leafed through his clippings and handed one to Lawrence dated 1st December 1888. Lawrence unfolded it.

"You don't expect me to read all of this?"

"No. I had a lot of time to think about these crimes in hospital. One of the doctors shared my interest in the case, and we swapped ideas. I hid references to myself within the theories that I outlined in this article. There should have been quite enough to alert the SPR to my presence. They would know I was not a man to trifle with."

"It makes no sense to me," said Lawrence scanning the article. "I don't believe in black magic. What does the cross represent?" He pointed to a large cross on the right-hand side of the clipping.

"The cross is a representation of the murders," said D'Onston. "I did not include them all — just enough to justify my theory. The purpose of the article was to flag my presence. It did not need to be accurate."

"Forgive me for asking," said Lawrence. "But your name is not on the article."

"It is if you look closely enough," said D'Onston. "I have referred to the great modern occultist Eliphas Levi, and I have drawn a cross. Levi was a Rosicrucian."

"Meaning?"

"It's an esoteric order — a spiritual movement. You don't need details, Harpham. I'm trying to explain how I gained their attention again."

"Go on."

"The literal meaning of Rosicrucian is rose coloured cross. Do you see?"

"No. I don't."

"I have chosen the name, Roslyn. It is not my given name. The female equivalent is Rosalyn which means Rose. Do you see now? Rose and Cross. Rosicrucian. And if that was not enough to make the connection, the Rosslyn Chapel in Scotland is important in the Rosicrucian movement. I did not select my name for this reason, but many have assumed it."

"I don't follow," said Lawrence. "It is a big stretch."

"For you," said D'Onston, "but the SPR members are well versed in esoteric lore. I knew the article would stand out, and it did. They contacted me again the next day."

"And you got your money?"

"I received fifty pounds in an envelope through my door. There was also a letter telling me to contact the police if I wished, and be damned, but the murders were over. The Ripper was dead, and I would hear about it in the papers very soon."

"Not what you were hoping for."

"I was furious but side-tracked for a few days as I finally left the hospital in early December. It gave me time alone to consider my next move. I had a plan, audacious and risky, but it would bring me into public contact with the police without revealing what I knew." D'Onston smiled wolfishly.

Lawrence raised his eyes heavenwards and shook his head. "What plan?"

"I collaborated with an amateur detective by the name of Marsh. Common sort of fellow, quite full of himself. I had spent many hours researching the murders by then, and after several discussions, he went running to the police convinced that I was the Ripper. As I told you, the police are stupid. They still don't understand much about the Ripper's methods, and they fell for Marsh's story."

"I can't see how interaction with the police helped your cause?"

"Scotland Yard is a leaky sieve. It always was. It put me in a position to help the gossip along a bit, of course. I reported to the yard to help with their enquiries and gave them a good dozen reasons why my Doctor friend, Morgan Davies, was a better suspect."

"I still don't follow."

"They questioned Davies at length. A perfectly innocent, professional man was under scrutiny by Scotland Yard, on my word alone. A handy demonstration of how it would be if I chose to reveal the connection to the SPR. And it worked. Finally, it worked. At the end of December, I received a large sum of money anonymously together with a note reminding me that the Ripper was dead, and a body would soon appear. On the last day of the year, they fished Montague John Druitt out of the Thames. The young man appeared to have killed himself."

"Was he a member of the SPR?"

"He may have been, for all I know," said D'Onston. "I don't have a full membership list. The point is that the Society knew. They warned me not once but twice of the impending discovery of a body. How did they know? I have contacts in London. It did not take long to find out that Druitt was a serious suspect for the Ripper. And the murders stopped, so I had every reason to believe it. I assumed he must have a connection to the SPR. How else could they have known in advance?"

Lawrence pondered the matter. "How else indeed?" he said. "But everything you have told me is old news. None of it explains the attack on Violet."

"I don't know anything about an attack," said D'Onston, rubbing his throat. "Who is Violet? Do I know her?"

"She is my... she is a friend. A man attacked her last night. He had a knife. This man warned her to stay away."

"Nasty," said D'Onston, "but her attacker could be any number of East End ruffians. There are plenty about who would slit her throat for a few coins."

"Would you feel the same way if I told you that she was in the Headquarters of the SPR earlier this week?"

D'Onston whistled. "That's a different matter. Good God. What was she doing there?"

"Visiting," said Lawrence.

"Well, if I had a lady friend, I wouldn't let her anywhere near that place."

Lawrence paused for a few seconds to think. He walked towards the window and stared outside, before turning to face D'Onston. "There wouldn't be any danger if the Ripper was dead. You must believe he is still at large?"

D'Onston nodded. His brow furrowed. "I first had my suspicions in July of '89," he said. "There hadn't been a murder since the double event — As I said, I don't count the Millers Court murder. It wasn't right. But in July 1889 they found Alice McKenzie with her throat cut in Castle Alley, not far from where Martha Tabram died. Throat slit left to right and cuts to the abdomen."

"What did you do?"

"Nothing," said D'Onston. "The police played it down and said it wasn't a Ripper murder. I had my own problems and was back in the hospital again with…" D'Onston's voice trailed off, and he looked furtively around the room. He took a deep breath. Lawrence noticed that his hands were shaking.

D'Onston continued. "Anyway, I decided it couldn't be, and no noteworthy killings happened the next year, as far as I could tell. But now, Frances Coles is dead, and the method is similar. He cut her throat from left to right. There were no abdominal wounds, but there wouldn't be if he was interrupted. Judging by the newspaper reports, a policeman only just missed him. No, I know as much about these murders as anyone outside the police force, and I think it is a Ripper murder. He is back among us."

"You should tell the police," said Lawrence. "You should have told them a long time ago."

"What do you think will happen if I do?" asked D'Onston. "If they believe me, which I doubt, who will they investigate?" He lifted a magazine off his bedside table and passed it to Lawrence. "That's October's SPR journal," he said, "one new member and eighteen new associate members." He flicked the magazine open and ran his finger down the page, muttering under his breath. "There, that's ten committee members too — twenty-nine names before the end of page two. The SPR is not a small organisation, Harpham. It is popular."

"The police have the resources to deal with it."

"You think the SPR will cooperate? Why should they? They could have called in the police and reported me. It would have saved them a considerable sum of money. No, we are discussing an organisation who have covered up the murder of one of their own. They are protecting someone who has murdered who knows how many women. They are not going to help the police make any progress. We need someone who can move among them without suspicion."

"Who?" asked Lawrence.

"Don't insult my intelligence," said D'Onston. "You enter my home, question me about matters that don't concern you and then you assault me. I may be a dipsomaniac and many other things of which I am sure you are aware but don't take me for a fool. You are a policeman, or you were a policeman. One of the two."

"I am a private detective," Lawrence sighed. "I was a policeman."

"Then investigate," hissed D'Onston, "while you still can. If they find out what has passed between us, we are both in danger, and so is your lady friend. This matter will not go away. Find a way to get close. You are far more likely to succeed by stealth."

Lawrence bit his lip. "You are right," he said. "I will do it. Have you told me everything?"

"You know everything you need to know," said D'Onston. "Don't bother coming here again. It is too dangerous now I have shared my secret. I will pack up and leave today and lie low for a bit — a different hotel perhaps, or even a hospital. I am not a well man, and I will not be a sitting duck. You are on your own. Do not underestimate the danger you are in."

Lawrence nodded and left the room without another word. If D'Onston was right, he needed to infiltrate the

SPR, and soon. But Violet was still in the hospital, and it was of the utmost importance that she was safe. Lawrence headed straight to the nearest post office and scribbled out a telegram which he addressed to Michael Farrow. 'Get the first train to Royal London Hospital. Violet is in danger. LH'

Chapter Twenty-Three

A CONSCIOUS CHOICE

July 1888

I found the summer of '88 gruelling. The weather was unremarkable, but my days passed in an endless stream of meetings and appointments. It was a busy time, both personally and professionally and I grew tired. Fatigue set in and drove me to self-medication. I found myself more disorientated then I had been in a long time.

I resolved the Gurney dilemma in June with help from a colleague. He assisted me, but not unconditionally. Against his interests, he insisted on an explanation, and a detailed one, at that. I unburdened myself to the most trustworthy of men in the certain knowledge that he would not betray me. Nor did he. Nor could he without bringing the organisation into disrepute. That reason was minor compared to the other self-interested reason he had for maintaining my integrity. He alone assisted me with the Brighton dilemma, but two others soon became involved. My benefactor felt unable to take sole charge of my future and needed help. The men he chose were familiar with my affliction and, at least on the surface, sympathetic. All were loyal to the SPR and swore to keep my secret, providing that I did everything in my power to manage the problem. I was confident in my ability to comply. I had stopped travelling by train and kept to my home whenever I did not have an evening appointment.

Then, in early July, a letter arrived at the SPR Headquarters. Anyone could have opened it, but fate intervened and placed it in the hands of one of the trusted three. The letter contained news of a most disturbing kind. How it had come about, I could not imagine, but a certain Roslyn D'Onston had intercepted my message to Gurney.

We knew him, of course, for we shared common interests, though his were of the darker kind. Rumours circulated that he was a student of black magic, if not a practitioner. He was a disreputable man and entirely without morals made clear from his letter containing a threat of blackmail. The trusted three managed the situation without involving me, and I was grateful. The letter had unnerved me, and I was beginning to suffer more seizures. I brooded over D'Onston as I went about my business, wishing him ill, wondering how easy it would be to exterminate him, as I had Edmund. But there were too many unknowns, and I resolved to leave my friends to deal with it. I tried not to worry, but it preyed on my mind.

Another woman was attacked early in August. This time, I was the culprit. I did not have to resort to the press to check my guilt for I remembered it surprisingly well. I had gone to Clerkenwell to visit an old friend, but I never reached his house. As I walked towards it, a feeling came upon me. My mouth grew dry, and my tongue felt too big. I smacked my lips together in that hitherto familiar way, then my recall became sketchy. Snatches of memory flitted out of grasp as I passed through Spitalfields and into Whitechapel.

When I regained my faculties, I was standing next to a woman in a dingy yard. She was plain and plump with an aroma of ale that made me queasy. I can only imagine what I must have said to her, for she turned away from me and lifted her skirts. I hesitated, repulsed and in a coarse cockney accent she told me to get on with it.

I did. I thrust my hand into my pocket and felt for the two knives I had taken from home earlier. One was a pocket penknife and the other, a ceremonial dagger that I kept in a display case. I put my arm around her chest and reaching from behind, I thrust the blade deep into her breast. She gasped, and I released her and let her fall to the floor. I discarded my coat and dropped the dagger. Her eyes fluttered shut, but her mouth gaped open as if she was snoring. Her neck was fat, and her fleshy double chin wobbled as she took short panting breaths. The notion that this woman expected me to engage in intercourse with her was insulting, repellent. The wound had left her half dead, but it wasn't dead enough. I took my penknife and rammed it into her throat. I pulled it out, and the sight of her blood made me angrier still. I thought of D'Onston and blackmail and Edmund and the unfairness of my affliction. I stabbed her over and over until I was too tired to continue. Then, I wiped the knives on her skirts, put on my coat and left the alley. I almost walked into the path of two soldiers coming down the opposite side of the road but managed to avoid them.

I walked the four miles home with a clear head. My thoughts and memories were lucid. Somehow there had been a sea change in my attitude. When I killed the first women, I had no control. It happened because of an automatism. I planned Gurney's murder, but with compassion. Tonight was different. Though I couldn't remember taking my penknife or the ceremonial dagger, there was no doubt that I had. This act indicated foresight. I had not been in full command of my faculties before encountering the woman in the alley, but I was when I murdered her. I chose to kill her, and I relished it. The pent-up release from plunging cold steel into flesh was exquisite.

By the time I reached home, I had concluded that something monstrous must have long dwelled within me. I couldn't pretend or hide behind my condition any longer. I cleaned the dagger and replaced it in the display case. Later that day, I purchased a newspaper. It did not take a long search to find news of the murder as it had previously. This time it was easy. 'The Whitechapel Horror' was emblazoned on the front page of the paper. The police had not yet linked the killings, but it was only a matter of time.

Chapter Twenty-Four

UNDERCOVER IN SPITALFIELDS CHAMBERS

It was six o'clock in the evening and Lawrence was on his way back to the East End of London. He had left The Triangle Hotel, pausing only to send a telegram, before returning to his room at The Regal. Once there, he opened his suitcase and searched for a small box in the inner compartment which he hoped he had the foresight to pack. His fingers closed over a square receptacle. Sighing with relief, he opened it and withdrew the contents. The object inside resembled a small animal but was, in fact, a false moustache and beard set. Lawrence placed them on the dressing table and ventured down to the hotel lobby. It was empty, so he crept downstairs to the basement where the odd job man had emerged the previous day. Lawrence ducked down the corridor pushing each of three doors. All were open and the end door led to a dark basement room containing a single bed and wardrobe. A dirty coat and hat hung from a hook on the door. Lawrence inspected them. The moth-eaten coat was missing a button, and a suspicious looking mark stained the hat. They were ideal. He bundled the coat inside his jacket and placed the hat on his head before returning to his bedroom.

Lawrence manoeuvred the false beard into a convincing position on his chin using a wire and spring arrangement. Then, he topped it with a greying moustache. Finally, he retrieved a piece of charcoal from the box and worked it into his fingernails and face. He smeared the residue on the coat borrowed from the odd job man and tried to ignore his nagging conscience, making a mental note to leave a few coins for the man to get the coat cleaned when it was returned. Lawrence covered his face with a scarf, draped the coat over his arm and concealed the hat beneath. Leaving the hotel by the back entrance, he scrutinised the gardens. They were clear of people, and he was relieved that nobody had seen him. When he was a suitable distance away from the hotel, he donned the grubby coat and stowed the scarf looking every inch a tramp.

Lawrence contemplated the distance between Lambeth and Spitalfields. It was touching three miles, but if he wanted to maintain the integrity of his disguise, he would have to walk. His lungs hurt with the ferocity of the bitter chill. But needs must, so he strode out towards East London thinking about the task at hand.

Soon, he would need to find a way to get close to the heart of the SPR, but that was a job for another day. The events of Wednesday night had foiled his attempt to gain access to 8 White's Row, but he still had an inexplicable urge to get inside. Two of the women had dossed there. Lawrence might have let the connection lie, had it not involved the most recent murder. D'Onston had convinced him that Frances Coles was a Ripper victim. The only way to find out more about her final hours was to visit her last known abode.

The walk took a little under an hour and Lawrence soon found himself in surroundings that were becoming depressingly familiar. It was pitch black when he arrived outside 8 White's Row. A chipped, metal sign inscribed 'Spitalfields Chambers' hung above the door. Lawrence checked his watch. It was seven o'clock, and the doss house should be full by now. He walked towards the entrance where a wooden door stood ajar despite the freezing temperature. He hesitated, then pushed it and stepped inside. The door opened into a dark, unfurnished hallway. Rotten floorboards squeaked as Lawrence ventured towards a welcome light at the end. The sound of laughter came from the room beyond. Lawrence opened the door and peered inside. Their voices quietened.

A matronly woman eyed him suspiciously. "What d'you want," she asked.

"A bed for the night," Lawrence replied in his best East End accent.

The woman thrust a grubby palm towards him. "You can have a room when I've seen your doss money," she said.

He reached into his trouser pocket and tossed a few coins onto the table.

She examined them. "They'll do," she said. "You can have one of the beds in the room upstairs on your right."

"It's cold," said Lawrence walking towards the fire. He held his hands in front of the flames, wincing at the sight of his scarred left hand. The disguise would have been unconvincing worn with his customary soft leather gloves which had been discarded back at the hotel. Lawrence felt vulnerable with his hand exposed, but it was unavoidable.

The woman put her glass down and patted the bench beside her. "You can come and sit here until you get warm," she said. "This 'ere is Moll," she continued, "and this one is Samuel."

Lawrence surveyed the room. It was long and narrow. A ring-marked table with two wooden seats either side was set close to the fire. Further down, two longer benches ran parallel with the walls. Men and women dressed in rags were sitting either side. A waist height length of coarse rope ran along one of the benches. Two men rested their heads on the line, trying their hardest to sleep.

Lawrence grunted and sat on the bench. Samuel took a slug from his glass and pushed it towards Lawrence. The glass was dirty. Something granular was floating in it, but Lawrence took a mouthful anyway. He grimaced as he wiped his lips on his sleeve but nodded his thanks.

"Never seen you around here before," said Moll. "I think I would have remembered a good-looking chap like you, wouldn't I Sarah?" She winked at the older woman conspiratorially.

"I'm sure you would," said Sarah. "Any new fellow's fair game for you."

"Don't mind them two," said Samuel. "They're only playing."

"It's a fair question. I've been dossing in Lambeth, that's why you haven't seen me."

"You're a long way from home," said Sarah.

"I don't have a home. It was Lambeth last month. It'll be somewhere else the next."

"Why are you here then?"

"Visiting," said Lawrence. "I've got a cousin in Fashion Street, and then I'm heading down to Swallow Gardens to see my nephew."

Moll and Sarah exchanged glances. "That's where Frances got herself killed," said Moll.

"Frances?"

"Don't you hear the news in Lambeth? Frances Coles — murdered. They thought it was the Ripper then they thought it was that stoker, James Sadler. It wasn't him though, and the murderer of that poor girl still roams the streets."

"Don't go on," said Sarah. "There ain't nothing we can do about it."

"Did you know her?" asked Lawrence.

"Course I did," said Sarah. "She stayed here often enough. She was with us the day she died. I was a witness at her inquest."

"La-de-da Sarah Fleming, court witness. You ain't no better than the rest of us," said Moll setting her glass unsteadily on the table. Half the contents slopped out and formed a pool of liquid.

"I didn't ask to be there," said Sarah, sullenly. "I had no choice."

"You don't have to tell everyone who will listen," snapped Moll.

"Why don't you just go to bed."

"Perhaps I will." Moll was slurring now. She finished her drink, slammed the glass on the table and staggered through the door.

"Don't mind her," said Sarah. "She's alright when she's sober, but a rotten drunk. He ain't much better." She pointed to Samuel. His head was resting on the kitchen table, and he was snoring softly."

"What was it like, in court?" asked Lawrence.

"I've been in worse places. They ask a lot of questions but nothing I couldn't answer."

"Were you surprised when they released Sadler?"

"No. He was a miserable specimen. I didn't like him,

but he didn't do it."

"You saw him that night?"

"Yes. Sadler returned after Frances left, whining because he had been set upon. Beaten up, he was and robbed. The cheeky blighter wanted to sleep here but didn't have any money. He had the front to ask if he could stay in the kitchen for nothing. I told him to sling his hook. He said I was a hard-hearted woman. Well, that's why they made me deputy lodging housekeeper. I would be pretty useless if I took in any old waif or stray. I don't have any sympathy for a man of his kind."

"So, you turned him away."

"I got Charles Guiver, my doorman to do it, God rest his soul."

"God rest his soul? Is he dead? How?"

"I don't know. It happened before the inquest. Apoplexy, the doctor said. Not that I believe him."

"Why not?"

"He was fit as a fiddle until recently. Never ailed, never complained."

"The Doctor should know."

"Well, he didn't. He should have talked to me before he decided how Charlie died."

"Why?"

"Because I would have told him that Charlie got himself coshed the day after the inquest. He went from hale and hearty to bed bound, just like that."

"Was he in a fight?"

"No. Charlie wasn't the type. I found him in the kitchen one night, rubbing his head and sick as a dog. He said he had been sitting there minding his own business when he heard footsteps. He didn't turn around because he thought it was me. The next thing he remembered was waking up on the floor with a lump on his head."

"Was it a robbery?"

"Don't be daft. This is a doss house. We're hardly rolling in money, and what we have, I keep. Charlie never had it."

"And he didn't see his attacker?"

"No. It could have been anybody. Can't trust no-one around here."

"The door was open when I came in."

"It always is, but Charlie was usually around, so it didn't matter. I 'spect they came in through the front door. It's of no consequence now. They got him, and now we have to find another watchman."

"Perhaps it was apoplexy, after all."

"No, it wasn't. Charlie got hit on the head. Pity the lump had gone, or Doctor Dukes would have seen it. Hang on a minute." Sarah stood up and clumped down towards the other end of the room. Two women had begun to squabble, and the younger had thrown a punch.

"Break it up, or you'll both be out on your ears," said Sarah.

"Witch," hissed one of the women.

"I warn you, Maggie Brown. One more word and so help me…"

Sarah glared at the women then returned to her place on the bench beside Lawrence.

"Drunken cows," she said.

Lawrence nodded.

"You were saying about the doctor. Did you get a chance to tell him later?"

"I tried, but he didn't listen. Just talked a load of mumbo jumbo about a blood clot pressing on Charlie's brain. He thought it might be caused by over stimulation. It wasn't. Charlie was hurt. The only excitement he'd had in a long time was chasing some fop out of the bedroom at the back end of January. God only knows why a gentleman would want to poke around in here, but Charlie found him and got rid of him sharpish."

"A gentleman? How did he know?"

"I don't know. Perhaps he was in tails and a top hat. As I said, I wasn't here. It was about midday, and everyone had gone. They don't stay here during the day. Charlie heard a noise and went upstairs to one of the dormitories. There are twelve beds - you'll see them when you go up later. A swarthy looking fellow had the end one the previous night. I've seen 'em all, but there was something about this man I didn't like. There are plenty of ruffians in the East End of London, but he wasn't that type. There was something different about him. Anyway, Charlie comes upstairs, and there's this toff, bent over the bed feeling around for something."

"What?"

"I don't know, and Charlie didn't know. He chased him away then he saw him a couple of days later talking to the same man."

"Before Frances Coles died or after?"

"I thought you didn't know about that?"

"I only know what you told me."

"You're a blooming stranger. How do I know that you're not Charlie's chap?"

"Do I look like a gentleman?" asked Lawrence holding his hands out in disbelief.

Sarah peered at his dirty nails. "No, you're as common as the rest of us," she said.

"So, was it before or after she died?"

"After, I think. Yes, a few days after. Why?"

"It doesn't matter. I'm only passing the time of day. It's a good story, and I don't hear many of them."

"I'm not making it up."

"I didn't say you were."

"You should go up now," said Sarah. "There are only a few beds left. You'll end up in the coffins if you don't watch it.

Lawrence nodded. He had heard of coffin beds. Passing the night in this hell hole was bad enough, but he didn't relish the thought of sleeping in a box too small to turn in.

"G'night then," he said and clumped up the stairs. They echoed under the impact of his boots.

There were three doors at the top of the dimly-lit stairs. Lawrence opened the door to the right. A flickering candle revealed a long dormitory containing a row of low metal beds topped with threadbare blankets. Sarah wasn't exaggerating. There were sleeping bumps in all but two beds. Lawrence waited for his eyes to adjust to the dark, then felt his way to the nearest empty bed. He pulled back the covers and got in fully dressed, anticipating a wakeful night. But after five minutes he found himself drifting effortlessly into a dreamless sleep.

Chapter Twenty-Five

A VISITOR

Friday 6th March 1891

Violet was cross when she woke. She had been in the hospital since the early hours of Thursday morning. Her lightly bandaged wound covered a superficial cut. Lawrence had been right. It was not serious, and yet she was still in the hospital. Violet had spent the whole of yesterday alone in the ward and was ready to leave. Lawrence, who treated her so tenderly on Wednesday night, had vanished. He hadn't visited or sent a message since she arrived. By Thursday afternoon she had had enough and decided to return to the hotel. But when she voiced her intention, the matron dissuaded her in a way that left no room for argument. Violet was not ill. She needed no further medical care. There was no reason to stay but getting out of the hospital seemed impossible. Violet was becoming paranoid, convinced that Lawrence had persuaded the nurses to stop her from leaving. The more she thought about it, the angrier she became. As a grown woman, she resented having decisions made for her.

The rattle of the breakfast trolley disturbed her thoughts. A bowl containing a gloopy mass bearing only a passing resemblance to porridge appeared before her. She took a spoon and tried some. It tasted like grout. She dropped the cutlery and pushed her breakfast away determined not to eat another meal in the hospital if she could help it. Violet concluded that the only way out of her predicament was to leave without telling anyone. If she didn't ask, they couldn't refuse permission. But when she opened the door of the single wooden wardrobe by her bed, it was almost empty. Her clothes had gone, and the spindly wire coat hanger contained only a scarf that didn't belong to her. She wrenched it down and stared at it, sure her clothes were in the wardrobe yesterday. Violet took the scarf and strode to the top of the ward where a young nurse was rummaging through a filing cabinet.

"Where are my clothes?" she asked, brandishing the scarf.

The nurse looked warily towards her older colleague who was dispensing pills into tiny pots.

"Your clothes are in the laundry," the colleague said. "You can leave this afternoon."

"I want to leave now."

"Sorry, matron's orders."

Violet was about to say that she would leave in her nightclothes if she had to when a brown-haired nurse with an obvious squint pushed the door open. She approached the older nurse. "Is Miss Smith in here?" she asked.

"I am Miss Smith," said Violet coldly.

"There's a visitor for you," she said. "In the waiting room. Follow me."

The older nurse sighed, opened a locker and removed a white dressing gown and slippers. She handed them to Violet who followed the nurse up the corridor.

"In here." The nurse opened the door and guided Violet inside. The small room contained half a dozen armchairs and a coffee table. And a man. A man who was wearing a dog collar and who looked vaguely familiar from behind. He was staring out of the window into the hospital gardens but turned around when he heard the door open.

"Michael," Violet exclaimed. "What are you doing here? It is so good to see you."

"I came as soon as I heard," he said. "You poor thing."

"Would you like a cup of tea?" asked the nurse, who had been waiting by the door. Michael nodded, and she left them alone in the room.

"Oh Michael." A wave of nostalgia rushed over Violet at the sight of her old friend. She struggled to keep her tears at bay. The last time she had seen Michael was at The Vicarage in Fressingfield where she had lived happily as Mrs Harris' companion. She had not realised quite how much she missed it. Seeing the young curate made her unexpectedly homesick for a place she would never live in again.

"Come here." Michael embraced her. Violet was not tactile, as a rule, but Michael was a man of God and her friend. He was dear to her, like a brother, and the familiarity they shared felt natural.

"I have missed you," she whispered.

"My fault entirely. I've been busy getting to know my new parish and have not made time to visit."

"You have your own parish?" she asked. "At last. I am so pleased. Are you still in Suffolk?"

"No, over the border," he grinned. "I'm a Norfolk man now."

"Then I will come and visit," she said.

"Of course — and bring Lawrence with you."

"I'm not sure I want to," she said, with a frankness that startled her. "Sorry, that must sound cruel."

"Have you argued?"

"No, but he is difficult to be around. He is selfish."

"He sent for me, you know," said Michael. "He cares about you."

"Lawrence is like two different people," said Violet. "He can be kind and caring, then he ignores me or vexes me. And he is very moody, and I am not. He can reduce my good temper to a boiling rage in a few moments."

Michael laughed. "I have never known you to be in a boiling rage about anything."

"Perhaps that's an exaggeration," she said, "but you know what I mean."

Michael nodded. "I have come to take you back to the hotel," he said.

"Thank goodness," I was beginning to think I was a prisoner here.

"Well, you're not. I'm…"

The nurse interrupted as she returned carrying a wooden tray. It held a pot of tea, cups and a plate of biscuits.

Michael took it and thanked her. He stirred the teapot with a spoon and offered the biscuits to Violet. She selected one feeling hungry for the first time in days.

"Where is Lawrence?" she asked.

"I don't know. He sent a telegram."

"He hasn't visited. We are partners, but I don't know what he is doing half the time."

"Are you unhappy, Violet?"

"Not unhappy. I like the work, and I am good at most of

it. I understand people in a way that Lawrence doesn't, but we are not on an equal footing. He offered a partnership, yet he makes all the decisions and is always in control."

"He is still grieving, Violet. He was not always the way he is now."

"I know. Lawrence must have loved Catherine very much, but he hardly ever speaks of her."

"He never forgave himself for living when they died."

Michael poured two teas and offered one to Violet.

"What happened?"

"I don't know the details. I wasn't living in Bury at the time. I was studying. Francis told me all about it when I returned for the summer holidays. Catherine and the child, Lily, perished in a house fire. Lawrence came home one evening to find his house ablaze. He tried desperately to save them, and his neighbours restrained him to stop him needlessly sacrificing his own life. But there was nothing he could have done. The fire had taken too great a hold. He ruined his left hand trying to break down the burning door."

"That's awful. Poor Lawrence. He must have loved them very much."

"He worshipped Catherine," said Michael. "He adored her, and the child. It was a tragedy, all the more because they weren't meant to be home. Catherine and Lily were due to visit relatives, and Catherine decided not to go at the last minute."

"How awful. Did you know her?"

Michael nodded. "Very well. She was a family friend. My brother, Francis was the best man at their wedding."

"They must have been very much in love."

"They were," he said, "though the strength of his adoration, must have been difficult to bear sometimes.

Catherine was only human…" His voice trailed away as he stared across the garden, lost in thought.

"I will try to be more understanding in future," said Violet.

"It's been three years," said Michael. "Things will improve. Lawrence will get used to it. Just give him time. Anyway, I've booked a room at your hotel, so let's get you back there. Then we'll wait until Lawrence puts in an appearance."

Chapter Twenty-Six

THE REGAL HOTEL

They did not have long to wait. Michael and Violet were sitting in the reading room of The Regal Hotel pouring over a selection of old newspapers when Lawrence burst through the door with no warning.

"Ah, Michael. Good, I'm glad you came."

"Lawrence, is that you?"

Lawrence gazed at the backs of his hands and touched his cheeks. They were rough with artificial hair.

"God, just as well there's nobody else in here," said Lawrence, releasing the beard. He peeled the moustache from his lip and removed the coat which he placed on the arm of the chair, then touched his hand to his head. "Damn it all," he said. "I've left the hat behind. That will cost a pretty penny."

"You look dreadful," said Violet. "What on earth have you been doing.

"Investigating," Lawrence replied. "Sleeping in a doss house, to be precise." He scratched his leg and pulled up the bottom of the grimy trousers exposing his calf. "Bed bugs," he grimaced. "I'm not surprised. It was an awful place. Pity anyone who has to sleep there more than once."

"Was it really necessary?"

"I wouldn't have got anything out of her, the lodging house keeper that is, if I wasn't a customer. My presence there had to be believable."

"And did you?"

"Did I what?"

"Did you get anything out of her?"

"I think so," said Lawrence slowly, perching on the arm of the chair.

"I wouldn't," said Violet.

Lawrence stood, but it was too late. A smear of charcoal decorated the fawn covered chair.

He sighed.

"Don't touch it," said Violet. "Your hands are filthy, and you'll only make it worse." She pulled a delicate lace handkerchief from the arm of her dress and dabbed at the stain, removing the worst of it.

"You seem happier," said Lawrence. "Has Michael been looking after you?"

Michael smiled. "She doesn't need much looking after."

"He has been wonderful company," said Violet. "Just what I needed after two days alone."

"I'm sorry," said Lawrence. "There was something I needed to do."

"Well, you didn't have to make me a prisoner," Violet said. "If it hadn't been for Michael, I wouldn't speak to you again. The matron wouldn't let me leave."

"It was for your own good," said Lawrence. "It's not safe for you to be alone."

"I'll decide what's right for me," said Violet.

"Well, we're all here together now," said Michael, in a conciliatory tone.

"Yes, we are," said Lawrence, "and there is much to discuss. But first I need to get out of this disguise before the odd job man sees me."

"You didn't," sighed Violet.

"I'll put it back," said Lawrence shortly, "with a few extra coins to make up for the missing hat. It was worth it. Give me ten minutes, and I'll tell you all about it."

Lawrence left the room and shut the door with a soft click.

"See what I mean," said Violet. "He is intolerable."

Michael spent the next few minutes defending Lawrence's behaviour. True, his friend had taken charge of Violet as if she was his wife or child. But Lawrence's concern for Violet was evident to Michael. He was both worried about her and passionate about his case.

"But what is he investigating?" countered Violet. "He jumps around from one matter to another, none of which I expect to see any income from."

"He has always been a little unorthodox," said Michael. "He was something of a maverick even when he was in the force, but his methods work. He has never failed to solve a case."

Violet took a breath and was about to reply when Lawrence returned looking cleaner and more presentable."

"Better," said Violet raising an eyebrow. "Are you going to tell us what you discovered over the last few days?"

Lawrence relayed the information as succinctly as possible. Violet and Michael sat quietly and listened to Lawrence speak without interrupting. When he finally finished, Violet rose and paced angrily around the room. "I simply don't believe it," she snapped.

"What don't you believe?" asked Lawrence, surprised. "I'm not making it up."

"I know. But the idea of a conspiracy from within the Society for Psychical Research is ludicrous. I've met them, Lawrence. They are gentlemen."

"Gentlemen are not immune from evil."

"I can vouch for that," said Michael.

"I daresay," Violet continued. "But why would you believe the word of a man like D'Onston over the actions of educated men. They are not as you describe, Lawrence. I will introduce you to Arthur, and you will see for yourself."

"That is out of the question," said Lawrence. "And you must not see him again, or any other man who belongs to this organisation. It could be any one of them."

"Arthur is taking me to Kew Gardens tomorrow," said Violet, "and I am going."

"You're supposed to be my partner," said Lawrence. "Your job is to help with the investigation, not to go swanning around London with your gentleman friend."

Violet gasped. "I do not know what you are implying, but there is nothing of that nature between Dr Myers and I."

"Yet," snapped Lawrence.

"She could always use the friendship to your advantage," Michael suggested.

"How?"

"She can learn as much from being an acquaintance, as she can from an investigation."

"Or she could be throwing herself into the path of a sinister society. Think of your safety, Violet."

"I am perfectly safe with Arthur. The man who hurt me

was rough and uncouth. He was not a gentleman. He is not someone I have ever met."

"How would you know. It was dark."

"His voice was rough, his hands coarse and the smell of him..." She shuddered. "I cannot tell you how I know, but he was not a gentleman. Not at all."

"You sound very certain," said Michael.

"I am positive", Violet replied, taking a seat.

Michael leaned forward and pressed her hand. She smiled.

"How will you move this investigation forward?" asked Michael.

"I have to get close to them somehow," Lawrence replied.

"I will introduce you," offered Violet.

"Don't be ridiculous," said Lawrence. "They can't know we are investigators."

"They don't know," said Violet. "I met Arthur and Mr Podmore in Chelmondiston. I was masquerading as an old friend of Alice Woodward's."

Lawrence sighed. "Who would I be, then?"

"My brother," she said. "They would be none the wiser."

"No, it's no good," said Lawrence. "They cannot see us together. They may have noticed me with D'Onston already. He is an extraordinary man. Quite unflappable, yet he intends to leave his hotel for a few weeks to be on the safe side. I cannot take any chances. We will have to think of something else."

"You can always go to the meeting," said Violet.

"What meeting?"

"The monthly general meeting of the SPR. It's at Westminster Town Hall," she said. "Look." She reached for a small pile of books beside the newspapers and peeled off a printed page. She passed it to Lawrence.

"That's tonight," he said.

"No time like the present," Violet retorted. "I would like to go. It sounds fascinating."

Lawrence gazed at the agenda. "If thought-transference and 'double personality of the ambulatory type,' is your idea of entertainment, then yes. Personally, I would rather go fishing."

"You hate fishing," said Michael.

"Quite. I will have to bear this meeting, I suppose."

"Why don't we all go?" Michael suggested.

"We can't," said Lawrence.

"Yes, we can. As long as you and Violet stay apart, there shouldn't be a problem."

"I see what you mean. You and Violet could go together, and she can talk to whoever she likes. I will sit alone and try to scrape an acquaintance with one of the other committee members. Anything that gets me closer to the organisation could be beneficial. Violet will be safe with you."

"I will be perfectly safe anyway," said Violet. "You are welcome to come with me, if you want, Michael," she continued, "but there is no need."

"I should like to," he said, "although I won't be wearing my dog collar. It wouldn't feel right. I can't relate to their way of thinking, but that is no reason to avoid attending."

"Jolly good. Then that's what we will do. Only the small matter of returning this." Lawrence picked up the dirty coat he had worn earlier and left the room.

"Are you any clearer about what we are doing?" asked Violet, "because I'm not."

Michael smiled. "I've seen him like this before," he said.

"He's happier than he has been in a long time, and what's more, he's on the trail."

"On the trail?"

"It's his sixth sense; an inner confidence in what he is doing. He has a goal and needs to work out how to get there. But he foresees danger, Violet. Whether he is mistaken or not, only time will tell. We should take great care, you especially."

Chapter Twenty-Seven

MEETING AT THE TOWN HALL

Lawrence thought of all the things he would rather do than sit in a draughty room in Westminster Town Hall on a cold March night. It was a long list. The three of them had travelled separately from The Regal Hotel. Michael and Violet took a tram while Lawrence walked. He underestimated the distance and arrived late. There were no seats left at the front of the room leaving Lawrence no choice but to sit in the back row. A stout woman with a large hat was directly in front of him and he struggled to see the stage upon which the committee members were sitting.

The hall was full, and the audience occupied about seventy seats, with latecomers still arriving. Lawrence wondered at their credulity. It was hard enough to imagine twenty people interested in this nonsense, but a full hall? They would be buying snake oil next. He had upset Violet with a similar remark earlier. She tried to persuade him that the SPR investigators used scientific experimentation. Lawrence countered that by denying that any test was capable of proving the existence of spirits and had continued arguing tactlessly. It was all very well pretending that spiritualism had a basis in psychology, but what was the point? What did it achieve? In the end, Violet walked away clenching her jaw. Lawrence had no intention of considering her point of view, and she had better things to do.

The crowd in the hall came from all walks of life. Some of them dressed in utilitarian garb, and others in finery. They represented all parts of society, sharing a common interest that Lawrence was wholly unable to appreciate. He decided to ignore them.

He scanned the crowd, looking for Violet and Michael and located them on the second row where they were gazing at the stage. A handsome man in a sharp grey suit waved at Violet. Even from his vantage point at the back of the room, Lawrence saw her beam with pleasure. He frowned. Violet's regard for the doctor was nauseating and made him feel physically ill. His heart pumped faster, and his ungloved right hand grew clammy. He felt unaccountably odd and wanted, no needed, to leave the room. His urge to flee almost got the upper hand and he had to muster every bit of will power to force himself to stay. Once the first speaker began the adrenaline rush left, and he tried to understand what had happened. Lawrence had no conscious desire for Violet Smith, so why had his body reacted so badly to her obvious admiration for another man.

The gentleman now standing on the stage sported a long, white beard and announced himself as Henry Sidgwick. The name was familiar to Lawrence from a leaflet that Violet had given him to read earlier that afternoon. Though he had only managed a paragraph, it was enough to know that Sidgwick was the President of the SPR. A natural speaker, Sidgwick addressed the crowd in a relaxed manner and joked that they were lucky to have avoided the committee meeting earlier that day which had gone on much longer than usual. Sidgwick announced the addition of another new member and nine new associate members. A further twenty-four new associates had also joined the American branch. Lawrence raised his eyes to the ceiling, then thought the better of it. He was here to observe and find a way into the organisation. Drawing attention to himself by being openly cynical, was hardly the best way to go about it.

Henry Sidgwick spoke again. "You've heard enough from me. Let me introduce Mr Frank Podmore. He will be talking to you about Dr Von Schrenk's experiments in thought-transference."

The audience clapped, and Podmore took to the stage. Lawrence watched closely. Podmore was younger than Sidgwick, wore a well-trimmed light-brown beard and spoke eloquently. There was something epicene about his appearance that Lawrence could not quite identify. Podmore's talk was long and tedious and described Von Schrenk's experiments in clairvoyance. It was too convoluted for Lawrence to comprehend fully. In basic terms, the tests seemed to involve one person drawing pictures and another using thought transference to predict the result. Podmore seemed pleased with the test conclusions, but to Lawrence's cynical eyes, there was little accuracy. It was all subjective. After ten minutes, Lawrence felt his eyes grow heavy and began to worry that he was in danger of falling asleep. He considered going for a short walk when Henry Sidgwick returned to the stage and thanked Frank Podmore. Sidgwick spoke of his regard for Von Schrenk and introduced the next speaker, a man called Walter Leaf who was another bearded gentleman.

Lawrence felt his clean-shaven face. He had never followed the trend for whiskers and disagreed with the doctors who prescribed facial hair for good health. Lawrence had once grown a beard and found it scratchy and unnatural. Besides, he had an excellent barber back in Bury. Claude Larke was an amiable man with a ready wit. Even in Lawrence's darkest, most introverted moments, he had always benefited from half an hour in the barber's chair. Larke had an uncanny knack of making him feel better about the world. Small wonder there was always a queue outside his shop.

Walter Leaf spoke of dual personalities. His talk was more interesting than Podmore's, and the concept seemed vaguely familiar to Lawrence. He puzzled over it for a few moments then remembered the stage play about Dr Jekyll and Mr Hyde. Of course. The story was sheer fantasy, but it had become popular in the theatres. Violet was a fan and had tried to make Lawrence buy the book. He had resisted at first, then read a few chapters to please her before discarding it halfway through. It was a waste of his time, but very much Violet's chosen reading matter. She would enjoy this talk.

Lawrence was glad when Walter Leaf finished speaking, but his relief was short-lived. He assumed it would mark the end of the meeting, but Henry Sidgwick returned to the stage and announced a second half. Lawrence bolted for the exit and into the gentleman's room. He finished his ablutions before returning to the foyer of the Town Hall. Sidgwick had announced a ten-minute recess, in his absence. Most attendees, including Violet and Michael, were directed to a side room for tea and biscuits. Lawrence could not bring himself to join them. The thought of watching Violet fawn over her SPR friends and Doctor

Myers, in particular, was too much to bear. He stayed where he was and contemplated his next move. Fate intervened when a dark-haired man, carrying too many books to negotiate the step into the foyer, stumbled. Books and journals tumbled to the floor. Lawrence detached himself from the wall on which he had been leaning and went to his aid. He collected the fallen books and passed them to the flustered man.

"Here you are Mr ..." His voice trailed away.

"Barkworth. Thomas Barkworth. Thank you for your help."

Lawrence picked up an SPR journal which lay splayed open on the floor. He examined it before placing it on top of the pile of books held by Barkworth. "Ah. Another article about double personality. I enjoyed the talk — fascinating and persuasive."

"Hmmm," said Barkworth. "It depends on how you approach it. I fear that Myers and I will come to blows on the matter of multiplicity of personality before long."

"Dr Myers?" asked Lawrence.

Barkworth stared at him. "Frederick Myers, of course. He is too reliant upon the testimony of those with recognised mental conditions. Well, outside the study of automatic writing, that is. Personality does not vary on a whim, you know."

Lawrence didn't know. The man in front of him could have been speaking Swahili, and it would have made more sense. But, now was not the time for honesty.

"Oh, I agree," said Lawrence, "though I only have a layman's understanding of the subject. That's why I came tonight."

"You're not a member?" asked Barkworth. "You should be if you want to know more. It is a difficult subject."

"I don't live in London," said Lawrence.

"Our members come from all over the country."

"Indeed? Well, in that case, I will consider it."

Lawrence was about to ask how to become a member when Violet and Michael entered the foyer together with Doctor Myers and Frank Podmore. Lawrence recognised Myers and scowled, glad that he was undercover and not required to acknowledge his presence or be polite.

"Ah, Barkworth," said Frank Podmore. "There you are. Are you speaking tonight?"

"No. I can't stay until the end. I have an appointment in Kensington."

"Bad luck, old man. There's a fine example of veridical hallucination in this month's reports."

Lawrence watched Violet as the men spoke. She had barely taken her eyes of Doctor Myers. Michael had almost given the game away by raising his hand. He realised his mistake in time and lowered it without waving, but he could not meet Lawrence's eyes.

"Were you interested in a membership?" asked Barkworth, resuming the conversation.

"Yes. I want to join if it's not too much trouble."

"Why don't you wait until after the case readings and I'll look you out a form," said Podmore.

"Oh, that's a shame. I have to go now," said Lawrence. "I say, I'm in town for a few days. Can I collect it from your Headquarters instead?"

"I suppose so," said Podmore. "Yes, why not. We're at the Adelphi, Mr, sorry. I didn't quite catch your name."

"Blatworthy," said Lawrence. "Alistair Blatworthy. Pleased to meet you."

Violet glared at Lawrence. She did not approve of his alias. The first rule of good detection was that pseudonyms should be commonplace. She had never met a Blatworthy, much less one who masqueraded as a quantity surveyor, whatever that was. Lawrence acknowledged her look of disgust. At least she had managed to tear her eyes away from Myers chiselled features.

"Come now," Arthur Myers had taken Violet's arm and was guiding her into the hall. Michael followed redundantly behind.

"Right," said Frank, "We'll see you over the next few days. It doesn't matter when you come as long as it's during the day. The doorman will let you in."

Lawrence nodded. He moved a few feet away before bending to tie a shoelace.

Podmore and Barkworth continued to talk about their movements for the rest of the week. Both were due at HQ within the next few days, and Lawrence grinned as he heard Frank Podmore discuss his plans for tomorrow. Podmore was going to Kew gardens which implied that he had invited himself to join Violet and Myers. Lawrence wondered how Violet would react. It was a small glimmer of levity in an otherwise tedious evening. At least he had managed to gain legitimate access to the SPR HQ which meant he could avoid the rest of the meeting. Lawrence whistled as he began the walk back to Lambeth.

Chapter Twenty-Eight

PSEUDONYM

Saturday 7th March 1891

The weekend did not get off to a good start. A heavy knocking at the hotel room door disturbed Lawrence just after dawn. It took a few moments for him to wake from a deep sleep. He peeled the bedclothes away, shrugged on a dressing gown and answered the door. It opened to reveal a plainclothes policeman.

"My guv'nor wants to see you," he said.

"Who is your governor?"

"Inspector Moore, and you'd better make it snappy".

"Tell him I'll be there by 8.30."

The policeman pursed his lips and nodded. "You'd better be," he said.

Lawrence mulled it over as he dressed. There were many ways he could have dealt with telling Henry about the D'Onston situation, any of which were better than the choice he had made. Lawrence's decision to say nothing left him in a quandary. On the one hand, he had promised to keep Henry informed. On the other, connecting the Ripper to the SPR might jeopardise his investigation. Not that he could count on Henry to believe any of it. The story scarcely seemed credible to Lawrence. And another thing. Lawrence couldn't remember telling Henry about Violet's attack which was bound to annoy him. He decided to stop speculating about why Henry had summoned him and put all his efforts into getting dressed.

Half an hour later, Lawrence arrived at Scotland Yard. It was quieter than usual. The policeman behind the reception desk waved him through, and he climbed the stairs, cleared his throat and knocked on Henry Moore's door.

"Come."

He entered.

"Where the blazes is D'Onston?" asked Henry, without his usual affable greeting.

"Ah," said Lawrence. "Has he gone?"

"You know damn well he has. Not completely. He obviously intends to return at some stage, but he's taken enough possessions to cover a lengthy stay somewhere else. I haven't the least idea where that could be."

"What makes you think I know?"

"We've been tailing him. You were the last person to see him. And I have it on good authority that you forced your way into his room. You haven't harmed him?"

"Of course not. He's probably gone to ground."

"Why?"

"Because he thinks he knows something. He believes there's a connection between the Ripper murders and the case I have been investigating in Brighton."

"Well I don't," said Henry. "Even Edmund Reid is having doubts about this last murder. The more time that passes, the less likely it seems. What did D'Onston have to say."

Lawrence unburdened himself. He abandoned his intention to avoid telling Henry Moore anything he didn't need to know. There seemed little point now he was sitting here in front of him. The story came out in a rush of words.

"So, you're telling me that D'Onston blackmailed the SPR because one of them killed a man who died an accidental death."

Lawrence nodded.

"And an inquest recorded this verdict."

"Yes."

"Furthermore, this man killed two women who we do not recognise as Ripper victims?"

"Yes…"

"And certain members of the society have conspired to protect their reputation, which they have done by concealing the identity of the so-called murderer…"

"Well, when you put it like that…"

"It's preposterous, Lawrence. I am surprised at you."

"It's no more unlikely than the suggestion that D'Onston was in possession of half a dozen bloodied neckties."

Henry shifted uncomfortably in his chair. "Miss Johnson withdrew the accusation yesterday," he said. "Her friend, Miss Collins, said she had made it up out of spite."

"That's one thing I am certain of," said Lawrence. "There was no space in his room big enough to contain a tin trunk. It is not in The Triangle Hotel if it exists at all."

"And neither is he," said Henry. "Which may be for the best. I am still not wholly satisfied with his innocence, but there will come a time when we have to stop tracking his movements. Perhaps this is it."

"He is telling the truth," said Lawrence. "At first I thought he had attacked Violet, but I don't believe it now."

"Violet?"

"Yes, my partner. A man attacked her the other night in the East End. She ended up with a cut across her throat."

"I heard about that. I did not realise you were acquainted. What has this got to do with D'Onston."

"I thought I saw him nearby, but he says he wasn't there."

"And this was Wednesday night?"

Lawrence nodded.

Henry rifled through the cards on his desk. "What time did it happen?"

"It must have been between 7.30 and nine."

"Then it wasn't D'Onston. He was at the hotel. He left briefly about 5 o'clock and returned within the half hour."

"I was certain. It looked like him."

"There are all sorts of thugs in the East End. They were probably after your friend's money."

Lawrence opened his mouth to protest, then reconsidered. He had done his duty by telling Henry about D'Onston, less the finer details. Henry clearly didn't believe a word of it. Neither had he associated the attack on Violet with the Ripper or the SPR. Lawrence could continue investigating with a clear conscience.

"You are probably right," he sighed.

"Yes. Wish Violet well from me. I think that's all, Lawrence. If you come across D'Onston again, then have the goodness to let me know. Send me an invoice for your work. When are you going back?"

"I'll be here for another few days," said Lawrence.

"Come over for dinner before you go. Mary would love to see you."

"I will," said Lawrence. "Thank you."

He shook Henry's hand and left the office, before heading towards The Adelphi and the headquarters of the SPR.

Lawrence didn't hang around waiting for transport and hurried along the Embankment arriving in Buckingham Street, slightly overheated. He climbed the small flight of steps and banged on the front door which opened, almost immediately, to reveal a lightly tanned, dark-haired man in his early fifties. Lawrence recalled his conversation with George Smith back in Brighton. The man in front of him must be the doorman with the exceptional memory. What was his name? Lawrence searched his own less efficient faculties. Ah, yes. His name was Elias Haim.

The doorman was an inch or two shorter than Lawrence and what remained of a receding hairline was slicked back under a layer of oil. His skin was olive and suggested Mediterranean origins.

Lawrence doffed his hat and explained the purpose of his visit.

"You can see Mr Podmore," said Haim, in a deep voice bearing traces of an accent. "He will help."

"I met Mr Barkworth last night. Is he expected today?"

"Mr Barkworth is in Chigwell. He won't be here until nine o'clock tomorrow."

"And Myers?"

"Mr Frederick Myers or Doctor Arthur Myers?"

"Dr Arthur Myers."

"He is indisposed," said Elias.

Lawrence hoped the problem wasn't too trivial. He was

tempted to ask why, but any further display of interest might look suspicious. "May I see Mr Podmore, then?"

The doorman nodded and showed him to a small room containing three high backed armchairs.

"You can wait here," he said.

Lawrence surveyed the room. Copies of the SPR journal lay in date order across a table. He took one and flicked through without reading it. Two minutes later a man appeared. Lawrence recognised him from the previous evening. It was Frank Podmore.

He shook Lawrence's hand. "Ah, Mr Blatworthy," he said. "You are keen to join our ranks if I remember."

Lawrence nodded. "Yes, I want to learn more," he said.

"Good to hear. Anything in particular?"

Lawrence tried to remember what Podmore had talked about the previous night. "The work on thought transference interests me most," he said.

The flattery worked. Podmore beamed. "Yes, I agree," he said. "It is a subject close to my heart. Now, join me in the library. I'll take your details there."

Lawrence followed. The library was empty of people, but bookcases surrounded the four back to back desks in the centre of the room. Every available shelf was full.

"You have an impressive library," said Lawrence.

"Yes. It's a testimony to our friend Edmund Gurney," said Frank. "He was the creator."

"My congratulations to Mr Gurney for a fine effort."

"He is no longer with us," said Frank, shortly.

"I'm sorry to hear that."

Frank ignored him and pulled a piece of yellowing paper from a tray near one of the desks. "Fill this in. I'll be back shortly." He left the room. Lawrence scribbled a fictitious address across the form. He couldn't shift the sense that he had displeased Frank Podmore. When the application was complete, he prowled the room scrutinising the bookcases. All manner of books and pamphlets about psychical research and esoteric teachings covered the shelves, enough to cure any amount of insomnia. Lawrence located a narrow desk nestled between two of the bookcases. A stack of wooden trays towered to one side. One was empty, and another contained blank subscription forms of the kind he had just completed. A third smaller tray held letters from the public. Lawrence rifled through them. There was nothing of interest, only reams of paper containing dubious accounts of spiritual manifestations. Lawrence pulled a face and put the tray away.

He turned to the narrow desk and saw a single drawer with a keyhole, then pulled the handle anticipating a locked drawer. It slid open. Inside, was a smaller drawer with an inverted 'J' shaped keyhole. This time, Lawrence wasn't so lucky. The door was firmly locked and impossible to budge. He extracted a handful of folded documents from the small drawer below and located a little ledger containing contact details for the committee. Lawrence opened the pages and read their names, muttering out loud. Henry Sidgwick, President, Eleanor Sidgwick — must be his wife. Frederick Myers — no doubt the brother of Violet's infatuation, the slimy Doctor Myers. "Hello, what's this?" Lawrence traced his finger down the page. 'Elias Haim, doorman, Gunpowder Alley, off White's Row, Spitalfields.' It can't be. He held his breath. Surely a coincidence? Lawrence didn't hesitate. He pocketed the ledger and left Alistair Blatworthy's application form on the desk. He waited until the doorman answered the call of nature and exited swiftly through the front door.

Chapter Twenty-Nine

THE DOUBLE EVENT

15th October 1888

By the end of September, I was a fully-fledged killer. I murdered quite deliberately, and it filled a void within me I had not known existed. During the day, I behaved as usual and was professional and upstanding — trustworthy. My affliction grew worse as the day wore on, becoming uncontrollable late at night. But it was no longer necessary for an episode to occur before I left, knife in hand, to fulfil my yearning for blood. Sometimes, it worked that way, but other times, it was a purposeful act within my control.

The murder in Hanbury Street at the beginning of September was both planned and unintentional. I had resisted the urge to carry a knife since the incident in Bucks Row at the end of August. But I grew tense and angry as the new month arrived. Only the sweet release of steel slicing flesh could reduce the urges that occupied so many of my thoughts. With this in mind, I purchased a new knife and placed it in my coat pocket. On Saturday the 8th of September, I used it.

I recall preparing for bed that evening. I was in my night attire, and I remember ascending the stairs and placing my hand on the door of my bedchamber. Then my tongue grew heavy and felt as if it were too big for my mouth and I knew it to be the sign of an impending attack.

I must have dressed in an automative state, for when I came to my senses, I was wandering the streets of Spitalfields in my usual apparel. I had not, at this stage, encountered anyone else nor committed a crime as far as I could tell from the cleanliness of my knife. Glimmers of memory returned, and I sought an anchor from where I might collect my thoughts. I found myself staring at a sign in Hanbury Street. The area seemed familiar, and I concluded that Aldgate Station was near and Liverpool Street, closer still. I could have caught a train home without difficulty, yet I did not. I chose to stay. Every previous killing had begun while I was not me, but here I was in full control of my faculties, fascinated by my condition. Though parts of my psyche repulsed me, I found the idea of self-assessment irresistible. Could I commit another murder when there was no impairment to my conscious state? I tried to think of it as a scientific matter though I did not deceive myself into believing that it was entirely experimental. I longed to see blood pulsing as it spurted from a wound wrought by my knife. To watch red-black pools leech from marble skin and settle in puddles on the ground. A work of art — my creation. So, I waited on the street corner and before long, one of those women, the working kind, came weaving down the road. She couldn't walk in a straight line.

I stepped out of the shadows and into her path, then took off my hat and allowed her full view of my face. It was a purposeful act and meant no turning back. She greeted me and offered to perform an act of the most revolting nature. Naturally, I accepted, having no intention of committing it. I followed her into a small yard, bathed in darkness. She made towards the rear, but I steered her into a recess between the yard steps and the fence. There was just enough light for me to work, but not enough for anyone to see me.

She was not afraid. When I stood behind her and reached for her chin, she did not suffer as my knife sliced cleanly through her throat from left to right. I am not a cruel man. I have never caused them alarm whether in my conscious or unconscious state. I have always tried to make the end quick and painless.

The woman was dead before I placed her on the floor. I positioned her, with legs drawn up and knees turned out, so I could gaze at the expanse of flesh beneath her clothes. Her abdomen was pale and swollen. I visualised where her organs might lay beneath the skin. Then, by the light of the pale moon, I plunged my knife into the side of her stomach. It slipped through her abdominal wall, and her intestines spilt through the hole. I pulled them out, and they slid through my fingers like slippery eels as I placed them over her shoulder and out of my way. I thought about taking a kidney but decided upon her uterus which I removed from her pelvis without difficulty. I placed it in my palm and held it towards a shaft of light from a nearby window. It lay there glistening, warm and wet in my hand. I marvelled at its beauty. It was round and fat and bloody with the appendages still intact — and it was mine. I decided to keep it and wrapped it in a piece of oilskin cloth which I had in my pocket. It felt warm against my trouser leg.

I returned my gaze to the body before me. What remained of the stomach was flat and empty and held no further interest. So, I left.

September was a busy month. The urge came upon me once again. I pretended to fight against it, to satisfy my conscience, but there didn't seem to be any consequences to my actions. On the last day of September, I gave in to my baser instincts.

My first attempt was frustrating though it should have been perfect. I did not lose one single minute to somnambulistic automation. My deeds were all within my control. I had expected to lapse at some stage having experienced many blank moments that month, and not only for short periods. Several severe losses of consciousness had occurred throughout the proceeding weeks. I found it surprising that my friends did not notice. At the start of the year, they had monitored my every move. The trusted three watched me constantly, and I was rarely left alone. I can only assume that they thought my indiscretions were over.

Remarkably, they did not associate the attacks on Ada Wilson and Annie Millwood with the more recent Whitechapel crimes. There was no reason why they should. The police had not connected them either. My friends discussed the Ripper crimes openly, suggesting they were the work of a monster. It was not for me to disabuse them. They would no doubt try to stop me if they knew. And I had no intention of stopping. Not yet.

In the early hours of the 30th of September, I selected a suitable victim. We walked together to a godforsaken yard off Berner Street where I struck. I pulled her head back using her checked scarf. It was a mistake. Seconds before my blade sliced through her vocal cords she cried out. Only once, but the sound shattered the still of the night air, and I heard the sound of heavy steps. I flattened myself against the wall as three men raced towards the yard. My heart was beating through my chest. I whispered silent prayers to the God responsible for my affliction, hoping he would not let me slip into an automative state, where I was vulnerable to detection.

One of the men saw the body and shouted to his friends in a language I did not know. Then they ran in separate directions, calling for the police. I took this opportunity to slink away, and I picked through the alleys and walkways until I was a long way from Berner Street. I loitered in front of Aldgate Station and contemplated returning home. Except I didn't want to. I couldn't. Cutting a throat wasn't enough. It was worse than having done nothing at all. It was like inhaling a full-bodied port, without taking so much as a sip.

Sweat trickled down my temples to the throb of a headache. I smelled blood, and I lusted for it. I could have, should have taken the train back west. But I had a job to finish, and I continued past the station, down Aldgate High Street and towards St Katherine Cree Church.

The sign for Mitre Street was near the church and just beyond it a woman leaned against the corner of Mitre Square. She was waiting for someone, waiting for me, as it turned out. The woman wore a black dress, a red scarf and a black bonnet. It struck me as wholly appropriate that the slick of scarlet silk would soon glow a bloodier red. As I walked towards her, a crowd of men strolled down the road. Their presence was off-putting and might have discouraged me had she not called out in a sing-song cockney accent, "Hello me old cock."

I turned away from the approaching men, stopped and tipped my hat, keeping my face out of sight. I was not wearing my usual head attire, but a felt flat cap I happened upon which was eminently suitable for my visits to the East End. I exchanged a few words with the woman, and she laughed, wholly confident in her safety. The papers were rife with horror stories about the London Ripper, but not one of my victims took a modicum of care. They were reckless and thought themselves invincible. Or their need for gin was more important than their need for self-preservation. Either way, it was of no concern to me.

The woman laughed as she placed her hand upon my chest and whispered in my ear. She made the usual proposition, and though I had no inclination for her offer, she was not unattractive. The idea did not turn my stomach inside out. I followed her into the dark square, keeping my head turned away. She reached behind and grabbed my hand. I became unbalanced and found myself looking directly into the faces of the men who, by now, were standing only a few yards away.

Two of them ignored me, but the third stared into my eyes. His pupils bore into mine, and after a few seconds he snatched his gaze away, put his hands in his pockets and continued walking, head bowed. I knew that he would remember me. He had seen something in my eyes — something that caused concern. Somehow, he knew me for what I was, and he was afraid. It was one thing letting the women see my face, but quite another to leave witnesses. And at that moment, a wave of anger rose within me, the like of which I have never felt before or since. I put my hand upon her shoulder and pushed her further into Mitre Square. "Steady on," she said, "show a little patience."

I showed neither patience nor pity. I sliced her neck left to right, nicking her ear lobe as I slashed a deep wound into her throat. It was a quicker end than she deserved for making me visible. Then I set to work on the body. I wanted a kidney this time, and nothing else would do. I removed it, tossing the intestines over her shoulder, trying to quell the anger but it never left me. Her face was serene above her mutilated corpse. It was the 29th of September when I set out on my murderous mission — Michaelmas Day. St Michael the archangel defeated the antichrist and transported all souls to heaven. Well, he could have this soul once my knife had prepared her. I carved two chevrons in her cheeks, nicked her lower eyelids and took away the tip of her nose. Better, but not good enough. I finished with a cut to the bridge of her nose and removed a large part of her womb. No longer in tranquil repose, she lay savaged and torn. God forgive me, but I felt better for it. Once I imagined myself a good man, worthy of St Michael. What was I now? A human devil? A cohort of Satan? Or a psychopath? The latter was a better fit. A condition of the mind brought on by my illness. An excuse for slayings beyond my control.

I had my fill for the evening and left her lying empty on the floor. I had taken a long time. The longest yet, and I felt calm and in control until I looked at my hands. They were wet with blood — a careless mistake. I had worn thin gloves on every prior occasion, but anger had made me thoughtless. I ripped a piece of an apron from the otherwise useless body and wiped the worst of the blood from my hands. But nothing short of water could remove the bloodstain. I couldn't use the main roads and risk detection, so I wandered through the back streets of Whitechapel until I found a trough in Goulston Street with enough water to clean off the worst of the blood. I wiped wet hands on my coat and dropped the apron to the floor. It fell on a piece of chalk stone which inspired me to mischief. The men I saw earlier had spoken a language I did not comprehend but was most likely Yiddish. The police would be out in full force looking for their killer, and the men had seen me. A little clue might divert them. I grasped the chalk and using lower class colloquial language, I wrote an ambiguous and meaningless message. 'The Juwes are not the men to be blamed for nothing.' Then,

I made my way back home. It was dark and quiet. Quite different to usual. The metropolis of London fizzed with energy. It was full of people, full of noise and disease and poverty and wealth — busy, always busy. Except at night. It never ceased to amaze me how easy it was to glide through the city undisturbed. I arrived home, satisfied and replete. In the early hours of the morning, I unlocked the door to my home, went inside and walked to my study where I unwrapped the oilskin from its home in my pocket. I placed the kidney in a jar next to the preserved uterus for my future enjoyment.

Chapter Thirty

A CANCELLATION

Back at the Regal, Violet was in a sombre mood. She stared despondently at a china teacup and stirred it repeatedly. Lawrence sighed as he placed his hand over hers and removed the teaspoon. They were sitting in the dining room looking out of the small window which overlooked an even smaller patch of garden. It was an unloved, unattended garden with a gravel covered area to the side of the lawn. Several bicycles in varying states of disrepair lay on the uncut grass.

Lawrence had arrived back from the Embankment just in time to eat a modest lunch. Michael had taken advantage of his presence to stretch his legs and spend some time alone. Lawrence attacked his bread and soup with relish, but Violet picked miserably at hers. She nibbled the roll and made a perfunctory effort with the bowl of soup.

"Are you going to eat that?" Lawrence asked.

"I'm not hungry."

"Then I'll have it."

Violet sighed and pushed the bowl towards Lawrence,

then picked up the bread roll and dropped it on his side plate. He raised an eyebrow. "What's wrong?"

"I feel like a dog on a lead," she said, irritably.

"You don't look like one."

"It's not funny, Lawrence. I'm bored. I was looking forward to going to Kew."

"Ask Michael to take you."

"It won't be the same."

Lawrence put his spoon down. "You seem to be more interested in your companions than the gardens."

"It is nice to go in a group."

"What happened? Why was it called off?"

"Frank Podmore can't make it so Arthur, I mean Doctor Myers, has postponed our trip until tomorrow."

"I saw Podmore at the Headquarters," said Lawrence, conversationally. "No sign of Myers, though."

"I expect there was a medical emergency or something like that. He is a very busy man."

"I daresay. Anyway, I made another discovery."

"Yes?"

"This." Lawrence took the little ledger from his pocket and placed it on the table.

Violet picked it up. "Lots of names and addresses," she said. There's nothing interesting. How does it help?"

"Look where the doorman lives." Lawrence pointed to the bottom of the page.

"Off White's Row? It's only a coincidence, Lawrence."

"No. It's more than that. Both Annie Millwood and Frances Coles had links to White's Row, and here it is again."

"I'm sure lots of people live there. That is no reason to connect it to the case."

"There's every reason. Elias is the most likely person to

have received D'Onston's blackmail letter. He is always in the building."

"Why would he bring trouble to his neighbourhood?"

"I don't know. That's why I'm going there.

Violet sighed. "You are frustrating, Lawrence. Why must you always base your decisions on instinct?"

"It's served me well up to now."

"What about me?"

"Michael will be back soon. He can take you out."

"I don't want to go out with Michael. I'm coming with you."

"No."

"I've hardly participated in this investigation. There is no point in being here."

"You'll have to bear it. I'm still worried about your safety."

"I am perfectly safe, Lawrence. It's clear you don't want me involved."

"Now who's being illogical?" The door opened, and Lawrence looked up. "Ah, Michael. Glad you are back. I'm going out."

"Nice to see you, Lawrence, albeit fleeting."

Lawrence ignored the sarcasm and left for the hotel basement where he misappropriated the odd job man's coat again. The poor man had noticed his missing hat and another, more dishevelled substitute was hanging on the door. Lawrence duly removed it feeling a moment of guilt. It did not last. Lawrence hurried upstairs, but as he took the stairs, two at a time, his shoelace became untied. When he stopped to fasten it, he yanked the frayed lace too hard, and a large piece came away in his hand. Lawrence swore beneath his breath. Karma had intervened. It served him right for borrowing things without asking. Time was short, and Lawrence didn't have any spare laces. He approached his room and noticed that the occupant of the opposite room had left his polished shoes outside the door. They were brown and a mismatch, but they would do. Lawrence abandoned his brand-new rule about taking things that didn't belong to him. He tugged a lace out and bolted to his room where he threaded it into his shoe before preparing his tramp disguise.

The rear door of the hotel was stiff. Lawrence put a shoulder to the swollen door and heaved. As he picked his way past the broken bicycles in the garden, he glanced through the dining room window. Michael was standing over Violet with a protective arm around her shoulder. She was sitting down with her head in her hand. Lawrence shrugged. She must have a headache, he thought.

Chapter Thirty-One

AN UNCOMFORTABLE NIGHT

It was late afternoon by the time Lawrence arrived in Spitalfields. The weather was cold but dry, and the streets were busy. Lawrence had hoped to locate Elias Haim's house without drawing attention to himself, but it was not to be. Having walked the length of White's Row several times, Lawrence realised that Gunpowder Alley did not have the benefit of a street sign. Several alleys were leading off, and it could have been any one of them. Worse still, there were no numbers on any of the houses. He would need help. By the time he had traversed White's Row for the third time, a group of women had emerged from Spitalfields Chambers. They sat outside the front door chatting to each other. A young boy dressed in frayed trousers finishing halfway up his legs rolled a wooden ball down a gulley which ended in a shallow pit in the middle of the street. Lawrence watched as the boy collected the ball and tossed it again and again. Eventually, it overshot to the cambered side of the Row where it rolled towards Lawrence. He picked up the ball. It bore heavy traces of wear and was no longer round, but a treasure, he suspected, to the poor ragged boy. He held it in the air, and the boy ran toward him. Lawrence ruffled the boy's hair and smiled. Then, remembering he was in character, he scowled towards the women as if the boy was a nuisance.

"Come 'ere Thomas." A young, sallow-faced woman eyed Lawrence suspiciously. "He didn't mean any harm."

Lawrence approached the group. He had not recognised Sarah Fleming from a distance, but she had seen him.

"You back again?" she asked.

He nodded.

"I thought you were visiting someone in Swallow Gardens."

"Been there and seen him," he said. "I'm going back to Lambeth tomorrow, but I've got business with Elias Haim. Know him?"

Sarah shook her head. "I've heard of him, but we've never met."

"I need to find him."

"Got an address?"

"Gunpowder Alley."

"I know Haim." Thomas was sitting on his mother's lap. She wrapped both arms around him and was rocking back and forward as she spoke to Lawrence.

Lawrence grunted.

"He lives over there, by the Tenter Ground." She pointed down the street towards one of the alleyways. "He's a funny one."

Lawrence raised an eyebrow.

"I don't want to talk out of turn if he's a friend of yours."

"It's business," said Lawrence, gruffly.

"He doesn't talk," she continued, "keeps himself to himself. We don't mind that, but he's not very friendly. We speak to him, but he doesn't reply. Thinks he's a cut above us, but he isn't. He lives where we live and breathes the air we breathe. There's nothing special about him."

"Which one is his house?"

"First on the left as you go into the alley. It's nothing special either."

Thomas wriggled free, and she watched as he resumed his ball game. She sniffed and wiped her hand across her face.

Lawrence nodded. "I'll be going then," he said and walked towards the unnamed alley, feeling the eyes of the two women boring into his back. He hadn't wanted to advertise his business, much less acquire an audience, but there was no choice. The East End was a far cry from Westminster with its well-mapped streets and numbered townhouses. Local knowledge took years to gain, and if he hadn't asked for help, he could have been wandering around for hours.

The alley was narrow and short. A terrace of dark-bricked houses loomed either side, their brick walls chipped and faded. The properties were identical. Each had a worn wooden door with a rectangular door light and one downstairs and two upstairs windows. The windows overlooked each other. But for the dirty panes, there would have been no privacy at all. Gunpowder Alley was grim and unpleasant. Lawrence wondered what drew a man like Elias to live somewhere so different from and with such a tortuous journey to his place of work.

As he hovered by the entrance to the alleyway, Lawrence noticed a flicker of light through the grimy window. It was after five o'clock and dusk was falling. The presence of a candle indicated that Elias had arrived home. Things were not going according to plan. Lawrence had hoped that Elias would be at the SPR headquarters for the entire working day.

His position at the front of the alleyway was conspicuous, and he surveyed the area looking for cover. Two wrought iron gates stood halfway along the row of terraces, one on each side. Lawrence strode towards the left-hand gate and unlatched it. The gate opened into a narrow, cobbled passageway which led to the back of the terrace and allowed access into a small yard at the rear of each property. The wall of the passage was about four feet high, and a corrugated roof ran along it across the width of the first two properties. A large tree grew at the end which might provide cover.

Lawrence hauled himself up the wall, wincing as tried to accommodate his bodyweight on his strong right hand. His useless left hand crumpled, but he managed to support himself on his elbow. Sitting atop the wall, Lawrence gingerly tested the corrugated roof. It took his weight, and he sat in the shadow of the tree watching the rear of Haim's property. The wooden back door was ajar, and the rear window was well-lit. Elias Haim was in full view, bathed in the soft glow of a lantern. He was sitting at a table and appeared to be reading. The outside light faded and as day slipped into dusk, the illuminated property became more visible. Lawrence could now see that Haim was reading a newspaper.

Lawrence fidgeted. He was uncomfortable and time slipped by slowly. It began to drizzle, and he pulled up the collar of the odd job man's coat. It smelled of glue and gave little protection from the elements. Lawrence shivered, wondering how long he would have to remain here. His presence would be pointless if he couldn't get into the house undetected. He thought about the investigation, as he waited. Violet's earlier words smarted. She had always valued logic over instinct, and it was one of the reasons he had asked her to be his business partner. They complemented each other in their approach. But if he listened to Violet and ignored his sense of certainty that the answer lay in the building before him, then logic would lead them away. In fact, logic would mean abandoning the venture altogether. From the discovery of Ruth Moss's body until the moment he entered Gunpowder Alley, was one long series of coincidences with little to connect them. He sighed. Perhaps Violet was right, and he was wasting his time.

Pins and needles tracked down his leg, his collar was wet through, and his thoughts were turning black. He recognised the early signs of depression and decided to do something physical to evade the cloud of gloom. He slithered from the wall and made for the wrought iron gate deciding to wander the streets for half an hour. If Elias had not left the property by the time Lawrence returned, he would abandon the idea, go back to The Regal and rethink his entire approach. He unlatched the gate and walked out, then quickly stepped back and squatted inside the entrance. He had almost walked right into the path of Elias Haim, who was locking his front door. Lawrence watched as Haim turned right and disappeared into White's Row.

Lawrence doubled back to the pathway behind the rear of the terrace. It was dark now, and the pale moon cast speckles of light across the wet cobbles. He spotted a wooden gate set into the low wall between the pathway and Haim's yard. The wood felt spongy as he pushed it open.

He closed the gate quietly behind him, inched towards the door and pulled the handle. Haim had locked it, and the door stood firm. Lawrence sighed. Even in this feral part of the East End, doors were usually left open, but not tonight, regrettably. He tried the window which moved slightly, but not enough. Then, he pushed against the upper window surround with his palms and tried again. A gap opened just wide enough to insert his fingers. One more yank and the stiff window moved freely. Lawrence ducked inside and eased himself into the same room he had seen Haim occupy earlier. He closed the window, noticing a newspaper laying open on the table. Haim had extinguished his lantern before he left, but a box of matches lay open nearby.

Lawrence turned the wick, struck a match and reignited the lamp. It cast a dim glow around the bare, tatty room. Lawrence searched his surroundings. A large section of olive-green wallpaper was peeling away over the door. The fire in the chimney breast contained a low, metal grate and weeks of ash spilt across the floor and coated a nearby threadbare rug. Apart from the table and chairs, the room was empty. Lawrence wondered if he was in the wrong house. Elias Haim had created a favourable first impression with his immaculate clothes and slicked back hair. There was not so much as a loose thread on his apparel. His shoes shone like mirrors, and the sharp crease in his trousers showed great attention to detail. His appearance belied the unkempt room.

Lawrence moved into the kitchen which was messy but not dirty with pots and pans spread across a small kitchen table, and plates in the sink. Lawrence opened a cupboard door, but there was nothing of note. Across the hallway and to the left he found the parlour tidily set out with two high-backed chairs and a fully stocked bookcase. This room was orderly and clean. Lace antimacassars covered the back and arms of the chairs and a small clock ticked on the mantlepiece. A book lay face down on one of the chairs. Lawrence opened it and held it to the light. The title read — 'The Methods of Ethics.' Lawrence had judged Haim as a man of intelligence, and his reading matter concurred.

There was nothing of further note, so Lawrence made his way upstairs. The floorboards creaked as he moved across the landing. The house was deathly quiet save for the tick of the clock in the parlour. Every footstep sounded like a claxon. Two doors from the landing lead to bedrooms, both open. Lawrence lifted his lamp and peered into the smaller of the two. It was little more than a box room with an unmade single bed and wooden chair. The next room was bigger and was dominated by a large double bed. Haim must have a penchant for oversized furniture. His chest of drawers looked too big to fit through the door frame. Haim's bed was unmade with sheets and blankets laying in a crumpled heap at one end. A small wooden crate containing a single book lay against the bed. Lawrence placed the lamp on top of the chest and pulled out the drawers one by one. He flinched at the smell of mothballs as the drawers opened. Haim had folded his clothes to exacting standards. They were clean and pressed. Lawrence continued opening drawers to find one full of books and another used for shoes. Both drawers were orderly. Lawrence tugged at the last one. There was no keyhole, but it would not open. He rattled it from the outside, and the contents settled. Inside were reams of paper and ephemera including documents and old copies of SPR journals. Haim had crammed a lifetime of memories inside including black-edged mourning cards, letters and old family photographs.

In the middle of the mass of paper, Lawrence found two

neat clippings attached to a copy of the Pall Mall Gazette. He held them to the lantern. "To the One Who Knows — Go to the premises of Gilbert Price, Butcher on the morning of the 14th inst. to receive news to your advantage." The other clipping was much the same. Lawrence gasped. The newspaper cuttings could easily be responses to D'Onston's blackmail demands. He had been right to come, after all. But Lawrence had no opportunity for self-congratulation. No sooner had he closed the drawer, then he heard the sound of a key scraping in the lock and the front door slammed open.

Lawrence extinguished the lantern and bolted into the back bedroom, flattening himself behind the door. His breath was heavy and laboured, and his heart raced. He listened while Haim prowled around the lower part of the house, opening doors and muttering under his breath. Lawrence felt a weight in his hand and realisation dawned. Haim was looking for the lantern that he knew he had left on the dining table earlier. Lawrence hoped that he wouldn't ransack the house looking for it. He waited by the door, cramped and uncomfortable trying to decide how to get out of his predicament. The window opposite provided no realistic means of escape. His useless hand would not allow him to hang down long enough to drop to safety, even if he managed to open it undetected. The same applied to Haim's bedroom. He could only hope that Haim would settle in the parlour with the door shut, so he had a chance to creep downstairs. Fate intervened. As Lawrence stood shuffling from one foot to another, the stairs creaked, and a candle flickered on the other side of the door. Haim was only feet away. Lawrence held his breath, clutching the lamp to his chest, willing his heartbeat to quieten.

Moments later, springs creaked as Haim slumped across

the bed. A noise like the sound of a cork popping preceded the clink of glass against glass. Then another, then another. Lawrence licked his dry lips. Haim was drinking in his bedroom, and the thought of liquid of any kind tormented Lawrence who, by now, had been standing for over an hour. His legs shook as he squatted against the wall beside the door to stop himself falling. He dropped to a seated position and held his breath hoping that Haim had not heard the faint squeak from the floorboards. To his relief, the chink of glass against bottle continued. Lawrence was in no doubt that Haim was getting quietly intoxicated.

Haim did not stay silent for long. As Lawrence settled with his back against the wall, the sound of sniffing began. Soft, rhythmic snuffles which in due course changed to deep gasps. It took a few moments for Lawrence to understand. The man next door was sobbing. Lawrence squirmed. His physical location was uncomfortable enough, but witnessing a grown man crying in the sanctuary of his own home, made Lawrence uneasy. He had not expected this. Lawrence covered his ears and tried to block the sound, but it was no use. The crying continued unabated for a long time — so long that Lawrence fell asleep.

He jolted awake in the small hours of the morning to the sound of a fearsome scream. He shook his head and blinked while his eyes became accustomed to the light, wondering where he was. The room was dark and unfamiliar, and the blood-curdling screech emanating from next door set his heart racing again. His first instinct was to run, but then he remembered where he was and who was with him. Was Haim hurt? Did he need help? Lawrence resisted the urge to check and stood up, wincing as he placed his hand on the small of his back. Cramp seared through his calves from long hours of sitting in the same position. He steadied himself on the door jamb and craned his neck into the landing. The door to Haim's room was still ajar, and Haim was the source of the scream. He was in the grip of a nightmare. Lawrence tiptoed into the landing and watched from a distance as Haim thrashed from side to side. He moaned, then silence settled like a shroud. As Lawrence took a step forward, Haim sat bolt upright in bed, "the blood, the blood, God help me." His eyes snapped open, and he looked straight into Lawrence's eyes.

Lawrence didn't hesitate. He ran down the stairs, two at a time, almost colliding with the newel at the bottom in his haste to get away. He rounded the corner and tore through the kitchen hurling himself at the door handle. But the door was still locked. Haim was fully conscious now and had leapt out of bed. Heavy footsteps thudded across the landing and down the stairs. Acting on instinct, Lawrence felt along the sill of the high window to the left of the door. His hands closed over two items. One was a key. He thrust it into the lock and, as Haim entered the kitchen, he turned it. Lawrence tore through the gate and vaulted the low fence. The risk of exposure was too high to turn right into the alley, so he attempted to pull himself up the wall again. As he jumped, he balled his left hand into a fist giving enough momentum to place his forearm on the wall. Haim was behind him now and lunged. He grabbed the bottom of the coat, but Lawrence pulled free. Haim tried again and seized his shoe as Lawrence scrabbled up the wall. Lawrence wobbled, almost losing his balance, before snatching a low-hanging tree branch. He pulled himself clear and slithered across the corrugated roof before dropping into a courtyard. It opened into White's Row, only a short distance from where he had entered that evening. Time was of the essence. Haim could arrive in White's Row at any moment.

He needed to hide — somewhere close and soon. The door of Spitalfields Chambers was still open. Lawrence slipped inside and brushed himself down.

"Who are you?" asked a voice.

Lawrence looked up. "We've met," he said. "I stayed here a few nights ago. We shared a drink."

"Oh yes. I remember you. What do you want?"

"A bed for the night."

"Show me your money."

Lawrence held out a handful of coins, and Sam swept them up.

"Oy," said Lawrence, "It's late. I only need it for a few hours."

"It's a fixed price." Sam was sullen. Lawrence had preferred him last time he had seen him, face down on the kitchen table. But it wasn't worth quibbling about the cost of the room with an angry doorman on his tail."

Sam smirked. "It's upstairs. On the left."

Lawrence followed his instructions and found himself in a different dormitory. He picked his way past sleeping bodies and settled on one of two free beds before rolling over and dropping off to sleep. When Lawrence woke a short time later, he was scratching like a dog. He looked at his watch. It was five o'clock, still dark outside and he was hellishly uncomfortable. Lawrence shuffled under the blanket, but sleep proved impossible. He put his shoes back on and clumped downstairs and into White's Row where he began the long walk to Lambeth. As dawn broke, it became lighter, and he pulled back his sleeve. Angry red spots littered his forearm — bed bugs again.

An hour later, he arrived back at the Regal, removed his clothes and prepared to go back to bed. As he hung the coat over the arm of a chair, something fell out. It was the other item that he had grabbed in panic as he felt around Haim's kitchen ledge looking for a key. He picked it up and examined it. The hairs stood up on the back of his neck. It was a scalpel — deathly sharp, with a nick on the side and a dark red substance embedded in the handle.

Chapter Thirty-Two

THE SIGNED CONFESSION

Sunday 8th March 1891

Lawrence decided against going through the charade of returning the coat and hat into the caretaker's bedroom in the basement. Though the room was usually empty, and he was unlikely to get caught, he had needed the disguise more often than expected. It was easier to hang on to it and give it back before leaving for Suffolk. As a sop to his conscience, Lawrence slipped into the basement and pushed a few more coins under the door. The man might need a coat — it was March, after all.

 Lawrence returned to the hallway to wait for Violet. He loitered in the hotel lobby before spotting a recently delivered stack of newspapers bound together with string. Lawrence reached into his pocket, pulled out a penknife and cut the cord from the bundle. He selected a copy of The Times and glanced at the headlines while shivering by the door. The temperature had dropped several degrees since yesterday. He had not felt the cold walking back from Spitalfields but standing still was another matter.

The door to the coffee lounge swung open, and Lawrence peered over the newspaper to see who was coming out. It was Violet.

"Hello," he said, tucking the paper under his arm. "I've been looking for you." The words stuck in Lawrence's throat as three people appeared behind Violet, two of whom were Frank Podmore and Dr Myers.

"Mr Blatworthy," said Myers offering his hand. "I trust you managed to get your membership approved?"

"Yes, I did thank you," said Lawrence. "Mr Podmore arranged it yesterday." He smiled at Frank Podmore while considering how he was going to explain his presence in the hotel. Being pleasant seemed like a sensible first move.

"You met Miss Smith at the Town Hall," said Arthur uncertainly, gesturing towards Violet. Lawrence chewed his lip. Myers was trying to make an introduction while unsure whether it was strictly necessary. He opened his mouth to reply, but Violet answered instead.

"Yes, you are right. We did meet at the Town Hall, and when Michael and I came back to the hotel, we found that Mr Blatworthy was also a guest."

Lawrence smiled. "A stroke of luck. It has been a pleasure to have companions with similar interests."

Dr Myers nodded. "Good, good," he said vaguely. "Well, my dear. We must be off." He took Violet's arm and guided her towards the door, then stopped and raised his hat. "Good day, Mr Blatworthy."

Michael nodded and exited with Frank Podmore, leaving Lawrence in the foyer. Lawrence watched through the window as the foursome approached a hansom cab. Dr Myers took Violet's hand and helped her aboard.

Violet took a seat and stared at the hotel window, flashing a look of fury at Lawrence. He sighed. He had wanted to let her know about Elias Haim and warn her, but she should be safe in Kew with Michael.

Lawrence's suspicions had settled firmly on Haim. He needed to know more about him and wondered if the Headquarters would be open on Sunday. Doubtful, but he had nothing better to do, and it wasn't far to go. He was in disguise yesterday, and it had been dark, so he shouldn't have anything to fear from Haim if he was there. Lawrence returned to his room, grabbed a heavy coat and a thick scarf then glanced down at his feet with the mismatched laces. Pity, it was Sunday. There was no chance of buying another set today. He thought about asking the Hotel manager if he could borrow some but decided against it. The owner of the brown shoes would have noticed the missing laces by now and might have reported it. Making a mental note to buy some more first thing Monday morning, Lawrence set off for The Adelphi.

Lawrence had been in disguise so often during the last few days that donning the soft tan gloves that he habitually wore felt odd. He wasn't able to wear the gloves in the doss house — they were luxurious and would have given the game away, so his hands were on show, scars and all. It had been good for him. His injuries no longer made him feel guilty. Other things invoked memories of Catherine now — smells, mostly. Perfume and the sweet odour of a certain kind of hand soap always produced vivid images of his dead wife. He considered abandoning his trademark gloves altogether. They belonged to a part of his life he needed to leave behind. He would never forget Catherine and would always wonder about the young woman Lily might have become. But if he was ever to free himself from the veil of melancholy, now was time to cast bad memories aside.

Lawrence arrived at The Adelphi, feeling lighter. His introspection had been beneficial, for once, like a tonic. Violet was with Michael, and she was safe. He had nothing to worry about for once. It was time to give the investigation his full attention. When he reached the SPR headquarters in Buckingham Street, he found the front door wide open. The weather was freezing, and Lawrence was still cold, despite walking for twenty minutes, so it was surprising to see the inside of the building exposed to the elements. All became clear when he went inside and almost collided with Thomas Barkworth as he supervised the removal of a large wooden cabinet.

Barkworth eyed him quizzically.

"Should I recognise you?" he asked.

Lawrence offered his hand. "Alistair Blatworthy," he said.

"Oh, yes. You're the chap that wanted to become a member. I'll get you a form if you can wait a moment."

"I've completed one," said Lawrence. "I was here yesterday."

"Then what can I do for you?"

"Mr Podmore said I could use the library," said Lawrence. Frank Podmore had said nothing of the kind, but Lawrence doubted Barkworth would challenge his word.

Barkworth sighed. "Wait a moment." He followed two workers in shirt sleeves outside while they deposited the wooden filing cabinet into a cart. Barkworth returned and closed the door gazing ruefully at the wallet in his hand. "I had the devil of a job trying to get them to work on Sunday," he said. "It has cost me a small fortune."

Lawrence smiled sympathetically. "I only came here on

the off chance," he said. "I'm surprised to see it open today."

"It's the popularity of the library," said Barkworth, and the lounge, if I'm honest. Several of the members are bachelors. They treat it like a club. There's usually somebody here."

"But a day off for the doorman?" asked Lawrence.

"No. Haim takes his day off on Monday. He's around somewhere. We're tidying up the rear rooms. We've got a delegation of American members visiting next week. We're getting their accommodation ready."

"Very good," said Lawrence. "Will you be open all day?"

"Until three," said Barkworth. "I'll be here for another hour, then Haim for a few more."

"A useful man," said Lawrence, "he seems so much more than a doorman."

"He is. And his loyalty is without question. He has longstanding family connections to some of our members. Not sure how, but perhaps through his father. In any case, he's been here longer than I have. Now, do you know where the library is?"

Lawrence nodded. "I've been before."

"Please don't remove any books. Read here as long as you like. I'll ask Haim to let you know when he is locking up."

Lawrence murmured his thanks and entered the library. He perused the shelves and picked up a couple of books which seemed basic enough to understand. Lawrence had little sympathy for psychical studies, but the number of books and journals in the library was impressive. He selected a dusty tome from the top shelf and sat down at the desk. Lawrence leaned over the book trying to concentrate.

The introduction was not as easy to understand as he had hoped, but it didn't matter. The book was only a cover for what he was about to do next. He listened for sounds in the corridor and heard nothing. Barkworth and Haim must be away from the immediate area, so he made his way to the narrow desk from which he had removed the address book the previous day. The drawer slid open again. Lawrence systematically removed every document studying each piece of paper in detail. They were disappointingly uninteresting — most documents related to membership in one way or another. There were lists of members, associate members, American and European members, contributors to the library and names of backers — men who had offered considerable sums of money towards the costs of running the SPR. Lawrence sighed as he thought about the many sensible things they could have purchased with their hard-earned cash.

After ten minutes of fruitless searching, Lawrence returned to the desk feeling annoyed. He had hoped to find something else to link Haim with the recent spate of deaths. First, there were the newspaper clippings and then the bloody scalpel. Lawrence shuddered. Haim must be involved in something untoward. There were definite links to the D'Onston blackmail attempt, and it had been reasonable to look for more evidence at the headquarters. But there wasn't any, it seemed. And now Lawrence was stuck with another two hours of pretending to research. The thought of wasting time in a place he didn't understand and with a possible psychopath only a few rooms away, left him weary. Lawrence wanted to go, but he had almost blown his cover this morning. If he behaved unpredictably now, there was no chance of recovering his credibility.

He read another page and another. His eyes grew heavy,

and he fixed his gaze on the opposite wall and tried to concentrate on the timeline of the investigation, so far. As his thoughts drifted, an idea popped into his head. Something was missing. When he opened the narrow desk draw yesterday, there had been another, smaller drawer nestling inside. He had examined every piece of paper in the desk today but had not seen the drawer.

He pushed his book away and approached the desk again, sliding the drawer open to a sea of paperwork, but no smaller drawer appeared. Lawrence placed his hands beneath the papers and felt around the bottom and sides. Nothing. He ran his hand along the top of the drawer. It was rough, and he felt a stab of pain as a splinter pierced the soft pad of his middle finger. He put his finger in his mouth and sucked the pain away then tried again, this time feeling above the back edge of the drawer where it sat in the carcass of the desk. His fingertips passed over a small bump which he pressed, and a tiny drawer sprang from the rear of the bigger draw. It was darker and locked with an inverted J shaped lock. Lawrence tried to prise it open, but it was sturdy and thick. Whatever mechanism held it was too strong for Lawrence to prise it away. Short of having the key, or destroying the desk, there was no way to discover what was inside. Lawrence sighed in frustration and shoved the drawer back. It slid into the mechanism and was swallowed into the back of the desk until hidden from view.

Lawrence sat down wondering how secret the drawer was. A stroke of luck had revealed it when he looked yesterday, but who else knew of its existence? All the members, or just one? The desk was well crafted and could have been in use for years with no one aware of the secret it held — if there was a secret. It could be empty for all Lawrence knew. Still, he would have liked to find out.

Lawrence spent a further hour trying to read his book. It was a waste of time. The words flitted around his head like bees in a hive, forgotten in an instant. It was not a bit like school, which he had, for the most, enjoyed. At the end of an hour, he couldn't face another page and returned the books before proceeding to the entrance. Both Barkworth and Haim were standing there discussing the building renovations. Lawrence's heart stopped when he saw Haim, but the man showed no sign of recognition. Nor should he have. Lawrence's disguise was excellent. He could have fooled his mother.

"Useful?" asked Barkworth. "I thought you'd be in there a bit longer."

"Very useful," said Lawrence. He sniffed and pulled out a handkerchief. "I would have stayed all day," he continued, "but I'm not feeling well. I seem to have caught a head cold."

"Hardly surprising," said Barkworth sympathetically. "We're in for some unpleasant weather. You've not been feeling well either," he said looking at Haim.

"No," said Haim. He did not elaborate.

"I'll be off then," said Lawrence.

"You've dropped this." Haim stooped down and picked up Lawrence's handkerchief. He returned it with a forced smile.

"Thank you." Lawrence shook Barkworth's hand and made for the door. He turned and waved as he stepped through the threshold. Barkworth smiled back, but Haim's face was ashen. He stood, motionless, eyes fixed and staring.

Lawrence walked back along the Embankment thinking about the hidden drawer. Then his thoughts turned to Haim, and in a sudden flash of realisation, he understood the expression on Haim's face. The dropped handkerchief had drawn Haim's attention to Lawrence's feet — feet that Haim had last seen scrabbling over the wall opposite his house. George Smith had been in awe of Haim's self-taught skills of recall. With a memory like that, there wasn't a doubt that he would remember seeing the mismatched laces the previous night.

Lawrence walked briskly towards the hotel hoping that Violet would have returned, but knowing that it was unlikely, given the length of the journey to Kew. His thoughts turned to Haim. What did he know about the man and what was speculation? The newspaper clippings were factual. While they did not name D'Onston, they were personal advertisements written as D'Onston described. Then there was the scalpel with the blood on the handle. But was the blood human or animal? And was the weapon used on poor Frances Coles a scalpel or a knife? As far as Lawrence could remember, Doctor Phillips hadn't specified the type of blade that slashed her throat three times. And that was all the evidence he had against Haim. The fact that the man dwelled in White's Row was circumstantial. He was sure of Haim's guilt but needed more proof and the best way to get it was from Scotland Yard.

Lawrence doubled back from Westminster Bridge and made his way towards the Embankment. He entered the open building and asked for Henry Moore. Henry was not available nor was he expected back that day. Lawrence asked to speak to Fred, who Henry had deemed the fount of all knowledge. But the young policeman behind the desk was uncooperative and viewed Lawrence as a nuisance. He refused to answer any questions or allow Lawrence to speak with a senior officer and there was no choice but to leave. Lawrence arrived back at The Regal, frustrated and angry. He paced the floor of his bedroom waiting for time to pass. desperate to make use of Violet's logic. She knew nothing about Haim. The opportunity to tell her had not arisen but Lawrence felt sure she would have something sensible to contribute. Perhaps a plan for what to do next.

At half past four, he ventured downstairs and sat fidgeting in an armchair until tiredness overcame him and he fell asleep. Michael roused him an hour later by gently shaking his shoulder.

"You were snoring," he said amiably.

Lawrence rubbed his eyes and focussed.

"Where's Violet?"

"I don't know. I hoped you did."

"But you went to Kew together."

"I know. We've been back for almost an hour. I popped upstairs to change. Violet was talking to the Hotel Manager when I left, but she's not in her room, and I can't find her anywhere else."

"Have you asked the Manager if he knows where she is?" Lawrence was on his feet now, pulling at the curtain as he peered out of the window. The street was empty.

"I can't find him either."

"Come with me."

Lawrence burst through the double doors to the dining room. A young lady was setting the tables for dinner.

"Where is Mr Brookbank?"

She pointed outside. Lawrence exited via the rear door with Michael following behind.

Brookbank was cooperative and told them that he had seen Violet and had given her a telegram which arrived just after she returned from Kew. She had asked him for directions to the nearest telephone and was sent to a nearby street containing the larger of the local hotels.

"So, she could be anywhere," Lawrence hissed when they were back inside.

"Don't worry. She'll be back soon," said Michael reasonably.

But she wasn't. They waited half an hour and then another hour, and at six o'clock, Lawrence pulled his watch from his pocket, checked the time and snapped it shut.

"I'm not waiting any longer. Follow me." He stepped into the street and hailed a cab. As they crossed Westminster Bridge, Lawrence told Michael about his encounter with Haim. He pulled the scalpel from his pocket and showed it to Michael who recoiled in disgust. They pulled up outside the Headquarters of the SPR and Lawrence jumped from the cab and knocked at the door. The building was unlit, and he remembered Barkworth saying that it would close at 3 o'clock. It had been a long shot, but Lawrence needed to rule out the possibility of Violet going to the building to see her new friends.

He turned to the driver. "Take us to Leman Street," he ordered.

The cabman nodded.

"Quickly," said Lawrence, and they sped off into the night.

The hansom cab pulled up outside Leman Street police station. Lawrence flung the door open and vaulted down, without waiting for Michael. He strode through the door of the police station and over to a red-bearded constable who was sitting behind a desk. "Yes?" he asked.

"Is Henry Moore here? Or Edmund Reid?"

"Inspector Reid is around," said the policeman.

"Well, fetch him then."

"And who might you be?"

Lawrence sighed impatiently. "Tell him Lawrence Harpham is here. I'm a friend of Henry Moore's."

The policeman left and returned moments later with Inspector Reid. "Mr Harpham," he said, extending a hand. "How can I help?"

"My business partner, Miss Smith, was the victim of an attack near The Paul's Head a few nights ago."

Edmund nodded. "I remember. One of my constables was first to the scene. I trust she has recovered."

"Yes, she is well. The cut was superficial, as you know, but she is missing. I cannot go into details, Reid. There is not enough time. But I am working on a case, and it concerns an individual, Elias Haim. He may have Violet. I recovered this from his house last night." Lawrence produced the scalpel. Edmund took it and turned it over in his hand.

"Those marks are bloodstains," said Lawrence.

"It is possible," Edmund said. "But why do you think he wishes to harm your friend?"

"I have reason to suppose that the organisation Haim works for has been protecting him. I believe he killed Edmund Gurney and it is possible that he's involved in the Ripper killings."

Edmund Reid raised his eyebrows. "That is a bold statement to make. Have you proof?"

"No. The only evidence I have is circumstantial. But I cannot risk it. Violet is missing, and I am going to search Haim's house, with or without your help. I would prefer it to be with your help. The man is dangerous."

"You have given me no justification."

"Look Reid. I was in the force for a long time. You know as well as I do that sometimes you have to take a chance. I am giving you justification. I am about to break into the house of a man against his will. You can come and arrest me if you want to justify your presence."

Edmund Reid sighed. "Where are we going?"

"Gunpowder Alley. The first house on the left."

"Peters, McCarthy — you heard the man. Get up there now."

Michael was waiting in the cab with the door open. He squeezed towards the window allowing enough room for Edmund Reid to join them."

The cab driver scowled. "Where are we going now?" he asked, defeatedly.

"White's Row, quick as you can."

The cabman cracked the whip, and the horses thundered up Leman Street. The three men held onto the seat and the window frame as the cab rocked from side to side.

"Michael, when we leave, get the cab driver to run you back to the hotel, just in case."

Michael nodded. Moments later, they arrived by the archway leading to Gunpowder Alley. Lawrence and Reid leapt from the cab and ran towards the terraced house.

Haim had locked the front door, and the rooms were dark. Lawrence peered through the front window but couldn't see anything. The house was silent.

"Come with me," he said, running towards the gate in the centre of the terrace of properties.

The back of the house lay in darkness save for a sliver of light from the pale moon casting shadows of spectral branches across Haim's yard. Lawrence opened the gate, and the latch clicked loudly in the still of the night. Both men stood side by side, surveying the cold, dead house and

Lawrence pulled up his collar. It was freezing, and a glassy frost was settling on the footpath to the back door.

Neither man spoke as they walked toward the house. Edmund Reid gripped the door handle and pulled, but it did not give. Lawrence approached the kitchen window, took his scarf and wiped the newly formed frost from the glass. He peered inside. As his eyes grew accustomed to the dark, they gravitated towards the floor. A pile of metal crisscrossed the tiles. He looked again, then turned to Reid.

"Is that what I think it is?"

Reid stared inside. "Stand back," he growled, then bent over and picked up a stone from beneath the window. He rapped it sharply against the glass, and the window exploded in a burst of sparkling shards. Reid put his hand through the jagged hole and opened the window latch, pulling the window to its fullest extent. He climbed inside. A few moments later, Lawrence heard the click of the back door, and Reid stood in the moonlight with an unfathomable expression on his face. Lawrence entered and crouched over the heap of metal on the kitchen floor. It was a pile of knives — a grotesque selection of every kind of blade from penknives to cleavers. They lay in a jumbled mess across the tiles.

"Haim must be out," whispered Lawrence. "He could not fail to hear that glass break."

"Find some light," said Reid.

"Follow me." Lawrence located the door to the dining room and opened it. The matches and a candle were where they had been yesterday.

"I don't know what you expect to find," said Reid. "The house is empty. Your young woman is not here."

"I don't trust him," said Lawrence, "and I'm not leaving

until I've searched every inch of this house. He might have a basement."

Reid stamped his foot on the dining room floor. He repeated it in the kitchen.

"There's no basement," he said. "The floor is solid."

Lawrence opened the door to the parlour. It was cold and his breath misted in the air. "He's not been in here tonight."

They climbed the stairs, treading lightly and walked past the closed bedroom doors. Lawrence opened the door to the larger bedroom. "Dear God," he exclaimed.

"What is it?"

Lawrence took a step into the room allowing Reid a clear view. In the middle of the bed, in the flickering candlelight was the bloodied body of Elias Haim. A savage wound gaped across his throat. Scrawled above the bed in red writing were the words 'God forgive me.'

Edmund Reid stood stationery. The enormity of the scene before him was sinking in. "Bring over more light, Harpham, for God's sake."

Lawrence returned to his hiding place from the night before. The lamp was where he had left it behind the door. He lit it using the candle and placed it on the large chest of drawers.

Reid approached Haim's body and lifted his hand to check for a pulse. Congealed blood covered both wrists. "Dead," he said, unnecessarily. "And he wasn't taking any chances. He cut his wrists and slashed his throat. Not long ago either — the body is still warm."

A glint of steel glimmered in the lamplight. Lawrence leaned over with his candle and pointed to a large, bloody kitchen knife.

Reid followed his gaze. "He did it himself?"

"So it would appear. What's this?" Lawrence's candle had illuminated a note tucked inside the book on the crate. Reid put his hand out to pick it up. At that moment, footsteps thundered up the stairs making the two men jump.

Edmund Reid wiped his brow. "About time, McCarthy," he said. "What kept you?"

McCarthy glared. He was panting so hard he couldn't speak then he looked past Reid and towards the dead man on the bed. He crossed himself. "Holy mother of God."

"Get a doctor. Bagster Phillips, if you can."

Peters had followed McCarthy up the stairs and was staring at the body. It took a few moments before his brain comprehended what his eyes were seeing. He put his hand to his mouth and retched. "Come on," said McCarthy and they escaped downstairs and set off to find a doctor.

"What does it say?" Lawrence gestured towards the note. Edmund Reid slid it out of the book and opened it. "It can't be…" his voice trailed away. Almost at the same time, Lawrence spied a glint of glass through a gap in the bedroom curtains. He approached the window and flung the curtains back. Two jars stood side by side on the window ledge. The lamplight did not stretch close enough for Lawrence to see their contents. He took the candle over and set it down by the jars. They were full of liquid, and a muddled, brown substance occupied the lower half of each. Lawrence opened the lid of the closest jar and recoiled at the smell of formaldehyde. He peered at the contents and almost dropped the candle. "Good Lord Reid, it's a kidney."

Reid nodded. "I would imagine that the jar next to it contains a preserved uterus. He waved the letter. It's a confession, Harpham. A signed confession. We've caught Jack the Ripper."

Chapter Thirty-Three

A NAGGING DOUBT

Monday 9th March 1891

The Ripper's death made the front page of every London newspaper. Reporters besieged The Regal Hotel, and everyone wanted to know more about the man who had found Jack. Henry Moore had arrived, triumphantly, and congratulated Lawrence on his success. In a private moment, he admitted that he would not have pursued the case any further left to his own devices. Lawrence's instinct was remarkable. His intuition had stopped the fiend of Whitechapel in his tracks. Lawrence was a hero and the most revered policeman in the whole of London. Lawrence listened to all the accolades, and yet, and yet...

It should have been perfect. Lawrence had spent his whole career waiting for a moment like this. A case not only successful but widely admired. And Violet was back. She had been waiting for Michael when he returned. The telegram she had received was from Bury Saint Edmunds. A new customer wanted to use their services and proposed a payment too good to ignore. Violet had left immediately to find a telephone with which to confirm arrangements. One call had led to another and another. By the time she returned, the situation had become so confused that she wasn't sure there was a case at all — more like a wild goose chase. But she was safe, and that was all that mattered. And Haim was gone and with him the threat of danger to Violet.

Lawrence prowled the hotel searching for peace. He was proud of the part he had played in exposing Haim but hated the attention. Violet coped better, holding court in the coffee room on their behalf and protecting him from intrusive questions. She was a natural with the Press and made the most of the opportunity to promote their business. Lawrence contemplated leaving for Bury. There was no point in extending their stay in London. Better to move sooner rather than later. He went to his room and pulled open his wardrobe wondering how much time it would take to pack. Not long, he decided. He could be out of London within the hour. He peered through the window. Some of the crowd had dispersed, but he didn't think he would be able to leave without attracting attention. It was windy outside, and the sky was heavy with dark clouds. It felt like a storm was brewing. He should go as soon as possible and hope that he could dodge the weather — and hope that life would be quieter back in Bury. No doubt the fuss would die away soon.

Lawrence slid his suitcase from under the bed and decided to give Violet another half an hour before telling her of his intentions. She might choose to stay in London a while longer, but more likely would join him. Michael had already taken the early morning train to Norfolk, content in the knowledge that Violet was safe. There was little left to make her stay unless she chose to spend time with her SPR friends.

Lawrence removed a spare pair of trousers from the wardrobe, folded them and put them in the bottom of the suitcase. Then he reached for the next item before realising that it did not belong to him. It was the hotel caretakers coat. He searched for the hat and found it on top of the wardrobe and decided to return both items without delay. Lawrence placed the jacket over his arm and walked towards the door wrinkling his nose as the familiar smell of glue wafted from the collar. It was a smell he associated with waiting — waiting for Haim to leave his house and waiting for sleep to come during his last visit to Spitalfields Chambers. How ironic that his sleep had been so fitful on the second occasion when he slept soundly on the first. Perhaps it was because he had occupied a different bedroom. Or that joining Sarah Fleming for a drink in the kitchen on the first occasion, had created a soporific effect. Spitalfields Chambers may have been a low doss house, but Lawrence had been warm, and the company had been friendly — and Sarah told a good story. They had chatted together for the best part of an hour. What was it she had told him? He had almost forgotten, but wasn't there something about a dead doorman? Yes, that was it. Charlie had died, and before he died, a well-dressed man had been poking around the doss house looking for something. Something left in a bed occupied by a swarthy, sinister man the night before. What could that be? For a moment, Lawrence considered dropping by White's Row for another look. Then he stopped himself. They had caught the Ripper, and there was nothing further to do. He shook his head and left the room, making for the basement. Who could the man be? Elias Haim was swarthy. In hindsight, he was sinister.

But why would he use a doss house only a few yards from his own home?

Lawrence reached the Caretaker's door and tried the handle. It was open, and he went inside. It would be sensible to hide the coat rather than leave it in full view where the caretaker would see it and wonder where it had been. Lawrence paused to think. Concealing something in an abode or place of work didn't make it well hidden. Far better to put it somewhere wholly unexpected — like the end bed of a doss house dormitory. Stop it. Lawrence rebuked himself as he felt the hairs on the back of his neck rise. He didn't like leaving loose ends, but Charlie's death wasn't a matter for him.

Charlie had died of apoplexy — natural causes. Only Sarah's conviction suggested otherwise — and what did she know? Instinct, he thought. She had known Charlie better than the coroner, better than the doctor. If it was good enough for Lawrence to trust his intuition, then it was good enough to believe in hers. All he had to do, was go back to the doss house and check the end bed. If there was nothing there, then he could go back to Suffolk. It would only take a couple of hours. And he didn't have to pretend anymore. There was no need to dress up. He would do exactly what Charlie's gentleman had done, slip upstairs when the coast was clear and check the bed. Lawrence felt more comfortable having made the decision. He hung the coat on the door hook and left the hotel by the rear entrance.

Lawrence found the absence of his tramp's disguise liberating. He boarded the tram with a spring in his step and alighted near Aldgate, before walking to White's Row. The journey was quick and comfortable although the unexpected presence of a group of women on the doorstep of the dosshouse delayed his progress. He loitered on the corner until they dispersed and watched them chatting together as they walked towards The Paul's Head. Lawrence looked over his shoulder, checking the street for signs of life. All was still and quiet. He opened the front door of number 8 and let himself in.

He had hoped that the building was empty, but it was not to be. Loud voices belonging to a man and a woman emanated from the closed kitchen door. They were arguing. Lawrence stood stock still in the hallway. If the kitchen door opened, he would be in full view with nowhere to hide. It was no time for caution. He padded up the stairs, wincing as they creaked beneath his weight and opened the right-hand door. The room was empty and icy cold. Lawrence counted the beds. As expected, there were twelve. He walked to the end of the bedroom where the beds were close to the window and stared outside. It had started to snow.

Lawrence crouched by the left-hand bed. The thin, dirty mattress topped a bed frame, and he peered underneath. The wood was solid with no apparent flaws, so he ran his hand below the bed and pulled at the sides. Nothing. He turned his attention to the opposite bed. It was identical and consisted of a wooden carcass with another grubby mattress inside the base. Lawrence glanced at the wood panel nearest the window. Nothing looked out of place, but when he pulled the edges of the wooden side, it moved. It was loose. Lawrence dropped to his knees and gave it a thorough inspection. The panel was spongy, rotten in places and the nails that secured it sat above the wood. He pulled it again but harder, and it gave a little more. The nails only served to pin the wooden panel to the frame. Anyone could prise it apart and re-affix it with ease. He popped the panel out revealing a void under the bed and swept his hand through the gap. It closed on a cold metal object which he pulled free and examined under the window. In his hand was a small bronze key in the shape of an inverted 'J'. It was unlike any key he had ever seen before, but he had seen a keyhole that shape recently. It was in the secret drawer in the library of the Headquarters of The Society for Psychical Research.

Killing time had become a way of life for Lawrence. He paced the streets of London again trying to occupy himself until the light failed and he could be sure that the SPR building would be empty. Quite how he would gain access, was another matter but it had to be possible. Lawrence spent the daylight hours walking between coffee houses. He could have returned to The Regal but knew it would be difficult to leave with all the press attention. Besides, it would be impossible to justify his hunch to Violet. He was putting instinct above business sense again, and she would disapprove. As dusk fell, he circumnavigated the streets surrounding the building. The weather was getting worse. Snow had been falling for hours and had settled into powdery heaps. Lawrence hoped that the bad weather might encourage the occupants to leave early. But every time he passed through Buckingham Street, lights shone from the windows. Nobody seemed to want to go home. It was hardly surprising, he thought, as he walked around the Adelphi for the third time. Some of the members used the place as a clubhouse, and some rooms in the building belonged to other organisations. Small wonder they needed a doorman. Lawrence wondered how they were managing today. He didn't know whether Haim's connection to the SPR was public knowledge yet. There was no evidence of reporters around the building, but it was only a matter of time until they came. If he was going to break in, it was now or never.

Finally, just before midnight, Lawrence trudged up Buckingham Street to find the building in darkness. He approached the door and soon discovered that the large townhouse was impenetrable from the front, but there might be access at the rear. Walking towards the Victoria Embankment, he turned left. The gap at the end of the townhouses led, as he had hoped, to a narrow alley providing access to the yards. Lawrence located the gate most likely to belong to the Societies' rooms. The latch on the door was open, and he entered with ease. The yard was small; less than the width of the building. He could have touched both sides with his outstretched arms. In front of him, was a door set halfway along the wall with double windows to the side overlooking a small square room. He tried the door which was solid and firm, and the windows were tightly shut. Lawrence felt in his pocket for the large rock that he had collected earlier. He had come prepared knowing that access was unlikely to prove easy. He wrapped the rock in his scarf and tapped it in the middle of the window. There was a muffled crack, and a jagged line appeared in the glass. He tried again, this time harder. Two large chunks of glass fell into the room. Lawrence cleared the worst of the remaining glass from the hole and reached for the latch. His thoughts turned to the actions of Edmund Reid at Haim's home the previous night. Breaking into two different properties on consecutive nights, was not something he had anticipated at the start of the week. He crawled through the window and slithered down, feet crunching on the broken glass beneath.

Lawrence pulled a candle and matches from his pocket and surveyed the room. He was in a storage area containing all manner of household items neatly stacked around him. On a high shelf, above a dressing unit, three lamps stood side by side. He reached up, and eased one of the lanterns to the front, then used the candle to light it. He opened the door and ventured into a short passageway leading to the main body of the house. The hall, which he recognised, led to the library and he reached for the door. It was locked, but Lawrence had already noticed a collection of keys dangling from hooks in the storeroom. He returned, collected them and tried each in turn. The third attempt proved successful.

The library was freezing and judging by the temperature, had been empty for several hours. A shaft of patchy moonlight glowed against the bookcases in front of the window. Lawrence held the lamp aloft. Fat snowflakes fluttered from the sky, twirling and dancing before his eyes as the wind buffeted them. He tore his gaze away, shivering as he approached the narrow desk. The lamp flickered as he set it on top. He pulled a wooden chair towards the desk, stifling a yawn as he sat down with a sense of relief. It was late, and he had been walking for hours. He opened the desk drawer and felt for the button. As soon as he pressed it, the secret drawer sprang towards him. With bated breath, Lawrence removed the inverted J key from his breast pocket and compared it to the lock. It was a close match. He inserted the key, exhaling as it unlocked with a satisfying click and he slid the drawer open. Inside were pieces of folded paper covered in scratchy handwriting. A sealed cream coloured envelope written in a different hand lay on top of the letters. Lawrence pushed it to one side and unfolded one of the documents. He scanned it, frowning, as snatches of sentences passed his eyes leaving no doubt of their provenance. He was looking at the writings of a killer. Lawrence opened another paper dated August 1888. The graphic details of the murder could only have come from the perpetrator. Haim must have written them. But why? And why had he kept them? No matter, it would be useful proof for Scotland Yard. Lawrence shoved the papers into his coat pocket. He could read them at any time. Better to finish as soon as possible and get away. He ran his fingers along the bottom of the small drawer to check he hadn't missed anything. It was empty, but the cream covered envelope still lay sealed on the desk. Lawrence reached for a letter opener and slit the flap before removing two sheets of thin paper. Writing covered both sides and the ink had bled making them difficult to read. Lawrence adjusted the lamp until it shone on the leaves of paper and peered at the pages. He read them, eyes wide, as the full horror of the words dawned upon him.

Chapter Thirty-Four

THE TRUTH ABOUT MARY

15th June 1889

I write these words in shame and apprehension. The shame requires no explanation, but my anxiety is borne of fear. Fear of the man I am sworn to protect.

What price loyalty? Does love outweigh truth? Or respect come ahead of honour? How are these things measured? Pity me, for I have chosen loyalty over life, prepared to risk my freedom to protect my friend. We have stood side by side for so long that I feel compelled to safeguard his interests, and if all goes according to plan, we will both remain at liberty. But the extent of his failings has become more evident, and my life may be at risk. I have chosen to record the truth for posterity though whether anyone will read it, I do not know.

Our friend, our dear friend, has ailed for some time. His affliction, though not widely known, was no secret from those of us who were close to him. But it grew worse, and the distortion of his personality became apparent, especially after dusk. We were wrong to conceal the murder of Edmund Gurney in June of 1888. We respected him, and he had been part of our organisation since its inception. There are some lengths to which I would not stoop. I want it known that I was not a party to Gurney's murder. I did not become aware of it until after the fact. Gurney had discovered our friend's involvement in the death of two women. Without wishing to sound trite, they were women of ill-repute. Their killings passed largely unnoticed. The police did not link the crimes to those that became known as the Ripper killings, and we did not connect them either. We would have been none the wiser if that weasel D'Onston had not become involved. D'Onston is a despicable man — a blackmailer and a fraud. I hold him partly responsible for the action I have taken which will be my undoing if my fragile mind survives it.

We paid D'Onston to disappear, and for a while he did. We thought the matter was over, but a series of brutal killings occurred in the Autumn of 1888. D'Onston came to suspect the truth long before we, who should have known better, realised. When a double slaying occurred late in September, D'Onston approached us again through the personal column of the newspaper. It wasn't until then that the three of us understood that the man they called Jack the Ripper was the man we were sworn to protect. We approached our friend and asked him outright, and he did not falter in his reply but confessed straight away. Our friend was contrite and terrified of exposure. He told us that a witness to one of the crimes had seen his face. He is not a monster, although he might seem like one. He is a good man afflicted with a terrible urge, but one that is containable. He trusted three of us with his secret, and we met that very night to discuss what we could do. We made two resolutions. The first was practical. At no time would he be left alone at night, and we arranged a companion to that end. The second resolution was to give him an alibi. To ensure his visibility elsewhere by reputable people in case D'Onston involved the police. It was a sound idea, but only achievable if there was another killing. We decided to manufacture one.

How cold that seems in hindsight. How clinical and calculating. It is far easier to make a plan than carry it out. For the best effect, the killing would need to occur on a particular day. We selected the 9th of November as it was the Lord Mayor's day and memorable. This death, unlike the others, must take place inside, where there was no chance of interruption. Somewhere that another man could replicate the previous murders. A man with no prior experience of killing. A man who had never even seen a dead body. A man who had never wielded a weapon in anger. I was that man. There was never any question of one of the others doing it. They were not practical men. Intellectual yes, but not cut out for the job in hand and the cold detachment it required. Neither, as it turned out, was I.

We chose Mary Kelly because she lived nearby. Other fallen women lived closer, but none of them dwelled alone. Nor were they as accommodating and friendly as she. The location was important. Although I lived my life privately, a woman who lived in closer proximity might have recognised me. The time of the murder would not matter as long as it took place on the designated day. I prepared well, committing to memory details contained in a journal that our friend had foolishly written. His earlier entries were useless, but he committed the later murders with full awareness giving me an opportunity to duplicate them.

Late on the 8th of November, I tracked Mary to her squalid room off Dorset Street. I could not find her, at first. She was out and had been drinking, so I waited nearby, and she went off with yet another man. She was absent for several hours. If she had been any later, I would have abandoned the task, but in the early hours of Friday morning, she staggered up the road, singing. I was standing in the shadows on the corner of Thrawl Street. I tapped her on the shoulder as she passed by and held out my palm containing twice as much money as she could expect to earn in a night. She reached for the coins, and I closed my fist. "You will have to earn it," I said. She giggled and took my hand and led me to her room in Millers Court.

It was that easy. Even with all the warnings and newspaper reports about the fiend of Whitechapel, she went like a lamb to the slaughter, the lure of money surpassing any fear. Yet it was that innocence, that willingness to please that almost stopped me in my tracks. When we arrived at her room, she reached for me, pulling me to her bed. She kissed me and began to remove her clothes. She was gentle and tender, and I recoiled from her. To commit the crime that I had steeled myself for, I could not afford to become attached. Her kiss, the feel of her warm hand on my face, had already unnerved me. It was the closest contact I had with a woman in a long time, and Mary Kelly was neither dirty nor unkempt. She smelled clean, and she dressed well. In another world, at another time, I might have been tempted.

She reclined on the bed smiling. "Don't be shy," she said, beckoning me towards her. I removed my heavy overcoat and hat, discarding them by the door and felt for the knife that I had secreted in the back of my trousers. I knelt beside her, and she reached towards me. Time froze as my heart thudded against my chest, and a momentary battle raged between my conscience and loyalty. Loyalty won. I grasped my knife and sliced it into her neck. She barely had time to register what was happening before a thick slew of blood gushed from the wound, and her head dropped to one side. Her dying eyes stared as I removed my shirt and trousers and steeled myself for what was to follow.

Before beginning, I reached into my coat pocket and removed the cork from a blue glass bottle I had stashed earlier. I drained the bottle dry and waited a moment for the laudanum to take effect. Then I stood over her and began. At first, I attempted to replicate the killing of Catherine Eddowes, but I knew little about the interior of a human body. I had memorised every detail of the injuries I was required to mimic, but when I slit her abdomen open, she became less human. Viewing her like an animal to butcher, overcame my repulsion but not my confusion at the volume of blood and the complexity of her internal organs. After a while, the Laudanum took effect. A wave of euphoria came over me, and I became careless, less concerned by detail as I worked to make this woman resemble the last Ripper victim. The task was all-encompassing, and time sped by. Memories blurred as if I was in a dream, but I was not afraid or even revolted, not while the laudanum protected my mind and induced a reverie.

After what must have been several hours, but seemed like a whole night, I stood up and surveyed my work. The mass of flesh before me no longer resembled a human being. I cannot bear to recount the details of what I did to that woman. Thank God some memories are clouded forever by the drug-induced haze. I can still recall dressing, leaving and walking home. And I have woken almost every night since haunted by the sight of her broken body. In every dream, I watch her through clawed hands dripping with blood. My hands, her blood, my living nightmare.

We made an alibi that night. The others were grateful, but we never spoke of it again, and they left me to deal with my demons alone. I never used laudanum again. My drug of choice was gin.

Though we cleared suspicion from the one we protected, his killings remained a burden for the organisation in general. D'Onston hadn't gone away. He kept needling, provoking us with his pointed newspaper articles. We met again. It was tempting to see D'Onston off once and for all, but he told us that he had made plans in the event of his sudden death. We had no reason to doubt him and decided, instead, to provide a murderer.

Montague John Druitt was known to the organisation and indulged in behaviours not approved of by many, but for which we were tolerant. The young man was a schoolteacher. An unknown member of staff had become aware of his conduct and was threatening to reveal what he was. The young man was in crisis and had written to us about his unhappiness. He was on the verge of suicide and felt there was no other choice. The last letter he wrote indicated that he was going to die. We took this opportunity to tell D'Onston that we had meted out justice to a killer who was one of our own and a body would soon appear. Whether Druitt took his own life, or we helped him, I cannot say for I was not directly involved. But his corpse weighed down with stones, turned up in the Thames in December of 1888. We gave D'Onston a final instalment of money. He must have believed that Druitt was the Ripper and to our relief, communication ceased.

Time has moved on and the summer of 1889 approaches. Our plan was successful, and our work continues. We are all safe. Our friend is still admired and continues to live as always. He is seldom left alone at night and will need a companion for the rest of his life. On the rare occasions, he is home alone, we lock his bedroom door at ten and open it at daylight. He has never reverted to the savage he became when allowed to prowl through Whitechapel. We three do not meet to discuss him anymore. There is no need, but Mary Kelly haunts my every waking thought, and I have nobody with which to share my burden. I tried, once, to talk about it. To relieve myself of the loneliness but I was the recipient of a stern frown and a shake of the head. I never tried again.

The voice of Mary Kelly is always with me. She beckons me still, calls me to her. I hold the knife sometimes, fingering the blade and imagine it plunging into my neck, slicing through my flesh until it hangs in ribbons. I expect it will end that way.

February 1891

Someone broke into my house in Gunpowder Alley recently. They ransacked it yet took nothing away. It has made me uneasy, distrustful. It might be him, though why it should be, I cannot say. Unless he knows about this letter, but even if he finds the drawer, he cannot access it without the key. As a precaution, I will move it from my house. I find myself torn between keeping his secret at all costs and preserving my life. I cannot predict which will come to pass, though I have planned for both. This letter has been cathartic. I have unburdened myself, and it helps mask the feelings of guilt. Perhaps that is enough. But for the sake of completeness, the trusted three are...

The gas lamps ignited with a click. Lawrence gasped

and dropped his lantern on the floor. Two men appeared in front of him, their faces covered by harlequin masks. "You won't be needing that," said a deep voice reaching for the letter. Lawrence stood and backed away.

"Give it to me," the man hissed.

Lawrence looked desperately around the room. The only exit was via the door, and the two men were blocking it. If he could only reach the window, he could wrench it open and jump through before they caught up with him. But there was no chance for action. One of the men rushed towards him, catching him unawares. The man raised his hand, and Lawrence felt a crack as something slammed against his head. A searing pain crashed through his skull, and the world went black.

Chapter Thirty-Five

UNDER ATTACK

Tuesday 10th March 1891

Lawrence opened his eyes. It was daylight, but his brain couldn't rationalise what his eyes were seeing. His face was cold on one side and something wet lapped against his chin. Where was he? He tried to move his hand, but nothing happened. He could not see his arms or feel them — and he was deathly cold. He blinked again and focussed on a riverbank, white with snow. Though stiff and uncomfortable, he was mostly dry and must be under shelter. He tried to raise his head but only managed to move it an inch off the ground. It was enough to see that he was under the arch of a bridge with his head almost in the water. He concentrated. Where were his hands? Not by his sides where they should be. His heart raced and he began an internal dialogue. Stop panicking. Think. He tried to move them again — nothing. Try one finger at a time. Yes. He wiggled the thumb of his right hand and finally realised that it was behind his back. His arms wouldn't move because they were tied together.

He raised his head again. It was snowing. He was numb with cold. He needed to get out of his bonds and soon.

Lawrence tried to shuffle to one side, but his legs weren't moving either. It didn't take long to understand that they were also bound together. He was trussed up like a turkey. How had it happened?

He peered across the river, squinting as light stung his eyes. His head spun, and he felt sick. The indentation in the ground in which his head had been lying was red with blood — his blood. His head screamed with pain. His body was stiff and chilled to the marrow. If he didn't move soon, hypothermia would follow. He must get help. He opened his mouth and tried to speak. "Help..." The word came out, but it was inaudible. He licked his parched lips and tried again. "Help." The word was a little louder this time, but there was nobody to hear it.

He tried to remember how he had got to this unfamiliar destination. What was he doing? He searched in vain for his last memory, but everything was foggy. Who was he? Oh God, he couldn't even remember his name. All he knew for sure was that he needed urgent help.

Lawrence wriggled his toes. They were numb, but not enough to prevent movement. He forced his legs towards the ground and the ropes gave enough for his feet to touch the surface. He ploughed the front of his shoes into the muddy ground and propelled himself forward a tiny distance. Gravel gouged his chin. Inch by painful inch, he wormed forwards across the riverbank until he passed around the bridge where there was a clearer view. A woman wearing a dirty coat and a threadbare shawl mudlarked on the banks of the freezing river. She had cleared snow from a patch of earth and was scraping it with a shovel. "Help." Lawrence croaked, but she did not hear. He tried again, but his head was swimming. He wanted to sleep. No energy — one last try. "Help." This time she turned her head. He gazed at her as she searched the river trying to locate the source of the sound. By the time she saw him and began her cautious approach, he had closed his eyes and succumbed to the cold. He was barely alive by the time she reached him.

Chapter Thirty-Six

VIOLET IN CHARGE

12th March 1891 – Violet Smith's Journal

They dragged Lawrence half dead from The Thames yesterday and he hovers between life and death. Poor Michael had only just reached his parish in Norfolk when he received my telegram. He has returned to be by my side while we wait to see whether Lawrence will live or die. Michael is writing a sermon as I sit here updating my journal trying not to think the worst. Lawrence's prognosis is poor. He received a terrible blow to the head and suffered from exposure to the elements during the worst week of weather we have seen for many years. Lawrence was the victim of a terrifying attack. The police think he was set upon, robbed, bound and tossed over the side of a low bridge. His attackers did not care if he lived or died. The fall could have caused fatal injuries. Instead, he escaped with a broken leg, broken ribs and a dislocated shoulder. Had he not fallen in the lea of the bridge, he would have died of hypothermia. But he has survived so far, and we can only hope that luck remains on his side. The doctors say we will know one way or another in the next few days.

18th March 1891

Lawrence woke yesterday with no memory of what had happened. In fact, he remembered nothing at all, nor did he recognise me. Doctor Naylor conducted extensive examinations and has concluded that Lawrence has amnesia. He believes it will be temporary, but only time will tell. Lawrence's injuries are mending well, but he is frail. Michael and I have spoken to him several times, but he keeps interrupting and asking who we are. His frustration makes him angry. He threw a glass of water on the floor in temper this morning. I telephoned the Society for Psychical Research yesterday hoping to speak to Doctor Myers to ask if he could give a considered opinion on Lawrence's prospects. Mr Barkworth will pass on my message.

21st March 1891

Lawrence has made some progress. He now recognises Michael and has remembered some of his earlier life. They talk together of their shared memories of Bury Saint Edmunds. Michael has steered the conversation away from the subject of Catherine. He worries that any mention of her will bring on one of Lawrence's black moods. Arthur telephoned me a few days ago and offered useful advice about coaxing memory recall. His duties leave him tied to his hospital at present, but he will visit as soon as there is an opportunity.

22nd March 1891

Doctor Naylor has expressed his concern at Lawrence's lack of progress. He thinks he is unlikely to show further improvement in this hospital. His physical injuries have healed, and there is no risk in moving him, but the Doctor believes he will fare better in a more familiar place. He has telephoned The Bury and West Suffolk Hospital and they have agreed to treat Lawrence. We will join him there tomorrow. Arthur called again and said how sad he was to hear that we are leaving London. I am disappointed too — more than he knows. But he has said that he will write to me and it has eased the pain a little.

25th April 1891

Lawrence has been in Bury hospital for over a month. He seemed to be recovering well but caught pneumonia after a week and went rapidly downhill. The outcome of his illness was uncertain once again, and we lived in fear of his demise. He has rallied this last week and is doing well. He recognises me and has begun to discuss aspects of our earlier cases. Michael visits when he can, and Lawrence takes considerable pleasure in their meetings. I have written to Arthur twice now but am yet to receive a response.

Summer 1891

Lawrence was moved to a nursing home in Felixstowe and will stay there through the summer. We hope he will improve enough to be discharged to his house, here in Bury. It is has become hard for me to visit as much as I would like. I have devoted all my time to the running of our business. It has been a baptism of fire. I have carried on advertising and have taken as many cases as I can manage. But with no experience and not having the benefit of Lawrence's guidance, it has been a slow, lonely process. I have come to understand his ways better. Recently, I took a case — a theft at The Willows cafe. The manageress did not want the police involved and asked for a gentle approach. I took my time to get to know the staff and deduced, eventually, that only three were present at the probable time. But narrowing the crime from three people to one proved almost impossible. So, I mulled it over and thought about what Lawrence might do.

I knew he would rely on instinct, but was mine the equal of his? I considered the suspects' characters and, free from the binds of logic, only one person stood out from the rest. The next day I questioned her at length. I was firm and direct, and to my surprise, she faltered and contradicted herself. Before long, she confessed. She was not a natural lawbreaker and took the money to help her ailing mother. She is repaying it bit by bit and still works at The Willows. The outcome of the case could hardly have gone better, and I learned that there is more to the art of investigation than facts alone.

It took several months, but Arthur replied to my letter. He had undertaken a time-consuming medical research project, hence the delay. But he has now finished and is looking forward to resuming normal duties. Mr Podmore and his SPR colleagues are still very busy, and his brother Frederick is writing another book. Henry Sidgwick and Thomas Barkworth are both well and have asked after me. The Chelmondiston investigation is now concluded and has been a great success. It is notable because the SPR members were there to witness the phenomenon making it unique in their annals. Mr Barkworth says it is a testimony to the importance of collecting first-hand accounts of paranormal experiences. A report will appear in the journal in due course, and it will remain one of their most important cases. I feel privileged to have been present.

9th November 1891

Lawrence returned to our offices in the Buttermarket last week. He is still too thin and walks with the aid of a stick, but it will not always be so. He sat on his chair with a cup of tea in his hand, and it was like old times. I have given him a case to look through. It is not too taxing and will not take him away from Bury Saint Edmunds. He pulled faces when I briefed him about my expectations, torn between gratitude for still having a business, and irritation about not being in control of it. His presence has lifted an enormous burden from my shoulders. I have someone to talk to, at last, and the world is not such a lonely place. The promised copy of the journal of the Society for Psychical Research arrived in the morning post and contains a full account of the Chelmondiston haunting.

5th May 1892

It has been many months since Lawrence's accident, but he still remembers nothing. His amnesia has been constant, and the Doctors think it unlikely that he will ever recall the events of that night. He cannot remember being in London, only Brighton. I have kept the press clippings from the week that he unmasked The Ripper, but they are meaningless to Lawrence. He stares at them for hours on end, trying to find something familiar, but it feels like it happened to someone else. Lawrence has been under medical care for such a long time, that his part in the Ripper's capture is mostly forgotten. The accolades went to Scotland Yard. It is for the best, and we can go about our business unrecognised. I cannot help but feel that a piece of Lawrence is missing. He is quieter, more introspective and tormented by something to which he cannot give voice. Nightmares still haunt him. They are as intense as they were in his first week in the hospital. He remembers snatches of dreams but cannot join them together. Since his return to work, he spends as much time trying to recall what happened in London as he does with our current investigations. At the beginning of the year, he fitted a cork board to the rear office wall and pinned up pages from the journal he had written in Brighton and all the Ripper press clippings that he could find. At his request, I spent endless nights recounting everything I could remember about our time there. I gave detailed accounts of all the information he told me about Roslyn D'Onston, White's Row and Elias Haim, but it was difficult. Lawrence investigated so much without me. I was oblivious when he left The Regal Hotel that day. I cannot account for why he left and cannot imagine where he went and what he was doing there. Unfortunately, neither can he.

10th March 1893

It is hard to believe that it is two years to the day since they found Lawrence lying on the banks of The Thames. Harpham and Smith Private Investigators grows from strength to strength, yet we still cannot deduce how Lawrence came by his injuries. He is at his physical best since we were first acquainted. All his wounds have healed, and he received medical attention to his left hand while in hospital. His hand still bears the scars, but it is stronger than before, and he has more use from it. His memories of Catherine returned piecemeal last year. They seeped through bit by bit and Lawrence bore it with quiet resignation. The lost memories of London torment him more than Catherine now. He has tried to find Roslyn D'Onston's whereabouts but to no avail. He wanted to go back to London and seek him out, but that was a step too far for me. I would not allow it. We have grown closer, Lawrence and I, since his injury and he listens to my concerns and respects my feelings. The suggestion that he might return to London upset me, and I took no pains to hide my distress. He reluctantly agreed to conduct his enquiries in writing, but so far nothing has materialised. It is good that he takes a more measured approach. The old Lawrence would have bolted to London with no regard for the consequences. He has memorised everything that I have told him about the case and anything else that he has read. He has all the known facts at his disposal. Only his memories are lacking, but it is his memories that hold the key.

7th January 1894

Everything has changed. We were beginning a new case and Lawrence wanted to gain access to a property in the guise of a tradesman. He was preparing himself in our office and had located his fake beard which had been mislaid. He affixed it using the mirror next to the cork board which had come away from the wall. A carpenter had been that morning and replaced it with glue and nails. He left just before

Lawrence arrived. From the moment Lawrence walked through the door, the smell of the glue bothered him. He held a handkerchief to his nose as the fumes caused him to sneeze, but donned the beard and moustache set anyway. Then he retrieved a charcoal stick from a tin in his pocket and completed his disguise. I watched him as he scanned the room. He kept wrinkling his nose and clasping his temples. He seemed in turmoil, and I pretended not to notice, fearful of what he might say. But his behaviour was so unusual that I asked him what was wrong, and he looked quizzically towards me. He approached his desk, sat down and put his head in his hands. Filled with alarm, I put my arm around him and again asked what had upset him. He looked up, brow furrowed. "It's the smell, Violet. The smell of the glue. I remember that smell." I asked him where he remembered it from, and he screwed up his eyes, trying in vain to sift through his thoughts. Then he raised the collar of his coat and sniffed. "It was almost there for a moment," he said, looking crestfallen as the memory slipped away. Lawrence hovered by the cork board all morning and did not leave the office when he should have. Then, after fruitless efforts at recall, he announced, in frustration, that he was going for a walk. The bell jangled as he stepped outside into the cold street. It had started to snow. A minute later Lawrence burst through the door, eyes sparkling, joyful. "I know," he said. "I remember. The old coat with glue on the collar, the disguise. White's Row. It was snowing Violet. The night they attacked me, it was snowing."

Chapter Thirty-Seven

DEATH OF A FRIEND

Lawrence spent the next morning in front of the cork board at the rear of his office. The flood of returning memories had taken him by surprise, and he sought to fit them into an orderly sequence. As one memory triggered another, he checked it against the facts he had amassed in the intervening years. But his mind ached with the bombardment of new information.

Lawrence sighed and stroked his chin. "What was I wearing when I left the hotel?" he asked.

"I don't know. I didn't see you," said Violet closing her journal. It had been an hour since Lawrence's memory had returned and he had been asking a slew of questions ever since.

"It probably doesn't matter, but I think it had something to do with a coat," he concluded. "I recall going to White's Row, Violet. That's why I left the hotel."

"I didn't know," she said. "Can you remember why?"

Lawrence bit his lip. "I was looking for something," he

said slowly. "And I found it. Yes, I found a key. I found a key, and I used it to open a drawer."

"Where?"

"In a desk in the library of the Headquarters of the Society for Psychical Research."

"You sound very certain."

"I am very certain. I remember now. There were documents," Lawrence continued, narrowing his eyes as he searched for the next memory.

"Dear God, Violet. Haim wasn't the Ripper."

Violet shook her head. "He was Lawrence. There were body parts in his bedroom."

"No. Haim was protecting somebody else."

"That's ridiculous. Why would he do that?"

"Loyalty."

"I don't believe it. Haim wrote a letter. He confessed."

"His confession was false. It is true that he killed, but he was not the Ripper. It was a deception to protect someone else."

"Who?"

"There were three names written on Haim's real confession. One is the Ripper."

"Which one?"

"I can't be sure."

"Lawrence. Think about this. What will we gain by bringing this up again? Nothing has happened since Haim died. There haven't been any other murders."

"Who is to say that there won't be? There was a gap in time before the murder of Frances Coles."

"How do we know Frances Coles was a Ripper victim?"

"We can only surmise," said Lawrence. "Haim killed Mary Kelly." The words were out of his mouth before he had even connected them with a memory. Now it was articulated he could see the words on the cream-coloured paper as if it was only yesterday. His thoughts crystallised, and his memories were knitting together nicely. Lawrence continued. "Haim killed Mary Kelly to provide an alibi. He did not kill the others. The man he was protecting functioned perfectly well during the day, but after dusk, an unnamed affliction made him a monster. He trusted three men with his secret and Haim was one of them. They worked together to ensure that the real killer was never left alone at night. That way, they were able to contain the worst of his excesses."

"And this man belonged to the Society?"

Lawrence nodded.

"You are certain?"

"There is no doubt."

"We should leave this in the past."

"I cannot."

"Then what will you do?"

"Flush them out," said Lawrence reaching for the telephone.

Wednesday 10th January 1894

It was just after ten o'clock when the train pulled into Liverpool Street Station. Lawrence opened the carriage and held his hand out for Violet as she navigated the step to the platform. She was pale and had hardly spoken through the journey. Her reluctance to return to London had given him a momentary pause. He owed her so much. She had kept his business going single-handedly for over a year while he recovered and had offered friendship when he was at his lowest ebb. Her visits had sustained him through the frustration of his missing memories. Her loyalty never wavered, even when he lost his temper or on the rare occasions he shouted. And now he was leading her towards a final denouement that could propel them onto the front pages again with the capacity to cause untold misery.

He had not revealed the outcome of Sunday's phone call, and she had not asked. One of the trusted three had answered the telephone and Lawrence had spoken succinctly before the man tried to end the call. His memory had been faulty for a long time, but now that it was back, it was as good as ever. Imprinted on his mind with alarming clarity, were names that had once eluded him. The memories were all the more powerful, as he was reading the letter when the unholy trinity had interrupted him. Their identities were the last words he read before they coshed him on the head and left him for dead. This time, Lawrence wasn't taking any chances. He curtly told the recipient of the phone call that a sealed envelope of detailed notes was behind the police desk in Bury Saint Edmunds. Lawrence wasn't bluffing. On Monday night he had walked to the new police premises in Saint John's Street and deposited the envelope with Inspector Andrews. They agreed that Lawrence would telephone on Wednesday evening. If Andrews had not heard from him by six o'clock, he would open the envelope and take action accordingly. The phone call to the Society for Psychical Research lasted only a few moments. During that time Lawrence left no doubt of the depth of his knowledge about the Ripper deception and the lengths he was willing to go to protect himself. He had done enough and was confident that Violet would be safe if she wished to join him. As much as she wanted to let the matter lie, she was not prepared to let Lawrence go alone.

They arrived in London, hailed a cab and twenty minutes later they pulled up outside Buckingham Street. "I don't know what to expect," said Lawrence, "or how long this might take. Do you want to come in?"

Violet shook her head. Her brown eyes were soft and sad, and Lawrence understood why. The last time she was at the Headquarters, she was in the midst of a budding romance with Doctor Myers. A fledging love affair that did not survive the distance between them. Lawrence patted her hand as he alighted from the cab, before stopping to ask the driver to wait. Then he took a deep breath, walked to the building and pushed the front door. It opened into the unchanged hallway which was much the same as it had been three years before. Haim's desk was still there but occupied by a blonde-haired man Lawrence had not seen before. The man approached him. "Are you Lawrence Harpham?"

Lawrence nodded.

The man reached behind the desk and retrieved an envelope. He handed it to Lawrence, then ushered him towards the door. "Leave now," he said.

Lawrence gazed at the envelope with his name inscribed in flowing handwriting. He did not argue and returned to the cab. The door shut behind him and he heard a key turn in the lock as he walked away.

"You were quick," said Violet as he sat down.

Lawrence nodded. He opened the sealed letter and passed it to her.

"It's an address," she said. "Who lives there?"

"I don't know," Lawrence replied. "Shall we find out?"

He opened the cab window and leaned outside. "Take us to Manchester Square?" he said.

The cab driver cracked his whip, and they set off towards Marylebone.

Half an hour later, the cab pulled up outside a row of smart red bricked townhouses set around a grassed square.

"Stop here," asked Lawrence as they trotted past number two. "I won't ask you to wait," he said, paying the fare. The cabman tipped his cap and rode away leaving Lawrence and Violet on the doorstep of the unfamiliar house. They looked at each other wordlessly, wondering what to do next. Lawrence seized the initiative and tapped on the door.

Moments later it opened to reveal a middle-aged woman standing in the doorway. She was clad in a black pinafore dress with a white apron and held a handkerchief to her lips. Silent tears coursed down her cheeks.

Lawrence searched for suitable words. "Sorry to disturb you at such a bad time," he stuttered lamely.

The woman swallowed and dabbed her eyes. "I am sorry too. What must you think of me? Are you friends of Doctor Myers?"

Lawrence and Violet exchanged glances. "Yes, we are," Lawrence replied.

"Terrible news," the woman said, shaking her head. "We hoped he would pull through, but it was not to be."

"We came as soon as we heard," said Lawrence, trying to appear as if he knew what was going on.

"Is he dead?" Violet's voice trembled as she asked the question. Lawrence pressed her hand in a gesture of support.

"I thought that's why you were here. Arthur died an hour ago."

"We assumed the worst." Lawrence almost crossed his fingers as he told the barefaced lie, which, for once, had not come easily. He glanced towards Violet. A single tear tracked down her face.

"I can fetch Doctor Drewitt if you like? He knows more about it." The housekeeper sniffed again. Her blue eyes wrinkled in another burst of silent sobs.

"Yes, please give him our condolences," said Lawrence," and tell him we would appreciate a few moments of his time."

The housekeeper opened the door and beckoned them through.

They followed her down a black and white tiled hallway and into an elegant sitting room at the front of the house.

"Wait here. I'll bring you some tea."

Lawrence waited until she left the room. "I'm sorry Violet," he said.

"It was a long time ago," she replied. Her eyes brimmed with unshed tears.

"Even so…"

"What do you think happened?"

"I don't know," said Lawrence. "Whatever I might have anticipated, it wasn't this."

"It feels like we are intruding," said Violet.

"It does. It would help if we knew why we were here. But this is the right address, and we must be here for a reason."

The door clicked, and a tall, moustached man appeared. The housemaid followed behind him carrying a tea tray. The man offered his hand to Lawrence.

"Frederick Drewitt," he said. "I hear you were friends of Arthur's."

Lawrence nodded. Drewitt gestured towards the couch. "Please sit down".

He pulled up a wooden chair, sat beside them and leaned forwards. "Were you close friends?" he asked.

"Yes," said Violet, hoping it was the correct response.

"Then you know about his epilepsy."

She nodded.

"Well, Miss... um."

"Sorry, forgive my manners," said Lawrence. "I am Lawrence Harpham, and this is Violet Smith."

"Oh, Miss Smith. I remember Arthur speaking about you." He smiled at Violet. She bit her lip.

"Well, I've known Arthur for, goodness, it must be over twenty years, and I have lived with him for the last two. Do you know how long he's suffered from epilepsy?"

Violet shook her head.

"His first attack was at university. It was manageable at the start. Sometimes he went for months without suffering, although it was always worse at night. Over the last few years, the attacks have been constant, sometimes several episodes a day. Such an intelligent man. A great loss to his profession."

Lawrence shook his head in sympathy. "A terrible shame," he said.

"When did you last see him?"

"Not for a long time," said Lawrence, vaguely.

"Did you know he resigned from his position at the hospital?"

"No," said Lawrence, "I'm surprised. He enjoyed the work."

"There was no choice, in the end," said Drewitt. "There had been an incident, you see. I cannot tell you more, suffice it to say that their knowledge of his epilepsy was mitigating. I don't know the details, but under any other circumstances, there would have been criminal charges."

Violet let out an involuntary gasp.

"I have said too much." Doctor Drewitt looked anguished as he apologised to Violet.

"Not at all," said Lawrence. "It is all so raw and upsetting," he continued. "But we want to know everything you can tell us, no matter how difficult."

"As long as you are sure," said Drewitt. "It isn't pleasant to hear. You've met Mrs Bull, our housekeeper. The poor woman found Myers on Monday morning when she bought in his breakfast tray. He was lying unconscious on the floor, and the room was in disarray. At first, we thought it was an epileptic fit, and he had fallen over, but Myers was insensible and unresponsive. His symptoms were incompatible with epilepsy on its own, so I searched his room and found an empty tumbler next to a bottle of Chloral hydrate on his bedside cabinet."

"Did he use the drug often?"

"Yes, but he was a skilled doctor and knew the correct dosage."

"And had he taken more than usual?"

"Much more."

"Are you saying that he deliberately over-dosed?"

"No. I don't think so. Arthur had packed his portmanteau ready for a visit and was bright and cheerful the night before. Perhaps his visitor brought bad news. I didn't see him conscious again, after that."

"What visitor?" Violet was alert now, leaning forward as she spoke.

"I don't know. One of his friends, I suppose. I heard voices when I was passing Arthur's room on my way to bed."

"Did he die from the narcotic or as a result of an epileptic attack?" Lawrence's question was direct and to the point.

"He died from asphyxia. My colleague, Doctor Colman, confirmed the diagnosis."

"But what caused the asphyxia?"

"The narcotics. An accidental overdose of Chloral Hydrate."

Lawrence sighed. Doctor Drewitt misinterpreted his frustration for sadness.

"I am truly sorry to be discussing his final moments. He was a great man, courageous and talented. A sad loss to humanity."

"You mentioned an incident," said Lawrence, "a criminal act. Did it make him violent? Was he ever aggressive in your presence?"

"Never," said Drewitt. "Not with any of us and he has shared rooms for many years. Another Doctor lived with him before I moved in. They got along famously until Arthur's illness became too much. The night time attacks grew so prolific that he locked Arthur's room at night. This was at Arthur's request, so he didn't suffer the indignity of witnesses to his fitting. But that was before my time. I refused to have anything to do with confining him. Arthur became frail, but his intellect never faltered. He was a giant among men, and I will miss him. I am sure you will too."

Violet murmured her assent. Her eyes were misty as she turned towards Lawrence. He gave a half smile, acknowledging her pain. "Thank you so much for your time, but we have disturbed you long enough," he said.

Drewitt shook their hands, and they left the building.

"What now?" asked Violet.

"Home," said Lawrence. "There is nothing left for us here."

Epilogue

Unsigned letter addressed to Lawrence Harpham dated 10th January 1894

Mr Harpham

Arthur is dead. I hoped I would never have to write these words, and if your memory had not returned, I would not be writing them now. If only you had stayed away. If only you had died by the banks of the Thames, we could have seen this thing through to the end. Arthur did not have long left. He was frail, and his epileptic attacks were increasing in frequency and duration. He had not been a danger to anyone but himself for many years. One momentary slip caused this anguish. We were assiduous after Mary Kelly's death. Two years went by without a single resurgence of the savagery inflicted by Arthur's other self. But one night in February 1891, we were careless, distracted. We left Arthur alone one night and, in his somnambulistic state, he returned to the scene of his previous crimes. Young Frances Coles encountered him as she returned from a tryst. One lapse and his carefully constructed alibi fell apart. We could have survived it but for you.

You will have deduced by now that Arthur killed Edmund Gurney. He had often treated him for minor ailments, so when he suggested a narcotic for Edmund's pain it was, quite naturally, accepted. Arthur slipped the mask over Edmund's face, trusted, as always. We later discovered that Arthur increased the dose significantly. His problem with the newspaper clipping vanished as Edmund drifted into unconsciousness. It was sheer coincidence that Arthur later spoke at the inquest. Hotel staff found a sheet of SPR headed paper in Gurney's possession and contacted Arthur to identify the body. It could have been any of us. Before the hearing, the coroner leaned towards a verdict of suicide. The final judgment was an accidental death. Speculation was rife that we had tried to influence the coroner's decision. It was not that simple. We worked to avoid a verdict of 'cause of death unknown.' It was too vague, and we wished to avoid the implication of murder at all costs.

Your doggedness paid off. Your persistent needling, like a vengeful mosquito, forced our hand. You will know from your conversation with Doctor Drewitt that Arthur Myers was more good than evil. His illness was an abhorrence of nature, an intolerable burden on a man with huge potential to offer the world. He was a force of good for humanity, an eminent physician of unusual skill and ability. And last week, we put him down like a dog because of you. Yes, of course, he didn't die by coincidence the very day after your phone call. We employed the same tactic on him that he used on Edmund. An overdose of chloral hydrate, forcibly given. He did not put up a fight. He knew what we were doing. He is not a monster. He never was. He succumbed to the narcotic, and sometime in the night, a fit made him insensible, and he lingered for another two days.

Now you know everything, it is up to you whether you reveal our secret. There will be no more killings. Will you ruin the name of a good man? It is your decision. Our work will continue, and memories of Arthur will remain with us, unsullied, forever.

Afterword

The Ripper Deception is a work of fiction based on the lives of real people. I am not a Ripperologist, and this is not an attempt to identify Jack the Ripper. Newspaper articles inspire me — I am drawn to accounts of real-life Victorian crimes, and they influence my writing. I am a keen genealogist, and my books often include my relatives, several of whom feature in minor roles in this novel. I generally set my books in East Anglia, and they involve local crimes. I ventured further afield on this occasion because the temptation to include Lawrence in the Ripper murders was too great to resist.

I am mindful of the feelings of living descendants of the characters in my books and hope not to cause offence. It is not my intention to implicate eminent physician Doctor Myers or his brother in the real Ripper killings and I am quite sure that historical records would prove it unlikely.

Next in the Lawrence Harpham series

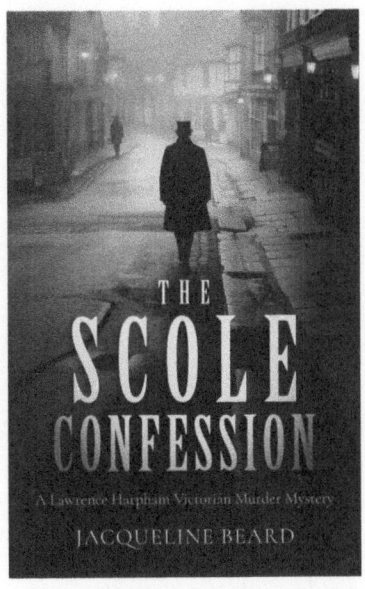

vinci-books.com/scole

A chilling confession, a string of murders and a race against time to uncover the truth.

Turn the page for a free preview…

The Scole Confession: Prologue

SCOLE, JANUARY 1892

"Repent therefore and turn again that your sins may be blotted out."
Acts 2:19

My fingers tremble as I raise the hand mirror and regard my features through faded eyes. A murderess, clad in the guise of a harmless middle-aged woman, returns my gaze. She has one foot on the path to old age, but will never arrive. Death is close behind her and catching up fast.

She and I were once the same — selfish, greedy and without compassion. But I have changed. We are different people now. A fleeting moment of regret made its home in my heart and nested there, bringing with it a conscience. A conscience that crept like a vine, infiltrating my memories, nagging and whining like a spoiled child. It thrived on sickness, revelled in infirmity and grew like the disease that ravages my body.

I am not yet fifty, but my face bears the marks of old age and a life poorly lived. My hair, once a lustrous brown, is grey and patchy. Heavy bags nestle beneath my sunken eyes

The Scole Confession: Prologue

and wrinkles furrow my face. I try to smile, but my mouth lingers in a permanent scowl, as well it might. My worthless life is coming to a lonely end.

I blink as a sharp pain sears into my eyeball and peer into the mirror to locate the source of my discomfort. The pain is from a loose eyelash which I brush from my eye with a gnarled finger, then I lower the mirror, and it falls onto the bed. The looking glass is brass, with a tiny bevel the only nod to luxury. It is not elaborate, but I appreciate it, knowing that not every woman can afford a hand mirror. It was a treat to myself with the money I received when Fanny died. It must be fifteen years ago now, but I remember as if it were yesterday.

I shake my head to dislodge the memories, but they will not leave. I find myself wishing that the disease had taken hold of my sanity as it did with Mrs Peters, who lives in the room below. Her mind went long ago, and now she croons to herself with a vapid smile on her face as she rocks the day away staring from the window without a care in the world. Her life is easy and pointless, but unlike me, she was always a harmless old bird. In the end, the good Lord gives us the end we deserve.

He came into my life three or four years ago, the good Lord, that is. I hadn't known I needed him, hadn't reached the depths of despair that followed later. Hope still glimmered, if not burned. But back then, I thought nothing of death and was quite content to profit by doing nothing. I did not consider my silence unreasonable, but self-awareness wasn't far behind.

The Lord entered my life one warm August evening. I'd been walking down Mount Street towards the Market Place on my way to perform a chore. I can't remember what it was. As I passed the Kings Head Hotel, I noticed there were

The Scole Confession: Prologue

boards propped up against a brick wall on the opposite side of the road. The printed boards announced an address by an American evangelist. He was due to speak at half past seven, and a small crowd had gathered to watch. I hastened along with no intention of listening, but entirely by chance, I found myself returning down Mount Street at a quarter to eight. The evangelist was in full flow, and the crowd had increased in size. They gazed at him with rapt attention. I found myself stopping and without giving it any further thought, I settled on a step and began to listen. I continued watching, fascinated by his words, and he held my full concentration. The preacher was not American at all but spoke with a distinct East Anglian twang. He could almost be a native of Diss, though his deep voice bore traces of another accent and some of the words he used sounded foreign. Not American, though – somewhere more exotic.

The evangelist was tall with high cheekbones and a full head of white hair. He wore a grizzled, un-trimmed beard that reached the top button of his threadbare waistcoat and he spoke confidently. Impassioned, honeyed words dripped from his mouth, leaving me spellbound. I hardly noticed the minutes pass by, and he finished in no time. One by one, the crowd departed until I was the only one left still sitting on the step and with no inclination to move. He approached me and held out a weather-beaten hand. His leathery skin was the colour of burnt wood and smooth to the touch. He smiled as he pulled me to my feet and asked me what was wrong. I remember wondering what he saw in me that made him ask. "I have sinned," I whispered as a torrent of feelings I had never acknowledged raced to escape.

He didn't ask questions or attempt to pry, but with a notable lack of curiosity, said, "Shall we pray?" and I nodded. We knelt together on the dirty pavement, and he spoke to God with fervour and faith. When he finished, he smiled at me, and I brushed my skirts and stood before him. But our reverent silence was disturbed by a rattle of stones, and I glanced across the street. Two boys, the Scott twins, were standing there pointing with percipient smirks on their faces. They were laughing at me, and my face reddened as I considered their interpretation of my actions. There was I, older than forty summers kneeling on a dirty pavement with a stranger. I had made myself a figure of ridicule. And it was at that moment that I realised what I had always known. All the secrets I had kept and the lies I had told, would never bring love or happiness or peace. My loyalty was misplaced.

The preacher watched as I wiped a tear away. Then, he turned and reached into a cardboard box tucked behind one of the boards and took out a Bible. He wrote in the front then handed it to me. Clasping my hands around the holy book, he quoted, "The love that lasts longest, is the love that is never returned." He watched me through weary, knowing eyes and I recognised a kindred spirit.

I stammered my gratitude and left for my home in Scole, barely remembering the journey back. The same night, I placed the Bible in a drawer where it remained for many months. But from that day, my conscience grew increasingly troubled. Time spent alone gave me opportunities to contemplate the unrequited love that had justified my silence. And as my health failed, and the object of my passion remained indifferent to my suffering, I burned with shame for the part I had played.

I reach for the hand mirror again and hold it to my chest. I cannot bear to see my reflection a second time, but the weight of the cold metal gives a strange, familiar comfort. Doctor Brown says that it won't be long now. My

The Scole Confession: Prologue

time is approaching, and my strength fails. I touch the brass to my lips and think of the man whose face I loved and the crimes I concealed on his behalf, though he never loved me. I should tell Sergeant Hannant and let him know what has lain undiscovered for so long, but old habits die hard. I cannot betray my love though I can and must salve my conscience before I die. The mirror slips onto the floor, and I leave it there, reaching instead for the Bible on my bedside table. I pick up the stubby pencil lying beside it, lick the point and write on a flimsy blank page at the end of the book. It takes an hour to get the words down – an hour of concentration and despair. But I finish it while I still can.

The words are clumsy, untidy, but written from the heart. They form my confession though I doubt anyone will ever read it. At least I can go to God with peace in my heart. I tear the page from the Bible, and it rips with an untidy, jagged edge. Then I fold it twice and roll it until it curls. It fits easily into the spine of the Bible, and I push until it is out of sight before using my last reserves of strength to place the book back on the table. I wonder if it is enough to save my soul, but it is all I have left in me. I sink back into my bed covers and wait.

The Scole Confession: Chapter One

AN OVERSTRAND HOLIDAY

Overstrand, April 22, 1895

"Well, that's awkward," said Lawrence. "You might have told me."

Francis Farrow put down his knife and fork and dropped a napkin onto his empty breakfast plate. Lawrence winced as a fishbone drifted onto the white table linen and wondered how long it would take before he felt compelled to move it.

"I don't see what the problem is," Francis replied. "Have you quarrelled with Myers?"

Lawrence sighed as he remembered the last time he saw Frederick Myers, a man he distrusted and feared. A man who had tried to kill him and afterwards had the nerve to ask for his discretion to cover a terrible crime. Lawrence had acquiesced, not from fear, but compassion. And because telling the story would benefit no one. It had been easy to conclude that the truth was not only unnecessary but vastly overrated. Which was all well and good, but it meant

The Scole Confession: Chapter One

that only Violet and Michael ever knew the full story. Violet, never comfortable with concealing information, refused to discuss it at all. Michael, being a clergyman, was bound by the restrictions of his profession. So, although Francis was a close friend, Lawrence hadn't told him about the events in London that resulted in his incapacitation for the best part of two years. Had he done so, he might not now be sitting in the breakfast room of a man who turned out to be an intimate friend of Frederick Myers, and more if certain rumours were true.

"Not a quarrel, exactly," said Lawrence, moving his hand towards the plate. He picked up the fishbone and deposited it in a cup while making a split-second decision to lie. "Myers and I had some business dealings, which didn't work out."

"I doubt he's mentioned that to Cyril," said Francis. "They will have far more important matters to discuss."

"Perhaps," said Lawrence, distracted by the fishbone floating in the coffee grounds at the bottom of the cup. He stood and walked to the window where he placed his hands on the sill and leaned towards the garden. "They all know each other, though, don't they?"

"Who?"

"Our host, Cyril Flower – sorry, Lord Battersea as he is now known. He was a friend of Edmund Gurney too."

"Ah, the chap who died in Brighton. I see. Didn't he form part of one of your investigations? Something suspicious, if I remember rightly? I hope you don't think Cyril was involved."

"Not at all. Cyril dined with Gurney the night before he died, but there is no question of any wrong-doing. He is a good man as far as I know."

"A decent man," said Francis. "An alumni of Trinity College. That's where we met."

"So, I gathered. It's good of Lord Battersea to extend the invitation to the four of us. I only wish he wasn't so well acquainted with Myers."

"That's the sort of generous fellow he is," said Francis Farrow. "As soon as I told him why I had declined his invitation, he said I must bring you all if that's what it took to get me here. A fine fellow."

"And when do we get to meet him?" asked Lawrence turning from the window. He scowled at the coffee cup and dropped a napkin over it. The fishbone was finally satisfactorily hidden from view.

"At dinner tonight. The Batterseas are in Norwich today. Constance has a long-standing engagement at the prison."

Lawrence raised an eyebrow. "Sounds serious?"

"Not at all. Lady Battersea is an advocate for women prisoners' rights and is seeing the board of governors to campaign for better conditions in gaol."

Lawrence grimaced and wondered how wise it had been to accept the hospitality of a liberal politician. While far from sympathising with the 'hang 'em and flog 'em brigade', he had seen enough appalling crimes committed by both sexes to be unconcerned about the conditions in which they found themselves incarcerated.

"Talking of Lady Battersea—"

The door opened before Francis could finish, and a young housemaid appeared carrying a large silver tray.

"Excuse me, sirs," she said, bobbing a curtsy. She placed the tray on the sideboard and began to clear the table.

"Oh dear."

Lawrence watched as she knocked the coffee cup that he

The Scole Confession: Chapter One

had hidden from sight under the napkin. A line of coffee grounds seeped into the white linen table cloth and dripped onto the carpet.

Lawrence bit his lip. "Sorry," he mouthed.

"I'll fetch a damp cloth," said the housemaid.

"What were you going to say about Lady Battersea?" asked Lawrence once the maid had left the room.

"Ah, yes. I didn't mention this before because I didn't want you to feel uncomfortable. After all, Cyril is much more down to earth. He knows men from all walks of life and status is less important to him."

Lawrence turned around. "Why do I get the feeling that I'm not going to like what you are trying to tell me?"

Francis walked towards the mirror opposite the sideboard and straightened his tie. "Lady Battersea comes from a prestigious family. She was a Rothschild before she married."

"Not the daughter of Sir Anthony, the merchant banker?"

"Yes."

"I didn't know."

"No reason why you should, old man. The point is that although she is passionately concerned for the welfare of the poor and needy, her natural companions are among the aristocracy. Lord and Lady Battersea entertain all manner of people from statesmen to royalty." Francis turned to face Lawrence before continuing. "As you know I am acquainted with Cyril from Trinity College. My father is a knighted high court judge; God rest his soul, so Michael and I have the right background..." His voice trailed away.

"I may not have advanced to your level in the police force," said Lawrence pursing his lips, "but my family have money and connections."

The Scole Confession: Chapter One

"You are not the problem," said Francis looking at his feet.

"I see. You are referring to Violet, aren't you?"

"She was a governess, Lawrence. She is from a different class."

"She is more of a lady than many I have known from the upper classes. And if it is such a problem, why did you invite us?"

"Please don't take offence. I have nothing but admiration for Violet. She is a friend and is welcome in my house at any time. The invitation was extended to both of you because I chose to honour our existing arrangements. I wanted to enjoy some time together, which is why Lord Battersea insisted that you come too. It's because I don't want Violet to feel embarrassed that I told Cyril that she was the daughter of a Scottish baronet."

"Please tell me you didn't. Violet hates deceit of any kind."

"Well, she's in the wrong job, then. Isn't that how you find things out?"

"Of course. Violet understands that it is necessary from a business point of view, but expects absolute honesty outside of that."

"I'm afraid she will need to treat this visit as if she was undercover. It will be easier for us all."

Lawrence shook his head. "I wish you hadn't misled Lord Battersea, Francis. Violet won't believe I didn't know."

Francis Farrow sighed. "It is done now. You had better find her and tell her the plan."

"Isn't this splendid, Cyril." Lady Constance Battersea beamed as she surveyed the dining room table, which was, as usual, beautifully laid out. Taking pride of place in the centre, was a whole salmon arranged upon a silver salver and surrounded by slices of cucumber. Caviar topped each slice, and the addition of giant king prawns and dressed crabs made a mouth-watering presentation.

"Yes, my dear. Cook has excelled herself. Please sit down." Cyril Flower gestured to his guests.

Lawrence Harpham took Violet's arm and guided her to a chair. When she was comfortably seated, he took his place beside her.

"Thank you," she said, biting her lip.

He patted her hand. "My pleasure."

"Well," said Lord Battersea. "It's good to see you at last, Francis. It's been far too long. What kept you away from us?"

"The Masonic lodge takes up most of my time these days," said Francis. "And I am on the board of Guardians for the Mill Lane workhouse, of course."

"Very commendable," said Lady Battersea nodding approvingly. "We also take a keen interest in the welfare of the needy. Cyril was in the village last week helping out with the Riseborough boy. So very sad."

"What was wrong with the poor lad?" asked Michael, ducking out of the way of the footman who was trying to fill his tumbler with water.

"He is dying from consumption." Lord Battersea shook his head sadly. "I delivered a box of food to his family. They are poor and in great want – but it is not enough to save him. A sad situation. His mother is widowed, and he is the eldest son and provides for the family."

Michael bowed his head. "God bless him," he said. Violet reached to her right and squeezed his hand.

"Your gardens are magnificent," said Francis trying to alleviate the gloom that had settled upon the room. He

The Scole Confession: Chapter One

scooped the contents of one of the crab shells on to his dinner plate and ate it with relish. "Delicious."

"Overstrand crabs are the sweetest in the country," agreed Lady Battersea. "These are fresh from the sea today. As for the gardens, the credit is due entirely to Cyril. They are far from finished, but I love the view of the poppy garden from the veranda".

"You love it now, my dear. It wasn't always so."

"But you have made so many improvements since we first came to Norfolk. That awful, draughty cottage. I was never so cold in all my life. And now we are about to join the two villas into one grand house."

"Really? That sounds like a lot of work," said Francis.

"And it will take a long time to finish," Lord Battersea replied. "But I have employed the services of Edwin Lutyens. His architectural plans are almost ready. It will be a grand residence when it is complete."

"And you can entertain as many people as you wish," said Constance. "Which will make you very happy, I am sure. Now, tell me about yourself, Miss Smith. I understand you hail from Scotland."

Violet lowered her fork. "There isn't much to tell," she said softly.

Lawrence watched her with concern. It was unlike Violet to be quiet. She had barely spoken during the meal and was showing signs of nervousness in the presence of Lord and Lady Battersea. Lawrence worried that the ordeal of masquerading as someone else had quelled her natural enthusiasm for being in company. Knowing Violet, she would feel like the worse kind of imposter. Under normal circumstances, Violet fitted into any social situation. Tonight, she should have shone, dressed in a royal blue dress with a delicate neckline and looking every inch a lady. Violet

The Scole Confession: Chapter One

Smith was no beauty. The kindest description would cast her as homely, but being in her early forties suited her. Clear unlined skin and delicate laughter lines enhanced her features. She had recently lost weight, but not too much. Her cheekbones now appeared sharper and her jawline firmer. Lawrence realised that he had been staring and took a sip from his tumbler of water wondering why the wine hadn't arrived yet.

"How do you know dear Francis?" asked Lady Constance, trying to put Violet at ease.

"Oh, we met in Bury Saint Edmunds. I—"

The dining-room door opened, and the butler appeared. "Excuse me, your Lordship, Lady Battersea. Mr Morley has arrived."

"Do show him in," said Lady Constance.

John Morley followed behind the butler. Cyril Flower stood, and Francis followed his lead.

"No, please sit," said Morley. "Carry on eating. It looks splendid."

"We have saved you a seat," smiled Lady Battersea.

Morley pulled out a chair at the foot of the table and sat down. "Please forgive me. I was delayed in London unexpectedly."

"Don't give it another thought," said Lord Battersea. "Francis, this is my good friend and colleague, John Morley. John, meet Francis and Michael Farrow, Mr Harpham and Miss Smith."

"Pleased to meet you," said Morley nodding his head. He sat down and helped himself to a plate of food while the footman poured water into his glass.

"How are matters in Ireland?" asked Lady Battersea.

"Complicated," replied Morley. "And not helped by the interminable disagreements within our party."

The Scole Confession: Chapter One

"Lord Rosebery again?" asked Lady Battersea.

Lawrence loaded his plate with another slice of salmon while Morley nodded in agreement. He wasn't especially hungry, but Lawrence had no interest in politics, and it created a distraction to disguise his evident apathy.

"We'll talk about it later," said Cyril. "The internecine disputes within the Liberal party are not an aid to a convivial conversation. How are you finding retirement, Francis?"

"Very agreeable. I don't know how I found time to work." Francis continued to regale them with stories of his last year as a senior ranking officer in the Suffolk constabulary. Meanwhile, footmen cleared the salvers away and replaced them with an array of mouth-watering desserts.

"And I still see my old colleagues at the Masonic lodge, of course," Francis continued. "And last week brought a nice surprise. The Social Design lodge invited me to join as an honorary member. They want me to assist in the organisation of a banquet in honour of the first Suffolk Grandmaster."

"Can you be in two lodges at once?" asked Michael.

"I won't be. The honorary position is for the Oddfellows, not the Freemasons. They are a friendly society composed, in the main, of town tradesmen."

"I am sure you will be able to offer valuable advice," said Lady Battersea eating a spoonful of cherries and cream.

"I hope so," said Francis. "Representatives will be arriving from Liverpool and Manchester next week. The planning has to be meticulous for an event of this magnitude."

"Ah, Liverpool. I wish you were going there rather than them coming to you," said Lawrence. "I have promised to visit Uncle Frederick next week and would have enjoyed some company on the train. And your Brougham is very comfortable for travelling to the station."

"I will be leaving Norfolk in two days," said John Morley, "and going straight to Liverpool. "If you decide to visit early for any reason, it is only a short journey to Cromer railway station. We could travel together."

"My uncle is expecting me next week," said Lawrence. "He is a creature of habit and not given to changes of plan. But thank you anyway."

"I understand. Let me know if you change your mind."

"Would you like to join me in the music room?" Lady Battersea finished her dessert and dropped her napkin on the table.

"I will, thank you," said Violet looking anxious.

"Are you quite well, Miss Smith?"

"I am well," she replied. "Just a little tired."

"Then you must retire to your room and rest. I will find something else with which to occupy myself while the men talk."

"Thank you, your ladyship. You are very kind."

She waited for Lady Battersea to leave the room, then followed behind.

Lawrence flashed her a smile as she rose, but she did not catch his eye and left the room with her head bowed.

As soon as the ladies had departed, Cyril Flowers got to his feet. "Gentlemen?" he said, gesturing towards the door.

Lawrence discovered why there had been no wine at dinner as soon as they retired to the smoking room. Lord and Lady Battersea were enthusiastic members of the Temperance Society and enforced the prohibition of alcohol after one of their staff committed an unmentionable act while under the influence. Though Lord Battersea alluded to it, the exact nature of the misdemeanour remained a mystery. Lawrence probed him on the matter, but Cyril was tight-lipped. John Morley was evidently in the know but loyally tried to explain the move to temperance in political terms. The Liberal party encouraged abstinence and its many members now embraced it.

Nevertheless, once in the safety of the smoking room, Cyril produced a decanter of whisky and offered it to his guests. Lawrence and Francis both accepted a glass while the others declined. The ensuing conversation was informative and free-flowing, despite the lack of alcohol for one half of the party. But after an hour, Lord Battersea suggested that they regroup on the veranda. By then Lawrence had consumed his third glass of whisky. One look at Cyril's anxious face and he concluded that Lady Battersea was unaware of the alcohol concealed in her husband's private room. It was clear that he was hastening a rapid departure before they drank enough to give the game away.

The tactic was well-judged. Lady Constance had not retired and was sitting on the veranda gazing into the distance with a contented smile on her face. It was approaching nine thirty, yet the evening temperature was still warm. Lady Battersea greeted them cordially and beckoned them to join her in the well-furnished outdoor space. After a few moments of small talk, Morley asked Lord Battersea to join him in a stroll around the garden. They meandered past the poppy beds and were soon out of sight.

"I expect they have party business to attend to," said Lady Battersea, by way of explanation. "Now," she said, turning to Lawrence. "What is wrong with your companion?"

The Scole Confession: Chapter One

"Nothing that I know of," Lawrence replied. "The journey might have overtired her."

"Yes, that is very likely. It is a pity that Miss Smith retired early. Now I must make conversation with three old bachelors." She continued, "What a shame that you have all missed out on the pleasures of married life. My dear Cyril is the most beautiful of men and such an amiable companion. I cannot imagine life without him."

"I'm not sure Michael qualifies as old," said Francis, "and Lawrence is not a bachelor."

Lady Battersea raised an eyebrow. "I am sorry. I did not realise that you were married," she said. "Francis failed to mention Mrs Harpham."

Lawrence drew a deep breath, unsure of how to reply without causing embarrassment, but Francis seized the initiative. "Lawrence is a widower," he said.

"I am sorry," replied Lady Constance.

Lawrence sighed. "Please don't apologise. You were not to know."

Francis diverted the conversation towards the arts and found himself arguing with Michael about the relative virtues of Byron and the American poet Emily Dickinson.

Lady Constance had been fidgeting throughout their conversation. With the brothers fully occupied in their debate, she turned to Lawrence again. "I have loved Cyril since the day I first set eyes upon him," she said. "And I know the pain of loss when I see it. I am sorry that I upset you."

Lawrence leaned back in his chair and observed his hostess. Her eyes shone with genuine concern. Talking about Catherine was never easy, but it was unavoidable without appearing rude.

"You are not the cause of any distress," he said. "But

The Scole Confession: Chapter One

Catherine died on May Day, and it is rapidly approaching. It will be the eighth anniversary of my wife's death – and also that of my daughter."

"You lost a child?" Lady Battersea's eyes widened, and she leaned forward. "I am so very sorry for you. What a tragedy."

"They died in a fire," said Lawrence, offering the information before she asked. "Catherine, my wife and Lily. She was only four years old. A beautiful little thing..." his voice trailed away, and he swallowed a lump. The pain of their loss had abated during the last few years, yet here tonight, it was raw again. He tried to speak, but the words stuck in his throat.

Lady Constance touched his hand. "In difficult times, we turn to our friends," she said. "It is so important to have loyal and compassionate companions." She smiled towards Michael and Francis.

Lawrence nodded. "I have known them most of my life," he said. "They are excellent men. Violet has also been a great comfort, although I have not known her nearly so long. But her kindness is inestimable."

Lady Battersea arched a brow, and Lawrence wondered whether she had misinterpreted his meaning. But there was no time to correct her as Francis had given up trying to persuade Michael about the superiority of Lord Byron's poetry.

"What's that about Violet?" he asked.

"Mr Harpham has been telling me about her many virtues," said Lady Battersea. "Ah, Mr Morley and my husband, have finished, it would seem. Hello, my dear," she said, rising to greet Lord Battersea who had emerged from behind the shrubbery.

The Scole Confession: Chapter One

"Come inside, it is getting cold," said Cyril, ushering them back into the house.

But Lawrence remained seated, in no mood for company. He stared into the darkness of the garden, brooding as he listened to the churning swell of the North Sea. It had been many years since the thought of Catherine had wrenched at his heart as it had tonight. Though he would always love her, he had become accustomed to her absence. His work as a private investigator had given his life meaning again. And because he was rarely alone, he seldom grew introspective and moody. Violet's influence had saved him from the worst of himself. Violet. She would know what to say to make the pain go away, though words were not what he needed. Being in her presence was enough and would take the edge off his misery. Damn Lady Battersea, for all her kindness. Without her interference tonight, the anniversary of Catherine's death might have passed without notice. Now, he was as afflicted by the yearly dread of May Day as he had ever been.

He looked at his pocket watch. It was a quarter to eleven. Violet's room was down the corridor from his own, and he must walk past it to get to bed. Lawrence entered the double doors in the dining room and slipped into the entrance hall bypassing the drawing room where his dinner companions were still talking. He climbed the stairs, then navigated to the west wing landing. Taking a deep breath, he knocked on Violet's door.

The Scole Confession: Chapter Two

A TRAGEDY

April 23, 1895

Lawrence woke to the shriek of gulls. Cold air enveloped him as he pushed back the bedspread and rubbed his eyes. The wind must have unhooked the latched window in the night, and it was now splayed open and showing signs of damage. He pulled on his dressing gown and slammed it shut, watching the trees tremble and bend in the blustery wind.

Lawrence perched on the side of the bed and poured himself a glass of water, then contemplated the previous night. His despair at the memories of Catherine had lifted, as he knew they would once he was in Violet's presence. She had a calming effect, and dark thoughts never intruded when she was near. But he shouldn't have gone to her — shouldn't have compromised her position. And now today, he had a new set of problems.

He decided to walk off his worries before breakfast. The weather was unusually cold for April, and dry but with squally winds. A solitary walk on the Overstand cliffs with the sea breeze whipping at his face would make him feel alert and alive. He would know what to do by the time he returned.

Lawrence dressed and descended the grand staircase into the spacious entrance hall. He removed his coat and hat from the stand by the door and made for the side entrance. A murmur of voices alerted his attention to someone in the morning room, and he craned his neck to see who it was. Violet and Francis Farrow were exchanging pleasantries across the table.

"You're up early," he said, popping his head through the door.

Violet was stirring a cup of tea pensively. "I couldn't sleep," she said.

"Nor I," said Francis. "I must have eaten something that interfered with my digestion. Damned dyspepsia. I didn't catch a wink last night."

"I am going to take a stroll," said Lawrence. "Would either of you care to join me?"

Violet looked up and nodded. "I'll get my coat."

"I'll walk part of the way with you," said Francis, wincing as he stood. "I don't think I can manage much of a distance, though."

When they were suitably attired, they strolled through the water gardens and into Gunton Terrace. A right turn at the bottom took them to the promenade where steep stone steps descended to the beach. The tide was out, and rock pools draped in seaweed covered the sand flats. They walked across the beach barely speaking, while gusty winds whipped past their ears ruling out any attempt at small talk. It was just as well. Both Lawrence and Violet were deep in thought, and Francis was grimacing in pain. At the end of

The Scole Confession: Chapter Two

the promenade, they climbed a further set of steps reaching the cliff top without uttering a word.

"That's enough for me, old man," Francis yelled against the wind as soon as they reached the coast road. "Are you coming back now?"

Lawrence shook his head. "No, I want to walk a little longer."

Francis raised his hand as they parted, and he set off towards the centre of the village. Lawrence and Violet continued in silence until they reached the Mundesley Road. Then, Violet stopped and took a deep breath. "Are we going to talk about it?" she asked.

"Violet. I'm sorry, I..."

Whatever Lawrence was sorry about remained unspoken. As he was talking, a man dressed in a white shirt and dusty work apron, tore up the road towards them. "Help me," he cried.

"What is it, man?" asked Lawrence. "What on earth is the matter."

The man stopped, caught his breath and put his hands over his face. "I think he's dead; God help him," he said. "Give me a hand cutting him down."

"Who?" asked Lawrence, but the man was already racing back the way he had come.

"Hurry," he called over his shoulder.

Lawrence and Violet exchanged glances, then ran after him, catching him up in a large yard about fifty feet away.

"In there," he spluttered, pointing to a large shed.

"I'll go first," said Lawrence stepping inside.

As Lawrence's eyes grew accustomed to the dark shed, a shape hanging from the rafter in the middle of the room swam into view. It was the body of a man with his head tipped forward, and snow-white hair covered his eyes. The early morning sun had dappled his dark apparel as it filtered through holes in the dilapidated shed. Stack after stack of neatly piled bricks surrounded the corpse, each one standing over six foot high. Closer to the body lay a set of smaller piles. Each block was staggered and fashioned into a rudimentary staircase giving access to the rafters.

"Don't come in," said Lawrence gruffly, but it was too late. Violet was beside him, staring at the hanging man in horror.

"Help me cut him down," said Lawrence, bounding up the brick staircase. He reached the top and touched the man's neck.

"He's still warm," he yelled. "Get me a blade."

The man in the work apron fumbled in his pocket, then pulled out a wooden-handled pocket knife. He held it towards Lawrence who began hacking at the rope. After a few strokes, the frayed rope split and the body fell crashing to the ground. Violet ran towards the man and cradled his head. His face was deathly pale beneath greying stubble, and small patches of blood had formed on his lips and eyelids. She gripped his wrists and felt for a pulse.

"Well?" asked Lawrence.

Violet shook her head. "He is beyond our help."

The man who had raised the alarm let out a strangled cry.

"Do you know him?" asked Violet.

"He's my father-in-law," said the man. "His name is Edward Bowden."

"I'm sorry," said Lawrence. "I wish we could have saved him. Can you fetch a doctor, Mr...?"

"Cotton, George Cotton," said the man who was now sitting on a packing crate looking shocked and pale.

The Scole Confession: Chapter Two

"I don't know. I'm—"

They were interrupted by the arrival of another man. "Oh, no," he said, clutching his chest. "Poor old boy. Have you told Mr Riches?"

George Cotton shook his head. "I've not long found him."

"Then I'll fetch him," said the young man, rushing away.

"Get the doctor, too," shouted Lawrence.

George Cotton scrambled to his feet, still pallid. "Wait for me," he said, stumbling from the shed.

"How are you feeling, Violet?" asked Lawrence, squatting on his haunches beside her. She was still holding the dead man's head.

Her voice trembled. "He looks peaceful," she said, "but I can't bear to think of anyone feeling so unhappy that this is their only option." She touched the rope still tied around his neck. "Should I undo it?"

Lawrence shook his head. "No, wait until the doctor arrives. Look, old girl," he continued, touching her arm. "You can't stay like this. Put him down."

"I can't leave him on the cold floor," she said.

"You must," said Lawrence firmly. He stood up and walked towards the door where he had seen a burlap sack earlier. Lawrence returned to Violet, moved Edward Bowden's head away from her lap and placed it gently on the sacking. "There is nothing more you can do," he said before holding out his hand. Violet grasped it, and he helped her to her feet.

"What's that," she asked, pointing to a second packing crate by the right of the brick staircase. Lawrence approached it to find a threadbare handkerchief, a few coins and a Bible.

"They must belong to him," said Lawrence. "He placed them there before..." Lawrence could not finish and stared mutely at Violet.

She bit her lip. "Poor, poor, man."

Without thinking, Lawrence picked up the Bible and opened the cover. "Another Edward," he said. "It's stamped inside. Edward Moyse, The English and Foreign Bible stall, Mann Island. Funny, that name seems familiar."

"What are you talking about."

"The inscription in the Bible. There's a verse inside, and the bookseller has signed it. He's from Mann Island. I know that name, but I can't remember where it is."

"Hmm," Violet half listened as she watched over the dead man, still reluctant to leave him.

"That's it," exclaimed Lawrence, clicking his fingers. "I jolly well ought to know. Mann Island is in Liverpool. It's not far from my uncle. Are you listening, Violet?"

"Yes," she snapped. "What does it matter. A man is lying dead, and all you can think about is the provenance of his Bible. Why are you so interested? And who is this other Edward?"

"Who indeed?" said Lawrence. He paced for a few moments, then returned to the packing crate and opened the Bible again.

"I knew it," he cried. "I must be getting old, Violet. Of course, the name is familiar. It's been all over the newspapers."

"What has?"

"The murder of Edward Moyse earlier this year in Liverpool."

"It can't be that Edward Moyse?"

"It must be. Moyse was a bookseller in Mann Island."

The Scole Confession: Chapter Two

Lawrence clutched his forehead. "Honestly, Violet. I'm losing my faculties."

Two men rushed into the shed before Violet had time to respond.

"George Riches," said the shorter man reaching out his hand. "I own the brickyard. Mr Bowden was one of my men. This gentleman is the coroner."

"I am Lawrence Harpham, and this is Violet. We are very sorry for your loss."

The coroner knelt and inspected the body. "I can confirm that life is extinct. He's probably been dead for a few hours. Did you find him?"

"No, it was George Cotton – his son-in-law."

"Thank you. There's nothing else you can do," said the coroner. "Leave us to it."

Lawrence nodded and guided Violet towards the door, passing by the packing crate. He waited until both men were facing the body, then discreetly lifted the Bible and placed it in his breast pocket.

Grab your copy...
vinci-books.com/scole

About the Author

Jacqueline Beard is a writer and genealogist living in Gloucestershire, with an East Anglian ancestry going back to the 1500s. She writes Victorian murder mysteries and is currently working on books in the Lawrence Harpham series and the Constance Maxwell mystery series. Jacqueline's books are a rare mix of true crime and fiction inspired by old newspaper reports. When Jacqueline is not writing or researching "dead people," as her husband so charmingly puts it, she is walking in the glorious Cotswolds with her dog. Jacqueline enjoys technology and spends far too much time on her computer. She dislikes flying, dentists and balloons – especially red ones.